Rachel was a history teacher for over a decade and after having her family decided to become a personal trainer. Her husband's job as an Army officer has moved her family ten times in twelve years.

Rachel has been writing since she was a teenager but this is her first novel. She is now settled with her family near London after finally saying goodbye to army life.

For Mike and Mum.

Rachel Lynch

THE DEPENDANTS

AUSTIN MACAULEY
PUBLISHERS LTD.

A CIP catalogue record for this title is available from the British Library.

ISBN 978 184963 926 2

www.austinmacauley.com

First Published (2014)
Austin Macauley Publishers Ltd.
25 Canada Square
Canary Wharf
London
E14 5LB

Printed and bound in Great Britain

'**Dependant**': a specific military term used to describe the official status of a military spouse and/or child.

Battalion rank structure:

Officers:

Officer Commanding (OC), a Colonel

2 i/c, second in command, a Major

Company Commanders (OCs), Majors

Platoon Commanders, Captains

Soldiers:

Sergeants (non- commissioned officers), Sgt

Corporals (Cpls)

Riflemen (Rfn)

Chapter 1

SEPTEMBER 2013

'News just in, three soldiers have been confirmed killed in action in Afghanistan this morning and seven further wounded, said a Ministry of Defence spokesman. Finally, in Nottingham, a lady dialled 999 to report her cat choking...'

Shit! Maggie fumbled with the radio dial taking her concentration away from the traffic and swerved. Shit!

'Shit.' Bethany's voice mirrored her own from the back seat.

'Mummy?'

'Yes, Darling?'

'Daddy is a soldier isn't he mummy?' Alex played with his toes absentmindedly as Maggie checked her daughter anxiously in the rear view mirror.

'Yes Darling.'

'Is he going to get dead?'

Thanks Dominic Byrne for your most sensitive handling of death at 8.30am on a Monday morning. Damn all of you media egos who report my life as if it is a goddamn statistic, she thought. Should she lie and say, no, daddy is not going to die for she herself did not know? Should she guarantee his safety for the sake of her daughter's undisturbed sleep only to have her resent her for the rest of her life should it turn out to be a lie? Why couldn't she guarantee her daughter that she couldn't keep daddy safe and that no-one could?

'Not today darling, he is coming home in eight weeks to see us and we are going to have so much fun!' Maggie fought to keep her voice from cracking and her hands shook as she tried to find a channel playing ELO or discussing cakes. She had lost weight, all the women had. Having no-one to cook for in the evening was no fun and she usually went to bed having

1

consumed half a sandwich and a bottle of wine. Funny how people said alcohol made you put on weight and was empty, evil calories; it was the best diet she'd ever tried. Bethany wouldn't let it go.

'What about tomorrow mummy? Will daddy get dead then?' Oh Christ, why did she have to be blessed with such an inquisitive daughter? Alex continued to play with his toes; his shoes having long since been strewn here and there. Why couldn't she have had two boys concerned only with their stomachs and their willies?

'Bethany, daddy is safe, I spoke to him only last night.'

'You talked to daddy?' Bethany wailed. Oh bollocks that was the last thing she should have said.

'I want daddy, mummy smells like poo poo.' Thanks, thought Maggie. I wipe your arse and feed you and hold you when you have a fever but I'm public enemy number one because daddy chose to fuck off and fight the world. Her stomach churned with resentment as she thought of Mark strutting around like a small Italian dictator as he prepared to depart six weeks earlier. His cam gear had cluttered her hallway and his side of his bed for months stinking of exercise and crawling through muddy puddles in Wales. She had thrown countless pairs of combats into the wash only to have to repeat the process on finding the whole wash contaminated by fag butts lying in wait in his pockets. He thought he was in *Platoon.* She hated herself every time she failed to become as excited as him about his impending knighthood for glory on the battlefield; he was to defeat the Taliban single-handedly and she was reminded of Tennyson's 600 as they rode into the jaws of death, cocks in hands ready to be slaughtered. It made her stomach churn and she remembered the moment when he had delivered the news like an excited puppy that he had volunteered to command troops in Afghanistan. Volunteered? What was wrong with her? What was so ugly and undesirable that he would want to leave her and his children to kill strangers and satisfy politicians and Generals in Whitehall? Something had died in her that day. He believed her selfish and unsupportive; she found him distastefully immature and irresponsible.

Their wedding day had been like any other; blue skies, beaming guests, flowing champagne, sword of honour and dreams. Her dreams showed in her long unrelenting smile that lasted all day long, so much so that her jaw ached when he finally carried her off to bed, to unpeel her from her very expensive gown, now in the garage. They had talked into the small hours of children and holidays and life together until old, grey age would inevitably bring it all to an end. She loved him with a passion so intense that she felt it deep inside every time he entered a room. She had beamed on his arm at grand Balls, and graced Generals and old Majors with her delightful banter fuelled by youth and hope. She had pinned her loyalty to him and the Queen. She had given up two careers, one after marriage and the other after children to follow him around the world in his quest for acknowledgement which, she was assured, would come once he was Captain...once he was Major...now it was once he was Colonel. Would that ever happen? Not if he got dead. Maggie wondered if the Taliban had wives and what they felt as they waved off their men in arms. She chuckled, of course they didn't have wives; they were lone counter insurgents living and breathing hate for their enemy who had dared to enter their country and the countries of their brethren. Had anyone ever won a guerrilla war? No. Those who had nothing to hope for and everything to die for made a formidable enemy.

Maggie had stopped watching the news. It was hideously one sided on the BBC and too raw on Channel 4. The whole media pounced like hyenas on titbits when a death occurred, each journalist dreaming of career defining moments, but Maggie just thought of the five injured, on average, behind every death, who weren't reported. Modern technology meant that even the most terrifying injuries were survivable now and men were being sent home as double, even triple amputees, and left to rot on benefits supported by a crippled mental health system. Mark had joked before he left that his Company was hoping to put together a Para-Olympics wheelchair rugby side on their return. It was the only way they could cope as they closed off from the reality of loved ones to the unreality of war. As Mark left on that cold, dark morning at 5am she had sobbed until Bethany padded down the stairs and she had to face the questions. 'Daddy has gone? How many sleeps?' A child's world is its parents and now there was one. She supposed it was similar to being divorced but with the added knowledge that he might come back and so they lived in the half light of uncertainty and her children felt it. Even Alex who was just two; had started taking off his nappy and shitting on the living room carpet just as Bethany had started pulling hair at nursery. They were barometers of her, she knew this but she couldn't help it. She couldn't help it that her devastation was written on her face and that her worst terror was being woken in the middle of the night by a priest knocking on her door. Phone calls made her jump, she went for days without washing her hair and she had started to smoke one cigarette before bed with her glass of wine outside in the freezing night peering up to the stars wondering if Mark would come back.

She often wondered if it was just her who had reacted so badly. Everybody else seemed to be coping just fine. When she saw mums at school, they exchanged pleasantries and told each other they were 'fine'. Now as she pulled into her driveway with Bethany screaming for her father and Alex now joining in, she thought she would go crazy. Chrissy was sweeping leaves and waved. Maggie rolled her eyes internally. She turned off the engine and got out momentarily relishing the peace as she slammed the door on her children. The noise resumed as she opened the children's doors and tried to find seatbelts. Bethany wriggled and was red faced now. Maggie ignored her, trying to keep calm.

'Let's go and eat some chocolate cake,' she soothed, and Bethany stopped for a moment to look at her mother wondering if this was a trick. Finally she nodded and so Maggie was able to battle with Alex. She set them both on the driveway and began searching for bags and socks and shoes displaced during the chaos. Alex fell over and Chrissy ran over the road to his aid. Maggie struggled to work out how she could physically transport two children and all of their worldly goods into the house in one but gave up and dropped everything to the ground to see to Alex.

'Thanks Chrissy. They're tired and grumpy.' Alex was screaming but it was an overreaction, there was no blood or indeed any kind of injury to speak of.

'Can I do anything?' Chrissy's children were grown up and gone and Maggie wondered what she did all day. She craved some peace and quiet and dreamt of what it must be like to have no children, often.

'What about a cuppa? The children can play; I still have some toys left for when people visit.' There was an element of desperation in Chrissy's voice and Maggie almost agreed but it was Alex's sleep time and she just needed to sit alone for a while and recharge.

'Thanks Chrissy but I can't, I really have to get Alex down before he explodes.' She thought she saw disappointment in Chrissy's eyes or was it judgement? There were benefits to living on The Patch, of course; you were surrounded by people going through the same thing, the children played together and everyone went to the same school and social events but it felt incestuous at times. Maggie had thought that The Patch was the perfect place to bond with other like-minded women and draw strength from them but the reality had proven to be different. There was plenty of chatter and smiles in abundance but no-one really talked or told the truth. That was saved for family visits; little snippets of sanity that popped up depending on their closeness and number. Sadly, Maggie had little family left and so her injections of normality were few. She got the same impression from Chrissy but it was never really discussed. Jane, down the road, on the other hand was always being visited by her mother or sister or this friend or that friend thus, Maggie assumed, easing her burden.

'Well what about tea? What time does Alex wake up?' She wasn't giving in. Maybe Maggie should take her up? What did she have to lose? Another afternoon on her own trying to keep two children from killing one another with soft toys and plasticine?

'Erm, about 3ish.' It was a strange feeling. Here were two women who had been thrown together by post code and their husband's occupation that probably would not spend a minute together normally, desperately negotiating their routine to tick off the hours until said husbands returned and life could start again.

'Well I will throw something in the oven and we can have some soup.' Soup. Maggie had once been a sales consultant in London. She had repped in Majorca and bunjeed in New Zealand and now her life had been consumed with poo, sick, separation and now, soup.

'Lovely. That's great.'

'See you later.' Chrissy seemed relieved. Why? She was an older woman who had clearly been through this many more times than a young Major's wife and yet she still showed the same desperation as her to reach out to another grown up to pass the hours. Why didn't she get a job or buy their own house and live in the country and raise chickens? Why was she still on The Patch?

Maggie put Alex down and he fell straight asleep. She looked at his face and once again wondered what Mark was doing and why he didn't want to spend more time with his son instead of playing big guns with his mates. She had to be careful; the resentment was consuming her. They'd had more than a few testing conversations over the phone where Mark had begun telling her of his desperately hard existence showering out of plastic bags and eating rations. She had wanted to scream, 'It was your choice ass hole'. But she had stopped herself. He was there and there was little she could do about it. Their marriage would have to wait alongside everything else. She was living in limbo waiting and waiting until the dust settled and they had some opportunity to make sense of the mess in which she found herself. Her Auntie Pat had helpfully informed her that she'd known what she was marrying, in other words, 'man up'. However, Maggie couldn't remember the vows that detailed months apart, raising children single-handedly and prostrating oneself on the altar of honour for her man whose ego rivalled Simon Cowell's. She didn't talk to her Auntie much after that even though her mother encouraged it. Aunt Patricia only lived ten miles away and her mother was convinced that this fabulous fact was proof enough to reassure herself that her daughter would be well looked after in this 'tricky period'. Her mother spoke in euphemisms like that. Maggie's problem though was that this was a 'tricky period' imposed by her husband and not some kind of unfortunate incident that fate had unkindly delivered.

Mark had been convinced that his future was safe should he volunteer for an Operational Tour. The MOD had been instructed to cut down swathes of infantry officers to save cash and everyone looked over their shoulder to see who would be next. An Op Tour would perhaps guarantee Mark another two years' employment which was a blessing with two young children to raise and feed. Meanwhile, Maggie seethed. Marrying the Army had seemed like a good idea at the time. Good pension, good travel opportunities, fairly good accommodation (compared to soldiers) and a bit of glamour. She had been seduced by many of Mark's uniforms and half smiled when she remembered making love on a tank with him in his combats round the back of the Colonel's house. Children had changed all of that, now they were lucky to get ten minutes together and that ten minutes had slipped to naught. She was surprised how much she missed him. Training had taken him away for months on end and she had filled her days with play dates and parks and the odd meal out with other wives. When the day came when he finally walked out of her life for seven solid months (excepting *Rest & Recuperation*), she realised that it had all been play acting; she wasn't ready at all, who would be?

At first she had kept his night clothes unwashed under his pillow but eventually she had tidied away his things and washed every scent of him out of their home. No cam kit lay about the place and no papers waiting to be read on counter-insurgency lingered annoyingly on kitchen surfaces. The fridge was full of her favourite foods and the bills were paid at a distance while she lived in a bubble. There was a man there but not there. She yearned for his touch in the middle of the night and agonised over the next phone call which would inevitably end in being cut off due to comms being cut because of another death or an acidic exchange of despair and need and bitterness. She received letters telling her how much he loved her but they made her stomach fill with bile, if he loved her why wasn't he there? He asked about the children and she made sure they drew pictures for him; paintings of blobs that she would label with names... hippopotamus... elephant... daddy... helicopter. He said he missed them but he still went. He said he was lonely but he still went. He said he couldn't wait to get back but he still went.

With Alex asleep, Maggie readied herself for the afternoon's next activity; keeping Bethany entertained. She flicked on *CBeebies* and sat next to her daughter while she munched on carrot sticks and hummus sandwiches asking incessant questions about the screen and the characters. Bethany needed to know everything about everything - Now. It had taken a while for Maggie to realise but her daughter craved certainty; labels itched, surprises led to tantrums and food felt 'funny' in her mouth. Every day she had to explain what was to happen during the next twelve hours with no surprises or unexpected twists. This is why the trip over to Chrissy's might be tricky; it hadn't been in their plan this morning, instead she had mentioned 'park'. When should she tell her?

'Bethany?' Her daughter looked up and stopped munching.

'Chrissy, the nice lady over the road, wants to cook your tea today and she has some toys for you to play with.' Bethany's eyes widened and she shook her head. 'No!' Maggie held her nerve but desperately wanted to scream. A tea date for Christ's sake was potentially going to ruin her day. She decided to take a different direction.

'She has rabbits.' At this, Bethany's eyes widened. Pets meant belonging and normality although Bethany was far too young to conceptualise the trauma going on inside her brain; pets meant something to care for and being in charge for a change; something to love to fill the gap where there was a space. Maggie knew that she should buy a pet but couldn't bring herself to have a needy dog or a snooty cat, rabbit hutches were expensive and hamsters vulnerable in Bethany's tiny but strong fists, she may very well over love them. But to visit someone else's pets, that was exciting indeed and now Bethany went to find her coat.

'Darling, we need to let Alex have his sleep first…'

'Now!' Bethany screamed and Maggie could have kicked herself for being so stupid however she couldn't have risked surprising her too close to the event for fear of her completely refusing; she had given herself time to work on her daughter not expecting such an easy victory.

'Let's watch the Zinzillas.'

'No!'

'Postman Pat.'

'No!' Maggie sighed. Not for the first time did she wonder if everything was well with her first born. Distracted, she failed to reach the plate in time before it was hurled across the room. 'Now!' Maggie was trapped; did she tell her daughter off for her manners or blame herself for mismanaging the situation?

'Ok, Bethany. If you don't say sorry to mummy for that and help me clear up, we won't go at all.' It was exhausting, the mind games and the tedium. Bethany stopped and surprised her mother by opening her arms for a cuddle.

'Sorry mummy.' Maggie drew her into her neck and kissed her cheek as Bethany sunk her teeth into her mother's shoulder. Maggie squealed and pulled back speechless. Every fibre of her wanted to slap her daughter's face but she knew that who she really wanted to do it to was Mark. They needed a normal life, whatever that was. She hated him. The uncertainty was sending her into a deep depression and her daughter could feel it too. Why couldn't she have given birth to a stupid soul and not an ocean of emotion reflecting her own? Maggie began to cry and Bethany stopped. She was only a child; she had pushed the only way she knew how and now Maggie blamed herself.

'That really hurt.' Was all she could say. Bethany touched Maggie's shoulder but she could not help but wince.

'Is Mummy going to get dead too?' Maggie's head whirled. She swept the child into her arms and said, 'no Mummy will never leave you. It's just that your teeth are really sharp and it is wrong to do what you did no matter how upset you are with mummy.' She could tell that Bethany was trying desperately to process this information but in the absence of an adult brain she was struggling to cope. It was up to Maggie to distract her.

'Maybe a kiss will make it better.' Bethany nodded and kissed her mother's shoulder. Maggie winced again not knowing if Bethany would do it again but she didn't.

'There's some ice cream in the freezer for the girl who finishes her lunch.' Bethany giggled and helped her mother retrieve the food from the floor.

Maggie sat back in the sofa, exhausted and empty. Would Mark come back and say he needed to go again to save another two years of his job? Was it worth it? If Bethany was reacting this way at four how would she react after another tour or another three tours? Maggie felt herself sucked into a precipice unable to climb out; she had no job, no relevant current skills, no money of her own and no energy; she was dependent upon Mark and his decision making for her own future and that of her children. She was scared; terrified that she had allowed herself to become nothing. She had become an Army wife and nothing more dragging herself and her children around after a man bent on promotion, and an institution that cared little for them. The precipice became a black hole and Maggie decided to visit the doctor the next day.

Chapter 2

The heating had stopped working and Jane picked up the phone to dial *Modern Housing Solutions.* Gone were the days when she could call the Families Officer and he would pop round with his screw driver, now that maintenance had been contracted out, one had to wait days if not weeks if the job was not deemed urgent. Jane wondered what defined urgent and toyed with smashing the window as well for good measure.

'The gas engineer is only in your area on a Friday, madam, and it is Monday today.' Jane felt like thanking the Liverpudlian accent for the lesson on days of the week.

'But it's cold and I have four children.'

'Have you tried the thermostat?' Does she think I'm an idiot, Jane thought.

'Yes, it's on full.'

'Well I could get someone there between 8 and 1pm on Friday the 24th, madam.'

'What! Can I speak to someone else please?' The woman sighed. Jane was irritated, it had only been a week since her cooker had been fixed after three weeks without it and the front door still stuck every time it was opened. She felt like kicking something.

'Putting you on hold.' Jane wondered how much this call was costing and was relieved that her husband was out of the country fighting for it and thus saving her money else she wouldn't be able to afford it.

'Hello? Mrs Blandford?' Said a new Liverpudlian voice. Were they passing her around the office?

'Sorry Mrs Blandford, all our engineers in that area are busy until that date but I think because you obviously have children then we could push it forward a bit. Have you an electric fire that you could use in the meantime? If not we could deliver some to you on Thursday.'

'This Thursday?'

'Yes madam.'

'I'm sorry that just isn't good enough, it really is very cold.'

'But cold weather emergencies don't come into operation until November 1st.' Jane was dumfounded.

'So what do you suggest I do?'

'Putting you on hold.' As the clock ticked, Jane imagined her BT bill climbing and wondered if they conspired with MHS to booby trap her heating.

'Hello, Mrs Blandford?'

'Yes, I'm still here.' I'm not doing this for fun she thought of adding.

'Do you have a relative or a friend to stay with in the meantime?'

'Are you fucking kidding me?' Jane blushed, had she really just used such vile language over the phone?

'There really is no need for that, Mrs Blandford; we record all of our phone calls.'

'Look, if you entered into an agreement with Her Majesty's government to maintain their properties then I believe that it is your duty to do so, I have four children, I have no heat in this house, I cannot wait until Thursday for electric heaters that will probably bankrupt me, I will have simply frozen to death with all of my children, is that what you want?' She was becoming hysterical.

'Mrs Blandford…'

'Do you want blood on your hands?'

'Mrs Blandford. Calm down. Putting you on hold.'

'No!' Jane screamed but it was too late. She rubbed her eyes. Why today?

'Mrs Blandford? My name is Katie, good to speak with you today now what seems to be the problem?' Jane couldn't believe what she was hearing. She retold her story with her eyes closed wishing that James was home. Not because he would have any better luck with MHS just because she could share her frustration with a sane adult. He would probably laugh but she couldn't bring herself to laugh right now, she wanted to cry.

'Ok, Mrs Blandford, it looks like we have a cancellation this afternoon.' Liar, thought Jane. 'Someone can be with you in two hours.' Jane stared at the phone. The bastards. She thought. How urgent do you wish me to be? If they hadn't the manpower, why not just be honest? Her blood boiled and she hung up at a loss as to what else to do.

She flicked on the kettle and held her hands over it as it reached boiling point. She wore a hat, scarf and gloves and peered outside at the gloom; the garden was grey, like the sky, and the trees were bare. Maybe she should go to her mother's? No, she was always running away and besides her mother irritated her after ten minutes fussing around her and insisting that she 'rest'. She chided herself for not getting to know the other wives better; she always had somewhere to go, someone to see to mask the singular emptiness of her life without James. James. Where was he? Was he twiddling his thumbs behind his desk looking at maps or was he out patrolling being spied on by a sniper? Stop! She couldn't allow herself to dwell too long on the subject; she had to remain strong for the children who looked to her as their only source of sanity. They had reached a point in their family life where Christian, their youngest, had finally gone off to nursery for five mornings a week; he was in the same class as Bethany, Maggie's 'daughter, but he had been taken home by another mother today to play and avoid the cold, of course. The other three were all at school and this should be the time when her and James could congratulate themselves on their lives taking a turn for the better; winning their freedom after four lots of nappies, teething, potty training and terrible twos. They should be having meals out together and planning holidays; their baby-making days well and truly over. James was due to have a vasectomy the week after she fell pregnant with Christian, and Milla had been a surprise too; they should have stopped at two, but she was forgetful when drunk, and James was petrified at having his bits played with by a trainee surgeon. When he had finally plucked up enough courage, along came Christian. She couldn't deny, though, that she would never turn back the clock, Milla and Christian had enriched their family and they brought even more joy to them all. On the flip-side single-handedly raising four kids was punishing, and she felt her life sliding by in a series of play dates, after school clubs, midnight sicknesses and complicated travel logistics.

Jane hugged her coffee and caught a reflection of herself in the window, her nose was actually red from cold and she could see her breath. She looked around her kitchen. It was large enough for a table and chairs and the view over the huge garden was a vision of middle-class prettiness, the flowered vinyl tablecloth and matching cake tins gave a sniff of Laura Ashley homeliness, but nothing could mask the knackered old cooker that had become her enemy of late, and the exposed pipes running along every wall; all a constant reminder of the temporary rental state she was trapped in. They were forbidden from improving their properties as every family was entitled to exactly the same and so should an improvement be made it would have to be ripped out again in two years when they moved on. Jane had spent many hours looking through *Ideal Home* magazine fantasising about what she would do with her own house, and the colours she would paint the walls. She was suffocating under a sea of magnolia and vowed that if they ever bought their own house she would decorate it in greys, mushrooms and mauves and never, ever, buy a *Mira* shower.

The phone pulled her out of her reverie, and she jumped, spilling coffee down her jumper. Well that was just fine, it could sit there with the milk from breakfast and the mud from Christian's boots.

'Hello?'

'Mrs Blandford? This is Kane Wolton from MHS, this is a courtesy call to let you know that I am approximately fifteen minutes away from your property.' Blimey, she should swear more often.

'Thank you, Kane.' She was amused by the efficiency and hoped Kane had what it took to fix her heating. Inside she expected him to take one look and say he needed to order a part and that it would take five thousand weeks like the cooker; meanwhile can you phone the job in again please? She was supposed to be dropping in on Chrissy for a coffee later so she might just be able to make it still. She rang her anyway.

'Chrissy? Jane. Look I've got bloody MHS coming round so I might be a bit late. Yes, great. No, No, that's fine. See you later.' She hung up. Chrissy had told her that Maggie was coming over too. Jane was pleased; she didn't know Maggie very well. After all they only had Bethany and Christian in common. Maggie was still bogged down in babydom with little Alex while her own dear Harry was ten and facing secondary school next year. Christ, where had those years gone? Jane pushed the thought away; James wanted him to go to boarding school to take advantage of the Boarding School Allowance but Jane couldn't face it, they would have that conversation another time.

Instead of thinking about such matters which always seemed to lead to a downward spiral of late, Jane busied herself with housework. Some Officers' wives had hired cleaners and even nannies for the tour taking full advantage of the savings they would make while their husbands lived in a ditch, but to Jane it seemed indulgent and she had opened a savings account instead. It already contained £1,200. Jane had been flabbergasted at how much more the bills were when James was around, eating steak, drinking beer, enjoying holidays, haircuts, mess bills and extra gadgets for him to play with that mainly lived in the garage. The phone bill was less, there were no dry cleaning bills for mess kit and the theatre trips and meals out had stopped. Sometimes, Jane was tempted to treat herself out of her secret account but the challenge to see just how much she could tuck away excited her and it had become an obsession; one needed such distraction in certain circumstances. She imagined James's face when she finally told him how much she had saved, and that it would take all of them on a trip away during post tour leave, maybe to *Sandals* in Majorca where the kids would be entertained and they could spend hours alone.

The doorbell rang as she had her head down a toilet trying to figure out how boys could piss over such a wide area and miss the loo completely. She hurriedly ripped off her marigolds and ran downstairs to the door. Kane grinned. He smelled of smoke, but he was still her Knight in Shining armour, potentially.

'Would you like a drink?'

'That would be fantastic, crazy morning, six emergencies like this on three different patches.' She let him revel in his own importance and took the coffee order; white, one. So now she was an emergency? She made a mental note to abuse more MHS staff in the future.

'It really is cold in here isn't it?' Moron, thought Jane.

'Yes. I wasn't making it up.' She smiled.

'Ah, they try anything to put you off; you just need to keep hassling them.' Jane was aware that he could probably lose his job over such indiscretion, but she let it pass; her silk was with Kane, not Mrs Liverpool from MHS Central.

'I bet I can guess where the tank is?' He chuckled to himself. Yeah, yeah, go on you cheeky little shit. Laugh away. Yes, it's upstairs on the landing over the army blue carpet with stains like all the others you've visited today, oh and watch out for the over glossed cupboard that might just hit you in the face if you pull too hard. She laughed back; a shallow half laugh that made her sad, at least she had bought her own curtains, and her lamp shades were slightly different to number 20's. She took the coffee upstairs and found him shaking his head. Oh God, please don't tell me...

'It's a tricky one, thirty five years old these old wrecks...' Yes I know, thought Jane, the last engineer told me and the one before that and the one before that.

'Don't know why they don't just pull 'em all out and be done with it.'

'It's called money.' Jane was becoming impatient.

'Well you can pick 'em up for a couple hundred quid you know.'

'Times 400,000.' Kane shut up and thanked her for the coffee before he stuck his head back into the cupboard. Jane went back downstairs and waited. She could hear clunks and the sound of metal on metal and thought of how cold the children's rooms would be tonight. Maybe she should make it into an adventure and let them all sleep in her bed, but Harry was a bit big for that kid's stuff, where had her baby gone? Even Lucas, at eight, was copying his big brother and recoiling from cuddles. Thank goodness she still had Milla and Christian to rely on for that silly but delicious baby stuff. She decided to clean another toilet - her quarters had several - and then mop the kitchen floor which always appeared dirty no matter how clean it really was. Jane wondered where the Army had sourced such vile lino; had they chosen the most impractical and ugly design on purpose? No, just the cheapest.

'All done.' Jane couldn't believe her ears.

'Really?'

'Yes, Really.' Kane beamed. Something in his eye warned her to look away. Cheeky sod, she thought, he must be twenty something and not a day older. Did he feel sorry for her or see her as easy because she was all alone and bored with her man away? Jane felt sick. She showed him to the door and almost forgot to sign the paperwork; he seemed disappointed. Had she led him on? No, surely not. As she closed the door the central heating whirred into life and she breathed a little easier.

She stood by the hallway radiator feeling it become warmer and thought twice about lowering the thermostat; no I'll leave it for now she decided. By the time she had picked up clothes from floors and tidied beds, collected cups, put away jumpers and gathered washing she was actually hot and it was wonderful. Life didn't seem so bad after all. She grabbed her bag from behind the utility door and walked out of her house towards Chrissy's.

Chrissy's house was the polar opposite of her own; no sign of children anywhere; they were long gone, and she felt sorry for her neighbour. The house was spotless but still marred by the exposed piping, magnolia walls and blue carpets; nothing could hide those. She followed Chrissy into the kitchen which she could have done with her eyes closed as the floor plan was a complete mirror of her own. Chrissy had put up pretty shelving for her cookery books and the room seemed a little warmer than the rest of the house; she clearly spent a lot of time in here keeping busy. Freshly baked bread wafted in the air and something was in the oven; cake maybe? Jane was trying to lose a few pounds before James's leave and although she had lost her appetite, her waistline had been stubborn. Chrissy was skinny and she wondered what she did with all that delicious home cooked food; gave it away probably.

'So, problem fixed?' Chrissy inquired.

'Yes! Thank god! It was freezing in there.'

'Well if it happens again I've got plenty of room, don't suffer in silence, I had no idea.' This was very sweet but they hardly knew each other; maybe she should take her up, after all how else would she ever get close to anyone? Was it the fear of revealing weakness that stopped her? That stopped them all? They had to all appear to be coping else they may all fall apart. Or perhaps the opposite was true? If just one person took the leap and admitted how shit it was then maybe they would all join in and could actually support one another?

'Thanks, Chrissy, that's really thoughtful, I'll remember for next time because of course there will be a next time.' They both laughed. Everyone knew that the remit of MHS was not to improve but to maintain and so after a while things broke again and again. Maybe one day their homes would simply fall down due to being stuck together with glue and tacks just too many times.

'So did you have a lovely time at your mother's?' Jane detected the slightest hint of envy in Chrissy's voice and wondered if she had family to rely on.

'To be honest it got a little oppressive at times.' She didn't want to appear ungrateful but she only visited her mother for any length of time for the sake of her children; whom she adored.

'Families. I suppose we can't wait to get away sometimes and then we realise that actually where we want to be is home.' Jane agreed although it was a bit deep for a Monday afternoon.

'What are you cooking? Smells divine.'

'Oh just ginger cake, I've had roasted veggies on for soup, I'm hoping Maggie will stay for some, tempt you?'

'Sorry, Harry has cricket tonight and Lucas tennis.'

'I'll box some up for you then.'

'No, don't be silly.' But inside Jane was thrilled at the thought of someone else providing for her.

'Ok well coffee and cake then?'

'I really need to lose weight.'

'Oh don't be silly, you look fantastic.' What is it with women who have to compliment all shapes and sizes just for something to say. She was overweight and she knew it, unlike Chrissy who looked as though she would snap; what did she know about diets and demonic scales? Chrissy was clearly a feeder and missed fattening up her strapping boys who were now fed by other women.

'Alright, just a little piece.' Jane relented to give Chrissy some thanks for her kindness. Chrissy plopped a chunk of cake in front of her and slid a cream jug within her grasp. Oh lord, what do I do now? Without voluntary movement from her muscular system her hand poured the silky liquid all over the cake and she tucked in, it was delicious.

'Any plans for the weekend Chrissy?'

'Well I thought I might do some Christmas shopping and I'm going to see a friend next week so I'll be packing for that.'

'Oh who is that?' Jane instantly felt nosy and a little bit jealous of her neighbour's freedom.

'An old friend, we were together in Germany. Her husband has just told her he doesn't love her anymore and he's seeing someone else half her age. Been together twenty one years. He's a General.'

'Oh my god, that's awful.'

'Yes, she's pretty messed up by it all but it's her kids who are feeling it most. I'm spending the week with her trying to work out a plan for their future, she doesn't work, hasn't in fifteen years and she simply doesn't know how she'll do it financially.'

'Surely he has to give her half of everything?'

'Half of what? They never bought a home and she's found out that he's been spending money on expensive gifts and hotels for the last two years.'

'Shit!' Jane couldn't help herself, she was swearing a lot lately. Chrissy didn't seem to notice.

'Exactly. But it's not the money that Jenny resents it's all those years wasted raising his kids and waiting around keeping the home fires burning while he was away on six or seven Op Tours. Apparently the new one is a military nurse who he met in Iraq. Jane saw a fire burning in Chrissy that she hadn't noticed before and was impressed.

'Nice.' There was a silence for a moment until the door rang; it was Maggie. The atmosphere changed instantly as a screaming toddler charged into the kitchen and another fell flat on his face.

'Bethany!' Screamed Maggie. Bloody hell, she's got it bad, thought Jane. She noticed the dark circles under Maggie's eyes and the deadness behind her weak smile and thought 'I've been there'. Six years ago when James was in Iraq. Harry would have been four and Lucas two with Milla on the way. She could remember meeting a neighbour for coffee for the first time and within minutes she had broken down in tears for no apparent reason. The neighbour had been older and wiser and took the toddlers away for ice cream for three solid hours while Jane slept. After, the two women grew close until another move separated them and Jane ended up in Catterick and Debs in Germany. They had never enjoyed the same posting since but tried to get together once a year. That small act of compassion had been the turning point that Jane had needed to pick herself up and she could see it in Maggie.

'Hey let me take Alex.' Alex sat on her knee and looked miserable. She was reminded of Milla's jealousy when Christian had arrived and how she teased him and abused him mercilessly until he had started to fight back only recently. Poor Alex, he had a few more years to go yet.

'Don't worry, one day you'll be bigger than her.' She whispered into his little ear. She took some cake off her plate that she really didn't need anyhow and fed it to him through his snot and tears. Funny how we find other people's children's snot such a turn off, she mused and wiped it discreetly with a napkin so beautifully folded by Chrissy.

Chrissy had spotted the same desperation that Jane had behind Maggie's frazzled appearance and took Bethany to meet the rabbits. Jane got Maggie a piece of cake whilst holding Alex on her hip with one arm.

'Oh I shouldn't really, I'm on a diet.' Oh god not another one, what had these men done to deserve this army of women obsessing about their figures for their glorious return, her included?

'Oh bugger it, you need the sugar, it will calm your nerves and perhaps even damage your hearing.' Jane smiled but Maggie still shook her head as if scared of the calories. Starving herself won't help, thought Jane. Maggie looked pale although that might be her normal pallor as Jane didn't see her much. She felt slightly awkward, how to get inside? Maggie had built a huge barrier, which was clear.

'So, how about we have Bethany round after nursery this week? My heating has just been fixed so I can guarantee that she will not freeze to death although she might be exposed to lots of sugar and hideous noise.' Jane ploughed on. Maggie's face relaxed and she stuttered.

'Oh, that would be nice, are you sure? Bethany is not… easy.' Jane was surprised.

'What children are?' She knew she had said the wrong thing. Maybe there was something peculiar about Bethany? Had she spoken out of turn? She had clearly denied Maggie her right to feel uniquely driven crazy by her own child as opposed to other mothers who just moaned. Jane found it difficult to decide whether Maggie was just feeling sorry for herself or if Bethany really was more than a normal female handful designed from birth to be bitches. Certainly Jane had been shocked when Milla came along. Boys were so much easier. Milla screamed more and threw herself on the floor in stubborn drama at the drop of a hat whereas the boys were so straightforward and no meant no. As for Milla, she knew better than her mother and challenged everything; she wanted to grow up before she could talk, indeed Jane was convinced that Milla was never even designed to be a child but should have been born straight into adulthood, that way she would be much happier. Her GP called it 'wanting to write cheques that her body can't cash'. That suddenly reminded her; she had thought herself at fault with Milla and had sought help. God she had forgotten, Milla had started to grow out of her drama around school age, but still showed signs of it, but with three other children to tend to Jane found it easier to ignore. She had forgotten the all-consuming despair experienced with a difficult child.

'You know, Milla was just the same. Nothing was ever good enough and she loved the sound of her own voice. We've had screaming matches in the street and I've waited thirty five minutes for her to get into the car.' Maggie smiled.

'Really?'

'Really. She drove us all mad, still does; she's such a drama queen. Instead of boarding school I'm going to suggest RADA.' They laughed. Jane didn't want to lecture and so left the subject for now, the last thing Maggie probably needed was some older, wiser wife giving unwanted 'advice'. However, she made a mental note to check in on her from time to time.

'All settled.' Announced Chrissy returning to the kitchen. 'Rabbits cuddled and now she's playing with an old sketch game I found last night, I knew I'd kept these things for a reason. Maggie, what time shall I do tea?' Tea. That singular English word that only mums can explain.

'You really don't have to.' Maggie's self-deprecation was starting to irritate Jane.

'It's all ready, no problem at all.' She smiled. Jane wondered whether Chrissy had thought similar thoughts about Maggie and had her over to distract her and possibly help a little. Maggie looked at her watch.

'Well, I usually do it for 4.'

'Ok, I'll pop it in now then; does she like chicken nuggets? Home-made of course.'

'Wow, yes. That's lovely, thank you.' Maggie was taken by surprise; she had never seen her neighbour as a thoughtful, easy-going person; in fact she had never seen her as a person at all. She always seemed to be super busy going out in the car for hours on end only to come home, drop something off and go out again. Funny how if we don't know someone we still judge, thought Maggie. She was feeling slightly uncomfortable under the gaze of these two far more experienced women and she felt inadequate. She would never be able to return the favour; when did she have time to cook soup and cake from scratch and Bethany was never treated to home-made chicken nuggets in her house, besides she had no clue how to make them; how did you make the breadcrumbs stick? Bethany had been such a dream feeder when a baby but now she would rather throw food and watch her mother's face than eat anything. Some days Maggie had put Bethany to bed on two *Babybels* and nothing else but still she had slept through the night. Food was a battleground and Maggie lost more battles than she won and wondered if the war would ever be over. She had told the Health Visitor who had simply said, 'she'll eat what she needs, don't worry.' But she was worried, that's why she'd spoken to the bloody woman in the first place. Alex giggled at Jane. Jane was nice too, thought Maggie. How can these women live a stone's throw away from her and her not appreciate that? She felt as though she lived in a cocoon but how could it be any other way when she barely had time for a shower never mind making new friends? She decided that it had been a good idea to come over to Chrissy's; she felt a little normal sat chatting with two other human beings in the small kitchen.

'This room is so homely, Chrissy; I love what you've done with your shelving.' Maggie's quarters looked unloved and she knew it but couldn't muster up the energy to create any kind of space that would merit being called a home. The magnolia walls remained blank and piles of letters lay unopened where dropped as she dealt with a tantrum or bottom wipe. Life was going too fast for her and she desperately wanted it to slow down. Chrissy had put up pine shelving and on them lay arranged pretty tins and pots; her spices and condiments were arranged on another and a cookbook lay open on a beautifully carved bookstand. There were framed pictures on the wall and patterned aprons and *Cath Kidston* oven gloves hung on hooks. Even the sink was tidy with everything in its place and matching *Molton Brown* hand wash and hand cream sat in a ceramic container. She could have been in anyone's kitchen; that is anyone normal, and not just plain old Army quarters.

'Well we've got to make some statement about the place haven't we?' Chrissy was obviously pleased with Maggie's observations.

'Yes to make us remember that we're not all living in the same cardboard box!' Laughed Jane.

'I hate my quarter.' Maggie regretted her hasty words after realising that she had just damned her neighbours' houses too.

'I mean, I just can't seem to make it look nice, yours is lovely, Chrissy. I just don't seem to have the time to put up pictures or keep everything tidy.'

'Woah!' Jane put up her hand. 'This gorgeous little man is still a baby; I'd say you're busy enough without beating yourself up.'

'Did you ever get time to wash your hair or apply makeup when yours were really little, Jane?'

'Can't remember. Don't think so. I remember always wanting to get them out of the house. Best thing for them I think if they're driving you mad is just get them out, anywhere; could be a park or a playground, anything to run off some energy. And yes my house was a tip, still is; stuff everywhere.' Jane laughed again. Maggie liked Jane's laugh it was frequent, open and warming.

'I agree,' Added Chrissy, 'I never had chance to do homey stuff when mine were little; it's only when they went to school that I was able to spend some time thinking where I wanted what. Don't be too hard on yourself Maggie.' Maggie was confused. She felt as though she was far too soft on herself if anything; she saw herself as listless, drained, and lazy even, and here were two women telling her to relax. It didn't make sense.

Chrissy put some potatoes on to boil and checked the nuggets; they were golden and fizzing temptingly. She popped some carrots into her steamer and carried on talking, making it all seem effortless. Maggie chided herself once again for falling short in comparison to others but she felt so at peace here and it saddened her that this feeling would evaporate when she got home. However, she also wished she could steer the conversation around to something a little more interesting than home and kids but she didn't know how to start. 'So, the bombings in Kuwait?' Seemed so aloof and patronising. She used to read *The Independent* every single day from cover to cover but now she only got the odd snippet from *Facebook* or *Sky* news. Did these women think the same or did they simply not care?

'Did you hear about the bombings in Kuwait last night?'

'Awful.' Said Chrissy, Jane shook her head in disgust. 'Those poor children.' So they did know! Why weren't they discussing it?

'I just wish I had time to read about it more.' Maggie looked wistful. Jane was becoming more irritated by this girl who sat and said a lot but clearly did nothing about it. Yes, we care about terrorism, she thought, but there's washing to do and kids to pick up and husbands at war to worry about, grow up and pull yourself together. She wanted to shake Maggie and decided to leave.

'Well I really better get going, thanks for the coffee Chrissy and of course your wonderful cake, same time next week?' Chrissy beamed.

'Absolutely, or should we go out? There's a lovely little coffee shop just opened on Brigg Street, looks fab.' Maggie felt a pang of jealousy, so these women spend regular time together? She spent regular time with no-one. Had they conspired to get her out because they felt sorry for her?

'Sounds great, let's do that. Maggie, lovely to see you and actually have time to chat for a change. If you need anything just shout; it does get easier as they grow up you know.' Patronising cow, Maggie thought, unkindly, her feelings of warmth disappearing. She smiled, 'Thank you, I will.' Not in a million years, she said to herself.

'I'll see myself out.'

Chrissy turned her back to see to the carrots and there lingered an uncomfortable silence.

'How many quarters have you lived in Chrissy?'

'Seventeen.'

'Oh my god, how do you cope?'

'Well I don't see that I've got much of a choice. Jeremy earns the money and we follow, like little ducks.'

'Don't you want to stop all the moving and settle?'

'What is 'settle'? My home is where my family is, I've seen some incredibly beautiful and interesting places, met extraordinary people, I always have a big house and a huge garden and my husband has a twenty two year contract of employment, I'd say I'm pretty lucky.' Maggie envied Chrissy but couldn't help the uncharitable thought that she was simply unambitious and old fashioned to let her husband call the shots like that.

'What about redundancy? Doesn't it scare you?'

'Jeremy isn't in the bracket, yet. Is Mark?'

'Yes.'

'Oh. Well I get the impression you'd like to settle as you put it so aren't you happy at the prospect?' Maggie hadn't thought about it like this before. Yes of course she would be happy to settle but where? And what if he couldn't find a job?

'Well I suppose so but still the Army is very secure isn't it? I think I'm a bit tired and grumpy, sorry.'

'Missing Mark? He will be back in no time, you'll see.' God, why does everyone assume that an unhappy woman is pining for her man?

'Actually no, I'm still angry with him for going in the first place.' Chrissy hid her shock.

'Ah, because he volunteered?'

'How do you know that?'

'Everyone knows. When Ben resigned they needed a volunteer to fill his place, it was very last minute.'

'Oh. Well he did it to save his job but I'm not sure what it will do to his family.'

'Oh you don't mean that, Mark loves you; it's so obvious.' What the hell do you know? Maggie's initial enthusiasm over meeting two new friends was quickly waning. Jane thought she knew it all and now Chrissy was playing Joan of Sodding Arc.

'Tea's ready, why don't you get Bethany and I'll set it out.'

Maggie remembered her neighbour's kindness in inviting her over in the first place and went to find Bethany, plus she was ravenous and couldn't wait to try the home-made soup. She stopped short of the door and listened to her daughter singing. It made her throat constrict; she couldn't remember ever hearing Bethany sing like that, it was tuneful and melodic and quite beautiful.

'Darling, tea's ready. Chrissy has made chicken nuggets from scratch!' Bethany stopped singing and Maggie's heart sank. She trotted into the kitchen and sat straight up at the table and said, 'mmmm.' Oh here we go, Maggie thought, I know your game. Chrissy served Bethany her food and mushed some up for Alex in a little blue bowl, how thoughtful thought Maggie. Bethany ate in silence and asked for a cup of water saying 'please'. Maggie nearly fell off her chair.

'Lovely manners! You can come here anytime Bethany!' Chrissy was beaming, again. Maggie was not in the least surprised that Bethany cleared her plate and added, 'thank you for my lovely tea.' Butter wouldn't melt. How could a four year old be manipulating her like this? And she was falling for it by letting her anger well up inside her, Bethany was winning. The soup was divine but she was aware of demolishing it like a hoover; she hadn't realised she was so hungry. She mopped up the last bits with a huge chunk of still-warm bread. Chrissy seemed pleased, like a mother looking after her starving son back from Uni.

'Can I box some up for you? I can't eat all this.' Maggie couldn't help but nod enthusiastically, most days she forgot to eat but being cooked for was luxurious.

As soon as Maggie said it was time to go, Bethany started to wail and flail her arms about screaming, 'No! Rabbits again!' Chrissy tried to soothe her and gathered their coats to help saying the rabbits were tired and she could see them again tomorrow, she had bought the damn things for Jake and Will ten years ago and they were still alive. To Maggie's horror Bethany kicked her shin and she screamed in pain.

'Bethany, that is no way to treat your lovely mummy.' Chrissy raised her voice and Maggie stared at her in shock.

'Young lady you will not be welcome here for tea if that is how you are going to behave, now say sorry.'

'Sorry mummy.'

'Good girl. Now put your coat on and I will ask mummy if you can come again, but only if you are nice ok?'

Bethany nodded. Bloody nora. The rollercoaster of emotions that Maggie had thus far felt that afternoon swung securely to 'respect'.

As Chrissy closed the door she wondered what sort of an evening Maggie had in front of her. God, that was exhausting, she thought.

Chapter 3

Chrissy closed the door and paused for a moment. There had been snippets of reality to her afternoon; mainly when someone smiled or laughed but the overwhelming undertone had been toxic; Maggie was desperately unhappy and refusing to accept any form of advice or help. She's a stubborn girl, she thought. Then she remembered how stubborn she had been when she had been her age; she moaned at Jeremy every night for this or that when the matter was entirely out of his hands. Why couldn't he just take the day off if a child was ill? Because it's not civvie street and you do as you're told, he would say. It had taken her years of anguish to realise the peculiar nature of the Army's hold over an Officer; if a Colonel says jump the correct response is, 'how high, Sir?' Now she found it amusing that Jeremy was a Lt. Colonel and she saw the job from a different perspective. With him presumably 'in charge' of the train set she expected him to relax, but if anything he had become worse, working longer hours to 'set an example' and now jumping through hoops for Generals or politicians. Chrissy had learned to let it go. He would have been as committed in any job he found himself in and she loved him for it. Her boys had turned out ok despite being 'third generation kids' or whatever they were called nowadays. She had found Maggie's comments hurtful this afternoon, it was as if Maggie looked down upon this transient life as if they all had a choice and Mark was making decisions to hurt her. Never mind, she was young, and had a long way to go yet before she really pissed Chrissy off, and even then, if she did, Chrissy wouldn't show it.

She could have chosen to live in the grand Colonel's quarters but she had found it cavernous and had insisted on staying on The Patch, which was unusual, but it was a battle that Chrissy had been determined to win. Jeremy had said it would compromise his position living amongst his Officers; that they wouldn't relax with him around. She had replied, 'darling with you training for eighteen months and deployed for eight I shouldn't think there'll be any men around to worry about.' That had caught him out and the deal was done. Some things she could not fight but she didn't want to be a Colonel's wife in an ivory tower; she had seen too many Colonels' wives make that mistake; they appeared aloof and uncaring and were bitched and gossiped about. She would rather gauge wives' feelings towards her face to face. This way, she got to walk around The Patch, go to the shops or hairdressers and bump into people and get to know them. Of course there would still be gossip; being the Colonel's wife was rather like trying to balance on a knife edge, sometimes she couldn't please anyone, not even a minority, but that came with the territory. At least she was amongst the wives, seeing them daily and getting to know them and them her; the more they saw she was human the less likely they would be to throw the knife. She was perfectly happy being where she was, and ideally placed to gauge the gossip about who was struggling and thereby act upon it. Sometimes, wives forgot who she was and she liked it that way. Familiarity worked to her advantage. Every time she came upon a tricky encounter, which was more regular now the men had gone, she tried to remember what she had thought of the Colonel's wives before her. She had seen many come and go and tried to take the positives and avoid the negatives. The position came with instant mistrust; if she spoke to someone she was suspected of prying; if she called round, she was accused of lording about; if she passed an opinion, it was examined acutely; if she failed to attend a function it was superiority; if she turned up unannounced it was arrogance. Chrissy had agonised for months before Jeremy took his current position, and in the end she had come to the conclusion that she would just be herself; as friendly and positive as possible. That's why she invited people round regularly; despite liking the company since her boys had gone, she wanted to get a feel of whether she was on the right path. Some women were nervous about coming to the Colonel's house but Maggie hadn't been; she was so wrapped up in herself that she clearly didn't give a monkeys who she was talking to which was particularly refreshing. She wanted to see more of Maggie but wasn't sure whether she would ever get anything back. She'd met the type before; probably used to be some high flyer in London and couldn't stomach the fall in fame and fortune; she'd followed her man for love and found magnolia walls and posting orders and naked, unforgiving loneliness. She had rarely seen anyone call at the house and wondered if she had family or close friends but how is such a subject broached without coming across as patronising or matronly? How could she make sure that Maggie got through this tour unscathed without seeming to pry? She began tidying toys. She smiled as she remembered Jake and Will playing with them; memories flooded back of Jake walking into a door holding that bananaman or Will running round the garden with that toy hoover; she had kept them for some sentimental reason and was glad, anything to remind her of the boys was welcome. They were men now; one in the city and one about to go off to Africa and save the world with the Red Cross, bless him. After all that moving as kids she expected them to stay put but they had blossomed and Will, especially had the wanderlust. Jake was more serious and had a girlfriend, she suspected he would probably stay on home soil but Will was and always had been her adventurer. The pain at seeing him go was excruciating; she could see Maggie's frustration with her daughter verging on distaste but when they go into the big bad world, it's only then that the love hits you like a train. Please keep him safe, she said to some unknown entity in the sky. Of course, Jeremy felt it too but if men are emotionless, soldiers are made of stone. The odd pat on the back or discussing rugby in the pub was the sum of Jeremy's fatherly love but that was his way; it didn't mean he was any less adoring of them. Thank god they had boys; a girl would have become so needy without daddy's affection, maybe this was what had happened to Bethany? She was an extremely clever girl and she bet her last penny that mealtimes never went off without a fuss at home; this made her smile but one thing was certain; Maggie wasn't smiling. She pined for a girl in the early days to dress her in pink and plait her hair but now she was thankful; boys are so much less complicated she thought. That reminded her of Jane who had a brood of boys and one lone, complicated girl but Jane was no Maggie and she somehow had the measure of her daughter and Milla knew it.

Chrissy had liked Jane instantly but had shied away from appearing too cliquey with a senior officer's wife; it was such a damn cliché. She hadn't wanted the other wives to feel as though she had a favourite but it was true; she did. Jane was grounded and in control and Chrissy liked that. Maggie made her feel uncomfortable and she got the impression that nothing anyone could do or say would please her. She was clearly an extremely bright young woman but that matters not when launched into the world of shit and snot and vomit; it's a great leveller having kids, she thought.

The phone rang and made her jump. Her house was so quiet now with Jeremy gone and the boys preferring to talk to girlfriends rather than to their mum.

'Chrissy.' It was Jeremy.

'Darling! How are you?'

'Oh you know. Just to give you the heads up....we've had our first fatality.' Jeremy always did this, spoke as if to a soldier; it was all he knew. He carried on.

'Sgt Dent. Comms will be cut any minute...just wanted to warn you, I know you'll be amazing.' The line went dead. Shit. Then it rang again. This time it was Dave Proctor, the Families Officer; well they called them Welfare Officer now thanks to someone earning their MBE behind a desk at the MOD but to her, and everybody else, he was still the Families Officer.

'Hello Dave. Jeremy just called.'

'Chrissy, it was Sgt Dent.'

'I know. What happened?' A knot was forming under her rib cage. Anita Dent had three young children and was a popular woman, always in the Families Office chatting over coffee or laughing with other wives. Chrissy wondered where she had been when the knock came upon her door; had the children heard? Who was with her now?

'IED, there are horrific injuries. It was well planned.'

'Where is she?'

'At home. Her mother and two sisters are on their way and her neighbour, you know Sandy Cooke? Yes, well they're best mates. She's with her and *The Casualty Notifying Officer* and a Padre.' God.

Chrissy knew the drill. She knew that shortly, Anita would meet her *Casualty Visiting Officer* who would support her for up to two years; he would arrange the funeral, sort Lee's affects and organise the repatriation of his body as well as put her in contact with any outside agencies that she may need such as *Relate, Cruse, Help for Heroes* or counsellors. Her body had sunk into itself and all her energy had been pulled from it; she thought she might be sick.

'It's protocol to go round, Chrissy.'

'I know.'

'Right away.'

'I know.'

'I'll be there in five minutes.' Her stomach lurched. She hadn't been trained for this but knew that one day it would come. She had put herself through a bereavement counselling course before Jeremy left with his blessing. He was so proud of her he had said. She hadn't even told Jane. She tried to remember the course and some suggestions of what to say. She remembered when her mother died and her world had fallen apart. Some people said silly things like, 'she's in a better place,' and this had infuriated her. Others had said nothing which was even worse; that was when she learnt that death is a plague that drives people away as Anita was going to find out. She busied herself with her coat, gloves and hand bag and stood nervously by the door; she would hear Dave's car.

Thankfully, when he pulled up, no-one was on the street and she could just slip into the passenger seat unchallenged. Maybe she should have taken the isolated Colonel's quarters after all? They drove past *Tesco* and she spotted flowers in the entrance and she wondered idly where the British tradition of buying flowers in sympathy came from; the Jews leave rocks and the Vikings burned everything. She would not take flowers; this wasn't someone's granny who had passed away in her sleep aged 95, this was a death borne of violence and horrific suffering and Anita and her children may never heal. They pulled up outside her small quarters and Chrissy's hands and cheeks were hot.

'Do the children know?'

'No, they think mummy is poorly – her GP has been and given her a shot of something, so she might be a bit groggy still. She can't face the children today; that's for another day.' Dave had obviously been told to go straight in as he didn't knock. Sandy was trying her best to entertain the children; she was watching a dinosaur movie with the eldest and colouring at the same time. The one year old played with cars. Chrissy took her coat off and joined in. Sandy's face was red and puffy and she smiled weakly. Dave disappeared upstairs and when he returned he said simply,

'She wants to see you.' Chrissy was terrified. She knew she would have to show her respects on Jeremy's behalf but she had never imagined that Anita would actually want to see her face to face. The shock showed on her face and Dave put his hand on hers with a 'you can do it' look. She rose and went through the door, her heart pounding. As she began to climb the stairs she willed herself not to cry; it was such a selfish act, the grief was all Anita's and no-one else's.

She found Anita on her bed on her side with a pile of tissues; a few empty cups littered her bedside table. A female professional sat on a chair in the corner of the room silently. Chrissy sat down gently and touched Anita's back. She let out a gut curdling sob and sank into Chrissy's lap where she stayed for a very long time. It was too soon for words. Anita was like a lost and innocent little girl and Chrissy stroked her tear-drenched hair and pulled it off her puffy face. She closed her eyes and seemed at peace and so Chrissy laid her gently back onto the bed and left the room. She had been there for over an hour. Downstairs, one of Anita's sisters had arrived. She eyed Chrissy suspiciously. Sandy stepped in.

'This is Chrissy; she's the CO's wife. As in, The Commanding Officer.' Chrissy hated her name in that moment, why couldn't she have been called something sensible like Margaret or Barbara; Chrissy sounded so flaky and upper class and why oh why did she have to say CO's Wife? It instantly put people's backs up. The woman made no attempt to introduce herself and so it was time to leave. She'd expected this, people deal with death in so many different ways; anger, fear, trauma, laughter; one had to choose what worked best. Who knew how she would react if it were her? In the car, Dave informed her that he'd already had several phone calls from wives wanting to help and that he had politely informed them that Anita's family was with her so please don't call on her. Of course; the vultures would come out now wanting to crush Anita with their sympathy and it was their job to protect her from this; they thought quickly; they had discussed the drill over coffee one morning four months earlier. Donations of food or toys should be delivered to the Families Office; Dave would pay for food to be delivered to the family so they had one less thing to think about. Dave's phone rang.

'Shit!'

'What?' Surely it hadn't happened again? So soon.

'It's already on *Facebook* thanks to Sharon Warmsley; name and everything.' Death attracts its vicarious spectators; they circle excitedly looking for titbits to share and fight over.

'That's disgusting.'

'I'll have a word.' Dave clenched the steering wheel tightly. Chrissy felt for him; his was a thankless task keeping four hundred wives happy, taking phone calls in the middle of the night saying that Corporal X is in the cells or Mrs Y has kicked Sgt Y out on the street for the fourth time this year. And now would come the most challenging point of his career to date; an Op Tour, not on the front line but in the firing line of, some would argue, an equally formidable opponent; women. Chrissy cringed at the thought of huddles of women whispering in the Families Office and shaking their heads, all offering advice. But thankfully, they were in the minority; this day would pass for most like any other apart from a generic text informing them of a fatality so they would know it wasn't theirs; they would chug along tending to their families praying it wouldn't be them next. After Dave had dropped her off, she felt weak and drained. It was dark now and a few lights burned in the close. Chrissy toyed with the idea of popping over to Jane's but she craved silence and privacy more. She poured herself a large glass of wine and sat in the lounge and wept.

HELMAND PROVINCE
22ND OCTOBER
1845HRS (1445HRS GMT)

A routine patrol leaves it's PB (Patrol Base) to clear an area deemed to be a medium threat. It is usual for a patrol to respond to local information once a threat has been ascertained and verified. As the patrol wanders through compounds with BARMA men at the helm, men wearing dusty combats and carrying 72lbs of kit (not including body armour) go about their business directing metal detectors and receiving information from receiving information from a UAV (unmanned aerial vehicle) flying 300m above them.

1915HRS (1515HRS GMT)

'HELLO. OVER. CONTACT: IED, REPEAT, CONTACT: IED. WAIT OUT.'

The net burst into life. It was Rupert Swan's voice.

A quad bike can be heard in the distance transporting the Coy (Company) Doc and shouting ensues as men take whatever cover they can without moving far expecting more explosions. They will have to maintain position for as long as it takes to clear the area which could be hours.

At first it is unclear who had stepped on the device and whether he was alive or dead. A path to the casualty will have to be cleared by an IED team before the Doc can assess the victim. Others in the Platoon have received shrapnel wounds to buttocks, faces and feet; they will be dealt with later; the Doc's priority is the ones who aren't moving. For interminable minutes, Captain Swan lay on the ground unable to reach Sgt Dent; his body was not moving and all the men could see and as the initial commotion settled, silence descended excepting the static of the radio and Rupert's voice demanding to know where the fuck the helicopter was.

1937HRS (1537HRS GMT)
Finally, the blades of a Chinook bringing the MERT (medical emergency response team) can be heard and rounds start pinging off in all directions. The IED team clears the area and finally the Doc can get to the body. Dent is clearly dead and as the Doc opens the body bag, men bow their heads in silent prayer. They cannot lose focus now; they have to get back to the PB.

As the helicopter leaves for SALATIN, Dent's men look for any military kit dispersed by the explosion that could fall into enemy hands: grenades, maps and medical kit and they carry out the grim task of looking for personal belongings that can be given to his family.

As they return to base, the men are in shock and as Rupert laments the lack of resources available to the British Army he curses what the men need on the ground and what they actually get. The defence cuts hit Rupert in the face and he feels bitterness well up in his throat.

A hasty memorial service is held soon after and a prayer of hope said for the five others that had been seriously wounded by shrapnel. Rupert goes over the orders time and time again; there had been little ambient light due to a sand storm and the area had been deemed safe by 5 Platoon who had patrolled there yesterday.

No doubt a Sgt from the SIB (Special Investigations Branch) would be on their way; already formulating questions in their head, what had gone wrong? Rupert cannot help but relive the orders from the early hours in an attempt to find something he'd missed. The image of Dent's body flying into the air will never leave him.

Later that day, Dent's friends would pack up his kit to be sent back to the Quarter Master and the personal belongings would be packaged for his wife. Sgt Dent had told his best friend, Sgt Ferris that he did not want his kit washed in the worst case scenario and Ferris was left the forbidding task of deciding what Anita should see and what she shouldn't. On searching through his things, Ferris found Dent's letter to his wife should anything happen; his hands shook, they had all written one.

1641HRS GMT
Anita Dent plays with her one year old son. He has changed so much; Lee won't believe it. The microwave pings and she leaves him to stir the sweet potato mush for his tea. The other two are at Sandy's for the afternoon and she loves afternoons like this; the delicious feeling of having Jacob all to herself. There is a furious rapping on the door and instantly Anita thinks something has happened to Tory or Dominic. She leaves the mush and rushes to the door. She stops short as the door is banged again. Sandy doesn't knock like that, she thinks. Suddenly she is alert and still as a fox. She looks at her watch: 4.42, and something within her memorises the numbers. Her gut turns over and her hands suddenly feel clammy. Slowly she peeps through the spyhole and sees several male figures. One of them is Dave Proctor. She manages to open the door in a haze and her knees buckle as Dave's eyes meet hers.

Chapter 4

News of the identity spread quickly and Jane had thought about visiting Chrissy several times but didn't want to come across as nosy. If Chrissy wanted to confide in her, she would. Jane wondered what kind of roll Chrissy was expected to take on if at all. Gossip had spread and Jane felt like all the others who hadn't known Anita. She'd heard of her and heard her bellowing laughter at the Family Office but she couldn't quite place her face. They said she had three kids under five and this made Jane feel ill. She imagined having to sit down and tell her children that they would never see their father again and what that might do to their little lives. She kept shaking her head and rubbing her eyes.

'What's up mum?' Harry was such a sensitive soul; he knew the moment that something was wrong.

'I'm tired, darling.'

'Milla playing up again? She really has no manners, are you sure she's my sister?' This made Jane smile; he was so grown up and proper just like his father. She ruffled his hair.

'Ten minutes.' He rolled his eyes; at the grand old age of ten he thought he should be staying up beyond 9 o'clock but it was a school night and Jane insisted.

The Tour seemed real now. The atmosphere had shifted and she wondered if everyone felt it. After Harry went to bed she picked up the phone to ring Debs. They hadn't spoken for a good few months.

'Jane! I was just thinking about you. Get ready; I'm coming for a long weekend next week if you'll have me. Of course, Ben is terrified of looking after the kids on his own, after all he is only their dad, but he's agreed, so start stocking the fridge girly.'

'Oh, Debs that's brilliant news. Perfect timing I'm feeling pretty low today.'

'Having a dip? Or is madam misbehaving?'

'The Battalion suffered its first fatality today.' She didn't feel right calling it just a death, it seemed more than that.

'Oh shit, Jane, that's horrendous. Do you know the wife?'

'No, thank god. She has three kids under five.'

'Oh my god, I feel sick.'

'I feel so helpless, Debs. I couldn't face it I would totally cave in.'

'No you wouldn't. Cheers.'

'What?'

'Well I'm assuming you've got a bottle open, so have I. Cheers.'

'Clink.'

'Don't tell the kids, they don't need to know.'

'Yes, you're right. Anyway, how are you?'

'Oh alright I suppose. Bloody mortgage fell through so back to square one.'

'Oh, Debs, I'm sorry, you really wanted that house.'

'No I want to stay in my beautiful quarters that were featured in *Ideal Home* last month because of their quirkiness; noisy boiler, mossy garden (north facing), creaky floor boards, paper lamp shades, dodgy plumbing and stained sage green carpets.' This made Jane laugh; a welcome diversion. Debs had had enough of moving and was settling the family in their own home but the house hunt and paperwork was tedious and frustrating. Jane wondered if she would reach that stage; yes, moving every two years wasn't ideal but she got itchy feet after a while in one place and enjoyed meeting new people, she liked making her houses homes but would it be better for the children to go to the same school for the rest of their childhood? She didn't know.

'So, tell me about The Patch, anyone interesting?' Debs giggled. This reminded Jane of when they used to share a bottle of wine together and compare notes on other wives. It was utterly bitchy but enormous fun.

'CO's wife has decided to live on The Patch and not Waterloo House.'

'What!' Debs nearly spat her wine. 'Fuck, that's terrible.'

'Actually, I like her.'

'That's even more terrible, Jane, have I taught you nothing?' Jane laughed.

'She's a genuine woman, no side, no agenda, just normal.'

'But how could that be? I bet she's an antelope at weekends or something.' Jane laughed again. This was doing her good.

'There's a new-in-green called Maggie who is tedious and self-absorbed.'

'Brilliant, get her round.'

'Two kids, world on her shoulders, hates her man for leaving her... you know the type.'

'Had an amazing job before marrying the army?'

'Expect so.'

'I can't wait; my visit just became more interesting. How are the kids?'

'Oh Harry is so grown up, Debs, he looks like a teenager already and gets embarrassed when I see him naked. Milla's a witch but an impressive and inventive one for which I salute her, Lucas is trapped in the middle and Christian has started fighting back.'

'No!'

'Yup, I pretend not to notice when he slams his sister against the wall or pulls her hair; it's sweet revenge for four long years of abuse and she deserves it.' Debs giggled. She had two of her own but older.

'What about yours?'

'Oh you think you know about private bathroom behaviour; Franky locks the door and Celia teases him about his voice and pubes; I think Celia and Milla were separated at birth weren't they?'

'How old is Franky now, Debs? Sixteen?'

'Oh yes, and Celia 18 and dating a twenty four year old. Ben went ballistic.'

'What did you say?'

'At least he's not one of your soldiers.'

They rang off, excited about their weekend together. Jane flicked around the TV but the casualties were being reported on two channels and stupid quizzes or reality shows blared on the others so she flicked it off. She had almost finished a whole bottle of wine, so she decided to go to bed; she'd probably be over the limit for the school run and have a hellishly sore head for the rest of the day which would make her irritable and snappy with the children. Well tonight she had wanted to forget and ease the fear and trepidation in her belly. She knew that comms would be down for a while but still James hadn't rung. Where was he? He'd said Afghanistan was beautiful and the night stars incredible, was he looking at them now? Was he thinking about her? Whose Company had Dent been in? Not James's she knew that much. She hoped beyond hope that Sgt Dent didn't turn out to have been in Ben Howard-Holmes's Company because they would all never hear the last of it from Titania. She could imagine it now; Titania worrying about her role as Company Commander's wife under pressure and obligation, counselling terrified wives, and bearing the white woman's burden for mankind while notching up injuries and fatalities in her husband's Company and secretly keeping a chart to boast of his singular bravery and commitment. Given the habit of Officers' wives shortening their names to Chrissy, Maggie, Twiggy, Fanny and Ginny, she secretly named Titania 'Titty' and thanked her parents for calling her Jane. They had decided to call their daughter Camilla without appreciating what it may one day become. To date, no-one had ever tried to call her Jany until that day over a year ago when Titty had said it once.

Jane had been to Titania's house to introduce herself and had instantly disliked the woman. She never stopped talking; about herself.

'Oh, fabulous to meet you Jany, I've heard so much about you.' Titania had gushed.

'What a job we face eh? When the boys have gone.' Jane thought she'd been about to get her Hunters on and practise tying knots and making fire; or, worse, baking hundreds of cakes for the Families Office and suggesting fund raising gatherings. She imagined Titania digging for victory in 1939 and posing for the papers then taking all the credit for single-handedly putting Hitler off the idea of invading, which, if Hitler had known Titty, might actually have been true. Jane found herself wondering if Titty had indeed been reincarnated just to piss everyone off. Jane tittered to herself and climbed the stairs remembering how she had been strangely nervous when she'd told Titania that she preferred plain old 'Jane'.

The house was silent. She used to find it unnerving when James was away but she was used to it now; except when it came to the moment that she went to bed, usually until then she kept herself busy, but when she climbed the stairs to the bathroom to brush her teeth and remove her make-up, she missed his idle chatter about her bottom or what he wanted to do when they were in bed. Her body ached and it surprised her because when James was around and available she didn't much care for sex. It was alright and she enjoyed the intensity at times when James gasped on top of her and they stuck together with his sweat, her knowing she still pleasured him with her post-four-baby figure. But now, in the silence of their large house and in her empty bed, she yearned for his muscular strength to pin her down, and turned over and over rubbing herself against her sheets, thrusting into nothing and running her fingers through her own hair. She found herself surprisingly wet and couldn't help but slide two fingers in and out, around and around; toying with her clitoris.

'Mum.' Shit! Jane popped up from underneath her dishevelled duvet and made out the silhouette of Milla in the glint of the moonlight flowing through her light curtains. Milla had been having trouble sleeping since James had left and had relapsed into being a small child again. Of course, she was only six, but it was as if she was four like her brother. She sucked her thumb.

'Can I come in with you, Mummy?' Jane didn't have the heart to deny her daughter this pleasure and comfort and opened the duvet for her daughter to climb in.

'Will you stroke my hair and do 'relax'?'

43

'Of course.' Jane had got into the habit of trying to relax the hyperactive Milla before bed time with a mantra of 'relax your eyes… relax your mouth… relax your shoulders…' etc. until she'd worked all the way down to her toes by which time Milla was usually asleep. It worked. Jane studied her daughter in the half light and noticed how at peace she looked when asleep - in total contrast to the whirlwind she became in daylight hours. Although a challenge, Jane admired Milla. The boys were boys; predictably uncomplicated and honest, Milla was manipulative, deceitful and wily; she'd make an awesome woman one day.

Jane woke to the sound of Lucas emptying his bladder; all over the bathroom floor no doubt. Milla had gone, probably watching the TV in front of which she would like to live given half the chance. Jane had noticed that she let the kids watch more TV now without a fellow cop to police the situation. She gave into other things, too, like enforcing teeth brushing so often and visits to *McDonalds*. She'd read about the man in the States who'd kept a *McDonalds* burger for fourteen years and it hadn't gone off. She shuddered at the thought and imagined the chemicals lurking in the so-called 'food' powerful enough to ward off nature's bacteria. However, tiredness and emotional erosion made her forget these little details when said chemicals kept her brood entertained for two hours on a Saturday.

Jane felt a stab of unknown fear and then she identified it. Anita Dent was waking up this morning knowing that she'll never see the father of her children again, or maybe she had never slept. Jane felt guilty that she had slept so soundly and wondered when Anita would sleep again without the help of a GP. There was a knock on the door and Jane quickly dragged on some joggers cursing whoever it might be. She checked herself in the mirror. After such a good night's sleep, her eyes were saggy and she had tram lines where the duvet had folded across her cheek. Bugger! But it was only Chrissy.

'Oh sorry Jane, I thought you'd be up with the children.' She hesitated. 'I'll come back later.'

'Don't be silly, I know I'm not at my best at 8am on a Tuesday but if you can handle it so can I. Coffee?'

'That would be wonderful.'

Jane led Chrissy into the kitchen and started to prepare proper coffee in the *DeLonghi* James had bought her for Christmas.

'Decaff or full bull?'

'Full what?' It was her and James's pet name for kick-ass full strength dark stuff able to strip the chest hairs off squaddies. She laughed apologetically.

'Full strength. Sorry.' Chrissy smiled.

'Full bull, please.'

'Coming up.'

'I suppose you heard about Sgt Dent?'

'Of course, jungle drums be loud in this part of the shire.' Jane put on her best West Country accent. Chrissy smiled again. Jane had got used to the CO's wife's smile and could tell whether it was genuine or forced; this morning it was forced.

'You look tired.' That was probably the wrong thing to say thought Jane but it was honest.

'I saw his wife last night, and their children.' Jane stopped.

'Oh God. I don't know what to say.' And she didn't.

'You don't have to say anything, Jane. Do you mind if I just sit here for a while and hide?' Jane was taken aback and flattered.

'Make yourself at home, there's your coffee. You know where the sugar is, I'm going to grab a shower and do the school run. I'll be back about 9.20 okay?'

'Thank you.'

When Jane returned she was pleased to see Chrissy still sat in her kitchen.

'You have beautiful children, Jane.'

'Oh, I'm not sure about that. You don't see them when night falls and they grow fangs.' Jane wondered when Chrissy would get down to business; she obviously wanted to discuss something.

'I'm not sure it was such a good idea staying on The Patch; I had three knocks on my door before 7.30 this morning and only made it over here by sprinting.' Jane was reminded of Debs' reaction last night to the CO's wife's decision, and wondered if she agreed or not.

'I don't know, Chrissy. It shows you care; that you're not likely to run away.' Chrissy laughed ironically and Jane remembered that she was going to see her divorced friend next week and how bad it would look if she had to cancel because of the funeral.

'Yes you read my mind. I promised Jenny I would be there but the funeral's next week.'

'Why don't you invite Jenny here and pay her train fare?' Jane knew she could afford it and that Chrissy wouldn't see the suggestion as rude. The CO's wife nodded. It wasn't such a bad idea.

'Jane?' Jane looked at her and a knot formed in her stomach.

'Will you come to the funeral with me?' Oh Shit. She couldn't help but be honest.

'Oh Christ, Chrissy, why me? I'd be terrible. What would I do with the kids?'

'I can arrange childcare here at your house paid for by the Families Office, that's the easy bit. I'm sorry to burden you but I want someone to dilute Titania's grief. Sgt Dent was Ben's Company.' God this just got worse. The thought of attending a full military funeral was bad enough but with Titania Howard-Homes? She rolled her eyes away from Chrissy's gaze. She thought of James and what he would want her to do.

'Ok, I'll come.'

Chapter 5

Maggie watched Alex playing on the floor of the GP's waiting area; an old couple stared lovingly and nostalgically at him. She wondered if she would see children in such a favourable light when she was eighty. He was very cute, she had to admit that, but she rarely got to enjoy him as his sister was always ruining her day. Bethany had been born with little fuss and Maggie had congratulated herself for being a near perfect first-time mum. The midwives all did too. She hadn't torn, stage two had taken around half an hour, and everything had gone swimmingly according to her pre-written birth plan, something the midwives hadn't seen in years. Admittedly, Maggie was stubborn and that coupled with a high pain threshold led her to believe that childbirth was a doddle. But then the fun began. Bethany was a hungry baby and screamed for food at 3am despite having been fed two hours before. She remembered with bitterness burping Bethany and rocking back and forth in her feeding chair crying tired, desperate tears as Mark slumbered peacefully on. Then came the weaning. Bethany would throw clumps of lovingly prepared food on the floor and look for her mother's reaction, she squelched avocado between her toes and stuck lumps of cauliflower and chicken patties to the wall. She learned the word 'no' before any other. Then the teething started. One night Maggie had patted neat whiskey onto her daughter's gums to stop the crying and Mark had admonished her because it had been a single malt. Bethany had been blessed with the misfortune of getting her teeth late but all at the same time and it had seemed like she screamed for weeks. By the time she was crawling and becoming more interested in the world around her rather than out-smarting her mother, Maggie had found out that she was pregnant. As the term pressed on, Bethany sensed her mother slowing down and took full advantage, running away in shops and screaming in Post Office queues. As Maggie became more stressed and embarrassed, Bethany seemed more hell bent on driving her into a deep depression which had hit shortly after Alex was born. When Mark brought them home from the hospital, Bethany had sunk her nails into the newborn's cheeks and drawn blood. Maggie had collapsed into tears and Mark had hit Bethany's bottom, hard, making her scream and look at them both as if they were monsters, which she supposed they were. At her 12 week check, it was official; Maggie was suffering from post-natal depression.

The feelings hadn't subsided but she had been weaned off Prozac by a helpful but short-sighted GP in Shrivenham. It had been too early. She had been torturing herself for months, telling herself that if the GP thought it was time to cope alone then he was right, wasn't he? The feelings of despair and frustration and worthlessness had begun to creep back. She resented Mark, off pursuing his dreams while she was left holding the babies, with a trashed figure, no friends and no job. She resented everything. She resented other mothers who seemed to cope effortlessly, or who actually even seemed to enjoy being a mother. She resented friends who had lived in the same house for years and had a readymade network of support from sisters, brothers, aunties, mums and dads; she had no-one. Dad didn't like driving far and mum still worked part time and always seemed too busy to visit. Mark's parents seemed to judge her every move and she felt examined under a microscope, like some startled insect desperate to get away; she would never be good enough for Mark's parents and visits from them were excruciating so she avoided them altogether. Mark had indicated that he would like them to stay during his mid-tour leave and she was trying to come up with a water-tight excuse to prevent it from happening.

Maggie sat staring into space and reminiscing on the last four years and how Bethany was destroying her marriage and her life. Every day brought new and interesting topics over which to fight with her daughter, and her attitude grew more intense and worrying. The old couple had shifted their gaze to her and they looked sympathetic; God how patronising, Maggie squirmed.

'It gets easier. I had four boys.' The old woman offered.

'I'm done,' Maggie smiled weakly. 'I only have two hands.' The dismissal sounded harsh but Maggie couldn't wait for Bethany to grow up and leave her alone. She felt instant guilt for Alex; if only she'd had two of him.

'Margaret Heston?' She hated when people used her full name. The Doctor waited in the entrance of her surgery, smiling.

'Hello! Come and take a seat. Doctor Stevens sat down in front of her computer screen and was presumably studying Maggie's notes. It must be like a production line, thought Maggie; one after the other of depressives, addicts, weezers and complainers; the thought depressed her more and her shoulders sagged.

'So, what can we do for you today?' Maggie wanted to ask for a spa retreat and a pedicure but held her tongue. She played with her fingers.

'How are the children?' Maggie was taken by surprise.

'Fine.'

'But you don't seem fine, Margaret.'

'Will you please call me Maggie?' Irritation bubbled under the surface and the Doctor looked intently at her.

'Why don't you tell me what's bothering you, Maggie?' Maggie started and quickly found that she could not stop. The bitter-tasting, foul-smelling rot that was inside her spilled out and then the tears came rolling down her cheeks, but still she did not stop. Dr Stevens nodded and passed her tissues. Eventually Maggie came up for air and blew her nose. Alex's brow was wrinkled and he watched his mother in silence; toys forgotten.

'You've been having a rough time. You know there are several events in our lives that are called critical; moving house, having children, separation are but a few of them, and you are going through them all. We aren't designed to cope with that much stress Maggie; I want to put you back on Prozac. I think you need it now to just ease the journey a little until things become easier in your life. Shall we talk about Bethany some more? Would you like to have her behaviour assessed?'

Maggie panicked. 'What does that mean exactly?'

'Well, a Health Visitor would come to your house over a period of about a month on two or three occasions and sit and observe Bethany or play games with her. She'd be on the lookout for any signals that Bethany was disturbed emotionally or troubled by something and thus expressing anger directed towards the only person in the world she can rely on; you.' Maggie had never seen it like this before; of course it made sense. Bethany didn't hate her mother; she was terrified of losing her.

'You know, children who move with the forces or with ex-patriot communities are more likely to have said goodbye to more significant people in their lives by the age of fifteen than most people will in their lifetimes. It seems to me, and I cannot guarantee it, that Bethany is displaying huge confidence issues related to belonging.' Maggie bit her lip.

'When can you get the Health Visitor round?' Doctor Stevens picked up her phone and dialled an internal number. 'Viv? Yes, I've got a patient who would like you to visit regarding her daughter's behaviour…she's four…yes…yes.' The Doctor covered her mouthpiece, 'Next Tuesday?' Maggie nodded. 'That works, Viv; what time? Two?' She looked at Maggie again who nodded. Maggie couldn't think of anything pressing in her diary, and the thought depressed her mood further. There was a time when Maggie's diary would have been full to bursting with dance classes, meeting friends, lunches out and cinema dates. Not now. Now she became excited over the weekly shop and what offers there would be on wine at Tesco. The Doctor rang off. She turned back to her screen and typed in some notes. 'So, Maggie, will you try the Prozac again for me?' Maggie nodded. Of course she bloody would; she would try anything. The Doctor turned back to her screen, she was updating some information and talking out loud…'non-smoker… height… let's weigh you… alcohol?' Maggie froze.

'Erm...I have a little glass most nights.' Big, fat, whopping lie. Doctor Stevens didn't seem interested.

'Ok try to have one or two grog-free nights a week just to give your system a break from it. You're staying well under fourteen units so that's good. Alcohol doesn't help depression.'

'Ok.' Maggie responded. Her weekly alcohol intake was closer to a bottle a night which equated to seven times eight units and seven times 800 calories, it made Maggie feel ill just thinking about the calculations. She was handed her prescription and the Doctor smiled warmly at her. 'Take care of yourself Maggie.' What did that mean? She wheeled Alex out of the surgery and went straight to the chemist. She felt a little lighter of step having shared a burden. When she got back home and checked herself in the mirror quickly she found that she had black streaks down her cheeks from crying and she had walked around *Tesco* like that.

She didn't always buy her wine from *Tesco* as she had got to know most of the checkout staff being in there daily. Sometimes she would drop into the local off-licence or even drive to *Sainsbury's* to avoid detection. She bought in bulk so she wouldn't have to visit the same counter with a bottle of wine every time she was there; in bulk, one could be having a party and she could have a lot of parties; lots of friends and family who visited often demanding to be fed and watered well. If only. Maggie had tried to 'detox' several times but failed. She would resolve most days to stay off the wine for a few nights but as her day ended and she fought with Bethany at tea time or was splashed on purpose at bath time or subjected to moans and excuses for Bethany creeping downstairs after bed time just one more time, she would cave in and pour herself a glass of the pale liquid which she would swill around her mouth enjoying the release it brought. One glass always led to another and another so that on not a few occasions she had found herself quite drunk by 9 o'clock. Even worse, the alcohol slowed her senses and made her lethargic and so she would skip dinner and simply fall into bed wishing her life away in chunks. If the phone rang late she wouldn't answer it fearing her words would sound slurry. If it had been Mark and he phoned again the next day she would just tell him that she'd had an early night again. No-one knocked on her door after 7 anyway so the habit had quickly and quietly developed until she found herself thinking about her first glass by 5 o'clock. Maybe the drugs would help; if she could just pull herself out of the hole she'd dug, maybe she'd be strong enough to say no to temptation. The Doctor had asked her about exercise and she'd admitted she hadn't done any for years. Exercise is good for depression, she'd been told; maybe one day she'd give it a go but not today.

The news of the death of Sgt Dent had shocked her and she'd responded in a time-worn manner by pouring herself a glass of wine which led to four or five and she'd woken with a hangover, again. Now, as she drove to nursery to pick up Bethany, she wondered if she could hold on until bed time because after that she didn't need it. She had swallowed two pills with water when she'd got home to kick start her recovery. However, Bethany had pushed her buttons on arrival home and hadn't come up for air. She generally collected her daughter in good spirits but five minutes in the car and usually Bethany would find something to get angry about. Today it was Alex who was singing a tune she didn't like. She hit him and Maggie had stopped the car and hit her back; and instantly regretted it. Bethany had wailed like a victim and it made Maggie's stomach turn over; she didn't know how hard the smack had been; maybe a bit too hard? By the time they reached home, Alex was screaming and Bethany was kicking him from her car seat. Why did she have to be so difficult? Did she hate her daughter or love her? Sometimes she simply did not know. She bundled Alex into the house and gave him a chocolate finger. Immediately Bethany demanded one too.

'No, Bethany, because bad behaviour is not rewarded. If you stopped hurting your brother then you would get chocolate fingers too.' She had no idea whether this was a legitimate tactic but surely by four, her daughter could decipher the difference between reward and punishment and how to avoid the latter and attain the former? Alex already grasped the concept and always said 'sorry' for being naughty without prompting. By four o'clock Maggie was emotionally exhausted and the thought of bed time made her heart lurch in desperation. If only she could fast forward this part of her day maybe she would still have part of her sanity left. Bethany began throwing the post around while Maggie attempted to warm some Bolognese sauce for their tea. Alex screamed again and she rushed to where the noise had come from. Bethany had taken one of his cars from him and was holding it up above her head with her tongue out.

'Bethany, give the car back. One day Alex will be bigger than you.'

'No he won't!' Bethany cried. Her facial expression was one of disgust and wrong doing and Maggie wondered where it came from; her face was red and she gritted her teeth in defiance.

'Bethany, please give him his car back and say sorry and me and you can read a book.' Bethany launched the car at her brother and it hit him on the temple; he screamed again. Maggie rushed over to him; there was blood where the toy had impacted.

'Why do you do this?' She screamed at her daughter who simply mimicked her. How could she protect Alex from this while making tea and running a bath? She had to defuse the situation but didn't know how.

'Go to your room please Bethany, this behaviour is not nice and it is wrong.'

'No!' Maggie lifted the girl roughly and put her under one arm; she was amazed by her own strength. She deposited her daughter into her room and slammed the door. Bethany began kicking the door and launching things towards it. Maggie dragged a chair over and hooked it under the door handle locking her in. She went back downstairs and turned up the radio. Alex played happily with his toys until tea was ready and came to the table when called, smiling broadly. Bethany screamed on and Maggie wondered where she got the energy.

As Alex started to eat, Maggie climbed the stairs but not before pouring a glass of wine which she had finished by the time she reached the top. She hated herself. And Mark. And Bethany.

'Bethany. You may come out if you are going to come downstairs and eat nicely, otherwise you can stay in there.' An object was launched at the door. Maggie went back downstairs. Alex had finished and yawned. She took him into her arms and took him upstairs for his bath. Bethany was still screaming. Maggie felt a huge sadness not just because of her daughter's unhappiness but that her son had become oblivious to it; anaesthetised as if it was common and normal. Bethany went quiet. Maggie left Alex playing in the bath and opened Bethany's door. She was red faced and her eyes were swollen. She rushed into her mother's arms and sobbed. Maggie shook her head, what was the point? Why did she work herself into such a state? To what end? What was she trying to communicate to her mother? She patted her head and asked gently if she would like to eat now. Bethany nodded and pulled her mother's hand.

'Darling, I can't leave Alex in the bath, you go ahead and I will be down very soon.' Bethany sniffed but descended the stairs looking utterly miserable. Alex played happily and got out of the bath when asked. She settled him in bed with a book and promised to tuck him in soon. Downstairs she sat with Bethany but couldn't think of anything to say. This girl was the cause of all her misery, she thought and not for the first time she imagined life without her. When Bethany had almost finished she got down from the table and skipped upstairs. Maggie didn't have the energy to insist she clear away or ask to get down or even finish the food; she sipped her third glass of wine and wanted the day to end. 'Can I sleep in your bed Mummy?' It was so wrong to say yes but she knew if she didn't she would have to face another battle and that would keep Alex awake who was virtually asleep already.

'Yes, but I will put you into your own bed when you fall asleep.'

'Can I have a jumper Mummy?' Bethany had taken to asking for something of Maggie's to get her to sleep, like a jumper or scarf; something that smelled of her mother. She took off her scarf and wrapped it around Bethany's shoulders. Once she was in her bed, she checked on Alex who was fast asleep. Alex missed out on so much because his mother was busy trying to control his sister or prevent her from hurting something or someone; it was a full-time job and Alex was neglected. She checked Bethany once more; she had rearranged her bed. Bethany couldn't stand the sheets too high or too low, and had to ruffle the pillows several times before they were just right. Maggie watched the ritual and wondered when she could sit in peace. 'Ready,' said Bethany. Maggie kissed her and snuggled into her shoulder which Bethany loved. She switched off the light and closed the door half way and prayed Bethany wouldn't get up.

She couldn't face supper. An ad was playing on the radio and she'd heard it before. It was the local gym offering free personal training sessions to those who joined for six months. She was tempted, but, as always, forgot about it as she poured another glass of wine.

Chapter 6

Chrissy had been dreading the day for months. She reckoned it would take three hours to drive to the funeral of Sgt Dent. Twenty Three wives had given their names to Dave Proctor who had arranged for them to travel by mini bus. Some of them were Anita's friends but some were not. They had gathered on the parade square huddled in coats and smoking last minute cigarettes. Some had hot flasks of coffee for the journey, others had brought food. Chrissy and Jane would be travelling with Dave in a private car. Titty was supposed to have been accompanying them - she had talked of nothing else for a week - but she had cried off last minute saying her irritable bowel had flared up again. Chrissy had not seen a coffin since the death of her mother and a knot of butterflies lodged in her stomach. Thank god Jane had agreed to come, she thought. When Dave finally pulled up outside Chrissy's quarters, he looked smart and formal; he held his hat under his arm and boasted six medals that told a sombre story. Chrissy wondered what he was thinking; this would be the first of many funerals and, like her, he would attend every one having dealt directly with the families of the fallen. Chrissy and Jane glanced at one another and looked serious. Chrissy thought Jane looked strangely beautiful in her black outfit; she felt uncomfortable in hers as if it no longer fitted. If she could just get through the first one with Jane at her side, she'd be alright, she kept thinking over and over again. The driver remained silent as Chrissy and Jane were escorted to the car by Dave. Chrissy had brought coffee and magazines to keep their minds occupied. Dave sat in front to give them some privacy which touched Chrissy. As the car pulled away from the close, Chrissy saw Maggie pushing Alex and could have sworn that she was crying. Whatever she was doing she certainly didn't notice the car; too wrapped up in her own world to notice she thought. The traffic was normal and people went about their business oblivious to the nature of the day. After all it was just one car; Sgt Dent already rested in his home town. Her thoughts turned to Anita and she wondered if the children knew yet. They weren't attending the funeral and she was relieved; she would have found it virtually impossible to look into their eyes. She had to stay strong. Jane caught her wandering eye and squeezed her hand.

'Says here that this woman breast fed her father to ward off cancer and it worked!' Jane was trying to distract her and it worked. There was a picture of said father and daughter and Chrissy put her hand over her mouth.

'That's disgusting!' Jane turned to an article on Gary Barlow and *X Factor*.

'Let's send the *X Factor* judges wristbands to wear.' Jane's idea intrigued Chrissy. Why not, they could only say "no thank you". Dave had organised personalised wristbands for the Battalion and they had gone on sale locally. Since then they had gone through seven hundred bands and raised money for the Families Office. Some things were paid for by the MOD but sadly it was never enough and the money would be used to support families and rehabilitation.

Later as they turned into the village that had been the birth place of Lee Dent, they noticed scores of people walking in the same direction and some lined the streets. Grown men could be seen rubbing their eyes and people shook their heads. My god, thought Jane. The whole town has turned out: young, old, men, women, all turning out to say farewell to a local lad who joined the army. The driver pulled up near the mini bus carrying the others and they got out to stretch. Some wives grabbed a quick fag before they walked toward the church. Chrissy badly needed the loo but she would just have to hold it. She turned to find Jane who had knocked on a random door. What was she doing? She talked away with the woman who answered and was now nodding and smiling. She opened her door further and Jane gesticulated to Chrissy who joined her.

'I don't mind at all, you've driven a long way, it's the second door on the right. So sad, lovely little lad he was.'

Chrissy couldn't believe it; Jane had asked to use the woman's loo! However, she couldn't thank her enough as the sweet release hit her. This small act of comedy was a welcome diversion as they shared the room and took it in turns. They smiled their thanks profusely to the old woman who was proud to have helped in even a small way. Dave looked puzzled. 'Where have you been? We need to go in.'

'Don't ask.' The walk to the church was sobering. Press lined the streets and the nature of the occasion assaulted the two women. There was a large police presence and people stood quietly shuffling their feet. The Royal British Legion stood proudly wearing medals and holding flags to pay their respects as the crowds grew bigger. The press clicked away and some stood on ladders to get a better shot. Chrissy and Jane were uncomfortable and looked away. They approached the church doors. Jane's heart beat loudly in her chest and she kept close to Chrissy. The church was almost full and Dave directed them to the front. Oh god, she hadn't expected this. The left hand side of the church was full of uniforms and medals; the right full of ordinary people and tears. How ironic thought Jane; just like a marriage but which side was more loyal? Organ music played almost imperceptibly and Jane couldn't think of anything but her wedding day. The military presence stood straight and silent on the left hand side and relatives and loved ones on the right; two families torn apart by tragedy. The left side of the church handled it better though, thought Jane cynically. Armies have been losing soldiers for centuries; this family will only lose their son once. The bearers arrived and the two women took deep breaths. Quiet, almost unrecognisable sobbing murmured around the church and Jane took deep gulps of air; her cheeks were burning and her hands were clammy. Chrissy fiddled with her wristband. Dave looked dead ahead. He looked a handsome veteran in his hat. Some of the other wives turned around to look and Jane thought this crass. 'Everybody Hurts' by REM began to play and people barely kept themselves together. A lump formed in Jane's throat as it constricted and she looked to the ceiling. Anita walked ahead of her husband and was flanked by mother and sister. Her face was covered with net but the dark circles could still be seen around her harrowed eyes; she looked ahead dispassionately towards the altar, not daring to meet anyone's eyes. She was followed closely by other family members who held onto one another. Some missed their step and an older man, probably the father, held onto the pews for support. Six men in full ceremonial uniform carried the coffin containing Lee Dent's body or what was left of it Jane couldn't help thinking. They stood tall and brave, honouring their comrade having been flown back specially from theatre to complete the task. The coffin was shrouded in the Union Flag and having seen it so many times on TV on previous tours; it took Jane's breath away. Her eyes stung; Chrissy found her hand. Sniffles and sobs resonated around the church as Lee's body came to rest in front of the altar.

The first hymn was introduced and Jane thought she might crack; *I Vow to thee My Country* was sung at their wedding.

'The love that asks no question, the love that stands the test,
The love that lays upon the altar, the dearest and the best;
The love that never falters, the love that pays the price,
The love that makes undaunted, the final sacrifice.'

Singing could be heard just off time outside and there must have been hundreds of people out there. As the organist finished, the air once again filled with sniffs and coughs. Chrissy got a tissue out of her pocket and wiped her nose; Jane nudged her and she passed one across discreetly. Jane pressed it to the corners of her eyes and she wondered how long this would last.

The eulogy was read by Colonel Mark Dalton in the absence of Lee's Company Commander, but it was Ben Howard-Holmes's words that formed the body of the message. Anita bowed her head when she heard details of Lee's bravery and commitment; his courage and honour and messages from his mates still in Afghanistan. The priest then took his turn and struggled over the human noise of devastation and Jane wondered if he found these occasions trying, or did he really believe that Lee's soul was resting with God...*'and there's another country I heard of long ago, most dear to them that love her, most great to them that know...'*

They stood for the next hymn and Chrissy took a sharp intake of breath; she had dreaded this. *Jerusalem* was sung at her mother's funeral and the haunting pitch and tales of struggle and beauty was a common choice and no surprise.

'And did those feet in ancient time...
'And was Jerusalem builded here,
'Among those dark satanic mills?'
'I will not cease from mental fight,
Nor shall my sword sleep in my hand,
Till we have Built Jerusalem,
In England's green and pleasant land.'

A senior Regimental Colonel marched up to the coffin and folded the flag which was presented to Anita; she accepted it and stared at it. It was over. The coffin was hefted once again onto six strong shoulders and their faces were fixed in solid unmovable masks as Eric Clapton's *Tears in Heaven* began. Anita walked unsteadily behind, supported by her mother who was crying tears that will not stop for a very long time. Music is truly the language of the heart, thought Jane and the words left nothing to say; words may never be needed again, but the memory of the music would live on forever.

Would you hold my hand, if I saw you in heaven?
Would you help me stand, if I saw you in heaven?

Slowly, the congregation made its way outside where the press took more photos. They stood on walls to get the best angles and talked on mobiles to their offices. The coffin was driven away to a private burial service, followed closely by the funeral cortege. Groups of people chatted quietly outside and Jane and Chrissy said hello to various military people they had come to know over the years. It was time to go. The lady whose loo they had used was in tears at her gate. They smiled warmly and she waved.

When they returned to the car they all sighed and Dave removed his hat and rubbed his hair; it was a distinctly military thing to do and reminded Jane of James.

'Jesus, that was horrendous.' Jane tried to make conversation. Chrissy looked pretty ashen. 'I feel as though I have run a marathon and my body aches.'

'Well done you two. The Col will be proud of you.' Dave was thoughtful as ever and it was hard to imagine him as a soldier in theatre although he had seen much action in his time. The rest of the journey was spent in silence apart from a *Tesco* stop and a loo stop; they hadn't eaten all day. Chrissy thought of Anita and doubted she would ever see her again. Her life was about to take a sharp turn away from Army life, although Dave would follow her progress and Chrissy would surely write.

'Thank you for coming Jane. It means a lot. I'm sure it wasn't easy.'

'No it wasn't but it was nothing compared to what Anita Dent is going through right now and her children.' There was nothing more to say. They were exhausted. As they returned to The Patch the day was giving up its light and matched their moods. Chrissy was suddenly thankful that she lived on The Patch; she would not want to be going into that cavernous palace that stood in splendid isolation on the periphery of the parade square. As it was, she knew Jane was three doors away. She would make it up to her someday. The thought of facing the kids exhausted Jane even more and Chrissy read her thoughts.

'Want me to help with bath and bed? It's been a while but I'm sure I'll cope.' Jane was shocked but grateful. 'Oh please, would you?' She said in relief. Actually Chrissy rather wanted to unwind from the day in someone's company even if accompanied by screaming children; after all the children weren't hers and so the stress would bounce off her deliciously. Jenny had turned down the offer to drive up and stay, much to Chrissy's regret, but she had understood. A full tank of petrol was an expense that a divorced woman could not afford. Chrissy had arranged for a baby sitter who could drive to pick Jane's children up from school and entertain them until they returned. Of course Christian had been home all afternoon but she knew the sitter well and she was more than capable. When they were dropped off, the normality of noisy children was a welcome one. Lucas and Milla charged around the house while Christian watched and Harry was locked in his room away from the chaos no doubt studying.

'Wine?'

'I was wondering when you'd ask.' The day deserved it. The children could wait.

'I wonder how many more. I'm happy to come with you again, Chrissy; it's easier in pairs isn't it?' Chrissy was grateful but she looked awfully tired. Jane had no idea how old she was but she looked over fifty today.

'Right.' Chrissy was decisive and Jane in no mood to argue. 'I'll run the bath, you round 'em up.'

'Yes, ma'am.' As always, Milla was the most difficult to catch but that was alright as Christian and Lucas could bath together and Milla could go last and daydream until the water grew cold while Jane tackled the others. When the children were settled, Jane put a plate of cheese, pate and dips out on the kitchen table with some crackers and chutney. It was a welcome sight; they were ravenous, all they had eaten all day was takeaway nibbles from *Tesco*. They were feeling distinctly tipsy and so the calories were welcome too. Both women felt as though they'd been through something together that day; they didn't necessarily have to discuss it, but because they had both been there it halved the stress and brought some kind of comfort. Jane was right, Chrissy thought, it is easier with two. She would take up Jane's offer again.

By the time Chrissy left, it was gone eleven and they giggled about something that would be forgotten by tomorrow. Chrissy noticed Maggie's light still on but she presumed the children still needed a comfort light sometimes. Should she knock? She crossed the road and tapped gently not wanting to wake a child; Maggie wouldn't be happy with that at all. She tapped again but she heard no noise behind the door. Should she knock louder? No, she left it and wrapped her jacket closer around her. She shivered as she opened her own door and was faced with a dark, gloomy, silent home. She wished her boys were closer. Her mobile buzzed. Who the hell could it be at this time? Jeremy only called the landline. A knot formed in her stomach. It was Dave Proctor; a young Rifleman called Ian Clark had died from small arms contact in Helmand Province. The first thing that struck her was that Dave was a machine; there she was getting pissed with Jane and he was still at work; she felt ashamed. The second thing that struck her was the context of these deaths; they were happening suddenly and consecutively, had something gone wrong? Or did this mean that Jeremy was taking the fight to the enemy as promised and casualties reflected the ground won not lost? She thought of Jem. Is this what he wanted? Would he want his sons to sacrifice life and limb for such a cause? She sighed. What cause? She couldn't actually pin one down, it was so enigmatic. The words 'terrorist' and 'extremist' were bandied about so thoughtlessly in the press that now everyone who was our sworn enemy must therefore be in the wrong. Who was it that said 'one man's hero is another man's terrorist'? By that logic she guessed that Hitler and Stalin could be classed as freedom fighters and Ghandi a terrorist. It was all so confusing and now that soldiers had started to die she didn't know how to feel. Her friends and relatives had always taken Chrissy's back bone for granted. She was made of 'stern stuff' and suited marriage to an Officer who would one day be General. But as her own boys had toyed with the OTC and joining up, it had terrified her, did this make her a hypocrite? She could stomach the deaths of other women's sons but not her own? But today she had found out that she couldn't stomach it; how could she? If she lost Jem then at least she'd be able to explain in adult English to Jake and Will; unlike Anita Dent who had to make pre-schoolers understand; it was an impossible task; those children were scarred forever. And now Rfn Clark, who was he? She couldn't place him. Dave had said he was 21 years old. The same as Will. The wine no longer seemed a good idea and she rushed to the toilet to throw up.

Maggie lay on her sofa humming quietly to the greatest love songs album, glass in hand; eyes glassy. The children were asleep, at last. The rapping at the door had startled her and she had dived for cover behind a sofa before she realised that her curtains were all drawn and she hadn't been spotted. She had peaked through the downstairs loo window and spied Chrissy tapping lightly on her door. What did she want? She wanted to open the door and fall at Chrissy's feet and spill out all of her hatred and loneliness, but at the same time she didn't trust her. Eventually Chrissy had slipped away and gone home so Maggie relaxed and poured another glass of wine. By 9am the next morning, 400 wives had received a generic text that sadly, another soldier had died yesterday. In her post-alcoholic haze, Maggie chided herself; what if Chrissy had been coming over to share her burden and the solemn news? No, surely she wouldn't confide in such a junior Officer's wife? By the time Maggie had taken Bethany to nursery and knocked on Chrissy's door, the house was empty as usual.

Chapter 7

Four weeks had passed since the death of Rfn Clark and seven more soldiers had died. Chrissy had attended every funeral and Jane had accompanied her to four. They told no-one and no-one asked; but word got around via those who volunteered to go on the bus. As a result there was a slightly perceptible shift in respect for Chrissy; women stood to chat for longer and looked her in the eye. Fifty women had attended the funeral of Sgt Page. His wife was popular and well liked and Colin a cheeky prankster in the Mess. The funeral had been hell; they had three teenage daughters who held onto one another and their mother, sobbing uncontrollably. More lives destroyed; more scars to bear. A silent and insidious killer lurked around the barracks. It was reported nationally but then forgotten as the journalists and camera crews moved on; but the shattered lives remained. Chrissy had guessed that there had been five hundred at Page's funeral. Jem had shown signs of fatigue when he'd called that day; he sounded tired and stressed, the tour was being reported in the press as a particularly tough one.

It was part of Dave's job to provide some sort of distraction for the wives during a tour and the success of this activity varied from officer to officer. Dave cared about his job and came up with some great ideas. Chrissy was wary of becoming too involved as she worried she'd put people off attending, gone were the days when the CO's wife led the way, it was a little more democratic now although she could name a few officers' wives who still wore their husband's rank and demanded preferential treatment. Chrissy couldn't avoid them altogether but gave them a wide berth when possible. Chrissy actually preferred the company of soldiers' wives; they were more real and less self-focused, except Jane of course. This was why she was looking forward to a Sunday roast in the

Sergeants' Mess. It had been Dave's idea and it was no ground breaker but it was working well. The children were catered for with something yellow and chips or they could go for the roast as most of the adults did. Dave charged a small fee of £2 a head and he had received a few comments indicating that anything laid on by the Families Office should be free but they missed the point; it was a nominal amount to cover costs; Dave needed all of his budget to cover travel to funerals, visiting bereaved families and sending presents to Amber Lynn, the country's most state of the art rehab centre in Hampshire; where, to date, forty five men had been treated from the Battalion. Some remained there still and would for a long time. Years of physio awaited some of them after that and then coming to terms with never running again, never doing push ups with their pals, never dragging a comrade over the assault course's seven foot wall and, for some, never making love to a woman. One young man had been a virgin when he'd had most of the lower part of his body blown away including his penis. Sometimes Chrissy wondered whether it was right to save them with such horrific injuries; in any other war they wouldn't have stood a chance; Iraq and Afghanistan had given rise to the ultimate sharpening of medical response times and hi-tech treatment that a civilian hospital could only dream of. Was this a good thing? Chrissy didn't know. One thing was for sure though - it wouldn't be a topic of conversation in the Sgts' Mess that afternoon. The chatter would be about babies, pregnancy, Saturday nights, *Strictly* and *X Factor*. It wasn't that they were uneducated women disinterested in current affairs; more that they had reached saturation level with reality and wanted to dip out of it sometimes. Chrissy enjoyed the conversations and she was seen as somewhat of an older, wiser Aunt who gave advice on weaning and teething. She was only 49 but felt older sometimes. Jem was four years her junior and his parents had not approved but here they were, still together after twenty four years with two fabulous sons who the in-laws loved to death.

The walk to the Barracks was a five minute stroll through the back gate from The Patch, and women joined together as they pushed buggies and shared stories. The price of food was a common theme as was children's behaviour. Maggie walked out of her house as Chrissy and Jane passed. They hadn't seen much of her lately but they both stopped and each noted how well she looked compared to that dreary afternoon in Chrissy's kitchen. Bethany scowled and Alex was refusing to get into his buggy, but Maggie seemed less suicidal about the whole affair; she spoke calmly and cajoled Alex into his seat, but Bethany still scowled.

'Hi Maggie you look great, what have you been up to?'

'I joined a gym.' And I'm on anti-psychotic drugs she thought but didn't say.

'Well it's clearly working, where is it?'

'Oh just the *Nuffield*, I got a few free PT sessions when I joined and I'm loving it, I was forever reading that exercise gave you more energy and trying to figure out the oxymoron but it's true.' Maggie couldn't help but prove her intelligence whenever she opened her mouth thought Jane, but she let it go.

'I've been thinking about doing the same but I don't seem to find the time.' Said Jane. In fact this was untrue; she was lazy and loved food and would rather eat a doughnut than lift weights. She had been the same all her life; at school she had joined library club rather than hockey and read for hours while her friends played in the street. James said he loved her curves but deep down she wished she had Maggie's figure. Now, looking at the transformation in Maggie whom she assumed had less time than herself to dedicate to sweating, she toyed with the idea of following suit.

'You've inspired me, Maggie can I come with you to have a look?' Maggie was pleased, she quite fancied having a gym partner now she had overcome her nerves and thought Jane to be fun if a little distant and judgemental.

'Well I'm going tomorrow after nursery drop off, I put Alex in the crèche and he sleeps for most of it, so I get time for a nice long shower afterwards and even a coffee if I'm lucky.' Maggie giggled.

'Right tomorrow it is, God I hope I don't regret this!'

'Oh I wouldn't worry, I was terrified at first but they're all really friendly and you must get Peter for your free PT, he's amazing.'

'Oh I'm not sure about that.' The thought of a young trainer watching her wobble only added to Jane's trepidation, maybe she'd give the PT sessions a miss.

'How do you stay so slim, Chrissy?' Chrissy had been asked this question all her life and she struggled to answer.

'Just because I'm skinny it doesn't mean I'm healthy, I'd love to build a bit of muscle but I struggle to put on weight.'

'Do you realise that's a stoning offence saying that in the company of women?' Maggie was enjoying herself. Chrissy laughed.

'I know, I'm sorry. I do try to eat more than they say but it disappears.' She shrugged her shoulders in apology; the others smiled an envious smile.

'What a lovely day.' It was. Despite being November, and a chilly wind gently teasing them, the sky was blue and the sun shone.

'Haven't seen you at the Mess on a Sunday before, Maggie.'

'Well I've kind of been a bit down, you know; didn't really want to mingle. But I feel much better now.' Of course, Jane and Chrissy had worked this out but how could they have helped without being patronising? 'Oh, Maggie come on, old girl, perk up! Come and have some mediocre roast potatoes and MSG laden gravy in the Mess and listen to other people's children scream, it will do you the world of good!' They had both knocked on her door regularly but she'd never answered. Jane could have sworn she saw Maggie go into her house one day only to face silence when she went over and knocked. Not even Alex could fall asleep that fast. As they neared the Barracks they chatted to other women and the mood was buoyant. Some soldiers' wives never spoke to officers' wives but most did despite viewing them as lofty and spoilt. Rank in the infantry was still a serious thing. Titty never attended Sunday lunch for exactly those reasons; she found soldiers' wives common and uncouth. She judged on accent and breeding rather than content which saddened Chrissy and made it harder for the rest of them. Titania was ridiculed by the soldiers' wives and Chrissy knew it; she'd heard it plenty of times. She would never interfere; she was in no position to admonish; if she had it would have implied that she was some kind of supervisor of behaviour which might have rung true in 1968 but not now. People were entitled to their opinions and no-one was cruel to Titania's face, no, it was much more fun to do it behind her back. Despite the appearance of togetherness, however, the wives walked in gangs: the officers' wives together, Sgts' wives together, and so-on. No-one planned it like that, and it wasn't malicious it just happened that way. The children played together regardless of rank and they displayed a pure interest for one another not based upon prejudices that were learned and nourished only by adults. Bethany ran along with a young daughter of a soldier and Alex pointed at a baby from crèche; what happened to humans when they grew up that they chose to socialise with those they saw as equals rather than just for the pursuit of fun? Children were so honest like that and Chrissy smiled. It was an ice breaker as well. A soldier's wife might shy away from conversation with an officer's wife but not if their children played together and Maggie chatted happily to a woman she had never met; she didn't know what her husband did and what rank he was, she didn't care.

As they reached the Mess a waft of old, fried oil lingered in the air and made them all hungry. Dave had erected a bouncy castle and the children rushed to it eagerly ripping off trainers and boots. A room was set up for older kids with a Wii and DVDs and the bar was open. With the children taken care of the wives could relax and let some of their domestic stresses ebb away for a while. Everyone prayed there would be no text today. Some of the wives flirted with Dave. He was an attractive man in a rugged manly way and one of the older wives called him 'dishy Dave' while he was within earshot. Chrissy thought she saw him blush.

'So, Dave what about those *X Factor* tickets?' Dave had organised a free trip to one of the live *X Factor* shows in December; he had tasked a secretary to write to Simon Cowell not expecting a reply but one had come from a private secretary and offered them 75 tickets. His dilemma was who to give them to. He thought of an auction, or possibly a lottery. Whatever he decided it wouldn't please everyone and those left out would whinge. There was a buzz of excitement round The Patch and tomorrow they would be given out on a first come first served basis, all they had to do was turn up in person and follow a simple treasure hunt. It was a distraction but one with a great prize.

'Make sure you get here by 8.30 tomorrow Lynne and you'll get your chance.' He winked. He wasn't above flirting back on occasion; it was just another way to keep wives sweet. Dave tried to get to know as many of them as possible; he came to fun days and coffee mornings and mingled. It was tedious but essential. If he was to have the inside track on what was happening to his families he had to work his way in.

Jane ordered a glass of wine. Her children had disappeared and she was in the mood. Chrissy was on orange juice; she couldn't let her guard down; Maggie chose gin and tonic (less calories). Jane felt like telling her to fuck off but didn't. What was it with people who discovered something new in their lives and had to share it with everyone? She was like Gwyneth Paltrow and it made her heave. Someone was complaining to Dave about the smokers being too near the children and the open doors. He agreed but had to take it carefully, he asked the offenders politely to move round to the front where no children played.

'For god's sake Dave can't we even have a fag in peace?'

'Sorry ladies, I did put it in the newsletter.' They moved and winged. Some women took the idea of 'child's entertainment' a little too literally and got steadily drunk and raucous while their offspring kicked empty cans and bullied younger children. Some of the more socially 'responsible' wives took it upon themselves to tell them off and received some verbal in response. It was all part of the banter and was harmless. Generally, everybody had a good time but there was always a decent mess to clear up afterwards; the chefs and Chrissy usually helped.

The chatter turned to birthing stories and Jane rolled her eyes. Here we go, she thought. Someone was reminiscing about her near death experience after a fifty hour labour and those around her made appropriate noises to register sympathy and shock. Apparently this is why she could never exercise again. Lying cow, thought Jane.

'My births were pretty easy; it was after they came out that the problems started.' Maggie was being surprisingly social and had had several gins.

'Which are easier? Girls or boys?' This led to intense debate. Some were adamant that it was boys but an equal contingency fought for the girls.

'Oh god it's got to be boys; girls are complicated, highly strung, bitchy, dramatic and manipulative.' Bethany heard her mother's announcement and wandered off to play. She hadn't understood many of the words but she knew by her mother's tone that she didn't much care for girls. She knew she loved Alex more and that's why she hated him. The women laughed.

'Just like us then.' They all laughed. Sadly, Bethany had neither the vocabulary nor the maturity to understand the conversation's irony.

'Can we just hold off on the hideous birth stories for a while girls?' Donna Cronin was pregnant with her first and terrified.

'Don't worry Donna, it's not that bad.'

'Not that bad! Jesus, trying to push a melon out of your fanny while trying not to shit yourself, no it's a barrel of fun.' Helpful, not.

'Ha, grapes falling out of your arse and bleeding nipples; nah it's a doddle.' Donna put her hand up.

'That's right, go on. I'm not listening any more, la la la.' More laughter. Someone got in another round and lunch hadn't even been served. Dave announced that it was time to get the kids sorted and mums queued up to fill plates for the children. Chaos ensued, toddlers refused to sit still, mums forgot gravy or ketchup, babies threw brussel sprouts and the tables were soaked in spilt coke. However, for the momentary relief for the mums to be able to eat in peace after the kids had finished and gone off to play it was well worth the mess. The luxury was rare with the men away; no second pair of hands to help out at meal times and so the women relished it and took their time. Some went back for seconds and even Maggie had dessert. It wasn't exactly award winning fare but it was hot and tasty and filling. Dessert was sticky toffee pudding; the chef clearly had a diploma in comfort food for lonely women.

They cleared away their own plates and wrapped up the rubbish in the paper table cloths. A few were unsteady on their feet and Maggie was one of them. Her cheeks were pink and she was laughing loudly.

'Maggie, I think that's your son crying.' She went across to him and realised she'd had far too much to drink. As a mum pleasure was transitory and she realised that she was not entitled to enjoy herself for more than 30 minutes at a time. Alex needed a cuddle; he was tired and had been left on his own. In truth, Maggie had forgotten all about her children she was having such a good time. She picked him up and rocked him on her knee. He sucked his thumb and yawned. She gulped a glass of water that she found and felt a little better. What she would give for a snooze now; she wondered if Bethany might have a little lie on the sofa watching a movie and she could shut her eyes and sleep off the alcohol before bed time.

Women had started to leave; generally the ones who never tidied up and forgot to pay Dave. Chrissy sat for a little longer chatting to a friend of Christine Page, the late Colin's wife. Patsy was telling her how Christine was getting along and it wasn't good. Patsy welled up when she spoke of the daughters.

'The eldest had stopped going to college and the youngest is in therapy but Christine is finding it hard to keep up because it's so expensive, there's a year long waiting list for NHS counselling. Her family are helping but she got herself into a right mess, Colin used to do all the accounts.'

'I'll talk to Dave; would she see us as intruding or not do you think?'

'I don't know, you could do it through me and I'll let you know.'

'Ok thanks Patsy, keep me updated. Patsy? Does she like flowers?'

'Yes,' Patsy smiled. 'She really did love the ones from the Battalion.' Chrissy would order some more. She didn't want Christine to feel forgotten. Sometimes Chrissy asked Dave to fund gifts and cards etc. but sometimes she did it herself. Her husband was a Colonel, her sons worked and she had no-one to feed; they could afford it. Patsy left and Chrissy realised that just her, Dave, Jane and Maggie were left. Maggie had sobered a little and was trying to find various bits and pieces belonging to her children. Jane was also a bit tipsy and carried on singing after the music was turned off.

'Are you going for *X Factor* tickets tomorrow?' Dave asked Chrissy.

'I don't think it would look good if I got one; smacks of preferential treatment a bit.'

'I don't envy you Chrissy.'

'Nor I you.'

'Oh I think Dave's job is definitely shitter than yours Chrissy.'

'I agree.'

'Well we won't be queuing for tickets, Jane, we're going to the gym remember?'

'Did I really agree to that?'

'Yes and you can't get out of it now.'

'If you don't kill me do you want to bring the kids for tea?' She didn't really expect Maggie to accept.

'That would be great, thanks Jane.' Maggie was looking forward to tomorrow already. She didn't really know what had happened but she knew that she felt more grounded and settled of late. Of course it helped that Peter looked at her so often in the gym. He couldn't be a day older than 25 but it flattered her, and anyway she wasn't hurting anyone. She thought of Mark and what he would say. He would be jealous of course but he didn't need to know. Some things were meant to be kept a secret for the sake of a bit of light-hearted ego massaging. He wasn't her jailer although she thought he'd like to be. She thought of him less and less and this made her sad when she remembered, which she did now. He was so apart from life now; she had built up a routine without him, ok it wasn't very interesting or mentally stimulating but it worked and she had pulled herself out of depression, she had done that and no-one else; Mark hadn't helped, in fact he'd just made it worse by making her feel inadequate for not being able to juggle all the shit the army threw at them. Shit usually slipped through fingers and wasn't solid enough to juggle. She still received letters from him most days but hers had become fewer and fewer. She apologised when he rang saying she was busy and tied up with a child or something and he always said that it was alright, he understood. This made her feel guilty. She was flourishing as a single parent but her husband still paid the bills. She had managed their accounts for years anyway; this wasn't a huge shift, she just had to forge his signature now and again. Computers didn't have an Afghanistan button so it was easier just to sign stuff on his behalf. Alex had stopped saying 'dada' and Bethany had never started. She'd tidied his side of their bedroom and stretched out in comfort every night. Nothing irritated her because things stayed where she had put them, she didn't find newspapers in the toilet and she wasn't woken by snoring. Distance quite suited her, or so she thought.

They walked slowly back to The Patch to walk off a bit of alcohol although Chrissy hadn't drunk. They talked about Christmas. They talked about when the snow would fall and how everything would be better in the spring. They talked of R&R and what they planned to do although Maggie went quiet at this point as she hadn't even thought about Mark's mid tour leave for weeks. She remembered how he'd wanted his parents to visit and her heart sank. She put it out of her mind and kept walking. The women said their goodbyes and Jane and Maggie prepared to do battle with over tired, sugar-stuffed children hyper-active on yellow nuggets and chips followed by doughnuts covered in hundreds and thousands and smothered in gloopy synthetic custard. In fact Harry looked after himself these days so Jane felt like she only had to face three but that was bad enough after too much wine when all she wanted to do was close her eyes in front of the fire and watch a rerun of *Pretty Woman* or something equally as facile. Chrissy wrote a letter to Anita Dent and phoned *Interflora*. Maggie let Bethany sleep with her and fell into a deep sleep. The Patch embraced the night once more; another day closer to the end, another day survived, for most.

Chapter 8

Considering the amount of alcohol consumed at the Mess, Jane felt quite fresh on Monday morning- until she remembered where she was going at nine o'clock. She hadn't been to a gym in years and wondered why she'd agreed. Maybe she was hoping to get to know Maggie better. Whatever the reason, it had been foolish and she bitterly regretted it, there were so many other things to do with her time today, she didn't even know where her trainers were. At least the first session was free, then she wouldn't go back making some excuse to Maggie; besides she would slow Maggie down, given the appearance of Maggie lately she was clearly working hard, something Jane found difficult to grasp. She had always shied away from weights and instead walked on a treadmill watching TV or rowed for a bit; Maggie had told her that all she did was weights and Jane didn't understand. What on earth did she do for an hour? Surely she couldn't be lifting weights, that was for men and besides it would make you fat; maybe she meant little movements with weight like *Callanetics* or something. When she dropped Christian off at nursery after taking the others to school, she secretly hoped for a stay of execution and that Maggie would be tired and hung-over.

Sadly the opposite was true. Maggie beamed as she deposited Bethany at nursery and seemed like Annika Rice on speed. What had happened? Maybe the gym wasn't too bad after all?

'Hi Jane! All ready?' 'Tits 'n' Teeth!' Jane replied through gritted teeth. Maggie giggled. She wished she could write down all the sayings that Jane came out with. When they reached the gym, Jane felt stupid again and wished the hour could be fast forwarded to coffee afterwards. Alex went to the crèche happily and was almost asleep as they left. Maggie was a pro; she wore matching top and bottoms and looked fabulous. Jane searched but she could find no evidence of fat anywhere on Maggie's body and seethed with envy. Her arms were lovely and slim and her bum stuck out proudly rather than her own which sagged sadly and followed her under duress. Maggie's skin was radiant and she looked the part; trainers said hello to her as they passed and Jane felt smaller and smaller; well, at least figuratively, literally she felt fatter and fatter surrounded by the beautiful people in tight Lycra. Lots of men said hello to Maggie too and Jane noticed that she was completely oblivious to her attraction; Maggie was gorgeous and she didn't know it which was an attractive quality to both sexes. Maggie said they should warm up first and she suggested a short run of about fifteen minutes on the treadmill. If that was the warm up, Jane dreaded the actual workout; she wondered when she could leave. Maggie pounded away at level 11 for the whole fifteen minutes but Jane had barely started to jog after ten minutes.

'It doesn't matter Jane, four weeks ago I could only walk as well; it's amazing how quickly you get used to it.' Maggie wasn't being patronising at all, she was so enthusiastic and genuine that Jane couldn't help feel some kind of internal challenge coming on thanks to Maggie's inspiration. Maggie then showed Jane around the weight machines and Jane looked terrified.

'Most people think that weights build muscle but actually it's the best way to burn fat as long as your weights are low and your reps high.' She spoke with authority.

'Reps?'

'Repetitions; how many times you push the weight.'

'Oh.'

'So if you concentrate on these three machines alternating legs, arms, legs, arms, four sets of 18 reps that will be a really good start.

'How do I know what weight to do?'

'You should start to feel it at 12 and shouldn't be able to do more than 20.'

'Right.'

'Look, I'll show you; sit there.' Jane positioned herself onto a machine and she vaguely remembered that it was to push weight away from the body.

'Try that.' Jane pushed and by 15 was wobbling.'

'Perfect.' This was hard work; she always thought that people on weights machines were just mincing around and looking good, she had started to sweat already.

'That's great, there's no point in coming if you're not going to sweat. I can't stand people who come to the gym to stand around looking good and chatting. The irony, thought Jane, and she wondered if Maggie ever sweated. Another two men smiled at Maggie and Jane felt invisible. After Maggie had suggested the other three exercises she should do, she went off and started her own work out. Jane couldn't keep her eyes off her; she was squatting down stood on a moon shaped ball, throwing dumbbells around and jumping on top of a step, she looked incredible. Now and again she would stop to wipe her brow or take some water; good, she did sweat. Jane could see the inches disappearing from Maggie's midriff. A trainer walked in and Jane had to stop her reps mid set (she was becoming used to the lingo), he was stunning. His physique was finely tuned and in balance like a wild cat; his muscles were defined and his skin like silk so that one wanted to reach out and stroke them. His bottom looked baked in cement and his face was chiselled but nothing prepared Jane for his smile, and he smiled at everyone, including Jane, who blushed a deeper shade of purple.

'Maggie!' She knew this Adonis?

'Peter, meet my friend Jane, she's thinking about joining.' Peter shook her hand, he was simply divine.

'Well I hope you do, I'm the trainer doing the freebees this month so you'll get three sessions with me to start you off.' Jane instantly made up her mind.

'I've already had a training session from Madam over there.'

'Yes she should be a trainer, she's excellent.' Jane wondered whether he thought Maggie was excellent in other ways too. Maggie grinned but shook her head.

'And what do I do with my kids? Sell them?' Maggie was trying to deflect Peter's insistence that she become a trainer. They all laughed.

'Oh wait till they go to School, Maggie, you'll get all the time you need, unless you have another of course.' Maggie screwed her face up.

'Ugh, no thanks!' A woman had stopped to talk to Peter and so he slipped out of their conversation. Jane looked at her watch, they'd been there 55 minutes and it had flown.

'Done?' Maggie swigged from her bottle and wiped her chest and forehead.

'Absolutely! Well I didn't expect to enjoy it so much! Thanks Maggie.'

'So will you join then? It would be great to have someone to come with.' Again, Maggie's enthusiasm rubbed off on Jane.

'Yes, I'll do it today.'

They stretched and Jane's body felt tired but exhilarated too. She looked in the mirror and caught sight of herself next to Maggie and was shocked; how had she piled on so much weight? She set a goal in her head, she still had some size 12 clothes somewhere; she would get into them for James's R&R.

'Am I allowed a coffee now?' Maggie laughed.

'I need to get Alex at 11 so we've got plenty of time, next time we should have a sauna and a swim.'

'I like the sauna bit, you can swim, that would count as two workouts in one day and that's just silly.' Maggie laughed. The café was small, well lit and nicely decorated and the staff very pleasant, they all knew Maggie by name. She was clearly a gregarious person but that didn't come across on The Patch, maybe she just couldn't relax around other army wives. Jane thought she could get used to this; she had washing to dry, toilets to clean, beds to make and an online shop to do but it didn't seem to matter, she felt vibrant and smug with self-satisfaction. She agreed to come every Monday, Wednesday and Friday with Maggie and inwardly she felt excited about it.

Maybe she would get to know the real Maggie after all; she hadn't found her at all irritating today.

The Families office was close to bursting. Dave had expected it but hadn't expected everyone to bring quite so many children who he was expected to supervise as the mums went off on the treasure hunt to find *X Factor* tickets. The hunt was easy, it was just a ploy to give the impression of fairness and it worked. Those who found tickets were ecstatic and those who missed out felt less robbed than they would have if Dave had just given them out and the affair passed remarkably easily. No officers' wives turned up and Dave wasn't surprised; Chrissy had been right, it wouldn't look good. Dave had arranged coffee afterwards and the lounge buzzed with chatter and laughter. Chrissy arrived and mingled easily congratulating the winners and commiserating those who had lost out. There were 75 very happy wives which was a rare occurrence in the office; most of the unsuccessful ones were leaving as Maggie and Jane arrived. Maggie hadn't wanted to come but Jane had persuaded her and she was enjoying her company. They found Chrissy.

'You're looking very pleased with yourself!' Chrissy commented.

'I've just joined a gym.'

'Well done you, so she didn't kill you then.' Maggie spread her arms as if to say, who me?

'Cake?' Maggie shook her head but Jane tucked in.

'I'm starving.' Maggie stopped herself from commenting that she would probably put back on what she had just lost and decided that Jane was a grownup who could make her own decisions. Chrissy tapped a spoon against her coffee cup.

'Ladies, now as you know I'm not one for bombarding you all with responsibilities but I wanted to get a show of hands regarding who might be interested in getting involved in fund raising for the Battalion.' There was a murmur of hush as women thought.

'What are you thinking Chrissy?' One wife asked.

'That's where you come in, I have no idea. What do you think?'

'What, like sponsored things, car boot sales, that kind of thing?' Asked another.

'Anything; anything that might raise a bit of cash for the Battalion to help out families who might not get much support from the powers that be. For example, we sent 20 iPods to Amber Lynn last week; the MOD doesn't cover that sadly.' She carried on. 'I don't want to be in charge, I just thought we could advertise a meeting, swap ideas and allocate roles then.' There was a widespread feeling of approval and Chrissy was glad she'd waited until this point in the tour when help could be seen as more relevant; now they'd started dying, she thought, but didn't say. Early on in the tour she doubted she would have got support, but now it was taking its toll, more women understood why it was necessary.

'As always, the children will be entertained, I've already cleared that with Dave, so let's say, Friday?' Lots of women nodded and started swapping ideas. Cake baking was mentioned, rattling buckets on streets, selling wristbands and competitions were all discussed. Maggie was impressed by how Chrissy had handled herself; she did so effortlessly and as a result got so many wives on side without them realising that it might involve some time and effort. Well done you, she thought. She might even get involved herself, she hadn't found coffee as scary as she first predicted; they were just a bunch of ordinary women really. As Chrissy left, Maggie found herself deep in conversation with two wives about running a race; they could involve the local community and dress up, it needn't be long, just fun. Even Jane agreed.

'I reckon I could run 5k if you put a doughnut in front of me and St John's was on standby.'

When Maggie and Jane left to get Christian and Bethany the sky was darkening already; winter was on its way which seemed to make the tour more foreboding and gloomy. As they reached nursery their mobile phones vibrated into action.

'Sadly a soldier was killed this morning and four injured. Next of kin have been informed.' My god that was quick. Had Dave known at coffee? Is that why Chrissy had left? Who was it? Had she been at coffee? Did they have children? How old were they? Did they suffer? Were the injuries horrible? Were they conscious? Jane and Maggie looked at one another; when one received a text it meant it wasn't yours and so brought bitter sweet emotions. The text system had been devised by Dave as a way to avoid unnecessary panic should wives hear it on the news first; as it happened they found out long before the press. It was a double-edged sword; on the one hand it enabled wives to prepare for the media interest but it also encouraged those - so inclined - to start gossip and make uninformed guesses that helped no-one. 'It must have been so-and-so, she wasn't at coffee and her children weren't at school...' Since the death of Sgt Dent, nothing had appeared on Facebook; Sharon Walmsley had had a thorough telling off and Dave had made it plain that if it happened again, the CO would step in and he had better things to do right now. They all got it loud and clear and the gossip had stopped for a while; but Facebook is just one medium, there is more than one way to skin a cat.

So now it was 9 dead and 49 injured. The statistics had caught the press's eye and The Tour was being reported more intensely. It gave Maggie a renewed edginess; she wondered where Mark had been and if it had been his Company. He wouldn't be able to ring her so when would she know? Did Chrissy know? She soon found out as Chrissy knocked on her door shortly after arriving home from nursery. She looked grave, but Maggie didn't fear the worst as she knew, like they all did, that informing would be done by Dave and a priest. However, her stomach flipped over.

'Can I come in Maggie?'

'Of course. Bethany, stop pulling your brother's top, you will hurt his neck, how many times?' Chrissy was patient and Maggie flipped on the kettle. The children went quiet and Maggie sighed. After such a lovely morning her day was about to be ruined firstly by her children, and, secondly, by whatever Chrissy had come to divulge.

'This morning, Maggie, the soldier who died, he was B Coy.' Maggie put her hand to her mouth. She had been here before, Mark had lost others but she knew what it did to him; he had become more and more distant and she feared she was losing him to this war.

'Who?' She dreaded the answer. She didn't know many of the wives from B Coy well but knew of them and had had many for BBQs or informal lunches before the tour, something that she detested but something that was expected of a Coy Commander's wife. The soldiers' wives pretended to like her and she pretended to host with ease. She hated it.

'Paul Hopper.' Shit. Paul was a young Captain and was engaged to Sarah, they had danced together stupidly at the summer ball. Paul and Mark had donned sumo suits and wrestled one another pissed. Sarah had showed her the ring and described her dress; the date was set for after the tour; it would be a grand home coming and his comrades in arms would provide the Guard of Honour. Shit. Shit. Maggie felt ill and began to shake.

'What do I do Chrissy? Do I get into contact with Sarah? Help, I have no idea.' She began to cry.

'If you can stand it, you could offer to go to the funeral. Let the family contact you if they wish, they usually don't; there will be a lot of anger and resentment at first but it is fitting for you to attend. Oh no. She hadn't attended the others from Mark's Coy because she hadn't known them and no-one had asked her to. Was it because Paul was an Officer? Paul. She thought of his cheeky grin and how he called her 'Chief of Staff Heston Domestic'. He had dined at their house many times and was one guest she did not dread; he was easy company and full of laughter and life. She couldn't imagine someone so strong and manly, dead.

'Will you go to the funeral too, Chrissy?' She hated to ask but couldn't do it alone.

'I go to all of them.' This was news to Maggie who instantly respected afresh this amazing woman. Her mouth dropped open.

'Jane sometimes comes too.' Something crashed inside Maggie; her self- indulgence, her self -loathing, her loneliness, her selfishness, all lingering on and festering away at her spirit while these women were attending funeral after funeral. This was no longer about her and no longer about Mark's decision to go. He was there and now it was all different. She would go.

'What about the children?'

'We've got an excellent sitter who will come to your home; she drives too so no need to worry about nursery.' They had it all planned. She hadn't imagined this side of the tour hitting her, hadn't seen it as real; she had been too busy feeling sorry for herself.

'When is it? Do you know yet?'

'No. It's usually the following week unless there are complications.'

'What do you mean, complications?'

'If there is any suspicion surrounding the death such as had they strayed from the orders or was the mission over risky?' So Mark could be implicated? Christ. She imagined him going over and over his orders trying desperately to find assurance that he hadn't ordered anything reckless. Maggie felt utter disgust as a thought formed in her traitorous head; she would get a day off the kids. She pushed it away and was horrified by her artificial demon.

'Maggie? Are you ok?' Maggie shook herself from her thoughts and busied herself with coffee.

'Yes…I'm just thinking about Sarah. Is it easier do you think when they don't have children?'

'He is someone's child.' She hadn't thought about that.

Chapter 9

Jane was on the platform waiting when Debs arrived beaming and laden with suitcases.

'How long have you come for?' They had had to cancel their previous meeting as Debs's youngest, Franky had broken his leg playing rugby and she had been keeping vigil until he was out of hospital.

'He's driving me nuts,' Debs had said in a long telephone conversation, 'I strut around the house like a manservant fetching things for him to keep him entertained while he languishes in front of the X Box. He's a cheeky little sod, he actually asked me to wipe his arse after I'd virtually carried him to the toilet.'

'What did you say?' Asked Jane, half chuckling.

'I told him to pee off, he just winked at me.' Brilliant, Thought Jane, it wouldn't be much longer until Harry was sixteen and growing hairs and scratching his crotch. Debs had put her foot down last week and announced she was spending the weekend with Jane. Ben had almost had a cardiac arrest and Franky was terrified. In the end, it had emerged that Franky could do a lot more than he'd been owning up to and was now moving about fine on crutches. They embraced.

'God it's good to see you.' Distance didn't matter between true friends and to Jane, it was like having mum come and make everything better; it had been a shit couple of months.

'You're looking good, Mrs, have you lost weight?'

'Well, I have a little secret. It is beauty on a plate, fit as a butcher's dog and called Peter.' Debs gasped. 'No!' She'd jumped to the wrong conclusion.

'No!' Jane laughed. The thought of her having an affair with someone half her age and as fit as Bradley Cooper made her choke.

'He's my personal trainer, idiot.'

'God, I thought you were playing away!'

'Tempting but I doubt he'd have me; he's 23 and so divine that I should think he only needs to breathe to attract drop dead gorgeous girls - which I am not.'

'But you look great.'

'Thanks, Debs, he makes me work my ass off and I'm quite enjoying it.'

'Things I thought you'd never say; number one.'

'I know; me and exercise are like Jeremy Kyle and TV - they should never be put together.'

'Well you surprise me.'

'Look, I'm parked over there. I know; I surprised myself. It's my neighbour's fault, she dragged me there and I couldn't keep my eyes off Peter's buns, they're like rocks.'

'Which neighbour? Can't wait to meet them all in the snake pit.' Debs had been married to the army long enough and had quit The Patch to buy this new house and she loved not having to smile all the time and say she was 'fine'.

'Oh, they're not that bad.'

'Don't you crave your own kitchen? Don't you fantasise about painting a wall or two and not looking at protruding pipe work all day?' Jane smiled.

'Of course I do but I just don't think we could afford to buy. And where we could afford I wouldn't want to live. I've got used to four bedroom houses with acres of garden and interesting little cupboards that were built because the builder was bored. So, how is the house?'

'I love it! It happened really quickly in the end and it's costing a fortune, but I'll save every penny just to be there. The removals cost the earth because we'd hoarded so much stuff over the years and of course the army doesn't pay for your final move.'

'How's Franky? Any more broken bones?'

'No, thank god. Celie is off at Uni so it's just me and Franky at the minute which is lovely, but challenging too. I caught him masturbating last week.' Jane covered her mouth and shrieked.

'No! What did you do?'

'I just walked out and now I don't go in his room without knocking.'

'Did you discuss it?'

'Kind of, he couldn't look at me, and I just said it's ok it's normal. He looked at me a bit funny as if he was the only sixteen year old playing around with his bits but now he thinks I'm dead cool.'

'God, I'm dreading that. Even Christian is obsessed with his dick and he's four.'

'That's men, they only have two organs and one cannot function in conjunction with the other which is why they don't think that much.' Jane was so involved in the conversation that she almost hit a pedestrian on the way out of the station; he swore and called her a whore. Jane gave him the finger.

'My, you are feisty. Whatsup?'

'Oh, it's been horrendous, Debs. I agreed to go to the first funeral with the CO's wife, as you know, and since then I've been to five more. It sounds so self-indulgent; I should feel lucky that it's not James's funeral I'm going to, but it just…you know…wears you out.'

'It was different when Ben was Coy Commander. They went to Northern Ireland, Germany, Bosnia...it was pretty safe, nothing like Iraq or Afghanistan.'

'Well I wouldn't say safe. How is Ben?'

'He's Ben. Next question.' Jane looked at her friend.

'Still married to the Army?'

'Oh, Jane, he pisses green. I've kind of given up. He stays in London for the week and then comes home at weekends and makes a mess. I cook for him and he takes Franky to rugby but we don't really talk. I actually think he might have someone in London. Some young secretary at the MOD that thinks his medals are fabulous.'

'Not just his medals? Oh, Debs, are you sure?'

'No. How can I be? Though I have found a few receipts from nice restaurants and there have been a few unexplained withdrawals from our account.'

'You don't seem bothered.'

'I'm not really, Jane. I think I would have been ten years ago but I quite like having my own space.'

'It's getting so common.'

'What?'

'Divorce in the army.'

'Well it's not surprising really is it? The quarters, the moving, the separation; it's enough to drive a truck through any relationship. Of course all anyone says is 'you knew what you were marrying', but we didn't, who does?'

'The CO's wife has a friend who's just divorced; he's a General, together 21 years, he shagged an army Doc half his age and just walked out one day. She's bitter as hell.'

'Don't you think about it?'

'What, an affair?' Jane shook her head. 'Who'd have me?'

'That's a cop out.'

'I know it's vomit inducing but, I love James. Always have. When he goes away I save up 'me time' and when he comes home I take spa weekends and stuff. It's not all about him. Like the personal training; it costs an arm and a leg but while he's away we're better off so it's ok. He's an amazing dad and I still fancy him.'

'Christ. You are special.'

Jane grinned. It was true. She was surrounded by disappointed middle-aged friends who had drifted away from their husbands as they concentrated more on nappies than sexy underwear, it just happened like that; but not for Jane. Her and James had 'date nights', when he was around of course. They would go to a fancy restaurant and she would wear no knickers and tell him just as he was stuffing a prawn ball into his mouth. They would be desperate to get back and make love but teased each other to increase the tension and need. Their love making was fresh and intense and she missed it achingly. She wished she had a penis so she could find quick release when he was gone but instead God had blessed her with an enigmatic G Spot; Eve must have been such a bitch. He'd bought her a vibrator before he'd left; a 'Rampant Rabbit' and she had been embarrassed at first – until she'd tried it. Jesus, it had blown her head off. She stopped short of telling Debs that if she were to have an affair it would be with a pink bit of plastic with a handy rabbit's head that didn't talk back. They'd been friends a long time but that was a bit much to divulge. James liked that she satisfied herself while thinking about him; he said that he wanted to watch when he came home on R&R. Jane laughed at the irony as they affectionately called the vibrator the 'RR' which was what she always thought of when 'Rest and Recuperation' was mentioned.

'So, takeaway tonight and copious amounts of wine?' Debs brought Jane back down to earth.

'No, I've got a lamb curry in the slow cooker, I've made chutneys too. However I did not make the wine before you ask and yes I've got enough to sink a battleship.'

'Oh, Jane, I miss your curries. Mine are never as good.'

'I sent James off with little spice mixes in old camera film cases so he can make his rations more interesting.'

'You are a good wife. I wish I was still interested in taking care of my man.' They drove in silence for a while.

'Have you been into London to meet him? Why don't you suggest it? Surely then you'll know one way or the other.'

'Maybe I don't want to know.'

Debs had brought presents for all the children. Christian had a light sabre, much to Jane's disgust, Milla a One Direction CD, Lucas a Horrid History book and she had bought Harry a £20 Waterstones voucher knowing that beyond 10 children don't want baby gifts anymore. It was incredibly thoughtful of her. They had all grown so much especially Christian who had been no more than a toddler when she last saw him; now he was babbling away and was even comprehensible. Jane was astounded at what a difference it made to have another adult to tackle bed time; she had got so used to doing it all by herself. Apart from Harry, who read quietly in his room, they were all fast asleep by 8.30. On their second wine, Jane and Debs breathed a sigh of relief and retired to the kitchen to tuck into the curry. Debs didn't know how she did it; it was better than the real thing.

'You should sell your curries.'

'I haven't got time for all that.'

'You'd be surprised. In Germany there was a woman who called herself the 'SpiceGirl', she would take orders and every Friday would turn up at the school gates with little plastic pots of sauces; made a fortune.

'But it wouldn't be really legal here would it?'

'You don't need to deliver at school; you could get people to pick up. Why don't you arrange a taster day in the Families Office and see if there's any interest.'

'Is it really that good? To me it's just cooking.'

'Jane, it's divine, I would pay for what I've just eaten, and the chutneys! Yum. That mango chutney? You made that right?'

'Yes, it's so easy.'

'See, to us mere mortals it's not easy and we are fundamentally lazy as a species which is why, of course, we will be extinct in the very near future once we have raped the planet.'

'My my, come down off that soap box.'

'400 women, alone, kids to feed and bored nights in- you would storm it.'

'Kids' curries?'

'Mine have been eating korma since they were 3 and now Franky loves a vindaloo.' Jane thought. She hadn't thought at all about working but the idea excited her and it wouldn't really be work; she would love it. It was true; everyone who tasted her curry loved it. The only thing was she wasn't sure she could replicate them to order; each and every one was different which is why she loved cooking them. She supposed next time she could write everything down and give them names. She was becoming animated.

'All you need is about 5 signature dishes to start with and then branch out into accompaniments.

'You want to be my manager?' They laughed.

'Speaking from experience; you need to keep busy. It will only get worse and they've done; what? Two months? That's five to go, six for some. Believe me, after Christmas will drag like hell and you will be scratching your eyes out watching the clock.

'Nice. Any good news?'

'It would pay to watch Peter's buns.'

The next day they planned to take the kids to the Zoo. Harry complained of course but Jane promised to treat him if he put up with the little ones for just one day of his life. Secretly, Harry liked Debs a lot, she seemed a lot younger than she was and told hilarious jokes. She also swore when she thought no-one could hear. Really, he wanted to go. They decided against sandwiches due to the high possibility of freezing to death in the outside picnic area. The kids could have nuggets and chips for a change. They all clambered into Jane's VW Touran (bought tax free in Germany) and Debs encouraged them to play 'I Spy'. Harry pretended that he was too old for that rubbish but he was enjoying himself. He made up particularly hard items that baffled the younger ones but Debs guessed every time. When they arrived at the zoo, Jane and Debs busied themselves wrapping everyone (except Harry) up warmly in hats, gloves and scarves. Harry in his Ted Baker hoody swore he was warm enough and refused to wear his jacket; he had blushed when Jane had quizzed him about it just as a teenage girl walked by equally embarrassed to be seen with her parents. Jane lifted an eyebrow, not long now, she thought. Eventually they paid and began their tour however, after five minutes, Christian needed the loo and Milla was saying she was cold. Lucas went missing and a Llama farted at them. Christian then fell and grazed his chin and Harry walked ten paces behind to avoid being associated with such social dimwits. A marsupial followed them through the penguin enclosure and nibbled Milla's coat; at which she screamed and Harry fell further back. Christian dropped his ice cream and Lucas threw up in the Camel enclosure which was, on reflection a bit niffy. All in all it had been an average day and Jane and Debs couldn't wait to get started on the wine again. Tonight Jane was cooking Jamie Oliver smashed creole chicken with sweet potato mash and asparagus. Debs couldn't wait, she could live here forever in fact maybe she would become a lesbian. Women made far superior husbands she decided. Her and Jane could start a commune and Debs might allow the boys in for good behaviour now and again. Bliss. Bed time went well again with two hands and they settled down to watch *Strictly* and *X Factor*.

'75 wives got X Factor tickets from Simon Cowell.'

'Wow! Not you?'

'No, it wouldn't be right would it for an Officer's wife to win.'

'Oh that's' a load of crap, Jane. Those days are over surely.'

'Not in a Battalion. Anyway, I couldn't be bothered; it's more exciting on telly.'

'God, look at those abs.' Jane had learned the correct lingo from Maggie. She had pondered on inviting Maggie over but had decided that she didn't want to share her friend; she was being selfish for once and loving it. She hadn't invited Chrissy either. Chrissy understood. Army wives went into caveman mode when they had a visitor and their house was officially out of bounds; everyone understood that they had real friends to stay; one from the outside. For two whole days, Jane could luxuriate in in her companion who had shared time with her in another life and who understood her more than anyone; it was decadent indeed. She would be sad to see Debs go but she would feel refreshed, recharged and renewed. They staggered to bed about midnight and hiccupped to one another up the stairs. Jane slept for the dead that night. In the morning there was another text.

Chapter 10

Mark was due home on R&R in two weeks and Maggie was becoming more and more anxious. What if he had changed? What would they talk about? Would he want sex all the time? Would he want his parents to stay? It had been a horrendous weekend. Jane had been off limits as she'd had her friend, Debs. Chrissy had been visiting Amber Lynn and her son in London. Maggie had agreed to the park with Titania and had felt sucked of life afterwards. Titania had a way of talking that left one feeling exhausted and dizzy. She had two children of similar age to herself and so she was an obvious park-partner but Maggie had found herself desperate for her own space soon into the playdate.

'You know Ben was saying to me the other day that the tour is punishing. I don't know how he does it; of course, he's been hit the hardest.' All the time she talked she looked into the distance as if who she spoke to didn't matter as long as she had an audience. Olivia and Tristan were actually very sweet but Titania spoke to them like a General and prided herself on their vegetarianism. Titania was a permanent fixture at Dr Stevens's and her conversation revolved largely about her lack of sleep and various aches and pains. Maggie suspected, uncharitably, that Ben probably preferred to be in a Patrol Base in Afghanistan rather than listen to his wife but that was probably true of them all; give a man a problem (such as a wife) and watch him run to the nearest war. She also looked at other people's children in a disdainful almost distasteful way and admonished them freely having read the complete works of Gina Ford. Maggie didn't really like her children being disciplined by someone else but Titania wasn't the kind of person to disagree with, besides it would have been a challenge finding a gap in conversation to register any annoyance or, indeed, any opinion of any kind. Bethany tore around the playground like a ferret on speed and Olivia copied her until

Titania commanded her to not charge around like an animal; clearly a veiled dig at Maggie's feral offspring. Tristan's grammar and diction was immaculate at three and he spoke like an Old Etonian. Alex still couldn't pronounce 'th' and Maggie didn't expect him to until at least five but she felt slightly inferior as a result and wondered how such a woman could have an impact on her. The conversation always went Titania's way and she found herself answering a barrage of interrogation rather than contributing to a casual chat. Titania didn't chat, just like she didn't slouch or serve Chardonnay. After twenty minutes listening to Ben's heroics and Titania's Christmas plans, she made her excuses and decided to follow Alex around pretending he was still a little unsteady on his little feet. Titania preyed on another innocent and Maggie could see her talking animatedly to another mum who nodded and smiled and grimaced as Titania talked and talked and …talked. Maggie just wanted a normal friend; somebody to laugh with and compare *X Factor* notes with. Jane was probably the nearest she had but it still irritated Maggie that Jane always seemed happy; how could this be possible with four children unless she was of a different breed? Chrissy was very caring and kind and she enjoyed her company but she was always so busy with Battalion stuff. Maggie had begun scouring her address book and phoning friends that she missed from various parts of the country. Most of them had children now like her so meeting up was tricky but at least they could spend time on the phone and afterwards she felt refreshed. She also spoke to her mum but mum and dad were so far away and dad didn't like to travel and mum didn't like to drive on her own. Sometimes she just yearned for her mum to sweep her up in her arms and rock her worries away. The nearest thing she had was Aunt Patricia, but she wasn't the hugging, rocking type. She was good for tea and buns in the afternoon, and she always managed to enchant Bethany with baking or knitting or some grand lost art that fascinated her. For this she was thankful. Pat was always offering to babysit and Maggie got the impression that she was lonely too. How many lonely people were out there that sat and wished for company but never sought it? Maggie thought of all the wives and wondered how many had nurturing friendships that comforted them and made them smile. She got the impression that soldiers' wives made friends easier but then they didn't move as often as Officers. Whenever an Officer's family moved they knew it was for a maximum of two years, Maggie and Mark had had two postings that lasted only eight months; how can one seek out, encourage and develop friendships in that time? Maybe she just wasn't very good at it. She had made friends at the gym. Peter was always super chatty and made her laugh out loud, Kate and Vicki on reception were lovely too and sometimes joined her for coffee if they had time; it made Maggie feel younger and civilian like when she was at the gym and wondered how long Kate and Vicki had lived in the area, all their lives probably. Her mind switched to Bethany and her lack of belonging and her resulting insecurities regarding routines and surprises.

'Titania, do you think Olivia and Tristan show signs of anxiety with all the moving and uncertainty?' She had found a gap in conversation and decided to get Titania's view; she fully expected it to be lengthy and dictatorial but it was another view and might be interesting.

'No. I moved all my life and there's nothing wrong with me. I got good grades, an excellent degree and worked in the City until I met Ben. I think they are grounded and content and take their lead from you; if you mope around, they will too.' The perfect irony, thought Maggie. Titania genuinely didn't see herself as a moaner. The concept was worrying; did Maggie want Bethany to turn out like Titania?

'I just think that their behaviour has definitely worsened since Mark went and it has got to be linked. It can't be normal what they are going through and they've got to deal with it somehow; they can't rationalise it so they express it in other ways like being naughty or wetting the bed.'

'Oh, mine were both out of nappies at two, straight through the night.' Titania had missed the point.

'Maybe they are developing food allergies, it can happen at any age you know; do they eat a lot of meat and dairy?' Oh god, Maggie couldn't take much more of this. She decided to give up and turn the conversation back to Titania so she could just switch off.

'So, how are the children? Are they any better?'

'No, what they have doesn't get better, although the GP refuses to diagnose them formally. She keeps telling me to give them meat.' Maggie raised an eyebrow. Why did she want to deny her children roast chicken and bacon? Her mouth watered at the thought. She thought of Alex sucking chicken skin and Bethany chewing pork crackling. Was it just so she had something to talk about? Complain about? She had heard Titania's birthing stories countless times and of course her mother's illnesses and even Ben's various career anxieties that could pass for ailments of a kind. Titania chewed up air miserably and left it heavy and stifling.

'I swear Tristen's allergies to protein were caused by stress in the womb; trying to rip him out after 27 hours and me nearly dying so not being able to hold him for a whole day, then, of course, he wouldn't feed because he didn't know me. It was horrendous.'

'Hmmmm.' Maggie nodded. So horrendous that you just cannot stop talking about it, she thought.

'Do these ailments run in your family Titania?' Titania looked serious and took a deep breath ready to launch into another diatribe for half an hour. Good thought Maggie that will keep her busy.

'Well, Uncle Willy is asthmatic, of course Mum has her shocking eczema, oh and on Ben's side his brother's all have allergies to wheat, cheese and nuts.' Maggie wondered idly if that was because they were all inbred.

'Oh look, Alex has fallen again.' She rushed to his aid and fussed over him for a long time. Bethany noticed and gave him a big shove. Maggie was reminded of *The Omen*. What was it with this child that she had to be so ungiving, nasty and vengeful? What was she trying to tell her? Of course, she didn't have to wait long for a theory.

'You're too soft on her, Maggie.' Here we go. Maggie braced herself for a lecture on her failings as a parent because Titania had read all there was to read on parenting.

'She controls you. She pushes your buttons on purpose and you let her walk all over you.' A knot formed in Maggie's stomach and she resisted the urge to punch Titania. She would have but for the fact that Ben was a more senior Major than Mark and had the Colonel's ear; it would look bad on his report. Wives were not explicitly referred to on 'confidential' reports any longer, not even in the Infantry, but the comments remained in invisible ink. Like poor Tim Curry who was D Coy Commander and 'Married Unaccompanied'. She presumed that Felicity simply did not want to move again for Tim not to be there anyway. Their kids were settled in school and they had their own house, why on earth would she want to come and camp out here as a single family when she'd made a life elsewhere. Apparently she worked too. However, everyone knew that Col Jem didn't approve of unsupportive wives. It was old fashioned but common; women should follow their men, or said men might become distracted and not perform to their best. In fact, Tim was probably having the time of his life living in the Mess before deployment, getting fed, no screaming kids and going down town with the subbies. Maggie and Mark had him round for supper regularly before the tour and he had the best of both worlds; single man in the week; family time at weekends, perfect. Titania was still talking.

'Watch this. Bethany! Come here now! Apologise to your brother as I feel that was a most terrible thing to do for attention, if you want mummy's attention then ask for it nicely, do you want to still play with Olivia?' Bethany nodded. Maggie stood speechless. 'Well then, you must show kindness and kindness will be received in return or mummy simply won't do the things you want. Olivia knows this don't you Olivia?'

'Yes mummy.' Maggie doubted Olivia knew what her mother was banging on about but got the impression that she said 'yes mummy' on cue regularly. Titania seemed terribly pleased with herself as Bethany trotted off hand in hand with Olivia and her impeccable manners.

'See? She needs a firm hand.' Maggie smiled. She wanted to scream. Bethany had played this other woman as well as she did her own mother. Maggie realised that she felt pride for her very clever daughter at outwitting such a vile woman. She learned in that instant never, ever to give advice to any other parent about their own child unless asked to; it was maddening and no-one but no-one knows your child better than you.

That night, Maggie drank a whole bottle of wine and phoned seven friends. She cried to all of them but didn't know why at the time. They all assumed she was scared for Mark and so let her blub away which was therapeutic if not accurate. She was just feeling sorry for herself. She had no idea how she had let herself be dragged into this world where she felt trapped by protocol and suffocated by bored women who had nothing better to do than talk about their husbands and children. Her head was fuzzy the next morning but she knew she could relax when she dropped Bethany at nursery and Alex went to sleep. She curled up on the sofa, but her peace was shattered when the doorbell rang. Maggie froze. Was it *that* call? It could be the postman, Interflora (fat chance), Chrissy, Jane, knock and run…but what if it was *that* call. It rang again and someone tapped at the same time. She swallowed hard and went to the door. Through the spyhole she saw Jane and let the relief wash over her.

'Hello! Your friend gone? I didn't see Christian at nursery.'

'Yes she's gone sadly and Christian has a temperature.'

'Oh no do you need Calpol?'

'No, just some company. I thought you'd be at the gym on a Monday morning.'

'Can't be bothered today.'

'That's not like you.'

'Can I make you a coffee?'

'Absolutely, let me go and get the monitor, I'm sure it'll work over here. He's fast asleep.' Maggie closed the door and went to the kitchen. She realised how different she felt in Jane's company and it hit her that maybe they had grown a little close. Their gym visits were fun and they spent longer and longer in the café afterwards. The thought excited her, maybe she had made a friend after all? When Jane returned, Maggie saw how tired she looked.

'I've been up pretty much all night. I'm clearly getting too old for this.'

'How old are you?'

'41.'

'Well you don't look it. Well you do today; you look like you need some TLC.'

'Thanks. Have you heard from Mark?'

'I got a letter this morning. His R&R is confirmed for two weeks yesterday.'

'What will you do? Escape on some romantic getaway?'

'Escape with two kids? I don't think so.'

'Haven't you got anyone to have them?'

'No my parents couldn't cope with both and all my friends have children already.'

'What about Mark's parents?'

'No, they see Bethany as a bit of a handful.'

'That's a shame she's such a lovely girl.' But that was the problem; no-one, not even Mark saw what she saw. No-one believed that Bethany could be so hurtful, angry and violent when she flew into a rage. They just saw an intelligent, quick-witted and energetic child.

'To be honest, Jane, I just want to stay here. I'm looking forward to Mark being able to lift the burden a bit you know, having an extra pair of hands just for a break.'

'Yes I know what you mean, I don't think we'll go away either; I should think we'll hide away and just enjoy it.' That wasn't what Maggie had quite meant but she let it go.

'When is James's R&R?'

'In a month.' Maggie smiled at Jane; they clearly had a strong, loving relationship, it was so obvious. Either that or Jane was hiding something. She was envious. Was it just that their children were so young? Did it get better as they grew up? Would her and Mark ever be like they used to be again? Bethany had consumed so much of Maggie's energy that she had little left for anyone else and Mark resented that. In fact she was dreading R&R.

'How was your weekend?'

'Fantastic. I feel so refreshed; I've known Debs for ages.'

'How did you meet?'

'Well I was thinking about that and it reminded me of you.' Maggie looked puzzled.

'I was struggling with two toddlers and pregnant by accident with Milla. I was exhausted and all I could see was a black pit. Five minutes after meeting Debs I burst into tears and she lifted me out of my pit.'

'And the connection to me?' Maggie felt nervous but at least the conversation was honest.

'Maggie, you need to give yourself a break. Your children are tiny; believe me it all changes when they go to school. Bethany winds you up because she can; that's what girls are born to do; it prepares them for later life when they have to compete against other bitches. Get a babysitter and let's go out. You need to laugh more.' Somehow, Maggie wasn't offended by Jane's words as she had been when they fell out of Titania's mouth. She smiled.

'I wasn't brought up to burden anyone; I always keep it to myself.'

'But if you open up then people reciprocate; not everyone, obviously, you need to be picky and not try and get on with everyone because that's unrealistic.

'The Dr put me on Prozac.'

'You and the rest of us.' Maggie was amazed.

'What?'

'I wish I could have a tenner for all the young mothers on The Patch who took happy pills, Maggie, I'd be a rich lady. You're not the only one going through a shit time; everything is relative, but the more you keep it in, the worse it will get. I'm going to make you cry before this tour is over.'

'What do you mean? Why would you do that?' Maggie was upset.

'Because you need it, we all do. I had a good cry with Debs last night and it made me feel great.' Maggie looked away, she couldn't look into Jane's forever stare but deep down she knew she was right.

'So, when should we go out?'

Chapter 11

The babysitter was lovely, as Chrissy had said, and Bethany warmed to her straight away. Maggie was happy to use Pat to go out in the evening, but for the funeral she wanted to avoid questions and enquiries on her arrival back home; she would have to share a cup of tea and relive her day before Pat would leave and she just couldn't face it, not today. Maggie had been to the funeral of her grandmother, 'Nanna May', when she was seven years old. She remembered looking at all the adults who wept and wiped their eyes with tissues and it had set her off too. She hadn't grasped the concept of never seeing Nanna May again; it had only hit her when she had continued to ask to visit her, eventually the message had stuck and she had realised that Nanny was gone forever. She had also attended the funeral of a distant cousin who died driving like a lunatic; his friends had been devastated and young girls had wept loudly. She hadn't known him that well and so it felt different to Nanny May but she still shed a tear as if that was what happened at funerals. The intensity of everyone packing into the Church together and the strength of mutual thought all imagining the same person at the same time was overwhelming and the sense of occasion always had the same effect. Princess Diana's funeral had made her cry and she had never known the woman; it was the nationwide sense of sadness and loss that she couldn't ward off and it penetrated her as much as anyone else. She had stood on Parliament Hill with friends, several of them gay, as Diana was wheeled past on the gun carriage. A hush befell the crowd and the wind died. None of them cried for Diana, just the passing of a good soul; she had emanated a kindness and selflessness that touched everyone, she also stood for the antithesis of the establishment and it was everyone's chance to stick two fingers up to the Royal Family who had become archaic and irrelevant, ironic that they were now so popular again. Then there was the funeral of Uncle Tom, dear

Uncle Tom who gave her sweets as a child and seemed a mountain of a man; his death was sudden and the funeral packed to bursting. She'd cried as an adult mourning for the first time and it hurt.

With the children settled and playing, Maggie checked herself in the mirror. She wore black trousers and a black jumper; she had dug out a cashmere black full length coat too; some funerals were excuses to be daring, giving the finger to death by wearing a red coat for example, but not today. Paul had so much life to live; he probably saw his time in the army as an opportunity to have some fun and derring-do before joining the well-trodden path to The City. Maggie thought about Sarah. Mark had been in Sierra Leone when she had planned their wedding and she hadn't thought about him not coming back, it wasn't something that had seemed a possibility. But combat was so different now, Afghanistan wasn't a peacekeeping mission, it was good old fashioned warfare involving actual combat sometimes on a daily basis. When they left their patrol bases, these guys knew they might not make it back, or perhaps they would but in a body bag. Or, even worse, they might return with bits missing. Mark had said that he'd rather die than be disabled for the rest of his life and Maggie had secretly agreed with him; she could imagine the hell of trying to rebuild his ego or having to wash him, feed him or lift him into bed; it would kill him inside. However, some of the stories of recuperation on the news were inspirational, but, she supposed, it all depended on character and who those people had around them to help. For every inspirational recovery, Maggie guessed there were ten others that would never recover mentally from their wounds.

She was nervous for several reasons. One, it was a funeral. No-one liked funerals. Two, she wasn't close family or a close friend for that matter and so she questioned the appropriateness of her attendance. Three, she couldn't figure out why this death had occurred, what was a young, attractive, vibrant, intelligent and funny man doing in such a hell hole? Her brain couldn't compute the contradictions; the wasteful nature of this passing. Finally, four, she couldn't guarantee that she wouldn't cry, and she had no right to, given all of the above. When she had spoken to Mark he had encouraged her to go without being too forceful; he was mindful of burdening her with some kind of 'duty'. But when she had said she was going with Chrissy he couldn't hide his relief and thanked her profusely. He would have liked to have been there himself, but, of course, that was impossible. She would be his representative, a fact that sat uncomfortably with her, she had no right to represent anyone not least someone in combat, she would run a mile rather than bear arms and fight with them bravely; courage to her was closer to stupidity than valour. She couldn't think of her attendance in these terms, Paul had died horribly, and she was there out of respect not responsibility. To her, he would always be Paul and not Capt. Hopper. She wondered what Sarah would be wearing and the butterflies started in her stomach. Chrissy rang the doorbell and it was time to go. Dave Proctor stood at the door of a 4x4 and opened it for her; she felt like a VIP but wished it had been in more glamorous circumstances. Chrissy climbed in behind her. The journey would take over three hours and Chrissy had advised her to take something to read and something to nibble on; Chrissy was a seasoned professional now and produced a flask of coffee to kick start their day. Bethany had barely looked up from her drawing as she had left and Maggie wondered idly if this meant that Bethany was a strong, independent child, or that she simply didn't particularly like her mother.

The day was cold and the sky grey. Exhaust fumes swirled in the air at traffic lights and people wore scarves and gloves and hats. They went about their daily business oblivious that another young man could be blown up today or tomorrow or had been yesterday. Why should they be concerned? After all this was a politicians' war not one of the people. Of course there was the spurious excuse given that by fighting terror abroad this somehow made the streets of Britain and America safer, but Maggie doubted that to be the case; it just gave the people something else to be scared of and another reason to vote-in the winners in the next election. It had eventually back fired on Tony Blair whose unshaken belief in his righteous ability had become as legendary as Maggie Thatcher's; ironic, considering their conflicting political persuasions. Maggie wondered if Chrissy questioned why they were there. Did any of them? Or did they all see it as a 'job' that 'someone' had to do? Words like 'honour', 'bravery' and 'glory' were constantly bandied about during war, but Maggie thought 'pride', 'rashness' and 'foolishness' would be more appropriate. Were these men who were dying in their scores brave? Or were they just following orders and carrying out their training? Maggie suspected the latter but that didn't take away or diminish their sacrifice, it was still tragic whatever the motive. Young men shouldn't die; old people die, starving people die, injured people die, diseased people die; strong, vital and successful men and women don't. But they do.

Dave passed them each an order of service and a picture of Paul stared back at her. She wondered who had chosen it, his beloved Sarah or Paul's family? He was out of uniform and smiling at the camera; he looked youthful and happy, a million miles away from the rape of a country blighted by war for decades. Did no-one tell Paul the chances of him being sent on an Op Tour and thus dying when he joined the Infantry? Why hadn't he joined the Signallers or the REME? He wanted the glory; the feeling of leading real men into battle on foot was too tantalising, why sit behind a desk when he could be a real man? And now he was a man no more. The thought chilled Maggie and she pulled her coat around her knowing she would not feel the benefit of it when they left the cocoon of the warm car. She silently flicked through the order of service which had a strong military flavour. The family were clearly incredibly proud of their son dying the way he had and they wanted to honour him.

'They shall grow not old,
as we are left to grow old:

Age shall not weary them,
nor the years condemn them.

At the going down of the sun
and in the morning,
We will remember them.'

Maggie read the memorial on the front page which accompanied Paul's photo. The only other thing on the face of the order was a silver bugle; the signature of the Light Infantry, it paced out their quick step matched by no other regiment, and had been hailed in the triumph of Wellington's Peninsula War. The Light Infantry (of course now called 'The Rifles') wore their bugle with pride, and Paul had been no different. Sarah was planning to decorate their wedding cake with bugles; their theme was to be green, red and silver to match Paul's uniform. The green would come from the foliage, silver from the tableware and various cleverly sprayed decorations, and the red from a poppy theme; aptly military, Sarah thought. She'd had no idea how apt. Maggie read the words, 'Entry of the funeral cortege' and had to swallow hard. What would be the worst bit - the entry of the coffin or its exit? She thought that the worst bit of a funeral must be the end because then one has to leave and re-join life; for a while, they'd all be allowed to escape down a lane of nostalgia and remembrance, but soon it would be cruelly over and one would have to brace up and move forward. She thought of the image that had done the rounds on Facebook, of the wife of a marine killed in Afghanistan who had slept by his coffin the night before his funeral. Had Sarah wanted to do this? How was Paul's death coming along on Facebook she wondered, cynically. Was it a good thing that the fervour applied to mourning the fallen had become something of a religion? Surely it just made the politicians more able to justify sending more and more youngsters to their deaths, or did it make it harder? She didn't know. All she knew was that as soldier after soldier was sacrificed, Mark might be made redundant in two years; then what would it have all been for? Would Paul have been made redundant too had he survived?

'Comfort stop.' Dave was talking. Maggie didn't need the loo; she wanted another coffee and so took the opportunity to dart into Starbucks for a hit. On the road again, she finished reading the rest of the order. Prayers. What to say? A full military funeral had to take place in a church and prayers had to be said in church, Maggie wondered if the family believed in God or saw prayers as a comfort or just didn't notice and accepted them as par for the course. '...Almighty God... Angels... Worthy of thy love Lord... your servants...your son Jesus Christ...' blah, blah, blah. Maggie wasn't particularly religious but even less so today. None of this crap could have saved Paul. Anyhow, how can a service celebrating violence legitimately use the message of peace to say farewell? Maggie shook her head; she was intellectualising again and irritated herself. At least Mark wasn't there so she couldn't irritate him too. Her trousers were too big and they sat rolled over on her belly; she rearranged them now and again. Readings, more prayers, tributes and poems passed by in a whir. The seriousness of the occasion began to dawn on her and her cynicism waned a little. She would tow the party line today, for all she knew, Paul might have been religious; they never discussed it, this might have been the send-off he wanted. She couldn't help adding that Paul wouldn't have wanted to be sent anywhere at twenty-nine, but there we go. *'I Vow to Thee my Country.'* How many times had she sung that at weddings? Especially military ones? She wondered if Sarah and Paul had planned it for their own wedding.

The car slowed and it was obvious they had arrived at the birthplace of the young Officer. She gazed out of the window and watched swathes of people walking in one direction, their heads bowed against the cold. No-one wore bright colours, although some were not particularly smart; she remembered Paul wearing ripped jeans and referring to them as 'the devil's cloth'. Would Paul want a sombre, sober affair? Who knew what he'd said in his last letter to his love. Maybe he'd written one to his parents too as they were still officially his next of kin. She could see the church and the road became busier; they slowed to drive through crowds and people looked in the window; weak smiles were shared as it was obvious where they were going. The driver found a spot to stop safely and said he'd meet them later rather than try to park amongst this chaos.

'You ok?' Chrissy asked. Of course she was; it was Sarah that wouldn't be fucking ok, or his mum, or dad, or sister, or his unborn child that he'll never have. Fuck.

'Yes, of course.' Chrissy offered her some tissues, she had forgotten. Maggie didn't really know what to do, so she waited around Chrissy who had clearly done this before. Dave put on his hat and they followed his lead. Maggie had been unprepared for the press but this was big news, she remembered. It is a tragic fact of war, and always has been, that far more soldiers die in war than officers; it is a statistical inevitability. To the extent that when an officer does die; the press go wild. They report on precedents and dig deeper into the details; attendees of the funeral find themselves on the front page and Maggie wondered how this affected the loved ones of soldiers who had been just as 'brave'. 'Click, click' Maggie looked away and down at her shoes, she wasn't wearing a hat but Chrissy was and attracted attention. Dave guided them to the church entrance and finally they left the glare of media and entered the cool church. Only mumbles could be heard inside the beautiful building and suddenly Maggie understood why one would want to lay a loved one to rest in this environment; it was peace personified and the perfect gate to the afterlife. An organist played a soulful tune and people stood and talked or hugged. Jane had told her that she'd probably be guided to the front left - the vanguard of the military family that mourned its brethren. The right was full of youngsters and family; some in awe of the military presence. Maggie noticed a lot of medals on the left side of the church. Just as Jane had said, they were guided to the front and there was a murmur as family and friends tried to work out who they were. It felt uncomfortable that one might be a minor celebrity at a funeral.

The organist stopped. The congregation stood and '*Fields of Gold*' began playing which took Maggie by surprise, she had expected all ceremonial stuff and not such a stinging reminder of flesh and blood as this. What would Sting the pacifist say? Maggie took a sharp intake of breath as behind the priest walking slowly and solemnly she saw Paul's coffin wrapped in the union flag. The bearers tried to keep balance as they shifted the weight to keep step. The coffin wobbled and the men concentrated. Maggie dug her nails into her hand as sobs resonated around the church breaking the previously serene tranquillity. The family followed; Sarah, flanked by mum and dad, Maggie assumed. Sarah looked ten years older and pain sat where youthful energy once had. The three of them propped each other up and they took steps uncertainly trying to follow pace, but each step stabbed their hearts as they watched the coffin being laid to rest finally before the altar. Maggie felt hot for the first time that day and screwed a tissue up in her fist, she controlled her breathing to prevent the tears from falling; she knew that if one fell then the rest would betray her and follow, and this wasn't her day. The right side of the church caved into an awful sea of sobs and sagging shoulders; the left stood tall and proud and immaculate. The service started and Maggie felt thankful for a short while; that was until the hymns started. She couldn't sing; her throat was constricted as she remembered Paul's laugh and the way he asked cheekily for more of her 'divine' lasagne. How he talked animatedly of getting married and where he was surprising Sarah for their honeymoon; she imagined him still and mortally wounded, had he shouted for his mother or his love? She thought of the once tall and strong flesh and blood reduced to a casualty and the doctors who must have tried to save him. She imagined Mark, blaming himself and cursing the loss and questioning why? She remembered a poem she had learned at Uni...*Dulce et decorum est*...and bowed her head; was it sweet and decorous to die? It made her throat worse so she looked at the ceiling. If she felt such pain and sorrow, how was Sarah coping? And his mother? And his father? His father's broken face would remain etched on Maggie for the rest of the day and a lot longer. Fathers aren't supposed to bury their sons are they? When they watched him pass out on the parade square at Sandhurst where he had carried the sword of honour, had they imagined this? Of course not. Maggie had to dab the corner of her eyes but still would not let the tears come as she knew that she wouldn't be able to stop. Finally, the moment she had been dreading arrived. She hadn't been able to open her throat enough on her wedding day to sing *I Vow to thee my Country* for reasons far removed from pain and sorrow but she had a similar feeling now; she just couldn't get the air in. She looked at the ceiling, she knew the words anyway. The first tears slipped down her cheeks and she began to shake. Chrissy squeezed her hand but she didn't mind. Before long, her nose was running and her tissues were all wet. Stop, Stop! She found a new wave of strength as the hymn drew to a close and kept the tears behind her eyes for now. It was over; surely it hadn't been long? She checked her watch; they had been in there for 45 minutes. As Maggie turned to leave behind the coffin in her place, she caught Sarah's eye; they smiled and Sarah nodded. She would have made a beautiful bride. No doubt her and Mark would have been invited. It could have been a wonderful day. Paul left the way he came; on the shoulders of men flanked by those he loved most in this world and they him. They would have a private gathering for close family and friends and Maggie would leave straight away with Dave and Chrissy to get home in good time. Maggie felt run over by a train but she also felt relieved; not that it was over but that she now knew it had been the right thing to do. By the time they arrived back it was already dark and they had spoken little in the car. Maggie was exhausted. She looked up at the sky and wondered what might be happening under the Afghan sky tonight; would more blood be shed or would they stay safe for another day? What could Mark hear as he wrote orders and visited soldiers? Bombs, whizz-bangs? Traffic? Normality or insanity? Whatever it was she was sure that it would be as far removed from what she would fall asleep to as physically possible.

Chapter 12

When Jane knocked at Maggie's the next day she half expected to be let off gym today but she was wrong; Maggie stood in all her glory and looked ready and eager; always a bad sign for Jane.

'Oh you tire me out just looking at you.'

'Oh come on you love it.'

'Only because it allows me to eat more - and guilt free.'

'Well there you go you've got something to look forward to then.'

'Mark's home soon isn't he? Are you excited?' Jane realised she'd said the wrong thing as Maggie looked as though she couldn't care less whether Mark appeared or not.

'Oh I don't know,' Maggie began as they walked to the car. They had decided to share driving as it was pointless using two cars all the time.

'I just dread the aftermath, that's all, Jane. Of course I'm looking forward to it but how will I explain to the kids that he's got to go again, it's almost cruel. I think it would be better if they didn't have leave.'

'But then they'd burn out. James sounds knackered and he's got another month to wait.'

'I envy you Jane; you always smile when you talk about him.'

'You're going through a rough time Maggie, pre-school is the hardest of all; it will get better I promise. When the kids get a little older and less demanding then you'll have time together again.'

'The problem is, though, I don't know if I want it.' Jane wished she could impose on Maggie her own experiences but that was impossible, Maggie would have to work it out on her own.

'Well, you'll only know for sure when he comes back for good; before then is unfair on both of you because you're living in an unreal situation, you couldn't possibly decide now.'

'I wouldn't tell anyone else, Jane. You don't judge me. I don't even discuss it with my mother.'

'What is there to judge? I'm not married to him. Besides, marriage is not easy, especially after kids.'

'I think it's unnatural.' Maggie had been thinking about this a lot. Jane wasn't surprised; they all had hitches and some lasted more than others. Men are fundamentally selfish little boys who get away with what women let them.

'To think that two people who change and grow over time can spend forty years in each other's company is nuts. Then add a psychotic daughter into the mix; it's all such a mess.'

'Is it really that bad? He's been away for four months, Maggie. How about getting some help with Bethany?'

'I've spoken to GPs, Health Visitors and I even had *Homestart* round; they all say the same thing, she's emotional, clever and will grow out of it. I've read books and scoured the internet and there's no magic pill; not even a diagnosis, she's just a bone fide pain in the arse. Bit like her dad, really.' They laughed as they pulled into the car park. Maggie winced as she thought of the Health Visitor appointment arranged for her by Dr Stevens; it had been a disaster, the woman had rubbed her up the wrong way from the start. She had suggested behaviour charts, rewards and stars and worse, Bethany had been beautifully behaved throughout.

'Have you thought about training?' Jane agreed with Peter that Maggie would make an excellent trainer.

'I looked into it and it's really expensive if I want to do it all at once. Otherwise it's night school and weekends which, as a single mum I can't commit to.' Maggie always had an answer for everything and wondered if she took the plunge once in a while what might happen; she might surprise herself. Leave it be, thought Jane.

'How was yesterday? You haven't mentioned it.'

'Hideous.'

'Concise.'

'Does it get any easier?'

'Yes I suppose so but then one comes along that surprises you and it feels like the first again.'

'Great.'

'Why? Are you thinking about going to more?'

'Well, I just think of Chrissy doing it by herself week in week out.'

'I know; that's why I do it too.' Maggie had already offered to go with Chrissy again, which was in some ways obscene as it referred to the inevitability of more deaths, but also a surprising comfort to Chrissy who was becoming weary.

Maggie threw herself into her training as always and Peter appeared as if from no-where. To Jane it was obvious; his feelings for her, but Maggie seemed oblivious. The age difference meant nothing; men desire a beautiful woman no matter what her age and Maggie was made more beautiful by seeming not to notice. Poor Peter, it must drive him mad. Maggie's body was becoming defined and everybody watched her inventive workouts; she was a natural and would breeze the course if she did it. Every time they went, Peter would teach her something new and she took to it quickly and enthusiastically. To Jane, enthusiasm should be reserved for the cinema or sex and not putting one's body in awkward positions and then adding weight, but Maggie was infectious and she always made the time go quickly. Jane never dreamt that one day she would be rubbing up and down an inflatable ball and rather enjoying it, but she was and she could feel her legs becoming stronger. Her belly was as stubborn as always but she was eating more as a kind of reward. James wouldn't care one way or the other anyway; she wasn't doing it to look like Elle MacPhearson (not that that was ever a possibility) but more because she enjoyed it. James loved her curves and her thoughts turned to sex. God she missed him. She planned to have her mother look after the kids during leave and take him away for a dirty weekend somewhere with her hard saved funds. She had now saved £3000. She would buy some new underwear and do a strip tease for him; she had been looking it up on the internet and toyed with joining a pole dancing class;

she probably had the strength now after all her work in the gym thanks to Maggie. James was in for a mighty shock. She had to change her thoughts as she could feel blood rushing between her legs and was losing concentration. All she had to do was close her eyes and she could hear James, taste him, smell him; oh God, not again. She had been fantasising for a good half an hour when Maggie said time was up. Wow; that was a handy distraction. They stretched and went to shower. Peter stopped them in the corridor and Jane said she would meet her in the changing rooms.

'You're looking great, Maggie.'

'Oh thanks Peter, I never thought I would get into it again after kids.'

'Well you don't look like you have two kids, that's for sure.' He smiled. She knew what he was doing; after all he was just a man with a penis; however it still shocked her that she could be seen as desirable by a man so much younger than her. She assumed men liked older women because of their confidence and wisdom and she was enjoying the ride.

'If you go ahead with the training, I have a brilliant book on anatomy and physiology. I could help you.' I bet you could, she thought. Ding dong.

'Thanks Peter that's really kind.'

'Every time you come in I'm going to teach you a new muscle and how to use it; where it begins and where it ends, so get studying.' Maggie wondered if the penis was a muscle but pushed the thought out of her sewer of a brain.

'Yes, sir.'

She was quite flushed when she went for her shower. Of course, it was unthinkable. The thought of having an affair was ridiculous. She hadn't undressed in front of anyone else but Mark for twelve years. But it was still good to play. Jane was out of the shower.

'You do realise that he adores you, Maggie.' She blushed.

'Oh, he's just a baby. He'll get over it.'

'I'm not so sure.'

'Jane, I'm old enough to be his mother.' As she walked away Jane wondered if the lady did protest too much. By the time Maggie joined her for coffee, the subject was off limits and Jane decided to leave it alone. If Maggie wanted to play with fire she would have to take out her own insurance policy; she was a big girl. The café was full of yummy mummies rocking prams, breast feeding and discussing teeth, toys and tits. Maggie wanted to read the paper but like everything in her life it would have to wait until Alex finally went to school. Was she a bad mother wishing their young lives away? Did she ever want babies? No, she'd wanted children; about ten years old would be perfect, old enough to reason with and have fun with rather than wiping arses and shouting orders. All she seemed to say at the moment was 'no.' Bethany had got worse. This morning she had got up to a whole tube of toothpaste down the toilet and a perfectly formed turd in the bath. Rather than stay calm as countless Health Visitors and 'professionals' had advised, she blew a gasket and wanted to drop-kick her daughter out of the nearest open window. Clearly, the situation escalated as Maggie reverted to childhood herself and a shouting match ensued that had made Alex cry.

'Now look what you've done!' She'd screamed. Bethany won again; she had managed to wind her mother up to a state of bursting and loved every minute; this was rich attention indeed. The thought of one o'clock loomed closer and Maggie's mood always took a downturn after lunch.

'Do you want to bring Christian round after nursery, Jane?'

'Yeah, sure. Why don't we walk to the park, get some fresh air down them?'

'Great.' Alex could forgo his sleep occasionally if it meant entertaining Bethany for a couple of hours. Maggie knew that the battle would begin again just as soon as they were alone but if she could delay the moment then she might not need her first glass so early. She hadn't reduced her drinking despite her fitness regime; she found she could do both and had even researched how women's bodies metabolise alcohol as heat rather than fat and so she could get away with it as long as she exercised. It had become a habit and she knew it. She worried what Mark would say when he came home and she popped a bottle open every night. She also wondered what effect it was having on her liver, if any. She felt healthy enough and if she got enough sleep she didn't get hangovers anymore, although perhaps this was a bad sign. She pushed the thought from her head.

'How about dinner Thursday night? We won't get chance once Mark's home.' Maggie had forgotten she'd agreed to go out and felt strangely excited at the idea, she couldn't remember the last time she'd 'dressed up' to go out. She was also slightly irritated by Jane's assumption that life would stop when Mark came back, but she was more irritated with herself rather than Jane as she knew that it would be true. No-one would call, not that many did anyway; like a plague victim, people would stay away as if she'd put a sign up in her window reading: 'husband back, shagging in process.' If only that were true. The thought of sex with Mark worried her; her feelings for him were confused. For one, he didn't deserve it. During sex, she gave herself up completely and she just didn't feel like doing that with her husband who had made her life infinitely harder by choosing to go off to war. She also resented the thought that he could piss off for four months and then waltz back into their lives and resume a routine which to her now seemed fake. He would get in the way; she liked her house tidy now his stuff had gone and they ate different food, she always ended up eating what he liked but now she had got used to a new diet full of fruit and vegetables and pulses and salads. He called that kind of stuff 'rabbit food' and wanted his meat like any other cave man. Meat, and his woman; a match made in heaven for any red-blooded male. The thought made her feel slightly ill. How would she react to his touch after so long? Had he been watching porn? Of course he had, they would all be doing it out there in their lonely tents, swapping the latest movies of gorgeous, slim, big breasted women being pounded from every angle; how could they marry that kind of attraction to loving their wives? She had watched porn once and she just ended up feeling sorry for the girls who had penises in all three orifices at the same time and looked as though they enjoyed it. She imagined Mark masturbating over a young blonde with massive boobs and dreaded sex even more. Maybe it would be a good idea to have his parents after all, then at least it would give her a legitimate excuse not to have sex; she hated doing it in the same house as them. At one time it had thrilled her, and she remembered Mark taking her across their dining room table and relished the impropriety. Besides, their cheap bed was creaky and even Mark's dad couldn't fail to hear a bit of shenanigans. She resented the thought of giving up her bed again; she had grown used to the luxury of spreading out. She had started to remember all the little things that irritated her about men's habits; the honking up mucus in the morning, the farting in bed and the hours on the toilet reading papers that would be folded and left by the loo for her to tidy up. She knew that Bethany would play them off one another like a perfectly tuned orchestra and they would fall for it every time, she imagined Alex's broken face when he realised that this was not forever and daddy would go again, and then the sleepless nights that would follow another early morning departure. All in all, it put her in a thoroughly bad mood.

'Do you ever get sick of the army, Jane?' They were sharing a pot of fresh coffee and Jane was eating hot buttered currant buns. She had learned to have snacks in for Jane should she pop over at any time; Maggie abstained as always and Jane marvelled at her will power.

'I just haven't got a sweet tooth.'

'You are just weird, you're not a real woman, Maggie, and you give the rest of us a bad name.'

'No, seriously, don't you wish James had a normal job?'

'What's normal? If he worked in the city he'd work the same hours if not longer, we'd have a crucifying mortgage and he would be just as committed.'

'Do you really think that? Wouldn't it be better to settle though no matter what it brought?'

'Well my friend Debs thinks so, she's just bought a house but she's not happy really.' Jane felt a little treacherous revealing this to Maggie.

'Really? Why?' Jane became vague.

'Well, let me put it this way; location does not a marriage make.' Deep. Maggie thought about this.

'So we're fucked wherever we live?' They laughed.

'Look. If you're unhappy about something then how is it the fault of some institution that pays the bills and gives you a nice house? I'm just saying that instead of looking elsewhere for reasons look at home first. We can only handle so much stress and we can't handle it separately, if you're so pissed off with Mark then try to find out why, don't blame your lifestyle.'

'I haven't got a lifestyle, that's the point.' Maggie would never have let someone lecture her this way four months ago but she knew Jane wasn't judging but just being honest and she appreciated it. If anyone else had said it she would have punched them.

'But it's not the army I blame, it's Mark for being so deferential towards the damn institution, and it is an institution; a mental one full of disturbed individuals that are a menace to society.'

'Ooh, hang on, Maggie, and you wonder where Bethany gets her drama from.'

'But he's like a child, so permissive and in awe of chunks of medal and rank. It grates me. I just wish he could stand up and say 'up yours' occasionally, my child is sick and my wife needs me. Is that so much to ask?'

'But you're a mum. He works and you run the house, that's the deal and you signed on the dotted line.'

'Well I signed it without reading the agreement and under the influence of something called love.'

'Foolish.'

'Yes I know. You need to meet my aunt Pat.'

'Maggie why don't you wait and see what R&R brings, go with it; he might surprise you.' Maggie doubted it. she was not sure if she loved him anymore, but these feelings had developed in his absence and so Jane might be right; surely he had a right to answer for himself but who wanted to spend R&R arguing when they might 'get dead' soon after? R&R really wasn't the time or place to be discussing their marriage; she would just have to pretend and then make her mind up after the whole thing was over. But did she have it in her to pretend?

Chapter 13

Chrissy was hosting her first fund raising meeting and it had attracted a slightly different crowd than the one she'd hoped for. For a start, Sharon Walmsley was there and then Titania walked in late with her children and expected everyone to stop talking while she sorted herself out.

'Sorry everyone.' As if anyone cared. A few rolled eyes were noticed by Chrissy but she carried on.

'So, like I said, I'm simply here to generate interest and gather ideas; minutes will be taken by the lovely Dora' (whistles). 'The basic idea is that, sadly, central government does very little, financially, for specific regiments and we would like to help give a little bit more, especially to help the families of those injured or…' she hesitated…' worse'. Lame; very lame. 'We want ideas that are fairly easy to implement and we need volunteers to make them work. Donna, you suggested a bring-and-buy sale and you know that the village hall is more than happy to host it for free, that's a great idea. We'll need someone to take charge of booking tables.' Hands flew up. This was a good start. 'Then we'll need someone to organise refreshments. Dave stepped in and said he'd sort that and any other housekeeping out.

'What about a raffle? We could ask local businesses to donate prizes.'

'We'll need about five volunteers, I think, to approach businesses.' Hands flew up again. Titania's hand remained down and she managed to busy herself with children every time Chrissy asked the question. Why had she come? Chrissy didn't dislike the woman but she was unpopular and did herself no favours. Maggie had told her what she'd said about casualties and it had annoyed her.

'What about a collection in the city?'

'Good idea. Dave do we have buckets or something?' He nodded. Dave was a man who could get his hands on anything, or, if not, knew a man who could.

'Do we have to register as a charity?' Titania stopped the conversation.

'I have no idea.' Chrissy looked at Dave who promised to look into it.

'Because I have legal training, I'm happy to take charge of the official side.' Chrissy blushed on Titania's behalf. The last thing she needed was being lectured to on what they couldn't do rather than what they could. Chrissy had a headache. She needed to get away. She hadn't heard from Will in over two weeks and Jenny had been ringing her in the middle of the night, drunk. She breezed over Titania's offer. 'So, any more ideas?'

'What about a cake sale?' Great.

'Take out an ad on *Garrison FM.*' Good idea.

'What about inviting *Pampered Chef* or *Avon* to do shows and get them to donate a commission.'

'Or *Ann Summers.*' A collective snigger rose up and Chrissy smiled.

'What about something for Hump week?' Chrissy nearly spat her coffee.

'Pardon?'

'Half way through the tour, dress up as hump backs or something and take buckets out.' Chrissy doubted the political correctness of such an activity and worried about offending hump backs.

'It might be less offensive to dress up as humped backed whales.' Dave was shaking his head.

'I worry about offending those whose husbands might be on leave that week; it might give the wrong impression.'

'Or the right one.' More laughter. Oh well, at least it was lightening their spirits. Titania wasn't laughing and looked distinctly unimpressed.

'I think I'll just take the children out if you don't mind.' Why did she even bother turning up? She could have left the children with Private John as all the others had but she was probably worried they might catch something infectious from a soldier's child. Chrissy felt sorry for her, if only she could relax a bit more.

'We could have a big brew like *SSAFA* has.'

'It's all good, keep them coming.'

'What about a calendar like calendar girls?' The room fell silent. Who would dare? Besides it had already been done. Chrissy took a breath.

'Can we have a show of hands?' More than 20 put their hands up. Chatter began animatedly about what month they'd each like to do.

'Chrissy, you could do March and march across the parade square naked.' Dave looked at his feet. Chrissy smiled and wished she could but imagined her husband's horror if she did. The most interesting fact that she took from the suggestion was that someone had dared suggest it; this was progress, it meant she wasn't seen as different or special. Good.

'I'll consider it if you do December and hang bells from those magnificent knockers of yours, Marjorie.' The room fell about and Marjorie did a bow and stuck out her chest. It was worth thinking about but there was no way Chrissy would do a naked shoot. However, it might not be necessary; the Calendar girls had done it tastefully, so why couldn't they?

'Any volunteers for looking into costs and marketing?' Hands went up again. Chrissy scribbled down names.

'What about a sponsored walk for the children as well?'

'Thank you, Sarah, for injecting some decorum back into the conversation. That's a great idea; can I let you look into that one?' Sarah nodded happily. Chrissy was exhausted and as she packed up, Dave patted her on the back. 'Well done, Boss.' The women separated into groups and chatted over their coffees and Chrissy made her excuses and left. She hadn't had a lie down during the day for years but when she returned home she climbed under her duvet and tried to dream of being the wife of a plumber. She dreamt of funerals and Will was shouting her; he was hurt and she couldn't get to him. Someone handed her a union flag and she found herself looking over her black clothes (of which she had bought more

123

of late) and she woke up sweaty and bothered. She called Dave.

'Dave it's Chrissy. I'm thinking of visiting a friend for a few days but I don't want to look like I'm running away.'

'Chrissy, even you need a break. You're not wonder woman; we will survive and I'll keep in touch should anything happen.' Christ she hadn't realised how much this would take out of her. She was trying to let it all wash over her for Jem; she didn't want to let him down, but she didn't want to burn out either. She needed a change of scenery. In the last three weeks she had visited Amber Lynn six times and written twelve letters to families on Jem's behalf. She was lonely too. No matter who she tried to relax with, duty always came into it. She found herself listening to conversations and trying to analyse them to try to detect the mood of the women as if she could sort it all out. She had lost more weight and her nails had started to crack. Maggie had noticed but she couldn't even open up fully to her or Jane. She'd noticed the two women becoming close and felt a pang of jealousy; could a CO's wife have a plain and honest relationship without it being a conflict of interest? No, she had decided not. Jenny would understand. Despite Jenny's own needs right now she would still allow Chrissy to be herself and wouldn't be interested in her role or how many funerals she'd been to or whether she'd attended Sunday lunch or a coffee morning that week. She saw it as a holiday from a toxic working environment. The Patch had become suffocating for her and she wished she'd taken the Colonel's house. She was a walking, talking representative of her husband; the man who was sending loved ones to their deaths. This morning had helped and most of the women had been relaxed with her but it still sat in the air like a bad smell. She knew that Jem was a hard boss, and some had had leave turned down when they'd wanted it, or he'd refused to give emergency leave to men in some cases when their wives had begged Dave for it. Julie Turner's daughter had taken an overdose and she'd demanded her husband to be sent home. Chrissy knew that he didn't want to come home; honour was even more important than his daughter (which was why she'd probably overdosed in the first place) but Julie thought that Jem had prevented it and she stopped attending coffee mornings and was suddenly cold with Chrissy. Sharon Walmsley was another thorn in her side and she contradicted Chrissy at every opportunity. Notably, she had left her alone this morning, thankfully. Sharon had cooled towards her when Dave had intervened over the Facebook incident and used Jem's name as a threat. It was true, Jem had been livid but it had been a stupid thing to do. Blame fell on Chrissy silently and she had begun to feel it. She wasn't doing enough; she was doing too much. She wasn't chatty or friendly; she was too chatty and over friendly. She wasn't interested in making friends; she tried too hard to be pally. Chrissy received gossip through various channels; Dave was one, Jane another. Titania clearly thought she could do a better job and couldn't wait to be a CO's wife herself which, no doubt, one day she would be, Chrissy cringed at the thought.

She looked on line for train tickets so she didn't have to drive and phoned Jenny to check. Her friend was beside herself. Funny, Chrissy had expected to be shunned by Jenny who had come to hate anything army but the opposite was true. No-one else understood the life and what Jenny had sacrificed to support her husband who had now dumped her and her children after fifteen quarters, seven schools, thirteen missed anniversaries, countless trips to the GP about Mattie's bed wetting and Harry's refusal to eat certain foods and twenty one years of holy matrimony that meant the square root of *nada*. Chrissy expected a barrage but she didn't care; it wasn't her barrage; she couldn't make a difference and wasn't expected to. She looked forward to curling up on the sofa with Jenny in their sloppies and watching *Strictly*, eating takeaway and drinking rose wine. She daren't let herself get drunk in front of anyone on The Patch; it would be too juicy a titbit to let go but she could in front of Jenny who didn't give a toss about the Battalion anymore.

The doorbell rang. It was Jane.

'You look tired.'

'Thanks.'

'Sorry. Maybe you should go away for a while and forget everything.'

'You can read my mind, Mrs Blandford, I've just booked first class train tickets to go and stay with Jenny tomorrow. I can't remember the last time I went shopping and Jem's loaded and I have the cheque book.' Jane giggled. She liked it when Chrissy was like this; she had become too serious as if she expected herself to save the world. She wasn't sure that going to all the funerals was healthy but she supposed Jem expected it.

'Look, if anything happens while you're away, me and Maggie will take care of it; please don't come back early, for anything.' Chrissy was a little piqued that she might not be needed as much as she thought but was grateful nonetheless. It was only really Maggie and Jane and , of course Dave, that knew exactly the role she had imposed on herself over that last four months.

'I came over to ask if you wanted to go out with me and Maggie on Thursday but clearly not as you'll be sipping champagne in first class.'

'I'm not sure first class *Virgin* rail is anything like first class *Virgin* air but at least it's better than driving. Fancy a cuppa?'

'Ok, just a quickie; I need to get the kids at four and Christian is at Maggie's. How did the meeting go today? I chickened out I'm afraid.'

'It went surprisingly well. There were some great ideas; a fairly well behaved affair, I think. I don't think we'll achieve everything but every little helps.'

'I'm perfectly happy to get involved and help but those open meetings make me uncomfortable, I don't know how you do it.' Several people had said this to Chrissy and it had started to irritate her; it's not as if she had a choice; she was the CO's wife, that's what they did. Maybe she had been foolish thinking she could be herself; it was an impossibility, which was what made her escape more appealing.

'What do you think about a naked calendar?'

'What? Oh my God. Never in a million years. Are they serious?'

'Absolutely. It's been done well before; we have plenty of volunteers so why not, I say. I don't think I'll be stripping off though; Jem would have a fit. Give the lads something to look at.'

'I wonder what the reaction will be; I think James would be horrified. Not that I'd posed naked, but that the whole bloody Battalion could get an eyeful.'

'Oh, we've got plenty of exhibitionists, don't worry I don't think they'll need you.' Chrissy looked cheeky.

'I'll try to make it as tasteful as possible, but I can't get in the way if they want to put buns in front of their bits. When's James home?' James was one of the officers that had had his leave cut by Jem, but it was because he was valued and for no other reason; she hadn't discussed it with Jane.

'Four weeks.'

'I get the impression Jem won't take any sometimes, it will probably be after Christmas at the earliest.'

'What will you do for Christmas?'

'No idea.' She lied. She had booked to go away on her own but didn't want to tell anyone lest they thought her a sad, lonely old hag going on a singles trip.

'Big family affair for us, join us if you like. I've invited Maggie.' Chrissy didn't relish the thought of remaining in this environment over the festive period that looked to be about as festive as a dinner dance at the local church. She was aware of herself becoming a little brittle, yes; a rest was just what she needed.

'I need to get back; I left Maggie on her own.' So? Thought Chrissy uncharitably. God she was cranky. What was it about women in threes? It never worked. She busied herself with packing once Jane had left and prayed that she got no phone calls before midday tomorrow. Once she was on that train there was nothing she could do about it. She wrote up the minutes from today's meeting and intended to give them to Dave in the morning. Maybe she could get away smoothly.

She hadn't envisaged running away like this and couldn't quite describe her claustrophobia. She wouldn't tell Jem unless he asked which he probably wouldn't because he was so wrapped up in what he was doing he rarely rang for a casual catch up. That night, the wind blew hard and the trees made shadows outside her window; she dreamt of Will again and mothers crying in church. She woke feeling grumpy and showered to freshen up. The phone rang at 9am. It was Dave.

'Don't be angry with me Chrissy.'

'What happened?'

'Two were killed at three this morning. Now, before you shout at me, you are getting on that train. I will deal with this.' Silence. She so wanted to run away but now she couldn't, how would she explain it to Jenny this time.

'That isn't an option, Dave.'

'Chrissy I will drive you to the station myself, I won't hear another word.' He hung up. She stared at the phone. How dare he! She grabbed her car keys and slammed the front door. Dave was waiting for her outside, grinning. She stopped.

'Dave…'

'I don't think you want to discuss this on the street.' Again she was taken aback by his firmness. She relented and walked back to the house and held the door open for him. She was sulking and both of them knew it.

'There is nothing you can do, Chrissy. Your actions are out of goodwill, you are not obligated and you need a rest.'

'Don't patronise me.'

'The Col said you'd be like this.' Her mouth fell open.

'I'm staying.'

'No you're not.'

'Yes I… I'm not playing games with you, Dave.'

'I know that.' He wasn't budging. She looked at her bags.

'If I remember Jenny Park as well as I think I do, I'd rather piss you off than her. You're going.' Dave had never sworn at her but she quite liked it. This was more like it; she needed a good scrap.

'You can't tell me what to do.'

'I'm not, I'm giving you advice.'

'I didn't ask for your advice. I am the CO's wife and...'

'I wondered when you'd use the rank card.' Chrissy felt an inch tall.

'Dave, I'm sorry, I...'

'I'll be back at 11.30 to take you to the station. If you run away I have the Col's permission to lock you up.' She glared at him but couldn't help smirking.

'Chrissy.'

'Dave.'

'I'll see you later.'

She had been thoroughly seen off and it felt delicious.

Chapter 14

Aunt Patricia drove a white convertible Renault *Zap!* with red
leather interior. Her nails shone from a recent manicure and
her lipstick matched the bright shade of *'Rockin Red'* recently
launched by Kate Moss. She had clearly 'had work' but she
had a good plastic surgeon who kept her natural-ish. She was
61 and looked the right side of fifty. Her hair sat, unmoving,
on top of her well poised head and her new shade, silver
bronze, suited her. She closed her cashmere jacket (camel of
course) closer round her against the cold afternoon and looked
slightly irritated which would worry most people, but to
Maggie it was her usual expression. She had the air of a young
Margaret Thatcher in her prime and Maggie would have liked
to have seen the pair dual; her money was on Pat. Her heels
clacked against the concrete and Maggie wondered if she'd
brought slippers as she'd never catch Alex in those things,
Alexander McQueen, no doubt. Aunt Pat shopped in *Harvey
Nichols* and nowhere else. Quinten, her personal shopper,
spent one afternoon a month with her perusing the latest lines
and matching outfits for this and that, or for no reason at all,
just that Aunt Patricia was stupidly rich and loved buying stuff.
Her late husband, Uncle Tom, had made it big in currency
dealing and invested all over the world; he'd died of a massive
stroke a year after retiring. They'd been on a cruise around the
Caribbean and the chopper took ages to airlift him to the
mainland where he'd died holding Pat's hand. They'd never
had children, Maggie remembered her mum telling her once
that Pat couldn't. They were going to cruise their way around
the world, trek Alaska and dive with whales and it was all
cruelly ripped away before it had really started. Pat rarely
talked about Tom but when she did a shadow of love warmed
her face and her eyes shone. Maggie didn't think she had a
new man but one never knew with Pat; if she did, she wouldn't
guess. Pat broke into a huge grin when she saw her niece and

opened her arms. Maggie sank into them. She was a wonderful Aunt in small doses, but most of all she was doting on the children, and Bethany adored her. Maggie always shook her head in wonder as her daughter who so terrorised her mother behaved beautifully for this old, formidable matron. She smelled of *Estee Lauder*, not only from her strong perfume but her rouge as well that sat on her cheeks beautifully. Quinten also gave her makeup tips.

'My lord, Maggie May, its freezing, I do hate the winter. I'm a sun worshipper you know so you're lucky to have caught me, I was about to book a holiday to see a good friend of mine in Portugal.'

'Well I'm glad you didn't, the children are so excited, Pat.' Patricia insisted that none of her nieces or nephews called her Aunt, it was so aging she said. However, Alex and Bethany were allowed to presumably because given her well-groomed looks, they could have been a niece and nephew unlike Maggie's generation which could be confused with sisters and brothers in the right light.

'Auntie Pat!' screamed Bethany. Pat took a step back as Bethany charged at her and got down on one knee to receive the girl. Bethany was swept up in a huge cuddle and Alex came trotting behind.

'Well, guess what I have in my bag?' The children's eyes widened, Auntie Pat always brought the coolest presents. It worried Maggie slightly as she didn't want her children spoiled, but she was just jealous, she supposed, as she could never remember Pat being like this when she was little. On the contrary, Uncle Tom had been the one who dished out the cuddles and boomed with laughter at his own kiddie jokes. He pulled toy rabbits out of hats and removed his false teeth making them all giggle. Pat had always been in the kitchen baking something delectable and had shown her love in that way, but now with her children, Pat had morphed into a gorgeous Granny figure and the kids loved her. She allowed herself to be pulled to the sofa and began taking out the gifts, all immaculately wrapped by *Harvey Nichols* staff no doubt.

'Go on Maggie May, forget about us, come back when you like, have fun.' May was Maggie's middle name and Pat always used it, always had. She thought she had scrubbed up quite well as she studied herself in the mirror. She had dared to try on an old pair of skinny jeans that had lain unloved for five years and they fitted her with room to spare. She slipped on some heeled boots and some silver bangles and tousled her hair; she was pleased. In fact, Maggie looked striking and Jane couldn't help a small gasp of breath when she saw her neighbour.

'Wow! Mrs fabtastic!' Maggie giggled modestly.

'Shall we?'

'Absolutely.' They both felt like they were going on a date and linked arms. The night was bitter but the walk warmed them; they were only going into the village but why not look nice too? They had considered cancelling when the news had come through about the two corporals killed but they had agreed that it was silly and self-indulgent; it was someone else's tragedy and they had no claim on it, besides what could they achieve moping about and feeling sorry for themselves? Neither woman knew the men. Neither was married. Death had become commonplace and the numbers mounted. They both agreed to go to the funerals as Chrissy wouldn't be there.

Jane had been a little pissed off with Chrissy lately. She was becoming irritable and distant and it was almost as if she wanted to carry the burden of the Battalion all on her own. Jane had called her Joan of fucking Arc on more than one occasion to herself and was glad she'd gone away for a few days; maybe it would do her good. In contrast, she had warmed to Maggie who was transforming before her eyes. The haunted look of a few months ago had gone and Jane wondered if Mark would notice; he'd better, thought Jane, because there were plenty of men out there waiting for a woman like Maggie. When they entered the restaurant Jane noticed men looking at Maggie who appeared not to notice. Wives and partners gave warning looks to their men as Maggie breezed by following a waiter who seemed more helpful than last time Jane had been in there. He guided them to a nice table for two by the log fire and they took their coats off; the waiter took Maggie's first and handed them their menus.

'Oh, this is bliss.' Maggie smiled.

'Cheers.' Maggie had already had three glasses by the time Pat arrived and so was well on her way but Jane didn't notice and presumed it was her first. They clinked glasses. They obviously weren't the only ones with the idea as three other wives walked in and to a table; they exchanged pleasantries and said something about the cold. They were soldiers' wives; it was obvious because all the officers' wives knew each other, there were so few of them. They were like two tribes that spoke two different languages, moved in different circles and discussed different issues. Neither group would have dreamt of asking for a table for five; both sides felt uncomfortable for different reasons, although neither was valid, but it mattered not; the boundaries had been drawn centuries ago and remained tight. Had they been civilian neighbours they might have become friends but the boundaries were etched deeper due to street name, too, and clumps of officers' housing sat apart from much bigger clumps of soldiers' housing. It was almost feudalistic; the CO sat at the top (along with his wife) then came the knights (Captains, Majors and WAGS), then the clergy (NCOs and wives) then at the bottom of the pile, the most numerous and hardworking, came the peasants and their families and the housing reflected this. Maggie and Jane lived in detached, four bedroomed Georgian houses with handsome windows and large front doors; their gardens were bigger than tennis courts and the street quiet. Sgts had fairly large gardens and the houses were smaller but very pleasant. A Corporal's house was usually a two up two down with a tiny garden on streets that looked like council estates made worse by the fact no-one tended their garden because why should they? This is where the playgrounds were, vandalised by teenagers abandoned by fathers, and shat in by dogs. It was rare to come across anyone who actually believed in this archaic system anymore but this wasn't a problem for rank rattlers such as Mrs Titania Howard-Holmes who made up for it in buckets.

Jane suspected that Titania actually imagined herself a different class of person to a soldiers' wife and therefore deserving of the four bedrooms. Maggie always joked with Mark that every time he got promoted they got another bedroom. Majors got four, Colonels could have eight and some generals had twelve plus staff. Their social life reflected this ancient tradition also, the balls and cocktail parties smacked of regency England when men talked of business and politics and belly laughed with the King (in the army this is called a 'career laugh') while the ladies gathered in the powder room and discussed domestic affairs. Of course the odd coarse girlfriend brought by a friend of a friend somewhere in Chelsea always reduced the tone a little, but for the most part, ladies were served by Privates calling them 'ma'am', and people danced in couples rather than rowdy crowds that one might see, say, in the Corporal's Mess.

The two tables of women were distant enough that thankfully they couldn't overhear one another so it didn't become embarrassing. If the soldiers' wives had been asked to judge who the least distasteful officers' wife was they probably would have chosen Jane or Maggie as they kept themselves to themselves and spoke normally in mixed company. By 'normal', they would have meant speech without squeaks, snorts, hand gestures and other such nonsense that gave away a privileged childhood which they all assumed they'd had. The stereotype was unfortunate but mostly true; as the officers themselves mainly went to public school, attended Uni, spoke the Queen's English and had friends called Ben and Sebastian; so their wives generally had degrees, earned large salaries before giving them up for babies, shopped at *Waitrose*, and had friends called Georgina and Farrah. The flip side of the stereotype was just as maddeningly true; a soldier usually signed up at seventeen, married at nineteen, was the proud owner of at least five tattoos (as was his wife) and had friends called Hicky and Doc; so their wives worked full time, called their children Tyrone and Britney, wore Ugg boots and had friends called Becks and Charlie. The three soldiers' wives laughed loudly from time to time in a 'salt of the earth' kind of way and were clearly becoming drunk. Maggie was as leaping as a lord but as an officer's wife, it was impossible to tell and their conversation remained about husbands, the gym and what was on offer at *Waitrose* because even though they shopped at *Waitrose* they could barely afford it which was why *Waitrose* had brought out their '*Essentials*' range for women who pretended they could. Actually Maggie shopped at *Asda* which was another reason why soldiers' wives didn't mind her as they regularly bumped into one another at the tills. The fact that Maggie bought *Asda Organic* didn't much matter; she had few airs and graces.

'So, are you getting butterflies at the thought of Mark walking in and ravishing you?' Jane was a bit tipsy which made her tongue loose. Maggie didn't mind, it made it more like chatting to a friend than one of her husband's colleague's wives.

'It's been a long time Jane; I think I've got cobwebs to be honest.'

'What, you mean you haven't got a toy to keep you entertained?' Maggie was puzzled. Was she referring to a vibrator? Her steak with blue cheese topping seemed tougher that particular mouthful. She glugged a long slurp of wine.

'No, why have you?'

'Of course! You've got to get one, stops the dark nights drawing in.' Jane laughed. Maggie couldn't believe what she was hearing. Jane, lovely Jane who baked brownies and made pots of tea and cooked curries from scratch and decorated cupcakes was getting herself off with the help of machinery.

'I've never tried it.'

'Neither had I until James bought me one as a going away present. It surprised me I can tell you, they really work.' My god, now they were talking about orgasms, conversation had progressed to alarming heights.

'Where did he get it?' Maggie had visions of James walking into a seedy back street shop in a trench coat wearing a false moustache.

'Online from *Ann Summers*.'

'Bloody hell. It's that easy! Weren't you embarrassed when it arrived?' For some reason she struggled over the derivative of the word 'come'.

'It didn't say 'sex toy' on the packaging, you numpty; they're very discreet. Postman probably thought it was another cook book.'

'Well, Jane you have shocked me.'

'Really?' No, not really; Maggie was fascinated and thrilled at the same time; she knew somebody's secret; this had to mean she had a real friend.

'No…just…jealous!' They both giggled (louder than the soldiers' wives' table).

'Well get one ordered then, we'll do it tomorrow on my iPad.'

'What if I don't know how to use it?' Jane looked at her curiously.

'Oh, I wouldn't worry; it's fairly self-explanatory.' Jane's laugh was dirty this time, Maggie was having fun.

'What does it look like?' Jane laughed harder but whispered;

'A massive penis with a rabbit on the side.'

'A rabbit?' Maggie's voice had become a little loud and Jane ssh'd her. They tittered away as they made their way through their second bottle of wine.

'It's called the '*Rampant Rabbit*', you know, it does the thing inside and the rabbit does the outside bit.'

'Oh.' Sweet Jesus. Mark would have a fit. 'Isn't James jealous that it's that good?'

'How can he be when he's been doing it since he was eleven, ok not with a rabbit but still. Besides it's totally different than with someone; it's just for fun, feelings don't come into it.' Maggie listened intently.

'Haven't the children ever found it? Is it noisy?'

'No and no.'

'Where do you plug it in?' Jane almost spat her Sauv' Blanc..

'It's battery operated, you idiot. And waterproof.' Lord above. Maggie was turning into her mother with her conservative expletives. She was lost for any normal words and took on a matronly huff to protect her innocence which was fading fast. She was intrigued.

'Do you think other people have one?'

'Well I don't think my £29.99 alone boosted *Ann Summers* profits last year and after Fifty Shades I read that sales had sky rocketed.' Of course Maggie had read Fifty Shades but hadn't imagined it to be taken seriously, after all; Christian Grey and orgasms like that didn't exist, did they? Visions of Chrissy using one suddenly popped into her head, and then the wives at the other table, ugh; she pushed them away. Maybe everyone was at it.

They paid their bill and gathered their coats to leave. They stopped at the other table and said goodbye; it was all very pleasant and they wondered what would be said when they left and hoped it wasn't too bad; better still, nothing at all. The walk back home was cleansing and they linked arms again. Maggie wobbled slightly and Jane thought Miss Fit clearly couldn't handle her drink; if only she knew. Maggie would down another half bottle before bed as soon as she had got rid of Pat. They laughed all the way home at Maggie's innocence and Jane swore she wouldn't forget to bring her iPad round tomorrow. Maggie didn't have one; of course she could have ordered it on her own laptop but Jane said the iPad was super quick and easy and she had an account. This was news, what else had she bought there? When they reached Maggie's door they promised to do it all again maybe fortnightly or something, it had been good for the soul and Maggie felt soothed. She watched Jane get to her door then turned in. Pat was watching a taped episode of *Frost*, her favourite programme. She fancied David Jason.

'Hello, dear. Did you have a smashing time?' Pat was a whole era of her own and it comforted Maggie.

'Yes thanks, Pat, it was great fun and I feel much more relaxed.'

'Well your two children are adorable, Maggie May. Please don't leave it long before you do it again. I'm going to

Portugal for a week and then I'll be back wanting to come and look after those little beauties again.' Maggie wondered which little beauties she was referring to and hoped that all children acted differently with those who weren't their mothers.

'Well, I'll get straight off, dear, I have this recorded at home and you look as though you need some sleep!'

They embraced and Maggie thanked her again. She watched as Pat climbed into her car and then peeled her boots off and padded to the fridge to find wine. She would just have one. She put her favourite CD on; the theme tune to *Gladiator,* and sighed. The fire was still on and she drifted off watching its red glow. She imagined herself in front of a beautiful log fire like the one in the restaurant; she could have stayed there all night. The cheap Army electric fire wasn't quite the same but belted out the heat. When she woke, her wine had spilled and she cursed. It was three o'clock in the morning, the CD player was quiet. She admonished herself and poured a large glass of water to take to bed; as well as another glass of wine. Alex woke her at 5.30 and she felt as though the Battalion had marched through her mouth after they'd marched through cow pats on Salisbury Plain. There was no way she could go to the gym today; it would be a miracle driving Bethany to nursery, maybe Jane would take her?

'Jane, was I really drunk last night? I feel terrible; I was wondering if you could drop Bethany at nursery?'

'Of course, you're not used to it are you? Too fit, that's your problem, but it was great fun.'

'Yes it was.'

'I'll come and get her at a quarter to nine.'

'You're a star.'

'We'll leave our shopping till later.' The memory rushed into Maggie's head and she blushed. Oh god, they had actually discussed masturbation. She wanted to die. Jane didn't seem bothered at all; no, because she was probably sober unlike Maggie who had been pretty much pissed before they had even eaten.

'Have a think about colour.' And she rang off. Maggie's mind boggled. Did colour affect performance? She shook her head and decided to head back to bed with Alex when Bethany was gone. Of course, hangovers go hand in hand with poorly behaved children; it's the law and Bethany was being particularly difficult getting dressed and brushing her teeth. At one point, Maggie had to rush to the toilet to wretch but nothing came up. When Jane finally came for Bethany she didn't seem at all embarrassed or hung over.

'Oo, you look...tired.' Maggie winced.

'Thanks for this Jane, I owe you one.'

'Don't be silly, go back to bed and I'll come over for a cuppa later, bye!' Bethany trotted off happily with Jane and Christian and Maggie wondered why she never got into the car like that for her. As sleep engulfed her she promised herself that she would try to drink less.

Chapter 15

'Young Doctor in the camp. Nothing will happen; it's all been hushed up because he's a Brigadier.' Jenny was talking and Chrissy just listened. The children were in bed and they had watched *Strictly* and discussed who should win this year; they had marvelled at the bodies of the dancers whose abdominal muscles rippled as they threw their legs around in impossible positions.

'I suppose he was flattered. Classic mid-life crisis.'

'Are they still together?'

'He denied it at first but Mattie is his friend on Facebook and there are pictures of them together.'

'Bloody Facebook, it's hideous. Isn't that kind of insensitive when Mattie can see?'

'Yes he's an insensitive, selfish, self-obsessed bastard. Mattie was devastated. Kept asking questions about why he didn't love us anymore and loved that woman more.' Chrissy shook her head. Idiot, was all she thought.

'How old is she?'

'25.'

'Christ. What's he doing? Does he think that she'll still fancy him when he's fifty? You wait, he'll come sniffing back.'

'That's the saddest thing, Chrissy. I'd have him back.' Chrissy shook her head again.

'Why?'

'Because I love him. He's all I know. I keep telling myself that he's just got to get this out of his system and then he'll apologise and come back.'

'Do you think he will?'

'The longer it goes on, the more I think not. He's taken her on holidays and tried to force the children to meet her.'

'How did they react?'

'Badly. Harry called her a whore. How could he do this to them, Chrissy? I hate him and I love him. I'm so confused. I could forgive the sex bit, that doesn't matter at all, after all we weren't having any; but what he's done to Mattie and Harry; I don't know if they'll ever forgive him. They've seen me cry; they've seen me shout and throw unpaid bills about and slam the phone down and call him unspeakable names.'

'That he deserves.' Chrissy interjected.

'That he deserves.' Jenny agreed. 'I've turned into an emotional wreck and I'm the one who's done nothing wrong.'

'What if you were to do it?'

'What? Have an affair...listen to me I'm talking as if I'm still married.' She looked at her empty wedding finger. For 21 years it had boasted large, glittering diamonds as testimony to the solidity of her life that had now fallen apart.

'I received my notice to vacate on Thursday.'

'What?'

'I've got to leave the quarters, I'm trespassing illegally and the MOD has given me 21 days to get out. Chrissy, I've got no-where to go.'

'You could move in with me.'

'What about school?' She was right, it was too complicated. Mattie was in the middle of A Levels and Harry GCSEs. What a bastard. Couldn't he have kept his dick in his pants until they were at Uni?

'I'm thinking of moving back in with my mother. Oh the shame.'

'Would it be that bad until you sorted yourself out and the money was organised?'

'What money?'

'Surely you're entitled to half of his pension and he'll have to pay maintenance.'

'I've been told that he would have to pay £1200 a month for the kids until next year when Mattie's 18 and then half of that. I won't see his pension until he retires and he's got years left in him the green bastard. He'll probably promote next year and he'll be on £90k. I gave up everything for him, Chrissy.' Chrissy tried to imagine how she would survive without Jem's salary. She could get a job; she didn't have kids to think of, but what would she *do*? She was like Jenny; she'd married the army and now they were pretty much unemployable. Not even *Asda* would take them on as their degrees would render them over qualified. But their degrees were outdated; Chrissy had studied English twenty years ago and Jenny Art.

'What about your furnishings?' Jenny was a gifted seamstress.

'I wouldn't know where to start, Chrissy. How would I advertise? How could I juggle starting a successful business with everything I do now?'

'Write a business plan.'

'What's that?'

'You write down the projected outgoings and incomings, materials, market, rent, premises etc. and get a loan.'

'Who would give me a loan?' Chrissy could understand Jenny's pessimism; she wasn't in the mood to discuss her future. She was still wallowing in despair; her confidence had been trashed. They sat in silence for a while and Jenny went to get something. It was a photo album. Mattie and Harry smiled into the camera; they must have been toddlers. Another depicted Martin bouncing one of them on his knee; another, him and Jenny laughing.

'It's as if it was all a dream. It meant nothing.'

'You're torturing yourself Jenny. Of course it all meant something; your life hasn't been rubbed out, things change but not the past.'

'My life has been rubbed out, that's how it feels. I look at the kids who were supposed to grow up to be confident, well-adjusted adults; happy and stable with their parents watching on and now I see Mattie getting drunk and Harry kicking things.'

'It's only to be expected, they don't know how else to react.'

'He's such a coward. He disgusts me.' Jenny's emotions were all over the place. One minute she pined for him, the next she wanted him dead. It was too early to see any future and she was at rock bottom. All Chrissy could do was be a friend.

'Have you thought about Christmas?'

'He wants to take them all to Devon.'

'Glamorous. What do the kids say?'

'They're refusing to go and I can't force them.'

'I'll cancel my holiday, come to me.'

'You can't do that, Chrissy; you'll need that holiday, but thank you anyway.' Chrissy had booked ten days in Fuerteventura, it had been cheap and cheerful; she intended to sunbathe, read and sip cocktails all on her lovely own. She reckoned she could afford to take Jenny and the kids too but was that a bit much and what would Jem say? She was supposed to be saving for an extravagant trip post tour. She could wring Martin's neck. How did he suppose he was going to conduct himself as a Brigadier and be taken seriously with a twenty five year old army doc on his arm? God it was embarrassing; like a pensioner buying a Porsche. What was it with men and their dicks? Jenny had said that Martin told her their love life was boring and he had gone off her. Of course he had; she'd gone off Jem countless times, that's what happens when you've been married twenty years but one couldn't just run away; a marriage had to be worked at, like a classic car, it had to be loved, nurtured and tinkered with on Sundays. And what was a middle-aged man doing on Facebook? Her sons had accounts and continually whined at her to have one but she refused; it was obscene, why would she want her business studied minute by minute by virtual strangers in some sort of popularity competition, Jane went on it, she was obsessed and wrote things like, 'baked my best pavlova today' or 'Christian has a temperature', her iPad was open on the kitchen counter every time she went round and she was constantly checking and receiving mail and chuckling over posts that she occasionally showed Chrissy. Admittedly some of them were funny like the one about this year's Prison Panto being good with Tarbuck, Hall, Davidson and Starr. Some of them were offensive and unnecessarily explicit but Jane chuckled along as did Harry who, at ten, Chrissy thought should be banned. Apparently Jane's 'feed' (Chrissy knew some lingo) went to all her 'friends' and 'friends of friends' so exponentially that could be thousands and it worried Chrissy.

'Are you on Facebook Jenny?'

'Only since Martin started. I want to know what my kids see. I can't help going on his page; I know it's masochistic but it's like an itch I have to scratch. She's pretty.'

'Everyone's pretty at 25.' Chrissy said wryly.

'What does she see in him? All I see is his saggy belly and grey hair, his huffing and puffing and his trousers getting too small. It's disgusting, she must be seeking a father figure and he's fallen for it.'

'Maybe you should get a toy-boy; you're an attractive woman, Jenny.'

'Not with my eye bags and chain smoking thanks to Martin.'

'You're letting him win. You'll only break free when you say up yours and start to look after yourself.'

'It's too early, Chrissy. My priority is the kids not me. Harry's school have called me and asked if anything major has happened as he's acting strangely.'

'That's a bit vague.'

'The subtlety is all mine, namely he has started smoking pot in break.'

'Bloody hell. How do they know that?'

'They say it's obvious. They can smell it and he looks spaced out when he comes back to class.'

'Have you challenged him?'

'How can I? How can I tell him he's not allowed to be angry and reckless because his father's a twat?'

'That's very liberal.'

'We have shared a few joints actually. He opened up to me and I'll do anything to find a way in. I have his trust and I'm thankful, I'm not going to straight jacket him with rules when inside he's screaming, maybe this way I can control it.'

'That's very wise. I wouldn't be that far sighted.'

'You don't know how you'd react until it happens, if you'd told me that I'd be smoking pot with my fifteen year old last year I would have choked in my ball gown and pearl necklace.

That's the worse bit you know; I never really enjoyed the life in the army; the balls, tattoos, official functions and tedious parties, I was always pleading with Martin not to go and I hated entertaining; he brought countless people home that I hardly knew and I stood and cooked for them for hours; I became what I thought he wanted; the perfect wife and actually it wasn't what he wanted at all was it?'

'Did you really hate it?'

'Yes, it's only now I realise that I gave up being me for him; I became an extension of him for his stupid career, I raised his kids while he trophy hunted and I always waved him off with a smile, little did I know that last time I waved him off he was ramming it into a young doc no doubt over his desk or in the portaloo, god knows where, I don't care anymore.' This was progress thought Chrissy; she had to get over the anger and go through the lethargy then she could kick some ass and start living again.

Chrissy used to like Martin. Jem had said 'there are two sides to every story' and it 'takes two to make or break a marriage' but that didn't apply in green. All's fair in love and war and they made up their own rules as they went along. She wouldn't speak to Martin again as long as she lived. Jenny had done everything right; she had waited longingly for her man on cold dark nights when he was training in Kenya or shooting in Wiltshire, she had raised his kids and understood his last minute flights to Winchester and last minute cancellations of family gatherings, she forgave him his absence at birthdays and christenings and births, she forgave him when he forgot to call when he'd said he would, she'd moved seven months early because he'd been promoted despite having made a good friend or found a job in the local library, she'd attended functions when the kids were ill so he didn't lose face by being 'unaccompanied', she'd smiled dutifully at Generals and Brigadiers who'd visited their house at short notice for a three course meal that she had prepared lovingly, she forgave him that the children waited up for him until nine and he still didn't come home because he'd been asked to do one more thing for the Colonel. Maybe it was her fault; maybe she had been too placating, maybe she was a walk over, maybe she should have stood up to him more and insisted on his attending the births of their children instead of understanding that this Colonel or that Colonel needed him. Maybe she should have thrown Valentines dinners in the bin instead of waiting up for him because he 'had so much paperwork to finish'. Allegedly, the British Army would falter if Martin Park took a day off to care for his wife who was vomiting every ten minutes whilst trying to feed a newborn and control a toddler intent on tipping the contents of a potty over the floor. Maybe she should have 'put out' more despite not feeling aroused because she was ignored and un-cherished and forgotten to the extent that sex became repulsive with a man who forgot Harry's school play or Mattie's swim meet because he was delayed at the MOD, 'I can't just walk out, Jen…it's not like that…we don't work to rule…integrity…honour…loyalty,' Ah, yes, loyalty. She deserved each and every one of his medals for putting up with him and those who owned him; he was a coward in so many ways; she felt sorry for him, he was not a leader of men he was a servant of assholes in Whitehall who never had to grow up; he was Peter Pan, Walter Mitty…he had been looked after by his mother from the womb, then by the army as a young man, then, stupidly, by her; he had never had to make a serious decision in his life, he had lived it as an automaton nodding and following like a lamb and she had been destroyed in the process. He had never had to drop everything to go to school to pick Harry up after an asthma attack; he had never had to return from Sierra Leone or Bosnia, or Cyprus, or Germany, or Kosovo, or Sarajevo, or Kandahar, or Basra because Mattie had a temperature or Jenny had miscarried; he was allowed to opt out of such loyalties on the basis that he was more important. Besides, why would he have wanted to return from Basra when he was banging a nubile 25 year old? Yes, it was good having Chrissy to stay; it had allowed her to see him for the arsehole he was. Their divorce would come through in December and she would survive.

Chapter 16

Mark stood in the hallway. He took Maggie into his arms and held her for a long time. There was a hardness to his body that hadn't been there before; his grip was vice like and she felt his biceps pressing against her shoulders; wrapping her up in a wave of lust and need. He was more handsome than she remembered and he had a tan. He smelled of work; a mixture of stale clothes, travel and faint aftershave. He was unshaven; it had taken him three days to get home from Camp Salatin because of various delays due to casualty priorities and paperwork in Dubai. He had landed in Brize Norton at two this morning and had hired a car and slept somewhere on the M6 when he could no longer keep his eyes open. His eyes were moist and he held her face in his hands.

'You look beautiful.' Maggie smiled; Mark was back and it was him.

'Where are the kids?'

'Asleep.' Mark raised an eyebrow; before he had departed, Bethany had been refusing to go to bed and was still up at 9 o'clock some nights. Maggie felt shy. He was a bundle of manliness and sex and she was intimidated; she could see the hardness inside his combats and swallowed hard. He came to her and lifted her top over her head; his mouth cradled her nipple and she moaned leaning backwards. His hands were everywhere smoothing her curves as his war weary hands gently caressed every inch of her body as he undressed her. Their breath came quickly and he hopped about as he tried to pull a boot off, he lifted her and she wrapped her legs around him and they fell on the sofa. When he entered her she gasped; he was hard and full and she was aroused and tight; she grabbed his biceps and he kissed her hard as he moved his hips around and around; his abdominal muscles tightened as he thrusted and she watched his new hard body on top of hers. His dog tags tinkled across her breasts and their bodies stuck together, he moved faster and faster and held his breath.

'I'm sorry, I can't stop...' She didn't mind, she wanted him to come inside her; she had forgotten what it felt like and she wanted to watch his face as he orgasmed deliciously; it would be her turn later. He quivered and his legs twitched and he gasped and bent his head to her neck. He sagged against her in relief and they lay wrapped up until their hearts slowed and Mark lifted his head.

'Hi.'

'Hi.'

'Is it weird?' She was surprised by his question; Mark wasn't a post-coital talker.

'A bit. It feels illicit and secret.' They laughed.

'God, I missed you Maggie.' She didn't really want to talk about that. It wrenched up issues that she hadn't yet dealt with.

'I'm cold.' He slipped out of her and they went to the downstairs loo. Mark had had a vasectomy and it meant sex was more intense but quite messy after. They got dressed and Maggie offered to get wine.

'I've been looking forward to a drink for four months.' When she came back Mark had put the fire on and had found some jeans and a jumper in his bag. He looked normal. She loved him in jeans; it meant he was off duty and all hers.

'Come here. You look amazing, Maggie, like when we first met. What have you been doing?'

'Gym, every day. Jane comes too.' Mark looked impressed. Maggie swilled wine round her mouth before talking a gulp and looked at Mark.

'There's a trainer there thinks I could be a personal instructor myself. What do you think?'

'Who's the trainer?'

'Well that's not the point; he's just some trai...'

'He?'

'Mark, don't be like this; I'm not a child I can look after myself.'

'Is he good looking? Do you like him?'

'Mark this is about me not some trainer…I don't know, I don't think of him like that.'

'It's not you I'm worried about, it's him looking at you every day looking hot, and god, Maggie, you look sensational.' He leant over but now she was pissed off and pulled back.

'What?'

'I was telling you about becoming a personal trainer, I wanted your support.'

'Are you serious?' He hadn't even thought her serious. She got up to get a jumper and tripped over one of his bags, she kicked it. She always allowed him to get her knickers off before she thought about what she was doing, now she looked at his stuff everywhere and felt claustrophobic.

'Maggie…where are you going?'

'For a jumper, I said I was cold.' Mark ran his fingers through his hair, what was wrong with her? What had he said now? Please don't tell me this is what it's going to be like for two weeks, he thought. The wine tasted good and he topped up their glasses. Maggie entered the room again and sat down heavily.

'I'm sorry.' He seemed genuine.

'For what?'

'I have no idea but I don't want to piss you off, not now.'

'I was trying to tell you about something that I could maybe achieve on my own that wasn't army related and might give me some shred of self-esteem back and you're just obsessed about who might be watching my ass at the gym, don't you think that's a bit shallow coming from someone who has been away for four months?'

'Maggie, there are no women where I work.'

'There must be; doctors, nurses, journalists, secretaries, translators.'

'Ok, yes but I don't see any of them as women.'

'That's not the point. You immediately assumed that I'm off gyming with other men who drool over me all day, and even if that was the case don't you trust me to handle myself or would you prefer I didn't go out at all? Should I just sit in the house like a good little army wife and wait for you?'

'Maggie I didn't mean it like that.'

'That's not the point! You said it, at least take responsibility for what falls out of your mouth.'

'I don't know what to say to you, I always say the wrong thing.'

'That's an excuse so you don't have to say anything.' He was baffled by her anger and she was livid with his immaturity. She gulped her wine.

'Should we start again?' Mark took her hand and she let him; it was easier that way. He went to kiss her and she closed her lips and kissed him on the cheek. He sighed; he wasn't out of the dog house yet. They flicked on the TV and Mark went to get another bottle of wine. They didn't talk again that night. They eventually got to bed around midnight having opened a third bottle. Mark left his kit in the hallway and they fell into bed; he'd started touching her but she pretended to be asleep and eventually he'd turned over and gone to sleep.

'Daddy!' Bethany screamed and jumped on Mark. Bliss, thought Maggie, let him deal with her. To her surprise Mark got straight up and bounced Bethany in his arms;

'Let mummy sleep.' He quietly closed the door and she turned over finding it hard to remember the last time she'd been able to stay in bed beyond 6.30. When she opened her eyes it was a quarter to ten and she felt fresh and alive, she luxuriated in the novelty for a while and simply stared at the curtains. She could hear vague noises downstairs which, she assumed meant that Mark had everything under control. Then she heard footsteps on the stairs and whispers and giggles and she hid under the duvet pretending to still be fast asleep. The door opened quietly and the three of them announced together;

'Surprise, Mummy!' She pretended to wake up and acted surprised and delighted.

'Wow!' Mark carried a tray with a fry up, giant mug of tea and a little jug containing what looked like weeds but would pass for flowers this time of year.

'Oh my goodness me! Thank you.' She kissed them one by one and the children looked very pleased with themselves. I wonder how long this will last, she thought. Her breakfast was delicious and Mark sat and watched her while she ate.

'What do you want to do today?' She asked between gloriously fatty mouthfuls of runny egg and crispy bacon.

'Nothing. Everything. No idea.'

'We could take the kids swimming and go for a pub lunch.'

'Ok, sounds good. I've been dreaming of that bacon for four months, I had mine earlier and it was divine.' She laughed,

'What, you mean rations don't cut it? How about I make steak and chips tonight?' Mark's eyes lit up.

'Stop, I can't stand it.' He rolled about on the bed in fake agony.

'I think this leave I will mostly be eating and drinking and making love to my beautiful wife.'

'I think this leave my new found waistline is going to expand three inches and I will enjoy every mouthful.'

'I'll give you a mouthful...' Shhhh!' Maggie nodded at the children who appeared to be oblivious. He was rampant which wasn't surprising considering he'd lived like a Neanderthal hermit for the last four months. He lay back on the clean sheets and caressed his pillow stretching fully. He looked happy and rested. The children became distracted and wandered off to Alex's room.

'How has Bethany been?'

'Next question.'

'I want to know, Maggie; I don't want you to deal with it all yourself.' Maggie laughed, she couldn't believe what he had just said, the glaring irony of it. He looked at her in his 'what have I done now' kind of way.

'Ok Mark, I'll say this once. By the way thank you for my lovely breakfast, I hope it didn't come with obligations attached and was simply a display of unselfishness and tender love on your part.' He started to say something.

'I haven't finished. Bethany is a girl who is insecure and hates change or surprises. She is intense and needy and impatient, in fact she displays all the insecurities of a single parent child. I have found out these things about my daughter since you decided to leave us to suck green cock.' Mark was smirking; he loved it when she was stern and sincere; it made him horny.

'If you were genuinely interested in helping your daughter you would stay around a while, ring some help lines, read some books, spend some time getting to know her, put your family first sometimes…just saying.'

'Have you finished?'

'Yes.'

'Come here.' He was doing it again. His hand was in her knickers before she could wriggle away.

'You are such an arsehole.'

'I love you.' He pinned her down and found her nipple with his tongue. She wriggled over so she faced her pillow and raised her hips up in the air; Mark thrust into her and writhed around and around while cupping her breasts and stroking her nipples with his thumbs. It always got her quickly like this but she had wanted to look at him last night. The bed was creaking but they weren't about to stop now, they prayed they could finish before being interrupted. Mark went faster and faster and pulled her hips towards him making it deeper; her nipples hardened as her womb contracted and she released four months of anxiety. She couldn't help crying out as he came and she could feel him pulsating.

'Mummy.' They were coming up the stairs. Shit! He pulled out quick and she found her t-shirt and threw it on. They hid under the duvet giggling and panting. Alex looked under and they surprised him with an almighty roar; he squealed and ran away then came back for more. Maggie went to the bathroom to clean up and looked at herself in the mirror; she looked alive, her cheeks were pink and her eyes sparkled. Bastard, she thought.

They finally got the kids in the car around eleven which was around the time they usually had lunch. Maggie had prepared for this and brought rice crackers, cheddars and juice. Bethany screamed when Mark opened her juice.

'Oh, she opens it herself now.' So much had changed, Mark felt surplus to requirements. Bethany's squeal grated his nerves and he ached to be with his wife alone.

'I don't like cheddars!'

'Me too!' Great, now Alex was in on the act. Mark stared out of the window and tapped his foot as Maggie drove.

'Do you mind?' He bellowed making the whole car shake. Maggie tried to concentrate on the bus in front. Jesus, what was up with him?

'Mummy has spent all morning putting some food together for you and this is how you act. Poor Mummy!' He was still booming and Alex began to cry.

'That's your fault Daddy; Daddy is mean, I don't want you home.' That was like a knife to his heart. Surely what he had just said was a good example of discipline was it not? Where had he gone wrong? Maggie rolled her eyes; well today was going just smashing, she thought sarcastically, she bit her tongue; they had never argued in front of the children but his tone was totally unnecessary; who the hell did he think he was? They weren't soldiers! Having another adult eased the physical burden but emotionally she felt as though she now had three kids to steer through the day. Bethany threw the packet of cheddars that Mark had forced into her hand straight towards the front of the car and one flew out and hit Maggie.

'Stop the car!' Mark roared. Maggie pulled over, shaking. He jumped out of the passenger seat and ripped Bethany's door open and belted her hard on her leg. She screamed. Maggie's thoughts were erratic; should she be pleased that she had someone to support her with her daughter's challenging behaviour or should she be livid that he had been so physical with a four year old. Part of her was secretly pleased that Bethany had managed to wind her father up so much; it wasn't her for a change, but parts of her hated him for reacting so mindlessly. The day slipped away from her and she questioned what she was doing waiting around for this stranger. Now she was in the middle of a war zone; ironic, he carried them with him wherever he went. Bethany was still screaming and her face had turned purple. Alex was laughing at her and this made her worse. Mark raised his voice even further to be heard above Bethany.

'How dare you throw things when Mummy is driving; do you want her to crash? Because if you do we will all die.' Slight exaggeration but he had a point. She wondered dryly where Bethany got her drama from. Maggie wondered idly if Bethany would be kept awake tonight with dreams of death again. She held on to the wheel and looked out of the window.

'Have you two finished?' She smiled a wide fake smile and Mark widened his eyes as if to say, what? You don't support me on this? He sighed and shrugged his shoulders.

'Right, I won't say another word then.' Oh Lord, she definitely had three kids in the car, in fact Alex was the best behaved of all three. They set off in heavy silence. Mark had got under her skin and the familiar feeling of revulsion at having made love to him crept over her. What was it with him? Why did she let him in only to be hurt and disappointed over and over again? She pulled into a parking space under the bridge where she had parked so many times this winter already but on her own. She got out of the car and still they didn't speak. Now, Bethany's screams had turned to sobs and she held her leg where Mark had hit her. Maggie moved her leggings to one side and looked to see if there was a mark. Christ, Mark's fingers could be seen perfectly framed in pink on the child's skin, he must have put some force into that slap. She held Bethany and wiped her face. Mark looked pale when he saw the mark; he busied himself getting Alex out of his seat. 'Apologise' mouthed Maggie. He spread open his arms as if to say, 'why? how?' and she could see he was out of his comfort box; a place he wasn't used to being. He approached Bethany with caution as if she were a ticking bomb.

'Bethany, Daddy is really sorry, but you shouldn't throw things.' Oh why did he have to caveat his apology? He almost had her and now she would close off to him again.

The walk was awkward and Bethany clung to her mother when Mark went near her. He distanced himself from them and they looked like a single family out with a friend. Alex had forgotten what all the fuss was about and sat on Mark's shoulders, Mark called him 'buddy' and Maggie was reminded how easy it is to love someone who loves you back. It was true; Bethany was hard to love but she needed them to just as much as Alex, men are so much better with animals and babies, they're uncomplicated and emotionally straightforward, they need feeding, watering and cleaning every now and again unlike Bethany who needed engagement and patience; two emotions that men and soldiers distinctly lacked and her husband was both. Maggie felt intense sympathy for Bethany in that moment and admonished herself for not seeing it clearer sooner; Bethany was crying out for attention, Maggie held her hand and the girl smiled up at her mother. Maybe it would be this unlikely relationship that would blossom during R&R as her marriage crumbled but then she remembered what Jane had said about haste; they were in no position to judge and would have to wait until it was all over to really understand where they were and if love still existed between them; of course this all went on inside Maggie's head and at no point did Mark suspect that his wife was contemplating life without him, he saw the blips as normal behaviour from a grumbling wife, after all, they all did it didn't they? His soldiers all came back from R&R moaning about their wives giving them a hard time; it was a universal truth that women cannot be kept happy and even if they are made happy momentarily the rules change so often that maintenance is quite out of the question. At no point did Mark even reflect that Maggie behaved like she did (as did his daughter) because she was unhappy: and unhappy for a reason no less.

They arrived at the pub and looked like any other family out for a walk and a quick pint; dogs sniffed around trees and canal boats moored up alongside the pretty lock. Families laughed and young childless couples recovered from the previous night with a steaming plate of sausage and mash whilst reading the Sunday papers. Maggie envied them. She remembered when her and Mark were able to do just that. They would wander through Smithfields market and grab a bowl of Thai then end up in some small pub down Brick Lane sipping Pinot Grigio and discussing politics. They continued to wander when Maggie was pregnant but their wanderings turned to Islington and Southbank where they would sit on benches or shop for antiques. She had breezed through pregnancy; she had bloomed and beamed and it had suited her. Then her life had ended.

Maggie sat down with a sigh. Mark noticed instantly and became defensive always turning the ebb and flow of the day to him. He mouthed 'What?' and she mouthed 'nothing.' Bethany found a dog to stroke and they chatted with the owners; an elderly couple who had probably lived here all their lives and sure enough they'd had Amber the dog for fifteen years and counting. How cosy thought Maggie, she knew what was coming.

'Can we get a dog, Mummy?'

'One day, maybe darling.' She smiled uneasily at the elderly couple.

'Oh, children love dogs don't they? Amber is our third bless them all, our four doted on them.' Thanks for that Mable or Doris or fucking Ida or whatever, butt out. She forced a smile.

'When? Mummy? When?' Here we go.

'Bethany, mummy said not now, you are too young to look after a doggie, mummy would have to walk it and look after it.' Mark snapped.

'I could look after it!'

'No you couldn't'

'Yes I could!'

'She's a live wire isn't she, got her own mind.' Doris stepped in again.

'She keeps us busy. Mark can you go and get the kids some drinks? I need a gin and tonic.' Doris winked at her, 'I bet you do my love. Go and sit down, your adorable daughter can sit with Amber for a bit.' Bethany almost exploded. 'Yes! Yes!'

'Oh I don't know that's really not fair on you...'

'Oh she's fine, look she's enjoying herself.' Maggie hated being forced into situations beyond her control and all she wanted was for her daughter to come and sit and colour some pictures and be with the rest of her family so they could at least try to look as if it were normal. She relented for the peace and quiet. 'Ok well we're just here.' Mark had disappeared to the bar and Maggie watched Alex in the outside play area. The day was crisp but dry and lots of people huddled around outside heaters in coats; it was bracing and warming at the same time. Maggie loved days like these; time stood still and calm descended for just a little while. Mark came back with a pint and a gin and two plastic cups of juice with straws. 'Oh they have beakers for little ones in here now.' Maggie felt a sting of guilt as she dashed Mark's efforts once again. She stood up but he said, 'No I'll go; where are they?'

'Oh don't worry, I'll go.' He looked run over by a truck and sat down to drink his pint. Doris looked at him and smiled.

When she returned they sat in silence and she swilled the cool gin around her mouth. The sun shone and Maggie lowered her sunglasses, that way at least he couldn't see her eyes; her eyes that carried mountains of despair and solitude. He reached for her hand and she recoiled internally. He did this. He thought touch cured everything. They sat.

Alex wailed and Maggie jumped up. He'd fallen and gathered a lump of soggy wood chippings in his eyes and mouth, Maggie swooped him up and Mark followed looking redundant.

'Mummy!' Why wasn't it 'Daddy'? But he knew the answer; he was on the periphery of his family and couldn't even find a beaker to put juice in. Maggie soon settled him and drained her gin.

'What are you having?' It was all he could think of to say.

'I think the quiche.'

'Oh.'

'What?'

'Well I was going to get bangers and mash.'

'Well get bangers and mash then.'

'Well if you're just having quiche…'

'Have what you want; I'm not losing all this weight just to put it back on again.' This clearly hurt him. She might as well have said, 'life doesn't stop just for you.' He ordered a sandwich and she sighed. A heavy weight spread over her shoulders and she ordered a bottle of wine. They both looked at Bethany who was happily chatting away to Doris and husband of a million happy years. The children's mini roasts arrived and Maggie set about slicing and blowing, Mark just got in the way; he put tomato ketchup over everything and chopped Bethany's potatoes too small.

'No,' she said too late.

'What?' He looked panic stricken.

'They don't have ketchup on roast.' He threw the cutlery down and turned his back to her. She wanted to cry. She gathered the children and Bethany's eyes widened at the red blobs near her peas; she didn't like vegetables to touch her ketchup.

'I don't want it.' Mark looked ready to burst and looked at Maggie as if to say, 'how are you raising our children?'

'Don't want it.' Alex joined in.

'Well there is nothing else and I can scrape off the ketchup, look.' The children eyed their mother with suspicion but eventually hunger overcame rebellion and they tried a potato. Maggie changed the subject to Amber and Bethany forgot about winding her mother up and ate with gusto, Alex copied. Mark tucked into his lunch and stopped trying to help. Maggie's quiche was getting cold but she was used to it besides the wine was good and she poured her third glass. Mark watched her and she saw judgement cloud his brow. She thought, 'fuck off.'

Between helping Alex with his cup and encouraging Bethany to use her fork and spoon correctly, Maggie grabbed mouthfuls of quiche. Doris got up to leave and Bethany almost knocked Alex off his chair in her rush to hug Amber goodbye.

'Bethany!' Mark shouted and Maggie cringed. She glared at him; well at least he'd enjoyed his lunch; a clean plate sat in front of him while hers was still over half full.

'Maybe you could take over now you're finished?' Her voice dripped with irony and it was not lost. Mark could feel his afternoon slipping away along with his wife and wondered if all women were like this after they had kids. Why was she always criticising him? Where had his Maggie May gone?

'Can I get another pint or am I driving?' He eyed the half gone bottle of wine.

'Sorry, you should have said, I think I've had too much.'

'I'll get a half then.'

When Alex started to fall asleep in his ice cream they decided to leave and bundled him into his push chair. Bethany climbed into the second seat which she still did occasionally when she was tired; maybe she would dose off this afternoon. By the time they reached home both were fast asleep and they carried them silently upstairs. Mark tried to be as quiet as he could, thinking about some time alone with his wife, but the bloody stairs creaked and Bethany woke. Damn! Maggie shut Alex's door and found Mark pleading with Bethany to have a little sleep.

'No!'

'Shhhhh! You'll wake your brother.'

'Bike!'

'No we are not going for a bike ride Bethany, we have only just come home; would you like to watch a movie?' She nodded and went to her mother. Mark could have sworn that he saw a look of triumph in the girl's face as she won yet again. Their afternoon was spent either side of Bethany on the sofa watching *Tinkerbell.* Mark fell asleep. By the time he woke up it was gone four o'clock and Maggie was outside on the trampoline with both children. He felt better but kicked himself for being so selfish. He watched his wife from the kitchen window, how to get in? Where had she gone? When had it happened? God she was beautiful. He ached to be alone with her. Instead, he joined them and asked Maggie if she would like a lie down. She smiled a genuine smile and slipped off to their bedroom. Once the door was closed, she shut off all noise from downstairs and drifted into a deep relaxing sleep; something she could get quite used to for two weeks.

Chapter 17

With Chrissy away and Maggie holed up in the love shack, Jane didn't know what to do. She had become reliant upon her two friends and it surprised her; she missed them. Her mind drifted to James's R&R and she smiled; heat rushed between her legs and she touched her neck absentmindedly. Maybe she'd pop to the Families Office for a coffee. She found Dave mulling over paperwork on his desk; he looked drawn and old.

'Hi Jane, brew?' No one else was around and she felt self-conscious.

'I'll make it, you're busy,' his phone rang. The community room was tidy and ordered and she idly picked up a glossy magazine. She should have gone to the gym but it wasn't the same without Maggie. She had said she wouldn't stop going just because Mark was home but Jane knew this wouldn't be true when it came down to it. It all changes when they walk through the door. She hoped Maggie and Mark were enjoying one another and that they had found time to just be and love. The kettle boiled and Jane made two coffees. Everyone knew how Dave took it; like a builder, white with two. She heard him becoming tense on the phone and wondered what hell today would bring him. She felt for his wife because even though Dave was here on The Patch still, he was absent in other ways and it must be just as bad if not worse for her. Sarah kept herself to herself and was rarely seen around The Patch. They had no children and rumour had it that she'd had several miscarriages and that she'd suffered a few nervous breakdowns but who can trust rumours? Dave certainly looked burdened but that could have been simply due to his job, no one asked. He walked into the community room looking tired.

'Do you get R&R, Dave?'

'Ha! On paper, but not likely.' He smiled broadly and his eyes twinkled; they hadn't broken him yet.

'So what brings you in here, Jane?' She quickly thought of an excuse to cover the fact that she was simply looking for some company.

'Well I was thinking I might do a curry afternoon, like curry and cupcakes, or something to raise a bit of money; you know, a bit like a coffee morning but a lunch.'

'On your own?' Jane hadn't thought of this.

'Er, well, yes.'

'Where would you cook it? We could open the cookhouse.' Dave actually thought the idea a goer and it pleased her.

'I was thinking of taster dishes, just little ones and could charge £1 or something.'

'But you'd have to fork out for the ingredients, I'm afraid there's not a lot of money left, could you make a profit?'

'I'm sure I could, maybe not a huge one but...' She had been thinking about the figures involved and if 50 turned up she could probably make £30, if 100 turned up she could make £70 for the Families Office. There were 400 wives on The Patch; where were they all? The meat would be expensive but using ramekin portions she could make it go a long way, besides many curry dishes were vegetarian and she already had more than enough spice. Cupcakes were cheap enough and she could get donations of those and have the children decorate them.

'Let's look in the diary. Let's see, Saturday 7th December?' The day before James's leave.

'Perfect. I could do a Christmas theme.'

'Wait a minute, why not make it a Christmas fair, we were having some sort of party for the kids anyway, that would draw more people and I could open it to the locals like last year. Jane was becoming nervous.

'How many are we talking?'

'Maybe 300?' Oh.

'Fine.' She gulped her hot coffee and burned her throat. What was she getting herself into?

'I'll get Chrissy to put it into the next meeting; you can't do it on your own. When is she back?'

'Tomorrow.'

'Good, I'm glad she went, she needed it.' This was a dangerous admission from the Families Officer but Dave knew who he was talking to and Jane thought, you need it, too, my friend.

As Jane made her way back to The Patch she turned her head as she noticed a flash of colour; it was Titty's bright pink pram being pushed up the hill. Jane was about to pretend that she hadn't noticed but as she drove past she noticed that Titania was crying. Oh Christ, this presented a real dilemma; Jane didn't like to see anyone cry and surely Titty had a few redeeming qualities that she just hadn't found yet? She couldn't stop the car in the street so she drove home and walked to Titania's house just as she was opening her door. Olivia and Tristen were asleep. Titty wouldn't put them into the local nursery where Christian and Bethany went as it hadn't received an outstanding Ofsted report last year.

'Hi, Titania.' She willed herself not to say Titty. Titania was taken aback and rubbed her eyes; she had been in a world of her own and had been oblivious to Jane driving past, shit, she could have ignored it.

'Have you been crying? I was just going to tell you about something happening in the Mess but is there something wrong?' Jane mumbled.

'Oh no, nothing wrong at all I'm just hormonal that's all and I miss HH who is soooo busy I could cry for him.' She called her husband HH after his double barrel surname; Jane wondered idly if she had pet names for the children too, Livs and Tris perhaps. She shouldn't have come, it was a mistake.

'Come in! Let's have a cup of Earl Grey!' The children slept on in the pram. They remained asleep; Jane was always flabbergasted at how well behaved they were, they lived like robots sleeping and feeding on demand and she guessed it was fear.

'Could I have coffee?' Jane was becoming a coffee addict; it soothed her and felt European and decadent. However, Titania's coffee left much to be desired, it came from a jar that looked as though it had been at the back of the cupboard for four years and had to be banged on the table to release a few grains, meanwhile Titania made herself a pot of Earl Grey which she covered with a *Laura Ashley* cosy. Titania's kitchen was freezing but she didn't seem to notice, the house was deathly quiet and Jane felt uncomfortable. Photos of her and HH adorned the walls and Jane was shocked at how much Titania had changed since they were taken and she guessed, correctly, that it hadn't been that long ago.

'So, busy busy.' Titania smiled at her and held her gaze. She felt under scrutiny.

'Not really, I think we've hit a dip.' Titania began to speak and so Jane closed her mouth.

'Oh, I know, at first it is the novelty of having to struggle on alone and now we're used to it aren't we? We just get on and do it although I think Ben will get a shock when he comes back and I leave him to get on on his own for ten days.' Jane almost spat her disgusting coffee.

'What?' She tried not to sound rude.

'Well I think it's the least he can do. I'm going skiing with darling friends of ours.' Titania giggled. Jane wished, again, that she hadn't come; there was no way in to this woman.

'Oh. Lucky you.'

'It's not luck, Jane; we keep points. My job as full time nurturer is just as important as his and I am just as exhausted; I need a break. Anyway he's looking forward to it.' Jane smiled. I bet he is, she thought. She made a mental note to take some curries round for him and offer to have the children to play. Ha, between them they might make normal kids of them in ten days, she thought, bitchily. Jane put away her uncharitable thoughts and tried to listen to Titania, which was difficult as she spoke like a whirlwind and one had just cottoned onto the theme when Bam! It was changed.

'Of course HH needs a rest too, as the senior commander out there in the toughest region, of course he needs to wind down, so he's going to Madrid for four days to see a good friend, it's a surprise so hush hush!' HH... Jane wondered where she had got the title senior commander and thought

James would find this hilarious. She wondered what Jem really thought of this illustrious Company Commander/second in command. Anyway what was a tough region? Weren't they all fighting? She was sure that James wasn't in the spa part of Helmand. Jane wondered if Titania would put the heating on but she made no move and so she kept on her coat. In the end Jane didn't get chance to tell Titania about the Christmas Fair. Instead, Titania told her about her Christmas arrangements, the children's dietary needs, her mother's gout, her father's hand carved walking stick that she had bought him for Christmas and the wonders of tofu. She had left intellectually richer, of course. She had learned that beetroot was good for gout, commercial noodles are coated in plastic, bamboo is harder than oak, that Titty once travelled extensively in Japan and the fact that Christmas was indeed a pagan ritual hijacked by Catholics. Finally able to leave, she walked slowly back to her house, low in mood. Mark was just parking.

'Hi, Mark! How are you? How is leave?' She smiled.

'Different! I think we've got the easy job compared to you lot.' My, Maggie has been working on him, she thought.

'I'm missing my gym partner! I hold you totally responsible for the guaranteed weight gain on my hips.' Mark laughed. He was so handsome, what was there not to like? But she wasn't married to him and Maggie was and behind closed doors he could be a demonic fetishist or something. Oh Jane stop thinking about sex! It was happening more and more as James's leave drew closer she just couldn't help it, she had had to replace the batteries on her RR three times and she wondered if it would melt.

'Daddy!' Bethany flew into her father's arms and it was a beautiful sight. Jane felt a pang of jealousy and reassured herself that that would soon be James and her children, even Harry would crack she reckoned. They said their goodbyes and Jane headed back to pick up the car to collect Christian. He chattered on about red paint and a monkey all the way home and yawned deeply as they neared their driveway. Maybe this meant that he wanted to sleep and today and Jane thought, I'm going to sleep too. As she was tiptoeing to her room the phone went, damn.

It was James. A flood of relief came over her and she smiled into the phone.

'James, I miss you.'

'I miss you too, gorgeous.'

'Can you tell me how it is?'

'Not really. I want to talk about leave. Tell me something good.'

'Who's listening?'

'Probably some spotty little Corporal in Camp Salatin, do you care?'

'No.' She giggled. 'God, I can't wait to get you home, I'm having dirty thoughts, constantly.' James felt himself go hard under his combats. He hadn't showered in days and he stank but they all did so it mattered not. A long queue wound behind him and they all waited to say the same to their wives; they wanted to fuck them, hard.

'Oh Jane, you're making me hard, I'll have to turn round.' He could hear helicopters nearby bringing much needed supplies and maybe letters from home.

'What I'm going to do to you...can you stand it?' She caressed the phone, she felt 20.

'Oh I think I can manage, I hope you're not expecting to leave the house for two weeks.'

'What about our dirty weekend away?' He grew harder and he ached for her. Porn was ok but nothing lived up to the real thing, especially not his wrist.

'We need to talk about that; I think the kids need you around.'

'I don't care where we are as long as I can abuse your body until you beg me to stop.'

'I won't ask you to stop, ever.' The line went dead. That was the way of things. She knew he wouldn't call back. She hoped the cut in comms meant no new dead bodies.

'Fuck!' His card had run out. Now he needed to top it up; they were only entitled to two hours a week and with all their filthy phone calls, James usually lost track of his.

''Scuse me, Sir.' Roberts squeezed past him and he hoped his boner had subsided. Back to work. He was exhausted and he needed a break but at the same time didn't want to leave his men behind. He looked up into the Afghan sky that was turning orange and ran his hand through his dirty hair. He imagined having a warm shower with his wife and felt a stirring in his pants again.

'Sir, you're needed in the Ops room.' He forgot Jane and marched to the Ops room; a concrete structure with tent doors, what now? They only had one unit out with A Coy. R&R was hitting the Battalion hard and they scrabbled round for infills where they could get them; it was a nervous time, the enemy knew their movements and knew they sent their soldiers home to recuperate; Christmas was the worst, soldiers would be off guard thinking about loved ones and the Taliban knew it. He had sent one section of eight men led by Cpl Hall to patrol a new area securing a new PB; there had been low perceived threat. The unit would rest tomorrow when the whole Company went out on patrol at 4am led by James.

The radio crackled. It was Hall's voice.

'IED, Sir, Crawley and Peters, Sir. Fatal times two, casualties times three.' Jesus, five out of eight.

'Get your ass back Col.' Colin Hall was a consummate professional and it must have been bad for his section to be hit, was intelligence correct? Had his men walked into a trap? Crawley and Peters were good men; he wondered how bad it had been. Colin Hall had dealt with fatalities before and James would commend him on his return. In one fire fight alone, he had nicked a jeep and driven it seven times under fire to retrieve men. He had come out with a dislocated thumb and no body bags, the guy was a legend. It was messy. He would now spend the night collating eye witness reports and trying to figure out what the hell happened, he would need to liaise with Mark, OC of A Coy. He liked Mark, he did his job and didn't whinge. He would be under just as much pressure right now and would be kicking himself for losing someone else's men. One day they would have a beer together but sadly not now. Two weeks before leave for Christ's sake. Then he remembered that Mark was on leave himself; someone was headed for an almighty pile of shit, who had he left in charge? Had a poor decision been made? He wouldn't phone him on leave but he could bet his life savings (if they had any) that Mark would be on the phone as soon as he could get through to London. He didn't envy Maggie. A call from the Col came in; Colonel Jem was a ball breaker and wouldn't take the news well. He shouted at various Sgts and Corporals and Captains within firing range and they set about making calls and then waiting. They couldn't leave the camp; they would stick to their planned patrol at 0400 and James hoped the bodies didn't return before then else morale would be screwed. He doubted he would sleep before the gates opened and they did it all again.

Chapter 18

Jane couldn't sleep now. She looked in on Christian who was fast asleep and she went to wash some pots and prepare their tea; spaghetti Bolognese. It was a winner, they always ate it and she never had dirty plates, pity she couldn't serve it every night. She had bought some ice cream for after but Harry probably wouldn't have some, he was too old for ice cream now. She flicked on the radio and listened to *Classic FM*, virtually the only station not to report the war. A text came in and it made her jump. It was Chrissy, 'back at ten tomorrow, fancy a coffee? x' Jane sighed with relief. She texted back.

'Absolutely x hope u had good time x'

'It was lovely, just what I needed, feel much better x'

'Good, see u tomorrow x' She was looking forward to seeing Chrissy again. It was turning out to be a good day; she had arranged to make curry for hundreds of women, spoken to James and arranged coffee with a friend. She smiled contentedly; she might even go to the gym alone tomorrow.

Dave Proctor buried his head. The Casualty Notifying Officer would be here in ten minutes. They would make the visit to Cpl Peters' house to see Ella. Crawley had been unmarried; his parents lived in Newcastle and it was being dealt with by their office. The MOD had Casualty Notifying Officers in strategic locations across the country to cut down notifying times; no-one wanted the press to get hold of information before the next of kin, although they were generally respectful and on the occasions they had got a name they had sat on it until the MOD had officially released information and given the green light. A car containing a priest and two officers would be on its way now to Mr and Mrs Crawley. Dave put on his jacket and braced himself. The Padre walked in and shook his hand.

'Dave.'

'Dick.'

Ten minutes later the female CNO had arrived and they got into Dave's car. Would Ella be in? She worked part time. Thank God they had no kids. The journey took four minutes and when Dave pulled up outside a group of mums with prams had stopped to chat. Shit, that's all he needed, they clearly weren't making a social call. They stared at the car as the three sombre faces climbed out.

'Ladies.' Dave nodded with a warning; they understood and covered their mouths.

'Best move off.' They nodded and walked a little down the street but he knew they wouldn't depart entirely; this was juicy indeed, they would hang around and start texting. If anyone found out before Ella he would personally batter them, he thought violently.

Dave knocked. Ella answered quickly; she was in sports kit with an iPod attached to her ear and was smiling broadly, until she saw who her visitors were.

Apparently Cpl Hall had held Peters' hand for forty minutes before the helicopter could get anywhere near but he wouldn't share that information with Ella. He was still alive when they loaded him but he slipped away three minutes before they touched down at Camp Salatin despite the efforts of the MERT. How much blood did he lose in that forty minutes? As he held Ella Peters close to him as she sobbed wrackingly into his jacket, forgetting who or where she was, he hated his job.

Three hours after the hideous deaths of Crawley and Peters, a text was sent to the wives informing them before the press. Tears rolled down Jane's face as she wondered who it was this time. The texts never contained names, that would have been crass, so one never knew if it was a neighbour or friend or someone you had had coffee with on Sunday in the Mess. That was what had cut James off after all. She had the morbid, obscene thought that as she was talking to her husband about sex someone had been dying and writhing in agony as one of their mates told them to hang on; they died without the face of a loved one, they died in the arms of comrades who had come to be their families but the faces of their near and dear were in their pockets and scorched on their brains. What did it mean to die in a foreign field? Did men shout for their mums as it says in poetry? Or does it all happen so quickly like in *Saving Private Ryan* that they hold on to their mates before slipping away, dirty hand in dirty hand?

Jane's mood became low and energy seeped from her body. How could she go on pretending in front of the children? Harry and Lucas in particular knew where their father was and they knew that soldiers were dying. She had caught Lucas weeping one night into his pillow although he had tried to cover it up. Did The Patch kids talk about it at school? She looked at the clock and then the fridge. A tiny glass of wine would soothe her and if she chewed a mint no-one would notice. She reached for a tumbler out of the cupboard and slid the yellow bottle out of their booze fridge which they kept in the spacious utility. Her hands shook as she poured. She drank the contents in one. She felt the warmth hit her stomach and spread throughout her blood vessels and her shoulders relaxed. Just one more wouldn't hurt. She poured another and her hand shook less. That's better. She sat at the kitchen table for a while and checked the clock. She closed her eyes for five minutes and thought of the mothers without sons; the women who lay awake at night remembering how they had held their babies and watched them grow, the smiles, the tantrums, the first steps, the first haircut. She imagined them holding old photos of innocence looking deep into their eyes bursting with life and promise; shattered, ripped away and dead in a ditch.

She reached for her hand bag and took out a mint and then thought 'I'll take a couple.' Where had she left her coat? The wind howled outside and it looked bitter, she found gloves and a hat too. Christian snuggled behind blankets and she put the pram cover on for good measure.

Why is it that kids are an emotional barometer of their mothers? All four were in terrible moods, even Christian who'd had a glorious sleep but now he was feeding off the others. Harry sulked miserably and said he wasn't hungry, not even for his mum's spaghetti Bolognese; Lucas kicked the fridge on his way in and caused one of Milla's pictures to fall and so she cuffed him around the head and a scrap broke out that Jane had to get in the middle of else blood would have been drawn. Milla blew a raspberry at Lucas and he responded by ripping said picture in half to which Milla screamed and ran upstairs slamming all the doors on her way; Jane hadn't been aware she had so many doors. Harry shook his head and seethed at Jane as if to register his shame; why couldn't she wave a magic wand and be in possession of well-mannered and happy children? Harry stomped off upstairs as well and slammed his own door, meanwhile Christian started throwing cars at the wood work; not that she particularly cared for the over glossed wood work but that was beside the point. She wanted to kick something herself but poured a glass of wine instead and let her children wallow in their misery for five minutes whilst she boiled spaghetti. Shit, she didn't have enough; it would have to be penne Bolognese for a nice change. She almost laughed knowing the reaction; a good old round of spaghetti slurping might just have saved the day but not now; she imagined that the penne would become missiles the way her evening was going. She set the table and listened to Milla wailing in her room, how could a girl be so loud? When the boys cried (rarely except Christian), they did it quietly and quickly but not Milla, her sobs could challenge earthquakes in their ferocity and they just kept going and going until her face grew purple and she got a headache; this would in turn create a new round of sobs because her head hurt so much and then finally at some point in the evening she would fall into an exhausted sleep, by which point Jane would be suicidal. This was when she needed James the most. She needed him to waltz through the door, throw his stinky combat ruck sack in a corner with his boots and take Lucas outside to kick a ball; Christian would try and join in and then she could concentrate on *Miss Emotional* giving Harry peace to read or do his homework. Not for the first time had she wondered why they had had four, it was a dreadful thought and she would be without none of them, but she only had two hands and with James away it was sometimes torture.

Lucas had put the TV on for Christian and they sat watching *CBeebies* together; secretly Lucas, although eight, liked to do this now and again and he could use the excuse that he was being kind to his brother. Jane smiled, two down. She tackled Harry first; Milla would continue to wail anyway regardless of her intervention. She knocked lightly on his door. He didn't say go away and so she entered. He was on his bed with his back to the wall and his feet up looking like a ball of anger.

'What's up?' She sat down and gave him space; he would talk if he wanted.

'I miss Dad.' He couldn't help himself; his chin wobbled and he rubbed angry fists into his eyes.

'Oh my sweet boy, it's ok, it's ok.' She soothed. He was ten, but only ten. He must miss James terribly; kicking a ball, playing *Risk*, discussing the rugby season. Boys need dads. Girls need dads. Wives need dads. She went to him and held him and he let her.

'Darling, he will be back so soon and we'll have the best time.' He nodded and tried to be brave, bless him.

'Then will he go again?' She couldn't lie.

'Yes, but not for so long and it will go quickly I promise.' She instantly regretted using those words, 'I promise.' She couldn't promise anything. Her gut wrenched at the thought of not being able to protect this boy, and all of them, from the reality of the world which is that people die and people die young and life is shit and cruel and painful and no-one could shield her children from those truths, not even her. She wanted to cry herself and it might have done Harry good to see it but she held her tears and held Harry tighter.

'Dad's so proud of you and so am I, you have been such an amazing help to me while he's been away and I know he thinks of us all the time. It is so very painful and I wish I could take that pain away, Harry, but soon we'll see him and soon the pain will go. I'm so sorry you feel like this, I wish I could make it better.' Harry nodded again; he was turning into a young man before her eyes, but it would take a few more years yet.

'Guess what?'

'What?'

'I've run out of spaghetti.'

'Mum!'

'I know; you've got to come up with a cunning plan that convinces everyone that penne is so much more exciting.' He laughed; good, he was almost back.

'Now to tackle madam.'

'Are all girls like that mum?'

'For a bit.'

'I'm never getting married.' He blushed.

'Well, you've got plenty of time to decide.' She left him. Jane sighed heavily as she stood outside her daughter's room. She went in.

'Get out!' Milla launched at the door thinking it to be one of her meany brothers come to torment her. Then she saw Jane and rushed into her arms almost winding her.

'Why do I have to have brothers? I hate them.'

'No you don't' Wrong thing to say.

'Yes I do!' Ok deep breaths, believe the drama.

'Ok let's say you do. I don't think they're that happy right now either and neither am I.'

'Why?' Milla looked puzzled.

'Well, mummy is tired and I feel torn between you all trying to sort all this out. I know you are grown up enough to help mummy when the others are being naughty.' Milla sniffed. How many more years of playing this game until they left home and trashed their own relationships in private? Jane cuddled Milla and her daughter let her. Sometimes she couldn't split herself between them and it was times like these that she saw them all as individuals, all wanting her, all splitting her four ways.

'Harry's thought of a new game.' Milla looked up questioningly.

'Well, silly mummy forgot to buy spaghetti today,' Milla's eyes began to widen, 'hold on... hold on... the new game is sucking the sauce through a pasta straw.' Jane beamed mightily proud of herself.

'That sounds stupid.'

'Well the others are doing it.' Milla was thawing.

'Come on, dry your eyes and let me see your beautiful face, I'll go and get the table ready and come and join us, I think I might have some lemonade left from the weekend.'

'Really?' Job done.

'Yes, now come on.' Milla jumped off her bed and wiped her nose with her sleeve; it turned Jane's stomach but she let it go, this wasn't a battle she wanted to tackle right now. Jane went downstairs and called tea time. Christian was helped to the table by Lucas and Harry took his place quietly. Jane put the food in front of them and announced,

'Ok, Harry, will you please explain the new game of pasta straws to everyone.' Harry smiled and Jane winked at him. He demonstrated beautifully and Christian and Lucas got stuck straight in.

'Milla, we're starting.' She shouted, she had begun to eat with the children occasionally because it was better than skipping meals altogether with James away and no-one to cook for late in the evening. Milla joined them and was fascinated by Christian's giggles. It was not her greatest idea and it was particularly messy but it passed in peace, arguments forgotten and by the time they had finished Christian was yawning and Milla sucking her thumb.

'I'll help clear up mum.' Harry smiled, her big grown up saviour, Jane thought. The other three ran away laughing and Jane promised them ten minutes of *CBeebies* before bath time, obviously with Lucas in the role of supervisor as he wouldn't want to watch a silly kids' programme really would he? The kitchen was a vision of red with smears on the table cloth and blobs on the floor but they had eaten two helpings and now they were calmer.

'Did some soldiers die today, mum?' Harry took her by surprise.

'Yes, they did sadly.'

'Who are they fighting?'

'They are called the Taliban.'

'What does that mean?' Christ, how could she explain the ideology of war to a ten year old then she remembered that Harry would be keener than most to understand. She remembered what James had told her.

'*Talib* is Afghan for religious student and these students believe different things to the government in Afghanistan and so Britain and America and a few other countries are helping to make sure they don't take over.'

'What business is it of ours?' Well put thought Jane.

'And why can't they just say they don't want them there?' Good question.

'I thought religion was supposed to be peaceful.' You should go into politics, my son. She took a deep breath.

'Well, some people, if they don't get their own way, begin to turn violent and they are called terrorists.' She was on shaky ground; if some foreign army invaded her country wouldn't she fight too? Harry was nodding, he had heard of this word. Jane continued, '...and if they succeed then it might make the whole of the Middle East - which is where Afghanistan is - unstable...'

'How?' It was late and she wasn't in the mood and the wine wasn't helping.

'Erm... well, it's good for everyone if all the countries of the world get along, they can trade and prosper, but war means these things are threatened and it's everyone's responsibility to not let this happen. Our government believes that they just can't abandon countries that are at war, they need to help.' That should do it; she was feeling quite proud of herself.

'So what has religion got to do with trade?' Oh Lord.

'Not all people agree that everybody should get along, some people want to mind their own business. I suppose it's like a game at school, if someone doesn't want to play you can't force them but sometimes rules have to be followed else it makes it hard for everyone else, like if you were short of a player on a rugby side just because they were refusing to play.' Even she was confused but Harry seemed happy.

'But why would you kill someone over an argument.'

'To some people, it is that important and that serious, and Dad is over there making sure they don't kill too many.'

'They sound horrible.' This made Jane sad but that was a conversation for another day. The adult world was so complicated, if children ruled the world then would there just be tantrums and loo stops and pretend fighting? Maybe.

To Jane's surprise, the night passed off without incident and by eight o'clock she was able to sit down in silence and have a final glass of wine. It was only her fourth and she hadn't touched any since tea time and so she felt the gloriously relaxing effect of this final glass and it made her warmer. She shut her thoughts away from the events of the day and tried to think about curry. She would busy herself tomorrow with making the various pastes that could go straight into the freezer. The cup cake mix could be frozen too. She almost nodded off; it had worked, her brain had been busied with something rather trivial and had allowed her to relax. She trod heavily on the stairs and yawned deeply. What a day. She didn't have the energy even to take her makeup off and quickly threw some of James's pjs on, she did this a lot. She was sound asleep within minutes.

Chapter 19

The atmosphere in Maggie's house had been unbearable all afternoon. When Mark had received the news he had sworn and paced up and down running his hands furiously through his hair. So much for *Rest and Recuperation*, she thought. She felt terrible for the families of the two soldiers but what could Mark do here? Surely the whole point of leave is that you leave someone in charge to deal with shit. But no, Mark was clearly irreplaceable, and, of course, if he had been there it wouldn't have happened; a heady belief indeed. His self-importance repulsed her. If only he was so animated about his own family. She had tried to placate him by telling him it was somebody else's business and that he was on leave. She had told him that they needed him too and it was their turn. He had responded by saying that she didn't understand, two men had died and it was his fault. She was exasperated. How could she make him see that he was just one tiny cog in a gigantic wheel that cared nothing for him; he might be made redundant next year! This had hit him hard and he'd said that was unfair and a low blow. He had spent the remainder of the day on the phone and from what she had overheard, getting nowhere fast. No-one could give him answers, comms were down and would be for hours; he couldn't add any value from where he was. She felt like stripping naked and running down the street to make him notice her but it was too bloody cold. In the end she took Bethany and Alex to the park, alone, as usual. She pulled her scarf closer around her neck and helped Alex climb trees; Bethany found a friend and played shops under a little play house. Maggie could have got into conversation with the other mother but she couldn't be bothered. She wanted to go to the gym and work off some anger; she admonished herself for giving up so much and now she was doing it again; Mark had walked through the door and she'd given up any shred of independence she'd gained in the last four months, why?

Where was it written that women should prostrate themselves across the altar of honour and duty for their men? Why did she allow it? Was it Mother Nature blessing her with the inferior hormones of her sex or was it some kind of need to please him. She laughed at this; when was the last time Mark had done something selflessly to please her? She couldn't remember. The anger was consuming her and the children irritated her, she wanted to rest and to be alone and felt red hot guilt at the thought of not wanting her family. She badly wished she could turn back time and remake her decisions, would she have married Mark? Would she have had children? At least his mother had left them alone; how ironic, maybe it would have been better if they had come to stay then she could have left them to it and disappeared for two weeks, none of them would have noticed anyway.

She looked at her watch. The day dragged as they all did. She felt trapped and for the first time in weeks felt like visiting the doctors to up her dose of happy pills as Jane called them. Jane; she wondered what she was doing. She imagined her beaming face when Mark finally left asking, so? Expecting her to say it had been wonderful and all her doubts had gone and they'd had teenage sex and she loved him with her life. How could she tell her that it had been an unmitigated disaster from beginning to end and that she felt like she was falling into hate with him? Someone once said that hatred was stronger than love and certainly it made her feel on fire and full of vitality unlike love which just plain hurt. Maybe she did still love him, but it wasn't this Mark, it was another; a Mark that had disappeared one day, she couldn't say when, not even what year, but she could not believe that she would ever get him back now; they were too far gone, their lives had ruptured and they had turned away from one another; him to his job and her to…what? Nothingness, self-loathing, boredom, disappointment and regret. She looked at her children and felt a pang of pain in her chest; they were beautiful children but their parents were letting them down; surely they must know that her and Mark weren't happy, not in the literal sense as their tiny brains wouldn't allow it, but they must feel that something isn't quite as fun as it should be, she rarely smiled and she always noticed other mums smiling, surely Bethany noticed this too? She could feel herself sliding into a downward spiral again; one that she had shaken while Mark was away. The revelation hit her like a concrete block; she had been content – to a point - when he was away, and now he was back she was miserable again.

She couldn't tell him on leave. Not even she could bring herself to be that cruel. It would crush him and ruin the rest of his Tour. How funny that she was so mindful of his needs even when she had just realised that they had no future. No, she would wait. It wasn't fair; she wouldn't lower herself, she would let him get out there and seek his glory and she would tell him when he got back after everything had settled down and the dust had cleared and she had made plans. A ripple of fear slid through her, how would she manage? She hadn't worked for five years, they had no savings and with two pre-schoolers she would have to live on benefits, her cheeks burned. No, she could make it work. Maybe she could go to mum's for a bit and think about it. Oh the shame. She felt trapped like a wild animal caught for the first time under a huge net trapping it and killing its instincts, there was no way out and no way in. The thought lowered her mood even further.

She walked back to the car silently and Bethany took her hand. She felt guilty again and smiled at her daughter and squeezed her hand.

'Is Daddy sad?' This was a shock. How could they be so selfish as to let their personal lives affect their small children who needed security and love?

'No darling, he's just very very busy. How about we make pancakes for tea?' Distraction: the jewel in any parent's armoury.

'Yay!!! Alex! Pancakes.' Alex giggled and toddled along, he would be out of his pram altogether soon; he had started to talk and put together little sentences.

'Pancake, chocolate!' She let them have Nutella and golden syrup which of course is why they were so popular. By the time they returned, the house was quiet; he'd gone out. Bastard.

For the rest of his leave they had sex once and she hated every minute of it. She did it because she felt sorry for him going back to that hell without her touch. She had taken him into her mouth and he had groaned thinking all was right again and they were as one. She could have bitten him. She caught him masturbating one day and had wanted to throw up; what if it had been one of the children she had screamed and Bethany had cried. Mark went out. If he would rather wank than heal their relationship then he could rot in his hell. One day she daydreamed about him never coming back. It was a shameful, tortuous thought but it would solve everything; he would get his glory and she would get his pension. She couldn't wait for him to leave, it had been a disastrous two weeks and she couldn't wait to get back to her life without him.

The evening he left his flight had been cancelled and so he waited around all day itching like a two year old to get back to his train-set. After the tedium of having to eat they embraced and he fought back tears. Please cry, she thought but she couldn't, she hadn't cried for a long long time, she realised with sadness and she remembered what Jane had said. She watched him climb into his chauffer driven car that would take him to a bus in the barracks and then onto Brize Norton to begin the arduous journey back to Camp Salatin where he would probably land under fire. Then on to his own FOB deep within Helmand where his brethren would be waiting and he could get back to the business of killing strangers where he felt most comfortable. Those around him would be grateful and excited by his return; he would be needed.

As the plane descended steeply into Salatin, Mark's stomach heaved, he hated this part. He thought of Maggie and how much he loved her and how he just wanted to hold her and her want to be held. He thought of his children who didn't really know him or he them. He thought of what he was doing; how did he end up so far away doing something so futile and yet so damned addictive. He had to focus. It would all be alright when he returned; they would survive, they would get back on track; Maggie was just struggling at the moment because she was on her own. By her own admission she had been to the doctor and was on medication, surely that should help? It was a pretty dramatic thing to do but if it made her feel better he wasn't going to stand in the way. He wondered if it was the pills that made her unhappier; anyway, she should drink less then she wouldn't be so grouchy with the kids. The plane lurched and he held on tight; the lights had been out for an hour and he imagined himself falling the last thousand feet wondering if Maggie would care.

When Maggie fell into bed she felt nothing; she couldn't cry. She was empty. Last time, she had kept his pillow case and smelt it, now she threw it off the bed and would wash it in the morning. In fact, after taking Bethany to nursery she had come home and started to clean everything from top to bottom. She scrubbed the bathrooms, she tidied toys and changed beds, she threw open windows and took in the cool, clean air, she hoovered the hideous army carpet and got on her hands and knees and scrubbed the lino in the kitchen so it looked cleaner than it ever had. When the doorbell went she didn't answer because she knew who it would be. It would be Jane wanting to know how it had gone and wanting to tell her how much she couldn't wait to see James. Was James such a different man or was Jane just such a different woman?

Jane stood at the door and rang again. The car was there and besides, Alex would be asleep so she must be in. A horrible thought went through her head; this was either really really good news or really really bad and her money was with the latter. Poor Maggie. Poor Mark. What had gone so wrong? Surely it was just a blip? She gave up and went to Chrissy's instead. When Chrissy had returned from Jenny's, she had looked fresh and rested but now she looked drained and harassed again. It hadn't taken long. Four more deaths, five more casualties. The total was at 13 dead and 54 injured. Chrissy had been to the funerals of Peters and Crawley with Mark accompanying her; Maggie hadn't gone. Mark had given nothing away; he had been pleasant and suitably chatty, Chrissy had said. He had given the eulogies at both and Jane wondered why Maggie hadn't gone to support him, it must have been one of the very low points of his career. He'd had to go to a tribunal with the parents of one of them as well who had wanted to know more detail. Details were read out in court that made Jane feel queasy; Chrissy had heard it all from Dave. There was a time when Chrissy kept most of the detail to herself but she confided more and more in Jane knowing her to be trustworthy and level-headed. Everybody needs someone to lean on thought Jane and her rock was finally on his way home. She had the Christmas Fair to get through and there he would be, although she didn't trust his timings one hundred per cent as one never could, things could change at any step of the way and they usually did and so she hadn't told the children the exact date, she had just said 'very soon' and crossed her fingers.

Jane's house stank of curry and the children had complained. Harry pretended to vomit and Lucas copied sticking his fingers down his throat, Christian and Milla thought this was hilarious and joined in. Jane admonished Harry as the ring leader but he performed all the more. For the first time ever, the Christmas Fair would be held in the cookhouse and Jane was a ball of nervous energy as hers was by far the most arduous task. Transferring hundreds of ramekins, cupcakes, icing, condiments and utensils on time and in order had set her on fire and she had become like a Sgt taking and giving orders and bossing Dave around which, he secretly enjoyed. Women had spent days decorating the huge hall with garlands and banners, kids games were prepared and Dave would make his entrance as Santa out of the little grotto that had been made by two Riflemen on leave. The head chef had given Jane a quick lesson in his kitchen (his pride and joy) and she hoped to god no-one ended up with food poisoning. The Barracks was open to the public and hundreds of raffle tickets had already been sold raising money for Amber Lynn. Chrissy had organised for the children to be taken to and from school so Jane could spend the whole day previous to the fair getting ready, she was excited. Only one thing nagged; she hadn't seen Maggie.

The day itself was a blur of smiling and entertaining and cooking for Jane who rather felt like she was in the middle of a monstrous dinner party although she knew few of the guests. She had made four main dishes, a beef vindaloo which had surprised everyone because in its authentic state it was not as hot as its reputation, it was actually tangy and sweet; a lamb dish fragranced with cardamom, cinnamon, peppercorns and nutmeg; there was a chicken tikka of course and a jerk pork reeking of ginger and lemon. She had made big pots of vegetarian sides much to the pleasure and approval of Titty who had still asked which ones were gluten, protein and lactose free and Jane didn't have a clue so she pretended they all were and Titty didn't seem to notice. There was a spiced potato, a fried aubergine, dahl, green masala lentils, cumin scented vegetables with almonds and a kidney bean curry. To scrape it all up, the Chef had done her a favour and baked countless chapatis and she had made her chutneys weeks ago to improve their flavour. The hall was packed by ten o'clock and people thronged around the tombola and children's games, there was card making, pin the beard on Santa, bean bag throwing and a bouncy castle all supervised by three Riflemen who took it all in their stride. *Pheonix cards* had set up a table as had *Barefoot books*, *Pampered chef* and *Avon*. But the star of the show was Jane and her curries, people went back for seconds and thirds and her main courses had run out by one o'clock. Some asked if she sold her chutneys and how much they were, a few asked her to cater for parties; she hadn't thought of that and had to scribble her number on the back of receipts and bits of wrapping paper. As the last pink cup-cakes disappeared, Jane realised it was four o'clock and suddenly she ached all over. Chrissy had brought the children and Harry had won a huge cuddly Santa that he gave to Milla. Their faces were smeared in coloured icing although she couldn't remember serving them but obviously somebody else had, Jane had had three wives helping her and over ten had made and iced cupcakes. Dave had made a stunning Santa although the wives stood around giggling trying not to let their children in on the joke.

After the last group left Jane sat down heavily and looked around; the place was a tip. Paper strewed the floor and dishes and cups filled every table and chair. Jane groaned. She needn't have, within ten minutes Dave was barking orders at seven Riflemen from rear party who set about tidying with black bags and brushes. By the time Jane had cleared her pots and loaded the biggest dishwasher she had seen in her life, the hall was clear. It was the same after any big event in the army; a secret army appeared in the night and worked until every trace of spilled wine glass, torn ball gown, melting ice sculpture, forgotten hand bag, marquee support had disappeared into the night and one wouldn't know of the debauchery of the previous evening's festivities. They did it silently and efficiently, just how they were trained to kill. Chrissy had been coming to Jane's more and more in the evening and tonight was no exception; putting children to bed was no trade for company to Chrissy, she rather enjoyed the chaos and then she could unwind with Jane when it was quiet, rather like having a husband really but one that you didn't have to have sex with. When they left the hall weary but satisfied Jane reflected that again, she hadn't seen Maggie.

Chapter 20

The gym was busy and it irritated Maggie; she wanted to get in and out and had a lot of angry energy to burn off. She gathered a medicine ball and some weights and set off to look for an empty squash court. She was in no mood to fight with poseurs sat chatting or checking their phones for a bench today. The male component secretly breathed a collective sigh of relief as she left; they could work less hard now they had no-one to impress. She threw the heavy ball over her head and it slammed into the wall bouncing with a heavy thud straight back to her waiting grasp. She did it again and again each time thinking about how Bethany had told her to shut up this morning when she'd asked her to eat her toast nicely. Where did she get the language from? TV, she supposed. Her daughter was angry, that much was clear and she guessed that it was because mummy was sad and she guessed that was because daddy left again and she guessed that was because he didn't love them. Daddy had hit her hard and his angry face was ugly and terrifying. He sometimes spat a little when he shouted and he didn't smile much even when she danced for him or made him a chocolate and jam sandwich with play doh. Maggie slammed the ball harder and felt some of the tension ease away. She thought of Mark on top of her and she found strength for just one more throw. The ball rolled to a heavy stop and Maggie breathed hard, she crossed to the side of the court and jumped and slapped the red line ten times on the left and ten times on the right. She gritted her teeth. She walked to the ball and slam dunked it, feeling her core ache as the ball was launched to the floor from full stretch. Thud-silence, thud-silence, thud-silence. She gasped. This time she jumped in the middle of the court, down into a squat and launching into the air, arms above her head, using the momentum to bounce down, up, down, up. Thud-silence-gasp, thud-silence-gasp… Now the ball was thrown over her head and when she caught it she twisted like an animal caught in a fight, this way, that way, throw, catch-again. Water. Towel.

She heard the door. Damn, she would have to carry on in the gym with the male stares stupefied by this woman who threw herself about, balanced on balls and handled weights like a pro. It was Peter. Her chest heaved up and down and she stood very still. He smiled, about to say something but stopped and looked at her squarely, hungrily. He strode to her and took her face. Delicious, hot electricity shot down her body as she let him have her, their tongues roved over each other's. What was she doing? She pulled away and looked around nervously; he could lose his job.

'I'm sorry, Maggie I thought…'

'No, yes, it's ok; it's not your fault. Not here.' He was shocked, he'd thought he'd stepped over the line but now was she saying he had read her face correctly just now?

'I'm married.'

'I know.'

'I've never done this before.'

'Meet me.'

'Where?'

'My flat, I live alone.'

'The children…'

'Use the crèche, I live five minutes away.'

'Personal training?' She smiled, she felt wicked and illicit and …thrilled.

'Kind of.' He smiled back.

'Leave me alone, I'm concentrating.'

'So am I.' Jesus he was luscious.

'I'm 36 years old.'

'Pleased to meet you, I'm Peter.'

'Go away.'

'Promise.'

"Go away, I'm busy."

'Promise.' He moved towards the door. He pulled the door and half walked out, waiting and smiling that smile. She nodded. He left. She leant on the wall and looked up to an imaginary sky that was the roof. Her heart beat fast and she couldn't help smiling. She was desirable. She was wanted. He knew she was married, what could it hurt just to play for a while? They'd be moving soon anyway. This would be her small diversion; a reward for taking so much shit.

When she arrived home, Jane was walking towards her house. Suddenly, Maggie felt drained and chained again as if she had been sucked back in to *Army World*. Would she see it in her face? Did she look different?

'Caught you, hello stranger.'

'What are you doing out isn't James home?'

'He certainly is, I left him tied to the bed, I needed a break.' Maggie was so envious of her friend's marriage; she couldn't work out how it was possible but it was undeniable; Jane was happy.

'I couldn't remember the day he arrived so I left you alone.' She lied. After Mark left, she couldn't stomach the thought of revealing to Jane what a failure she was.

'Are you going to ask me in then? James is still asleep.' Maggie regretted avoiding her now and she thought that Jane probably knew that it was no coincidence and she realised that true friends don't judge. She lifted Alex out of his car seat and he beamed at Jane, he showed her his toy.

'My, that is a handsome doggy.'

'Monkey!' Alex looked puzzled.

'Of course it is! Silly me.' Jane smiled. Inside, Maggie flicked the kettle on and took Alex out of his layers of winter garments.

'God, these houses are cold.' She flicked on the heating; with Mark away, she could afford it. The last time someone from MHS had been to fix her boiler he'd told her that her heating bills were probably three times those of a modern boiler due to the age of the system. She'd wondered if *The Daily Mail* might have been interested in such a story; that their boys were paying over the odds for heating whilst fighting for their lives in distant lands but Mark wouldn't hear of it, he'd be mortified if she sold any story to a national newspaper, like for example the fact that he was risking his life to save his job and his one per cent pay rise while the politicians who sent him there enjoyed their thirteen per cent, cash expenses and long summer breaks as guests of the rich and famous. She rubbed her hands together.

'So how was it?' Maggie expected the question and had thought long and hard how to answer it but in the end she could think of nothing to say.

'Pretty crap really.' Jane's face screwed up.

'Oh no, it can't have helped that he lost those guys on leave.'

'Oh, I don't know, I think he rather enjoyed the attention.' Jane looked shocked. She had gone too far. She kept forgetting that Jane was happy in green.

'Oh I don't really mean it, I'm just tired. No to be honest I think he was rested and caught up on sleep, the kids loved having him around although now they've gone back into fighting and crying, do you really think leave is a good idea?'

'Absolutely. I know it's a nightmare when they go again but they need it so badly, otherwise they'd burn out.' That was not quite what Maggie meant but she let it pass.

'The Americans are out there for over a year, though and they cope.'

'I don't believe they do, they have a lot more suicides.' Maggie raised her eye brows as if to accept the point.

'Mark was saying that the locals get sick and tired of so many different faces making empty promises; they just get somewhere with rebuilding schools or bridges or whatever and then a new Battalion comes in and relationships have to be built from scratch again; it must make them less trusting or hopeful for the future. At least the Americans are there for longer.'

'Bombing the shit out of everyone for longer.' They laughed.

'Did you go to the gym in my absence young lady?' Jane looked sheepish.

'Clearly not, I don't blame you. I missed you today.' The memory of this morning flickered across her brow and she turned away from Jane and made coffee.

'Now I'll be taking another two weeks off and I'll be back to where I started.'

'No you won't, it was my first day back today and I got back into it quickly.' Rather too quickly, she thought and felt ashamed.

'We are at slightly different levels though.' Said Jane ironically.

'I really meant to go when Mark was here but we just kept going out for meals and lazing around, well, until the funerals and then he completely changed. It was like one minute he was relaxed and Mark and then he got all serious and started saving the world again. Isn't James like that?'

'Erm, I don't know really. He switches off easily; he can't wait to get out of his combats and hang up his helmet usually.' They burst into laughter. With Jane around conversation usually turned to sex.

'Oh god, don't tell me, you've been screwing on the kitchen table and it's like when you first met.' Maggie placed her palm dramatically on her forehead.

'Well if you must know, yes.' Jane giggled filthily.

'Sorry to drag you away from your favourite subject but how did your curry thing go?'

'Amazing! I loved it but I was knackered and James came home the next day. I've sold seven jars of chutney already.'

'That's brilliant! Well done! Are you going to do it seriously then?'

'Well, I don't know. It's a lot of work and the profit isn't great although we did raise over £500 for the guys at Amber Lynn.'

'Wow that's incredible Jane.' Maggie was sincere but she also wanted to vomit. Jane was such a true believer; they were such unlikely friends. She wondered what her friend's opinion of her would be if she knew she was about to embark on a torrid affair for a bit of fun. She hated to compare people because one never knew what went on behind closed doors but she wondered what made James so special or was it just that Jane was extra tolerant? The woman had four kids so she must be a little bit batty.

'I've got a present for you.' Maggie looked puzzled. Jane went to her bag and pulled out a box. Maggie's hand flew to her mouth. She actually blushed. Jane fell about. Alex waddled in.

'A box!' Oh no.

'No darling, it's a book for daddy; I'll just put it away.'

'Big book!' Did her two year old just say that?

'Let me see!'

'No sweetie it's a surprise now don't tell daddy.' He smiled and put his finger to his lips.

'Shhhh.'

'Good boy.' Jane giggled and Maggie stared at her. Alex waddled back off. They had ordered it weeks ago before Mark had come home; Maggie had chosen a bright yellow and silver one with flashing lights as they had shared a bottle of wine and Jane had said it would be like fucking the 80s. They had agreed to get it sent to Jane's as Maggie wasn't ready to tell Mark yet. She had wanted it to be fun; she had wanted to tell him on leave but had never found the right moment and then things just deteriorated.

'Oh my god I had completely forgotten.' Maggie didn't know what else to say.

'I didn't get to tell Mark, it wasn't, erm, that kind of holiday.'

'Oh well, good timing then. I hope you've got lots of batteries.'

'Jane!' Jane's phone beeped and she looked at a text lovingly.

'Well, my husband is taking me to lunch so I will love you and leave you, just wanted to say hi. Oh and enjoy your new toy.'

'Sod off.' She saw her to the door; she'd hardly touched her coffee. It made her feel sad that her friendship came with conditions; their husbands always came first. A simple text had sent Jane scurrying back home and she realised that their lives were punctuated not only by their children's' needs but by the movements of their husbands, they saw so little of them that the moment time became short, everything else was dropped like rubbish onto the side of the road; nothing could be permanent or real in this parallel world, women's hearts beat to the rhythm of marching and they fell into line along with all the other foot soldiers to the tune of their masters. It's all a pile of shit, she thought. Her phone beeped.

'12 Heatherfield court. No sessions between 9&11. x'

She knew that she would go and she would enjoy every single second. She pressed delete and checked that her phone didn't keep deleted messages. No: good.

Chapter 21

Chrissy had recharged on her short visit to see Jenny, even though the visit had been under dire circumstances but Jenny would survive, women had survived much worse and would continue to do so, it just seemed hard at the moment because it was raw. She felt anger towards Martin but who knew what had driven him to stray? It happens all the time but why couldn't he just have had his fun discreetly? What made him leave his beautiful children? That was the puzzling bit. Why couldn't he just have had his fling and his fun and then return to his responsibilities? Coward, she thought. But then would it have been a lie? Better to give them all a chance to move on, maybe. Jenny was writhing in agony right now but maybe he'd done her a favour; she was young enough to fall in love again, God, they all were, although Jenny had turned distinctly into a man hater of late so she would be surprised if she looked at another but give her time. They had laughed and it had felt liberating. Chrissy hadn't thought of The Patch at all, she hadn't thought of families and moaning wives, of men knocking on doors in the middle of the night; she had just thought of herself and her boys, especially Will. She had received a letter that had taken three weeks to get to her; Will was coming home for Christmas. She had almost cried with relief. Of course, Jake would be spending Christmas with his girlfriend which was only to be expected as girls always go home, she had once joked with Jem that she hoped at least one of their boys would turn out to be gay and then he'd always come home for Christmas. Well, one out of two wasn't bad. The news had lifted her and even those two awful deaths over Mark's leave hadn't managed to send her into the gloomy spiral that she'd been in before she saw Jenny. She was slightly ashamed and felt that she'd almost let Dave down but he'd admonished her telling her not to be silly. She wondered what Dave really thought of her; did he see her as competent?

She hoped so. She hadn't seen Maggie, which wasn't surprising considering that Mark had been on leave but she was irritated that she hadn't accompanied Mark to the funerals. She liked Mark; he was manly and modest, qualities that she loved in the Infantry Officer. That had been what attracted her to Jem. They had met in London twenty two years ago and he intrigued her. They had both smoked then and they puffed away in clubs, bars and restaurants like everyone else. He was quiet but had a glint in his eye that she found irresistible. He was a strong lover and very demanding. He was a gentleman in company but utterly commanding in the bedroom; that heady mix hooked her and they married a year later and shortly after that Jacob arrived and then her baby Will. Jem had been promoted quickly but it took him away for great chunks of their marriage but she quite liked her own space and she enjoyed her boys. Maggie's self-indulgence annoyed her; Mark was clearly gutted that she hadn't supported him but like any gentleman he had made excuses for her and kept his counsel. Everything in Maggie's life depended on the Army; she put all her energy into hating it and one day it would bite her back.

She left the house and looked over the road; she really didn't want to see Maggie right now, she had other things on her mind.

Helmand Province
9th December 0510 HRS (0110 HRS GMT)
Two five tonne Mastiffs leave their Forward Operating Base taking engineers to build a bridge in the neighbouring town of El Shahook. Heavy rain fall during the night had made the journey slow. Cpl Martin Somors manned the cupola; a small dome on the top of the vehicle from which the two machine guns and grenade launcher could be controlled, he carried a Bowman radio to communicate with his Ops room and with the driver, Rfn Col 'Curry' Cooke. The ambient light was crap and Somer's uniform damp. There were other places he would rather be. His thermal imaging struggled under the

conditions but he could be secure in the knowledge that kick-ass troops were watching him form their sangers (watch points, usually on high ground, made of sand bags). 5 Platoon had been through yesterday and the threat was deemed minimal. The journey passed one blind spot that left them out of vision of the sangers but no untoward movement had been logged overnight. Somors tried to concentrate. The radio crackled.

0600 HRS (0200HRS GMT)

Curry tried to follow the lead vehicle exactly in its tracks but it was impossible, there were no fucking tracks; just mud.

The huge vehicle lurched to one side and Curry thought they'd been hit. The six engineers in the gut of the beast woke up and panicked. The next few seconds seemed to be played out in slow motion and Cpl Dickie Light, Commander of the lead vehicle, would re-live them for the rest of his life. He watched from his cupola as the great sandy coloured hunk of metal slid over onto its side. The road had simply disappeared. He heard shouting and Somors shouted into his radio. It was indecipherable and became a series of blurred noises, like gulps of air.

The vehicle was fully upside down. Cpl Light shouted into the back of his vehicle,

'They're trapped! Open the fucking doors.' The engineers in his vehicle looked at one another, was it a trap? What was protocol? Dickie charged over them and kicked at the back door, once open he raced around to the second vehicle; its nose was under water but the back stuck out of it. He could hear faint screams. Thank god the door was easy to get open; if it had gone down the other way they wouldn't have stood a chance. Two men grabbed at him and a third shouted for help. By now, the lads from the other vehicle had joined them. They set about pulling gasping bodies from the mud. Ammo and supplies had fallen to the front of the beast and one guy was stuck upside down. They dragged at his legs but the vehicle was slowly sinking. They pulled two more out but the Mastiff lurched and settled blocking the back door. They dug with

their hands but it was useless. Dickie felt sick; he kicked a
wheel. 'No!' He held his head in his hands. Someone was
shaking him.

'Chinook's on the way with the MERT. We did everything
we could.' They stood back helplessly knowing that the four
men inside the metal coffin might still be breathing.

Dickie had been through basic with Curry. Every Saturday
they would go down to the local curry house and get the
nearest table of girls to bet that he couldn't eat the 'ring
stinger' a vindaloo so fierce that it made men cry. Each
Saturday he would win. Ever since, Cpl Cooke had been called
'Curry'. Even the CO called him Curry. Even his wife called
him Curry.

0627 HRS (0227 HRS GMT)
The MERT scrambled from the Chinook but they knew it
was too late. Four men had perished in the most awful way
imaginable. No-one thought you could die of an accident in
war; surely you got shot, or blown up? Who could tell their
wives and mothers that they'd drowned?

Curry and Somors were in Jem's Battalion. The other two
had been engineers and so their own OC Rear party would deal
with the news. For Curry and Somors it was left to Dave.
Chrissy walked in.

'It's almost worse.'

'I know.'

'You need a break, when are you going to take one? Me
and Major Hicks can cope, you know.' Dave raised his
eyebrows. He felt like saying 'you were in your dad's bag
when I was in Baghdad' but let it go, besides, Tommy Hicks,
OC Rear, didn't know the families like he did; he had been
drafted in specially from Northern Ireland. He knew that the
families appreciated his familiarity.

'It goes with the territory, Chrissy. I'm not even out there;
my job is to make it easier for them, not harder.' She sighed.
He was just as stubborn as her but she had seen that haunted
look before. Dave Proctor wouldn't forget this tour in a hurry

and she wondered if he would ever be rewarded, unlikely. The gongs would go to those on the ground and her husband, of course. She thought about Jem less and less; he was in his element, he had waited for this his whole career and she had pushed him. She remembered when the boys were small and he would call saying he'd be late or that he had to go to London, or Belfast or wherever. He never gave specific details and she never asked; her Army was a different world to now; wives like Maggie wanting to know ins and outs and demanding what their men couldn't give, not now at least. Confidential reports were not made from men who looked after their domestic arrangements; they were made from thrusters, and those who didn't play the game were simply left behind. Jem had told her of dinner nights (all male) where he had met contemporaries from years back who were still Captains; of course they were still on good money but they didn't pull the rank; they jumped through the same hoops but not quite as fast, and it was final salary that dictated pension, and a General's salary was pop star stuff compared to a Captain.

She wanted to ease Dave's burden but she knew that she couldn't. 'Is there anything I can do?'

'Curry's wife has gone to her parents; you could arrange the flowers for Somers' family for me. The usual, I'll get the address. The funeral is next Friday and Curry's Thursday.'

'Where?'

'One in Sunderland and the other in Middlesbrough.'

'We should stay overnight; it's crazy to drive all the way back.'

'I agree, I've already booked three single rooms.' The two of them plus the driver.

'Thanks.' Dave no longer even asked if Chrissy was attending, she always did.

'We have a visit to Amber Lynn coming up; Monday I think, let me check.' Dave turned to his computer and put his glasses on; he looked old but she guessed she did too. She wondered what the men would look like on their return; would their eyes have changed? She remembered Jem returning from a rough tour in Belfast and she had noticed something missing in his eyes when he smiled. It emerged later that a fifteen year old boy had thrown a petrol bomb at their vehicle and he'd been shot dead. She wondered how long it would take Jem to open up this time. Of course, he wouldn't have seen much from HQ, it would be the Sgts, Cpls and young subbies that would bear the awful scars of witness first hand, no, Jem would bear another pain; that of the awful responsibility of sending them out to die in the first place. It was Jem's Ops that they were all implementing; the plan belonged to him and then the command travelled down the chain until it reached those who would enforce it with limbs, hearts and minds.

Her mind switched to Amber Lynn; she always dreaded it but always left heartened by the courage and determination she saw, and she was always staggered by the loyalty. She had felt embarrassed the first time; who was she to be gracing brave soldiers with her presence? But they had thanked her warmly and told her how much it meant that they hadn't been forgotten and she had felt a connection somehow with the men that had suffered horrific wounds under the command of her husband. Some didn't fare so well and psychological therapy was tight; one had committed suicide which had led to the hospitals supervisory and night watch being overhauled. This time, they were taking more XBOX games, IPods, DVDs and various crafts. This had surprised her at first but a lot of them liked to do puzzles or even sew. They were also taking Christmas treats; Chrissy had been gathering gifts from the wives for weeks and they had an almighty stash to squeeze into the back of the car. Donations had come in from local businesses too; toiletries, port, whiskey, cheese and crackers, lights, puddings and an enormous cake decorated by the local bakery on top of which stood a soldier dressed as Santa next to a helicopter with the words, 'Thank you and Merry Christmas.'

Dave's phone made her jump. He nodded. He rubbed his brow. She could tell that he badly wanted to swear. Oh no. She felt hot and needed air. She left Dave on the phone and went to stand outside. Tiny snowflakes were falling gently from the grey sky and the Camp was still. Her breath left her in clouds and she wrapped her arms around herself. She thought about smoking for the first time in years. She returned to the warm and looked at Dave questioningly, bracing herself for more bad news.

'Two idiots have got themselves banged up on leave. Picked a fight with some bouncers twice their size but still managed to break a jaw and a nose.' Chrissy was almost relieved, she wanted to laugh.

'You are joking.'

'Sadly not. They'll get a shock when they realise they'll be tried in a civvie court.'

'How come?'

'Happened outside the barracks so they'll be dealt with by the local police. They've already been charged and one has been refused bail so he can't go back to theatre.' What an idiot, Chrissy thought. It was probably a drunken brawl over hardened vets being wound up by disrespectful locals and they'd bitten; of course they had. Jem would be fuming.

'I'm having a coffee then I'll get going. They're in Watford for Christ's sake!'

'You're not going without lunch; I'll be back in ten minutes, please wait.' She looked him straight in the eye and he knew that he would wait.

'Am I right in thinking that you keep a secret stash of fags in that desk of yours?' He looked caught out.

'Well if it is true, can I have one?' Dave hesitated; he didn't want the CO breathing down his neck for encouraging her to smoke.

'I'm a big girl, give me one.' He reached into his desk and got the packet.

'Come on.' They stood outside in silence only punctuated with puffs. It was the best cigarette she had ever had, she thought. She stubbed it out and Dave held out his hand; typical soldier tidying up his fags lest the enemy find them. She passed it over and left, shouting behind her,

'Don't you dare leave.' Dave laughed, went back into the warm and started to log off his computer and check his diary.

At home she made him a bacon and egg sandwich with brown sauce and wrapped it in tin foil, she grabbed a smoothie from the fridge and a packet of crisps and a chocolate bar, it would take him ages to get to Watford. On her way out she touched a picture of Jem and the boys, laughing on a fishing holiday that she had sent them on. They had come back tanned and healthy, full of stories and exaggerations about fish-size. She smiled. Come home safe, Will. She couldn't wait to see him. Jem wouldn't make it before Christmas now so it would just be the two of them; she had booked theatre tickets and planned to cook his favourite meals. . She had cancelled her holiday; a crazy idea anyway.

She would spoil him terribly but she didn't care. She kissed her finger and held first to Jem then Jake then Will and swallowed hard. She gathered her bundle and jumped into the car; Dave better have waited, and he had.

Chapter 22

They had thought about not sending the kids to school but had finally decided to stick to normality taking the odd day off for trips. James had been taking the kids to school and Christian to nursery which was luxurious; for five days, she hadn't got dressed until gone ten. He would come back with cold hands and tuck them straight into her nighty making her giggle. 'Get off! You're freezing!'

'But you're so warm.' He would flash his eyes at her and convince her that being groped with cold hands was rather novel. She couldn't get enough of him. He had come back hardened and tanned, but despite this manly, rough exterior, he had treated her body gently and lovingly; the combination made her desire him even more. They lay in bed having made love. His head rested on her chest and he played with her nipple.

'Haven't you had enough fun for one morning?'

'Never.' His ability to make love two or three times consecutively had surprised her; he was like a wound up spring ready to burst and no matter how much he came, he was ready for more. He licked her nipple and stroked her thighs and she felt aroused again. He was hard already and she rolled him over and took him into her mouth; he groaned. She went faster and faster holding the base of him in her hand and sliding it up and down to the rhythm of her mouth. She was panting but kept the rhythm; he held her head and forced it deeper and deeper. He was warm and hard and she wanted to suck harder; he let go of her head and tensed, his arms above his head; she felt the end of him grow bulbous and she knew he was close, they knew each other's bodies so well. She wasn't going to stop now; it would be her turn later. Warm liquid squirted forcefully to the back of her throat and she closed her eyes and concentrated on not gagging; no matter how much she loved him, come was disgusting. She eased off and her mouth felt full; where did he get it from? She swallowed and it stung her eyes; she reached for a glass of water and gulped deeply. James lay gasping and held her towards him.

'Thank you.'

'No problem but I only take cash.'

'Oh, Jane. I love you so much. I wish I didn't have to go back.'

'Shhh. That conversation is off limits. What shall we do with the rest of our morning?'

'Get drunk?'

'We have four children.'

'Oh yes. Erm huge, obscene lunch with a tiny glass of champagne?'

'Where?'

'Oscars.' It was their favourite restaurant.

'I don't think we'll get in.'

'Already booked.' She beamed. Sly dog.

'Can you leave me alone long enough to get dressed?'

'Ok.' They showered quickly and for once she held him back when he became aroused in the shower.

'We'll never get out and you'll make me sore.'

'We wouldn't want that.' He threw on his old jeans and a baggy jumper and she felt herself tingle; he looked so hard and handsome. She felt slightly embarrassed by her wobbly tummy that had come back since she stopped visiting the gym but he didn't seem to notice, he just kept telling her he loved her.

'I heard some hideous gossip yesterday when I went to *Tesco.*'

'What was that?' James hated army tittle tattle.

'That Curry and Martin Somers drowned in an upturned lorry.'

'It wasn't a lorry, it was a mastiff and, yes they did.' Gossip was usually agonisingly close to the truth in the Battalion; he was amazed at how fast bad news travelled. Jane was shocked.

'How?'

'It's quite common, the roads are so crap, the mastiff weighs about five tonnes and the road gave way due to a ridiculous amount of rainfall and it sank upside down.'

'But couldn't they climb out of the windows or the thing at the top.'

'The thing at the top, called a cupola, Jane, went under first, the windows at the front are armoured but luckily the back door came open and four were pulled out.'

'My god, how many were in there?'

'8.' Jane looked puzzled.

'Engineers travelling to a village to build a bridge.'

'Oh.' What a way to go. They got ready in silence after that and Jane reflected on how many abominable ways one could die in war.

By the time they reached the restaurant, they had resumed easy conversation. James insisted on getting cabs everywhere; he wanted to enjoy the money he'd saved and wanted a drink. They felt decadent lunching in such luxury midweek during the day. They talked of the children; James would talk about his job when he was ready.

'Harry struggles the most, I think because he understands where you are and what you are doing; the others have still got that gorgeous selfishness and I'm afraid Milla getting to watch her favourite programme comes higher than you most of the time.' James smiled.

'Good. Maybe I should take Harry out on my own.'

'That's a great idea; you could take him to tree runners, mind you that might cause some jealousy with the others.' It was tricky; they all needed him in different ways; Lucas wanted to play fight, Milla wanted to be tickled, Christian wanted to do puzzles and Harry, well, he didn't know. Every time he played a new Wii game with him, the others wanted to join in.

'Should we get Harry an XBOX for Christmas?

'Harry or daddy?' He smirked. Of course he was thinking about playing it himself, loads of the soldiers had been sent the new *Grand Theft Auto* and it looked amazing, he had tried once but had been killed early on much to the amusement of his soldiers.

'When is the Panto?'

'Saturday afternoon, I didn't think Christian would last an evening.'

'What is it?'

'*Beauty and the Feast.*' He raised an eyebrow.

'Oh you'll love it.' She laughed. 'But we've got to get back earlyish to watch *X Factor*; 70-odd wives are at the live show.' He rolled his eyes and took her hand. They were on their second glass of champagne but she didn't care, nothing worried her when James was around; she would have to deal with nothing on her own and that was all that mattered.

'It must have been hard, Jane.'

'Yes, it is. I wouldn't want to do this again as long as I live but that's life, this is how we roll, baby. I'm ok, honest. I have down days, the day Crawley and Peters died was horrific and I was on the wine at three o'clock.'

'That hit us hard. How was Mark?'

'Frustrated, I think is the word. Maggie said leave didn't go that well, he was so focused on Afghanistan.'

'I think I would have been too. But there's nothing he could have done and it wouldn't have turned out differently had he been there. That's how it happens.'

'Is it going to carry on like this? The news says you're the hardest hit Battalion in fifty years or something.'

'It's a difficult one, Col Jem is determined to make a difference and leave his mark and he is achieving amazing things for the local people and they appreciate it; it doesn't look good from the outside but we're having successes all the time.'

'The funerals are horrendous James.'

'I know, I'm so proud of you for going.'

'I feel silly, rude almost; going to funerals of men I've never met but Dave said it makes the families proud to be honoured by so many connected to the Army. Generals turn up from all over the place.'

'That's the worst part about losing a man.'

'What?'

'Not being able to go to the funeral and pay your respects and say thank you and good bye; it's the lack of closure, especially for their close mates.'

'I went to one and there were soldiers there on leave in uniform and not one of them could control the tears; it was so powerful.'

'They get so close out there; they become each other's families, brothers really. They look out for one another and it hits hard when they lose a mate.' Their food arrived. James had ordered scallops to start and she had crab. She thought he was determined to eat as much luxurious food on leave as was humanly possible and who could blame him? Army ration beef stew with dumplings warmed on a camping stove didn't really cut it even with Jane's spice mixes. Now and again, chefs would be sent to the FOBs and would bake pizzas and cook roast dinners but when they were out on the ground they relied solely on rations. James said that a typical ration pack contained something like four thousand calories; that's how much they burned in a typical day. They carried armour, ammo, supplies, radios, rifles, grenades, helmet, food and water. Water was the most crucial thing; the late summer had been punishing out there and men collapsed from dehydration if they weren't careful.

'I love your boxes.' Jane had fun putting together weekly shoe boxes of treats for James.

'I am the envy of the Company; I've always got people sniffing round for my jerky or my Rolos. You are famous.' He meant it sincerely; Jane's packages were a godsend and he shared them generously despite joking to the contrary.

'On patrol, that jerky is perfect. I love it.'

'Not as much as scallops though eh?'

'Oh they are divine.' James closed his eyes and chewed. He swilled champagne around his mouth and looked contented. He had ordered belly pork for main and she skate wing. She loved going out with James, he was so decadent and generous; he thought nothing of ordering a bottle of champagne if that's what he fancied. They didn't think they had room for dessert and so ordered two Irish coffees instead.

'God, we're going to roll to school.'

'You stay at home, I'm enjoying picking them up, I don't get to do it very much.' The words stung; what if he never got to do it again? No! Stop! She pushed the unwelcome thoughts from her brain but the alcohol was making her emotional.

They walked hand in hand to the cab station. The sky was dark already; he put his arm around her and she felt like screaming down the street, 'look! I've got my man!'

James sensed her morbidity.

'What should we do for post Op leave?'

'Well, I've got a bit of a surprise for you.' Oh no, she wasn't pregnant? She smiled; he looked nervous. She hit him playfully; 'it's good news!' He looked even more nervous.

'I've been putting a little bit of money away - do you realise how much you eat? Anyway, when I have a spare few pounds or something doesn't cost as much as when you are around - which is a lot...'

'Get on with it Jane, how much?' He was so relieved that she wasn't pregnant, he loved his kids but five?'

'£4,200 so far.'

'What!' James looked as though he would collapse. Jane giggled.

'It just kept growing and then I got addicted and started starving the children.'

'Bloody hell. Can I have a *Rolex*?'

'No.' She rolled her eyes. 'I thought we could splash it all on a fantastic holiday, you know one of those five star places where they have kids club.'

'At this rate there'll be money left over as well.'

'Well that can be our Christmas fund then; when we get to celebrate it.' It made her melancholy to think of Christmas without James. It just wasn't normal, she felt particularly sad for the children; it would take away the magic although she knew that James had made them a DVD message to play on Christmas morning.

It was a rush to get back in time for Christian but it had been worth it. She might almost allow herself to fall into a mini routine for two weeks it felt so comfortable. Christian was weary and so they all had a nap which was an opportunity to sleep off the alcohol before they started again. Jane prepared a family meal while James went to collect the others; it was heavenly being able to take her time to do something instead of always rushing to meet deadlines and bells. She made moussaka lovingly and hummed to the radio while Christian played cars on his mat. She knew they were home because she could hear their laughter down the road; they stomped their boots and made puddles on the kitchen floor, it had begun to snow. Scarves, gloves, hats, coats and school bags were dumped in the kitchen and they disappeared to jump on James and enjoy him. They ate together and Jane wanted the moment to last forever. James told funny stories and Milla looked at him in awe as if he was her Prince. Harry got the more grown up jokes and Lucas sat on his knee. As Jane tidied away she looked out into the dark garden that now glistened with silver snow. Maybe they would give the children the day off tomorrow to build snow men.

Chapter 23

Heatherfield Court was tucked away from the main road and Maggie breathed a little easier. She had dropped Alex at the gym and pretended to go into the changing room. Thankfully the toilet was by the entrance, so she went in there for five minutes and then slipped out. Karen, behind the desk would no doubt be on her phone to her boyfriend anyway. She was shaking. Was she crazy? Should she turn round and run now? She still had time to change her mind. Bethany had scratched her arm this morning and it had bled. Alex had cried and stroked her gently; Bethany simply glowered at her from her bedroom door. Maggie had stopped asking herself why her family was falling apart. She sometimes wondered if she would have time to put it back together once Mark returned, some days she doubted that Bethany could ever be healed of whatever was wrong with her. Surely it couldn't just be anger? The explosive violence and rage was unsettlingly weird, there had to be more to it. She had read about defiance disorders, the autistic scale and various other labels and they all made sense but there was no pattern; some days she would morph into a normal little girl and go to bed like an angel, others she would scream and kick and punch all day long. It was days like these that led her to feel justified in indulging herself. She had checked herself in the mirror a thousand times before leaving the house this morning; she had to stop asking why a twenty three year old would desire her; leave it, she told herself, and enjoy it. She took a deep breath but her stomach wouldn't stop from turning over. She pushed the button for number 12; there was no going back now. Peter's voice came across the intercom. 'Hello.' She hesitated.

'It's Maggie.'

'I'll be right down.' Oh god, oh god, oh god. He opened the door and smiled broadly. He was dressed casually and he suited the jeans and sloppy jumper, she had only ever seen him in gym kit.

'God, it's cold out there.' He rubbed his hands together; he was gorgeous. She smiled nervously. She followed him, he smelled of warm body and mild cologne. Her gut turned over; what was she doing? As he opened the door to his flat, she nearly ran but didn't. He shut the door. She started to take off her coat but he was on her. His kiss burned her lips and took her breath away; she was breathing hard. She felt stupid in her gym kit now but it had been part of the cover up. Everything happened so fast, her head whirled and her body did things she had forgotten were possible. He pulled her hair away from her face and kissed her neck; she sighed and let him, then he was pulling her top over her head. She undid his jeans and could see he was hard already; the anticipation was killing them both.

'God, you're beautiful, Maggie.' She didn't want him to talk. He threw his jumper off in one move and she was shocked to witness what was underneath; his body was hard and smooth, a tattoo of a dragon curled around his bicep and his stomach was as flat and smooth as ice. She touched it and he lifted her sports bra up. Clothes were thrown around and she remembered his belt hitting the floor. The curtains were only half drawn and so the light was sexual; they fell onto a sofa and he heaved her leggings off; they got stuck on her trainers but he pulled them off too; how did he do that? They were naked and he moved on her with the grace and beauty of a stag; he was in command. She let him sink between her thighs; she surprised herself by how much she wanted him there. Months of anguish melted away as he played with her, my god, he knew what to do; where did he learn that? She didn't want to know. She groaned and the sound was alien to her. He was so attentive and gentle and thoughtful. He came up to greet her and smiled, she could feel him against her.

'Have you got a condom?'

'Yes.' He reached for something, strategically placed earlier perhaps? So what; he knew what she had come for and they were consenting adults. They were on his rug now, it was deep and silky and when he entered her she gasped; her whole body tingled, she had not expected any of this. He moved slowly and held her close only moving inside her to go around and around and it was heavenly. She let herself go and felt his buttocks, his arms, his shoulders and his face. They looked at one another and she saw his longing. Bloody hell. She wanted to get on top or move or do something but he wouldn't let her; the pleasure was to be all hers. She felt a burning deep inside and it grew more intense; it lingered maddeningly and then she held her breath as the tension was released and her body twitched. He moved faster now and she was covered in man. He started to groan with each thrust and his face was set in concentration; her own orgasm had subsided but it still burned. He let a loud breath go as he came and slowed down. Good, no mess; she could lie here for a bit. They were both sweating and warm and they laughed as they ran their hands through their hair. God that was good. Better than she ever would have expected; he was a talented young man indeed. He kissed her and asked if she would like some water. He strode confidently to the kitchen; he was clearly happy naked, but who wouldn't be with that body? She was more modest and she slipped his jumper on. Was that too cosy? She didn't know the rules. He smiled when he returned.

'Where has that body gone?' She laughed, he never gave up. She wondered how many older women he had seduced.

'Thank you for coming.' They both fell about laughing.

'I need to go soon. I have left my son in the crèche; I am going to hell for this.'

'Aren't we all?'

'Will you come again?' I should think that was in the bag she thought.

'Yes. Can you be discreet?'

'Of course. I know what this is, don't worry. I would love nothing more than to take you out, Maggie, and show you off, but sadly I know that's never going to happen. Just to be with you is enough.' Did she just hear that? Was he human?

'Stay for a bit longer.'

'Ok.' He disappeared and reappeared with a huge furry throw and some pillows. They huddled underneath and she told him about her past life. He never asked about Mark and she didn't offer to discuss him.

Enough time had elapsed and she was becoming dangerously close to over staying. She got dressed in front of him and he watched her; it was most distracting but edifying too; he appreciated her. He sighed and pulled his clothes on as well. She went to the bathroom and looked in the mirror and smiled. I did it! Her face was a little red where he had kissed her and she ached in her groin, she shook her hair and went to say goodbye. She hadn't decided yet when or if she would go back.

'Are you at the gym tomorrow? I have PT all morning; we could meet in the afternoon.' Shit, don't spoil it, she thought.

'Hold on, let me get my breath. I have the kids in the afternoons, I can't.' He looked accepting but disappointed. Jesus, she couldn't do this every day, it would kill her and besides she had to show up in the gym sometimes.

'I'll let you decide then, let me know. Don't wear anything too sexy tomorrow; it really puts me off my work.' She laughed. He went to kiss her but his door was open and she whispered, 'best not.' The walk back to the gym was bracing; the wind blew and the ground was covered in last night's snow; her feet crunched satisfyingly making big prints behind her. She couldn't help smiling to herself; she hadn't felt so liberated in years. Thankfully, Karen was still on the phone; she couldn't keep this up, it would become obvious but what else could she do? Auntie Pat. It was safe; Pat had no idea who her friends were and would never think to question anyway. She should be back from Portugal and she did say anytime; the kids would be happy too and she would miss bed time. She would leave it a couple of days; she didn't want anything intense, just some fun and she could see it in Peter's eyes; he was a man possessed. She would have to cool him off.

Alex was still fast asleep when she walked into the crèche to collect him after her shower. She loved her time alone with him; he was her saving grace, without him she would have thought that Bethany's character was all her fault, at least with one normal, loving child she could feel at least a little proud of herself. She kissed him lightly as she put him gently in the car not wanting to wake him. When she got into the driver's seat she realised that she was sore between her legs and she felt a flash of guilt, but most of all she felt delicious, satisfied, selfish pleasure. She had done something just for her and it had felt good.

'Hi Patricia.'

'Maggie-May! How lovely. So tell me all about Mark's holiday. I left you two love birds alone, you know I've been back from Portugal three weeks and I've been dying to call.' *Holiday*. Apt.

'Oh he was very relaxed and loved playing with the children, he got off ok and it won't be long now. Just got Christmas to get through.'

'Oh that'll be a doddle, my dear, the children will keep you busy and he'll be back in no time at all. I would have had you all here but I'm going on a Caribbean cruise.' Phew.

'Oh lovely! On your own or with friends?'

'A dear friend, can't wait; now when can I come and see my little ducks?' Evasive, did she have a new man?

'Well that's what I was calling about, I've been invited out again and I was wondering…'

'Of course! Anytime, Maggie-May, I told you that.'

'Well it's next Friday night.'

'Just let me check my diary.' Pat fumbled around; her diary was much more interesting than her own, thought Maggie, wistfully.

'Oh! Look at that! I have nothing in, there we go, you're all booked.'

'Thanks, Pat, I really appreciate it.'

'Not at all, now, are you going anywhere nice?'

'No, just a restaurant I think, but it will be nice to get away for a bit.'

'Well, dear, you go off and have a wonderful evening and don't think about us, we'll be dappy-doo.' Pat spoke like a *Disney* character but it was part of her charm; she wondered if she had her own dictionary with things like dippety-dop, and wobbly-woo in it.

'Bye, dear, must rush; I'm going Christmas shopping in *Harvey Nicks* and I'm going to spoil you rotten this year. Kiss kiss.' Maggie smiled. What a whirlwind life her Auntie seemed to lead; older people seemed to glean such joy from life, they had grafted all their lives for the pleasure and most found new freedom in their autumn years, unless your body let you down, of course.

She wouldn't tell Peter yet; she'd save it. She didn't want him to think she was over keen else she'd never be able to get rid of him when the time came. She felt weary - unsurprisingly - and lay down on her bed. The adrenaline from this morning still hadn't worn off and she couldn't sleep but she closed her eyes and went over the series of events piece by piece from Peter's body to his hands on her and what she had done to him. It didn't seem real and she wondered if it had happened at all and then she felt a twinge deep inside and she knew it had happened. She didn't dwell on what he saw in her that was so attractive; maybe he used his position at the gym to woo lots of ladies her age and even older perhaps, perhaps he was with one of them now. Yes; she was probably a notch on his bed but she had got what she went for and she felt somehow serene and satisfied.

Alex woke her up by climbing out of his cot and bringing a teddy to her and rubbing it into her nose; she looked at her watch and realised she'd been asleep for over an hour. She swept Alex up onto the bed and tickled him and he giggled endearingly. His little body was warm and he nuzzled into her; he showed love so effortlessly compared to his sister who seemed to want to only punish Maggie for some unknown crime. Her stomach sank; it was time to get Bethany. She wondered if she would sustain an injury this afternoon or what new vile word she might come out with. It always started well; Maggie always tried to wipe the slate clean and appear bright and happy with her daughter, but as the day wore on and Bethany became more cruel and tormenting and Maggie's demeanour sagged, she ended up reaching for that cold bottle of wine in the fridge, placed there earlier, knowing that it would come to this eventually.

The nursery was pretty and the staff seemed kind. Bethany always skipped out with a smile; it was in the car that it started. She would complain that her belt hurt or that her coat was twisted and start to scream. Then she would throw something either at her or at Alex, then Alex would cry and Maggie would try to be calm at first asking what the matter was; this usually made things worse and she struggled to understand Bethany's peculiar needs and at what point to draw the discipline line and be harsh; she had tried both and all shades in between but nothing worked for a sustained period of time. She had tried reward charts, penalty points, gifts, treats, the naughty step, the naughty room, the naughty teddy, hide the teddy, throw all her toys away (or, pretend to), threats - no TV, no ice cream, no chocolate, no play dates etc. she had threatened to tell her teachers, a doctor, the police, Mark and nothing had worked in the long term; of course they all worked in the short term - what child wouldn't be stunned into behaving with the threat of the police? But, after a few minutes or hours, the behaviour that had landed her into trouble would be repeated as though Bethany suffered from a lack of memory and then the whole process of reward and punishment would start again. Hours of this, days of this, weeks and years had taken its toll and sometimes Maggie couldn't fight at all and she simply locked her daughter in a room. Once she had stupidly locked her in the utility room and after a few minutes Maggie had smelled chemicals; she had opened the door to find washing powder, softener and floor cleaner running like a river across the floor with Bethany sat on top of the freezer staring at her. A hundred years ago she would have been beaten or given away, Maggie supposed. She vaguely remembered corporal punishment at school; it had disappeared as she had moved to secondary school but older children still gossiped about it and everyone knew the 'hard' kids who had received the cane from Mr so and so who seemed to enjoy it- so stay out of his way. Now, teachers seemed to sing their way through their day with their green pens, didn't they get tired of smiling and ticking boxes and praising children for the slightest thing; didn't failure exist? What had the Labour Party re-named it? 'Deferred success.' Was this why defiance in children was getting worse or had it always been so? Children seemed to know that adults could not do anything against them that was truly hurtful or particularly scary. But surely Bethany didn't get this at her age, or maybe she sensed her mother's fear and indecision in dealing with her behaviour and as a wolf sniffs weakness so did she? One thing was for sure, she did not underestimate her daughter's intelligence; she did not dismiss her as 'only a child', she was wily as a fox and was becoming more menacing by the week. Doctors had told her that she'd grow out of it after the 'terrible twos' but these doctors never saw Bethany for more than a few months and then they were off again to the next post and she had to repeat her story; no-one had seen Bethany's emergence as a child, they had seen snippets and it didn't help that she was very pretty and sat angelically in any Doctor's surgery making Maggie out to be either a fraud or simply neurotic. With Bethany suffering from the terrible threes and fours and highly likely to suffer the terrible fives, sixes and sevens; Maggie drove to nursery with a heavy heart.

She greeted her daughter with a big smile and a cuddle. Bethany had painted a picture of an elephant which was, in fact, a grey blob with funny dots but Maggie said it was amazing. She thanked the teachers and waved goodbye. As they walked to the car, Bethany screamed. Maggie closed her eyes and took deep breaths. She had become anaesthetised to Bethany's screams and so until she put Alex down she would have no idea whether it was serious or not. It was not. Her brand new painting had a tiny fold in the corner. Bethany was turning purple. Maggie tried to soothe her but Alex had started to cry too.

'Darling, it's ok; I can iron it so it will look like new.'

'No!' She ripped up her painting and threw it all over the car park. Maggie thought of the scene in *The Exorcist* when Regan's head spins round. She bent over to pick up the pieces mechanically and as she was distracted, Bethany pulled Alex's hair.

'Bethany! That is so unkind. Say sorry.'

'No!' She pulled her tongue at her mother. Bitch, thought Maggie; what have I done to deserve you? Damn you, Mark, I hope you're enjoying playing war while your daughter gets committed to a mental institution. She bundled Bethany into the car, which was difficult as she was becoming a strong little girl and was no longer a toddler; she held her down in her car seat and Bethany's body lurched up and down making it a nightmare to fasten; click. Maggie dreaded the day when she worked out how to open her car seat belt but for now, she was restrained still screaming but at least she could hurt no-one and Maggie could ignore the screams. She tended to Alex who was still tearful. She put him into his car seat beside his sister and sagged into the driver's seat. Her last thought before leaving the car park was that if anyone had just witnessed that they would probably call social services and report her for child abuse.

Chapter 24

The journey to Amber Lynn was long and the roads were treacherous. Snow ploughs slowed the motorways and the smaller roads leading to the once great estate were still and silent as the ploughs hadn't touched them yet; abandoned cars littered the pavements, probably left in desperation by people thinking they could brave the conditions, but *Mother Nature* had beaten them as she always did. They travelled in a 4x4 and so they made progress but it was still slow. Amber Lynn sat in huge grounds; it had once been the home of some Lord or other and had been sold to the MOD in the 1970s, then it had been used as a medical training facility and now it boasted some of the world's leading prosthetic and rehabilitation knowledge and techniques. It boasted a staff of highly trained Physios, trainers and consultants who usually did yearly stints there before going off to a less harrowing post. As they parked up, Chrissy felt the familiar knot in her stomach. Dave had worked tirelessly on his lap top and phone for the whole journey and now stretched in the cool air. Nothing moved; the grounds were blanketed in white and the trees looked majestic in their white glorious cloaks fit for kings. The Patches of black leaves and branches made them look like ermine and they nodded in the wind at her acknowledging her presence.

They were greeted by Col Farrow, a senior consultant. He wore a suit and was extremely charming, he brought a calm efficiency to the place and she felt in safe hands. The Colonel called for some staff to unload the car; there must have been fifteen boxes rammed into the rear of the vehicle.

'Tea?'

'Lovely, thank you.' They took tea in his office and the Colonel offered them cake. How civilised. They always did this; the formal, polite chats and the refreshments before they got down to business.

'Well, we've had seventeen new admissions since last time and of course they are mainly your Battalion, Capt Proctor.' No matter how informal the surroundings or domestic the arrangements, Army men just couldn't use first names.

'We have discharged some too. Wellen, Stevens and Gamble have all gone home although there is a question mark over Gamble's psychological well-being and he is being monitored.' He made it sound as though they were new prototypes that needed the odd tweak - so commonplace was his work now.

'Laithwaite has progressed most spectacularly and I think he'll be leaving us soon. He actually jogged around the grounds on his running legs.'

Men and women received different sets of prosthetics depending on their life styles; a far cry from the First World War when it was one leg each and it was a nasty tan, plastic monstrosity. There were running legs, walking legs, legs for the shower, legs for skiing, legs for cricket and legs for wearing shorts; the same applied to arms and hands too.

'Says he wants to be a Para-Olympian and I think he will do just that.' Chrissy was overwhelmed; the spirit of someone like Laithwaite astounded her.

'So, shall we?'

Chrissy took off her coat and laid it across a comfy chair, she kept her hand bag.

'I think I'll just visit the ladies'.'

'You know where it is.' Yes, she did. She checked her make-up and noticed dark circles around her eyes. She would make a note of the quiet ones and the overly chatty ones; they were the ones to look out for. Some went irretrievably into themselves and some took on a nervous energy to fill the gaps where their limbs used to be. The halls were decorated with old paintings of distinguished surgeons and the like and a waft of disinfectant could be made out, flowers graced the window sills and music could be heard.

'Pilates.' The Colonel explained. Amber Lynn ran daily classes for those who were well on the road to recovery.

Their first stop was a new arrival. Chrissy recognised his face.

'Rfn Christian.' The young man straightened as if he wanted to stand and salute. Chrissy saw pain behind his eyes and she could tell that he was new.

'This is Mrs…'

Thank you, Sir. 'I know.' Of course he knew. 'Hello ma'am.'

'Will you please call me Chrissy, I insist.' He looked uncomfortable with this but nodded. The drill was to split up so as not to overwhelm anyone and real conversation could take place and so Dave and Col. Farrow moved off.

'Wow, you have a lot of cards and flowers.' Christian smiled.

'Big family?'

'Yeah, too many.' He laughed.

'Will you be able to spend Christmas with them?'

'Not sure.' He looked at where his legs used to be. He looked uneasy in the wheel chair; she had seen it before, it took time.

'What happened? You don't have to tell me but it might help.' She believed in being direct; most of the time it was appreciated more than fannying around the fact that they didn't feel like men anymore. He seemed to relax.

'IED ma'am.'

'Chrissy.'

'IED, Chrissy. Me- mate Johnno shot up in the air like a fire cracker. We were out patrolling and doing the usual stuff you know, looking around and trying to walk in line, then, just, bam! It went off. The sound was amazing, me ears rang for hours after.' Chrissy nodded.

'Johnno weren't moving.' Christian rubbed his eyes.

'I'm sorry.' It seemed lame but it was true.

'I could hear shouts and orders and it was all like a thudding in me ears and that's when I realised I couldn't feel me feet.'

'How long ago did it happen?'

'Six weeks. I never thought they'd piece me together.'

'They've done a good job.'

'Oh the nurses and Docs were amazing. It was hard, like, at first. I didn't want to recover.' He looked down and shook his head.

'I think that's what anyone would think at first.'

'But then I started thinking about me mam and dad and brothers and sisters, even though me sisters are a nightmare.'

'Aren't they all? Girls are women in training, we bite.' They laughed.

'Has your mum been to visit?'

'Oh yeah, they all have. Never leave me alone.' He laughed again. He was a handsome young man who had clearly done a lot of soul searching lately, the anguish still sat in his eyes.

'I walked yesterday, Chrissy.'

'Yay! How far?'

'Ten steps. We have this mean PTI who's as big as a house and he was shouting at me and telling me to do just one more. It was brilliant.'

'Did it hurt?'

'No, it just felt weird like when I first woke up and still thought they were there.'

'So that's it now, you've taken your first steps, you can't get away with anything now; what's next? Did you play any sports before?'

'Rugby. I always joked I'd do Para-Olympic rugby and now look.'

'I heard Laithwaite ran yesterday.'

'He's a machine that guy; if I can do half of what he's done I'll be a happy man.'

'Do you want to come with me to see him? You can show me round.' Christian smiled and was happy to be useful. He wheeled his chair with ease; his discomfort forgotten.

'That's the day room where we can play pool or just watch TV.'

'Oh that reminds me, we brought new Xbox games.'

'Get in.'

The room was filled with sunlight and people milled around in chairs playing chess or cards or simply talking.

'Dan, losing again?' A young man who couldn't have been older than twenty looked up from the chess board and grinned.

'Out to play, Grayson?'

The soldiers looked at ease in this environment; she had heard that the Military wing in Coventry Hospital was manned by civilians and many soldiers had complained of their treatment there and there had been that horrible case where a few nurses had actually abused them for what they perceived as misguided politics, but here it was different and the banter was free and easy. There were no civilians at Amber Lynn and the residents felt more at home. Besides, Coventry was only the beginning of their journey; a casualty would see a field hospital first, possibly Salatin, then maybe a European unit and then onto Coventry and finally Amber Lynn and so the soldiers that wheeled themselves through these doors had come a long way in terms of acceptance and despair; recovery was a long and painful journey and by the time they reached this haven of peace and hope, many of the casualties had already faced their worst horrors. It wasn't all plain sailing though, the suicide last year had hit them hard and shown that the final stage of their journey was by no means easy; the most difficult challenge would be integrating back into the real world, possibly alone and unemployed.

They found Laithwaite in the gym. He was laughing with Dave having become quite the celebrity.

'Hi, Chrissy. Nice to see you.' She was glad that they remembered to call her by her first name, she hated being called ma'am but of course on some occasions it had its place, though not here.

'Well well, Mo Farah.' They laughed.

'Word has got around. You are famous you know.' He shook her hand and looked embarrassed.

'That is fantastic news, how did it feel?'

'Pretty amazing.' Chrissy noticed that in the absence of the likely expletive adjective that they all really wanted to use, 'pretty' always came a good second given the company.

'Lunch is served and it's curry day so I hope you like it as hot as these chaps.' Col. Farrow ran a tight ship. Chrissy was ravenous and would have eaten anything. The men made a path for Chrissy and someone said, 'Ladies first.' She was escorted to lunch by Christian and Laithwaite who continued to talk openly,

'Don't you get your walking leg today?'

'Yeah, tried it yesterday and I didn't fall over.'

'Oh you will.'

'Thanks.' Chrissy wondered about their darker moments and how the staff managed to keep them buoyant. There were regular counselling sessions and the night duty officer was informed of anyone who might have been placed on suicide watch; it was nothing unusual or sinister just a head in a door to make sure all was well; the patients never usually noticed.

When it was time to leave, Chrissy felt a familiar pang of regret; she always wanted to stay longer but they had to get up to Tyne side tomorrow and book into their hotel before two days of funerals. She hadn't packed; it was such a desperately sad thing to pack for she had put it off and put it off. She would miss Jane and was still angry with Maggie so it would just be her and Dave again but he was good company, he told her stories from the old days when Dave was a Corporal and Jem new in green. She was ashamed that she didn't remember him but he remembered the first time she had entered the Mess on Jem's arm; all the Mess staff checked out the wives and girlfriends and noted who threw up and who would be taken upstairs by a single subbie for some after curricular activities. They also remembered which Officer's soup they'd spat in, or worse. She probably wouldn't sleep well tonight, there was too much in her head and she hadn't heard from Will since he'd left Morocco. He was saving money by flying budget airlines through random countries and she was terrified that he would end up in the wrong part of some foreign city that didn't care for tourists. She shivered. The boxes had all been unloaded and they would let them unpack them in their own time, it was more fun that way. The Christmas boxes were labelled with either 'decorations' or 'presents' and would be opened accordingly. She had yet to do Jem's box. He had told her how pissed off he was with random members of the public sending boxes containing pot noodles and socks, he had stock piles of bloody pot noodles that no-one wanted and wished he could bomb the enemy with them; certainly they would die if they ate them that's for sure. These misplaced acts of kindness also delayed post from family and friends which was a crucial part of morale. Soldiers would rather receive one letter from a loved one than ten boxes of flap jacks and shampoo.

She took Christian's hand and said 'good luck', he smiled warmly and nodded. He would be ok; he had that determined look behind his eyes and he had his family. All too often, the ones who struggled had either no relations or very poor ones. She had even heard of one family who spent their son's disability pay out on a holiday to Greece. As they pulled away Chrissy felt confident that it had been a good visit. Her and Dave had little to say and remained in their own thoughts. She rarely talked to the driver and he in return expected nothing of the sort and so she was able to sit back and close her eyes. The next three days would be punishing but she reminded herself that for the families of Somers and Curry, the punishment would go on and on for months, years and probably a life time. Last year the father of a fatality on another tour from a different Regiment had committed suicide six months after the death of his son; he simply couldn't cope; Chrissy had thought of his wife who had lost her son and husband so close together.

It was dark by the time they arrived back to Chrissy's house and she couldn't wait to get inside, drink a gin and tonic and fall into a bath. The house was cold and silent. They were setting off early and so she faced packing tonight; she couldn't put it off any longer. She longed to chat to Jem, not about casualties or duty but just some small talk about their plans for the spring or the children. They weren't children anymore but they would always be hers. She wondered, as she did often, where her husband was. He was her silent resident. Dave had said that it was likely that Jem would come home in the New Year but she knew that his diary would be full; he would be off to London and still trying to run things from home. He would be with her but not quite and she fully expected that; Jem always said one should manage ones expectations and she was very good at doing just that. They would get the odd night out perhaps or even a trip away and maybe he might even give himself a lie in if she pushed it. Jake had said he would visit with his girlfriend and she looked forward to having men to feed again. If only Will would call. After nurturing babies so closely and having them rely on you for everything, it was tough letting go but she knew she had to and she just looked forward to having them in her life again if only for a short while. She planned to take Will Christmas shopping; gone were the days when she could surprise him, she always got it wrong.

It seemed that she was spending less and less time in her home and as a result it had become more and more alien to her, she had a relationship with her kitchen and her bed and that was about it; the rest of the house sat idle and unloved. A woman came in weekly to wash, clean and iron so she knew the rest of the house existed but she rarely saw her or checked her work. Morale on The Patch was uncertain now; they were over half way but the weather didn't help and bad news kept coming in, daily it felt sometimes. The dark mornings and nights kept women inside behind their curtains praying that the door wouldn't be knocked on in the early hours. Children were nearing their holidays and were exhausted and belligerent; women were preparing to leave to visit family and friends for the festive period to take their minds off their men and Chrissy predicted a very quiet and sombre Christmas indeed.

Chapter 25

Jane looked at her family as the coloured lights lit their excited faces; they were shouting at the comic actors on stage, 'he's behind you', they giggled. Even Harry had got into the spirit and allowed his inner child to emerge strictly for the purposes of the younger ones of course. She watched as James lifted Christian onto his lap from where he could see better, he encouraged them to join in and Milla was so animated that she missed her seat on one occasion and fell to the floor laughing out loud. She jumped up and down and thought she might burst; Jane wished she could freeze time so they never had to leave. She felt a burning inside her chest and emotion overtook her. Please don't rip my family apart; please. She spoke to no-one in particular and knew that it wouldn't make a difference but she said it anyway.

Afterwards, they had eaten noodles and chicken at *Wongs* on the high street and they had all fallen on their food; Harry had tried to teach the younger ones how to use chop sticks but they were all useless, including Jane and James. When they arrived home, they were all exhausted and the children were not forced to bathe. It was dark and no stars shone; even the moon was hiding behind a cloud away from the piercing cold. Christian was asleep and had to be lifted to bed by James; Milla had started to complain and whine but it didn't last long as even she had to admit that her bed was indeed very warm and comfortable. Lucas tried to play his DS under his duvet but fell asleep before it could be taken off him and Harry said he was going to do some homework but after his door closed she didn't hear another sound. It felt like Christmas already; with the door shut and the country on holiday and expectant for the man in red; fires burn, chestnuts roast, stockings hang and good will is spread to all men, even those at war. Jane turned the fire on and got a blanket and James opened a bottle of red.

'I'm getting my pjs on, I'm freezing.' He laughed at her but relished the thought of the easy access.

'Me too, I'm just pouring.' They cuddled under the blanket and the wine warmed them; they were a little late but *X Factor* had been recorded so they fast forwarded the awful adverts and became excited about the acts and the mock-judge fights. Jane thought that Sharon better not have any more plastic surgery or her nipples might end up on her chin, James found Nicole rather interesting and Gary looked ding dong merrily on high as always. Louis was Louis. The crowd screamed for each and every act and it was all staged to perfection; more coffers for the Cowell millions. After one break, Dermot said, '… and we have, Ladies and Gentlemen, some very special ladies here with us in the audience tonight. Ladies and Gentlemen, please shout it out for the Wives and Girlfriends of 7th Battalion, The Rifles whose husbands and boyfriends are serving in Afghanistan right now.' The crowd screamed and the cameras hovered over hoards of screaming, waving women.

'Oh my god.' Jane recognised nearly all of them, they were going crazy. James hid his head in embarrassment. He was not good with public displays of emotion or zeal, unless on the battlefield. By the time the fourth and final act came on they had sat through hundreds of adverts and guest acts and Jane was feeling a little tipsy. She leant against James's arm and snuggled into him, he held her close. The final was only two weeks away and by then, James would be back in theatre and Major Blandford again. She felt sad and became quiet; they only had one week left, it was going so quickly. Her thoughts turned to Christmas. She had told Maggie that she'd spend it here but now looking at the children with James and how excited they were to be part of a busy chaotic house again, she wanted to get away; even going to her parents would be better than wallowing here. Her sister would be there with her kids and it would pass by in a lovely chaotic, messy haze with a lot of alcohol to help. She hoped Maggie wouldn't be offended. They each had to make their own decisions based on what was good for them individually and now she'd had James home, she realised that staying holed up on The Patch was not what was good for her or the kids. She would attend the Christmas parties but would ring Mum and Dad and arrange to go on the last day of term if the weather held and snow didn't scupper her chances. She half hoped that James would be delayed by snow but knew that he would be psyching himself up to get back too. By Wednesday of next week, she knew she would have lost him again and that it was necessary; he couldn't go back soft, it was too risky. It only took an absence of thought to find himself in a situation that he couldn't get out of and she would rather lose him for three days than forever. Forever. What a word, she struggled to imagine it.

The last *X Factor* act was distinctly average or was it her mood? She was sure that the wives would have had a fantastic evening and would hear all about it in the WO next week. They were planning a fund raising activity in the city dressed as Christmas elves; were they mad? They would surely freeze to death, but all in a good cause and the local people had proved generous before. The calendar had gone ahead and James had said predictably that he was relieved that Jane hadn't taken part, no officer's wife had. It was tasteful enough but Jane knew first hand that the gossip in Helmand was mixed with husbands of those featured having the piss ripped out of them, especially Shelley Brown's husband; she was the only one who appeared entirely naked except for a few strategically placed rifles and helpful tattoos. Jane had bought one anyway to show support and had giggled at the imaginative poses; she wished she were that brave. One girl, with a very nice figure (which helped) sat astride a cannon on the parade square and another dangled provocatively from a bar on the assault course, it was very well done and the national press had got hold of it boosting sales via the internet, they had their own *Facebook* page and *Twitter* account and the desperately needed money rolled in.

'Right, Mrs, take me to bed and lose me forever.' Forever. She allowed herself to be led upstairs and James brought the blanket. They undressed quickly as the heating system had been designed with evil intent and went stone cold the minute the radiators went off which had been some time in the afternoon. Under the sheets, James stroked her and despite the red wine, she became aroused. Their love making was painful; emotionally not physically, they looked at each other intensely and with each thrust willed themselves to hold on. Their bodies stuck together but they were not aware. Jane didn't think he could go any deeper and held onto him with her legs, 'I love you, Jane.' It was as if he was leaving tomorrow, they had crossed midway and now she knew that it would disappear in a flash. She made herself promise that she would hold onto every moment and carve memories into her brain to hold onto for the last long, arduous months. She prayed for spring; as new life emerged with each lengthening day, she could imagine the nearing of the end and as the birds returned and the trees grew green she could look forward to the day when he would walk back into their lives for good. He would in all probability go again but the British Ops were winding down and he would promote meaning next time might be a desk job. 'I love you too.' They didn't want to let go and drifted off in each other's arms. At some point in the middle of the night, they untangled themselves and Jane pulled her knickers on but she couldn't remember.

She woke with a heavy head, it was almost ten o'clock and she couldn't hear a thing. When she tiptoed downstairs to make a cup of tea a note had been left by the kettle, 'morning gorgeous, we're at the park, join us if you like or put your feet up xxx.' She smiled. She decided to have a shower and get dressed and then see if they were still there. James had left the heating on and so the house was warm and she felt an overwhelming sense of peace. By the time she was ready, they showed no signs of coming home and so she walked the short distance to the park. Snow crunched under her feet and she carried a ruck sac with hot coffee, chocolate and biscuits.

James was playing football with Harry and Lucas and Christian was trying to join in. James ran with him in his arms and kicked his tiny legs against the ball and scored and Christian shrieked. Milla had found a friend and was playing on the fire engine. Jane waved and they all came to her knowing that she would not have come empty handed. Their breath came in huge bellows of steam and their cheeks were pink; she handed hot chocolate around and fixed James a coffee.

'Thank you for my lie in, I can't remember sleeping for so long.'

'You were out of it so I thought I'd leave you.' The children had disappeared once more and Jane and James sat on a bench and held hands; she felt adolescent and in love. Other fathers played with their children and she noticed the usual absence of mothers on a Sunday morning; something that she usually resented but not today. They had built a family of snowmen and had gathered stones, leaves and various props to make them come to life. 'You have been busy, super-dad.'

'Oh it's a doddle.' She hit him.

'Oh god, it's Titty.'

'What?' James spotted Titania and rolled his eyes at his wife's nick name for her. 'Jane!'

'James! Hi.' She gushed. Titania knew more about Army Ops than the average Rifleman and so Jane left them talking about how things were going, pretending to run after Christian. Ten minutes later they were still at it.

'Ben tells me that this Battalion has created more PBs than any other.' Jane didn't know what a PB was but guessed it didn't stand for pork belly. Ben had already had his leave and they'd disappeared for the fortnight. She genuinely hoped they'd had a lovely time, she meant no malice towards Titania but it was fun teasing her. She'd idly wondered at the time what had happened to her solo skiing holiday but left it. The less questions she asked Titty, the better, and the quicker they could escape.

'Ben has had Christmas cards made of his soldiers in Santa outfits; they are super! As if he hasn't got enough to do, but that's Ben, work, work, work.'

And that's the rest of us, thought Jane, 'pleb, pleb, pleb.'

Tristen woke up and finally Titania disappeared to check on him and that was their opportunity to clear up and move out; it was lunch time anyway.

'Good luck James and give my support to everyone out there doing such a splendid job!'

'Of course I will, Titania, lovely to see you.' That singular Army phrase bandied about like sweets at a fourth birthday party. James had driven the car to pack in all the extra kit; he'd decided to cover every eventuality so they squeezed back in and the windows steamed up on the short run home. Hunger had set in and instead of turning the engine off, Jane whispered '*MaccyDs*?' to James. He nodded.

'Who wants *McDonalds*?' He bellowed. A collective cheer deafened them and he pulled back out of the driveway.

Jane tucked into her *Big Mac* greedily and thought about her waist steadily moving outwards. Well, she thought, it's nearly Christmas anyway so she would restart her regime in the New Year; only dull women have only one dress size in their wardrobes. Silence fell upon their table as they devoured the hot, salty food and mayo dribbled down their chins. It didn't last long.

'Let's vote on a film.' This was always rather tricky and involved Harry giving way to the younger ones, but he would be rewarded for his tolerance with extra pocket money in secret which he knew.

'*Sound of Music!*' Milla's new favourite.

'Booooo!'

'*Mulan!*' It was dramatic enough even for Harry and he agreed; there was even the chick element to satisfy Milla.

'Settled then.' James licked his salty fingers and finished the children's chips.

The children knew that for a family movie the curtains would be drawn and they could bring duvets, pillows and teddies downstairs where they would camp in front of the fire for an hour and a half. The lamb would go in the slow cooker so Jane wouldn't have to move until later when she would peel a mountain of potatoes to roast for her hungry family. When they returned home, the children threw piles of gloves, hats and jackets into a pile but Jane didn't mind; they had their dad and that was all that mattered. They got comfy on the sofas and the floor and the film began; the children were silent and within ten minutes James was fast asleep.

Chapter 26

The door knocked making Maggie jump. It was Jane.

'I wondered if you were coming out of hibernation.' Maggie smiled; Jane was so forward.

'Isn't Mr Lover Lover man still here?'

'Yes, he's got work to do so I'm going to the fund raising meeting and you're coming with me.'

'No, Jane, really.'

'You're not allowed to sulk on a Wednesday, it's against the law.' Jane strode into the house.

'Coffee; white, one please.' She would have thrown anyone else out but she knew Jane only meant well. Could she stomach the meeting? Maybe she could detach herself from the fact that she would be suffocated by army-wives and their talk of nobility and duty?

'Alex is fast asleep.' She lied and made coffee.

'Stop making excuses; you need to get out.' Maggie was finding the intrusion unhelpful and sighed.

'I need you to protect me.' Jane pleaded.

'Bollocks.'

'Oh come on I haven't seen you in ages.'

'So stay here and drink coffee all morning.'

'I promised Chrissy I'd go because we're arranging Christmas bucket rattling dressed as elves.' Maggie almost spat her drink.

'What!'

'You heard. Elves.'

'Where are you getting the costumes?'

'Some company in the city sponsoring the buckets of course.'

'Can you wear a beard to hide behind?'

'Aren't elves pre-pubescent?'

'I don't know any.'

'I thought it would be quite fun.'

'Mine and your ideas of fun must be very different then.'

'Ice queen, ice queen.' Jane taunted.

'Is that my new nick name?'

'I wouldn't know; I'm not one for gossip.' Jane had cheered her up.

'Ok I'll come…but under duress and I cannot promise I'll break into a smile.'

'Chrissy got quite mad last time; some of the women were taking the piss and making stupid suggestions.'

'I suppose if you put a bunch of sex-starved, child-harassed and abandoned women in one room then it's only to be expected.'

'Do you really feel like that, Maggie?'

'Which one?' She knew the answer.

'Abandoned.'

'Well, I get it; I do. I get the whole 'it's not their choice blabla…' but I don't know what James is like but Mark puts everything into his job, his energy, his passion, his commitment…so I feel there's none left over for us.' Jane felt sad; could he really be that bad?

'Maybe he's just bad at showing his feelings, after all he is a soldier and his emotion gene was probably cauterised at Sandhurst.'

'Can we change the subject?'

Jane held her hands up and admitted defeat; what did she know?

'Come on then, it starts in half an hour.' Maggie rolled her eyes and went off to get ready.

Jane looked around Maggie's kitchen, it was quite bare. Letters lay strewn across the work surfaces and she noticed, not for the first time, one single empty wine glass. She wasn't about to judge, after all hadn't she done the same thing? There were a few pictures on the fridge of the children and some she didn't recognise. Bethany was such a cutie, as was Alex. The house was quiet and she felt alone, didn't the silence drive Maggie mad? Jane couldn't live without noise; if it wasn't a child screaming it was the radio or her humming or laughing. She had thought that Maggie had let her in but maybe she hadn't, there was such a lot to this woman that she didn't know; she was so much fun when they had gone out and she had seen her let herself go at the Mess and at Chrissy's but now she wasn't so sure. Jane was worried about her friend but didn't know what to say.

The meeting was packed and Jane guessed, correctly, that women were becoming more and more desperate to fill their time as the New Year loomed and they faced the final push. Dave Proctor rarely attended the meetings, he let Chrissy communicate to him what had been agreed, he had attended one and found the noise and cackling unbearable; also the veiled comments about his bum had led him to conclude that he best stay away.

'Ok, Ladies, please.' Chrissy tried to bring some order to the groups of women sharing stories, chasing toddlers, spilling coffee and generally being loud and rowdy. At first, Maggie had regretted coming as she fought through the sea of faces, it was so noisy too and she felt slightly overwhelmed but soon Alex had found someone to play with and she had got chatting to some of the wives she knew. Karena Hughs had come with her new born baby and women cooed over her and her undeniably very ugly baby. Maggie couldn't find one single pleasant word to say and would have rather said to the new mother; 'welcome to the world of sleep deprivation, sore nipples, unwanted hair, saggy vagina, screams in the middle of the night, teething, potty training and wiping up bodily fluids' but she thought that might burst her bubble. The same women who cooed over the new born shouted at their own off spring and she supposed that it was something to do with babies being so unspoilt; give it time, she thought. She listened to a group of wives talking about their appearance on *X Factor*; she had watched and laughed with delight on Saturday night and Maggie, despite her promise to Jane, found herself smiling and even laughing as the subject of the elves' costumes came up. Chrissy gave details of pick up and drop off times and various women volunteered to hold buckets and/or count money. Someone suggested they go out afterwards and would Dave organise a crèche all day? Chrissy was sure he would; it would only involve a few Riflemen in the gym with some fizzy pop and nibbles. She scribbled the point down in her pad. Where did they want to go? The Eat-as-much-as-you-like Chinese on the high street looked good; there was a general murmur of approval so Chrissy made a note.

'Ladies, I have some fantastic news; the total of the calendar sales so far are…wait for it… £5,675!' There was a woop and women shook their heads in disbelief. It was a truly outstanding achievement.

'Now, *Party Nites* have kindly delivered twenty Elves outfits of varying sizes so I'm going to ask groups of five to go and look through them, please only take one if you are definitely coming with us.' Many women with young babies did not get up as childcare was impossible so it was mainly women with school age kids who looked through the costumes. When it was Jane's turn, she grabbed Maggie's arm, 'come on.' Maggie couldn't make a scene and so she laughed it off and followed meekly. There wasn't much left but that wasn't a problem for Maggie whose figure was fairly uncommon on The Patch. Jane was left with a baggy green smock and red leggings, they fell about.

'At least I can hide behind the belt…and look! A beard.' Maggie slid hers over her top.

'Oh god, put it away, only you could look cool as an Elf. You've got to come, Maggie, you'll raise a ton looking like that!' Maggie giggled; maybe it would be fun and, more importantly, time away from Bethany. Dressing as an Elf might just be worth the break. Jane was very persuasive. Back in the meeting, Chrissy was suggesting that if they had more than twenty volunteers they could do shifts. Secretly, Chrissy was hoping that she would have enough volunteers to prevent her from dressing as an Elf; Will would be here and she wanted to spend every moment with him. He had finally phoned from Zebrugge from where he was hitching a ride in a lorry across the channel. She knew that right now he was on British soil and she breathed a little easier. From the meeting she would go to the butchers and buy two fat fillet steaks, she found steak always tasted better when it had been frozen. He was arriving this Sunday and she could hardly contain herself. Indeed, she was in unusually good spirits, especially compared to the last meeting which she had ended early after being heckled about money. Some of the wives had felt that after all this fund raising some of it should pay for a day trip out or something, they had suggested *Legoland*. Chrissy had been disgusted; even if they took only one coach load they were probably looking at £2,000 for the tickets and the transport, did they really think that one day's amusement was worth blowing that much? It was sheer greed. She had remembered that she couldn't please everybody and she would always get a few disgruntled wives wanting more and it had taken a coffee and a fag with Dave to calm her down. She knew that Jem would be smoking anyway; they all did on Op Tours because of the boredom. Yes, they were at war but 90% of their days were probably spent reading, cleaning weapons, waiting and wanking. She had left it to Dave to explain to some of the wives that after the Christmas party, presents for all the children and the return parade and fair, there wouldn't be much left over for a day trip. He also reminded them that whenever anything was organised, a free crèche was always available. He received the expected grunts but at least it bounced off his Teflon shoulders rather than Chrissy's. Dave had reminded Chrissy that the vast majority of the wives were decent, ordinary women who caused no trouble at all but from his experience there was always a small group who couldn't be pleased and this was part of the territory and not a bad average. As always, Dave had calmed her and she even laughed about it afterwards. She knew she wouldn't tell Jem, he thought she did too much anyway.

The meeting was over but most women hung around for coffee (free) and cakes brought in by wives; they took it in turns and today the offerings were a *Tesco* sponge, home-made brownies, cup-cakes and gluten-lactose free banana loaf (guess who). Titty had stopped coming to the meetings but still sent cake when it was her turn. Jane had thought of dropping in to see how she was but remembered the last occasion and how much it had drained her; 'stop it, Jane, you can't save everyone.' Chrissy had admonished her. 'Pot calling kettle.' Jane had retorted to the woman who visited Amber Lynn, went to two funerals, wrote five condolence letters, bought seven bunches of flowers, arranged childcare for eight families, sat in on the Padre's weekly moan session and had dinner with the Mayor all in one week. Jane wondered if James would ever make CO and she dreaded it.

As usual, the officers' wives drifted together.

'Maggie! You're smiling!'

'Fuck off' she mouthed to Jane.

'How are you doing, Chrissy? I haven't seen you for ages.' It sounded so lame.

'Oh busy. Will comes home on Sunday.' Jane and Maggie wooped and Chrissy's face looked radiant when she spoke of her son.

'What are you two doing for Christmas?' Jane looked guilty; she wanted to speak to Maggie about this alone.

'I'm thinking of going to my Mum and Dad's, it's a long drive but it will be good for the kids, I think this place will be like a ghost town. I hope you don't mind, Jane, I know you invited us.' Maggie turned to Jane. What a relief!

'No! In fact I was thinking the same. After having James around I've got used to having spare hands around to help. That's if we can get through the snow.'

'How is James?' Asked Chrissy.

'Good. Really good.' Jane looked far away and Chrissy and Maggie smiled to one another.

'So, you won't be dressing as an elf on Sunday then?' Jane asked Chrissy, changing the subject.

'No, but we'll put in an appearance for sure. I'm sure Will will want to witness twenty women dressed as elves rattling buckets in the snow.'

'How old are your boys Chrissy?' Maggie asked.

'20 and 22.' Christ, not much younger than Peter. Friday night was date night and she hoped it didn't show on her face.

'Oh.' Jane thought Maggie's reply odd but moved onto something else; she had been caught taking another brownie and was in deep conversation about her curries.

'I'm sorry I didn't make those funerals with Mark, Chrissy.'

'Oh, it's alright, I looked after him, they were tough. You know he never shuts up about you.' Maggie looked shocked.

'You're a lucky woman, Maggie. He's a hard worker and worships you as well. I bet he's a great dad as well, always talking about Bethany and Alex. I bet he didn't want to leave.' Maggie was stunned.

'Laura! Quick question.' Chrissy moved away. Maggie went to look for Alex and found him playing happily with two little girls. She fell into conversation with one of the girls' mother,

'Butter wouldn't melt eh?'

'Until they get home.'

'Yeah right you are! Wouldn't be without them though, would we?' The woman laughed.

Really? Thought Maggie.

Chapter 27

Christmas Day in Helmand was a day like any other although the patrols were for presence and focus rather than to take a new position or attempt anything risky. Hopefully no new medals would be won today. The enemy was highly likely to strike if only to catch the men slightly off guard and damage morale. The patrols had been split into two and so everyone would get a chance to enjoy a Christmas dinner, albeit made from rations. Some form of reconstituted turkey had been supplied along with powdered gravy, packet stuffing and pre-cooked sprouts; but the roast potatoes were real and some of the lads' Christmas boxes had contained squeezy tubes of cranberry sauce which they shared around. Family and friends had been sending parcels for weeks containing miniature Christmas puddings, plastic miniature whiskeys, silly hats, crackers, mini-trees, flashing snowmen and cheese and chutneys. The cookhouse looked festive and the mood was light. Men had been queuing since early morning for one of the three sat-phones that had run out of charge around midday. The line moved slowly as soldiers had been saving their credit for weeks. Some lads on leave had passed their phone cards to friends to use on Christmas day. Men smoked and chatted about what their families were up to and what they'd do if they were at home today. Each soldier secretly prayed that when their turn came, someone would pick up the phone or comms wouldn't be cut; just to hear a missed and treasured voice was enough to keep going for another week or so, especially today. At least a couple of soldiers left the phone listless and head down as no-one had been home or they had got their timings wrong which, with the time difference, was understandable especially when the clocks went forward or back. Some men sought privacy when their turn came or a conversation turned into an argument; women trying to hear over screaming kids became impatient and irritated; the call might have happened at a particularly tough moment or a wife might want to talk about money or going out; two subjects guaranteed to end in conflict. On these occasions, men handed the phone to the next in line and shook their heads; friends would pat their back, knowing exactly how he felt, no-one had good calls all the time; a few had disasters; soldiers had been dumped by girlfriends on the sat-phone, men had been informed of miscarriages, deaths of pets, deaths of neighbours, tragic world news and financial disorder over the sat-phone and it could seriously damage morale. The OC (Officer Commanding a Coy) generally wouldn't get involved; however, a well-run unit was crucial for maintaining mettle and pride. The back bone of a soldier's support network was his mates; usually his room-mates; they slept six to eight in a room on cot beds and watched movies together on iPads and shared music and porn. If there was bitching to do about the officers, they would spend less time being mates and be less likely to drag one another out of the desperate pit of longing for home or losing a dear friend in action. Their cot areas were decorated with Christmas cards, silly posters and bells that span around and the like. Some had downloaded Christmas songs and took their iPods to the cookhouse; they discussed what their mates had been doing last night and shared photos on Facebook of mates getting pissed and clubbing in Manchester, Newcastle and Nottingham, that's just what they'd be doing, they'd say.

Christmas dinner was traditionally served by officers dressed in silly hats and was eaten greedily. They drank water and imagined it was a can of beer. They pulled crackers and told stupid jokes. The officers tidied up afterwards and ate their dinner; then they chatted about home and what their families were doing and which part of the country they had gone to or if they had stayed at home. The older officers talked of children and showed photos; the younger ones talked of sport and climbing holidays, they talked of nights out and each other's girlfriends. It was a much quieter affair given there were around ten of them compared to over one hundred and twenty soldiers. After dinner, the cookhouse became quiet and groups would return to their rooms or gather and watch films; the sat-phone queue built up again and those who hadn't been successful before tried again hoping their families would answer. As it grew dark, men would leave for stag or turn in early ahead of an early patrol in the morning. They had survived Christmas and a new year would soon begin.

Colonel Jem tried to call Chrissy. Chat in HQ around the sat-phone was a little more subdued than in the FOBs and PBs; no-one wanted the CO to hear their conversation and the jokes were cleaner. Will answered.

'Dad! When are you home?'

'Maybe soon, can't really say.'

'Of course, sorry.' Chrissy hovered, smiling.

'How is the job? How is Africa?'

'It's amazing. We live in a tiny village with no running water - one of our main projects - and all of our food is gathered by hand, it's incredible, I love it but I think we're making a difference too.' Ironic that both father and son were pursuing conquests half way round the planet in the name of progress, both built bridges and roads, both won hearts and minds but one saved lives as the other took them away; both for the perceived greater good. Men found small talk difficult and so conversations between father and son were always short. Chrissy took the phone gratefully.

'How long have you got?'

'Don't know about five minutes, I think. I'll talk till it runs out.'

'Merry Christmas, darling.'

'Merry Christmas to you too. Has it been merry?'

'Not bad. I'm working but the guys are relaxing, I hope.'

'Can't you relax too or are you too important?'

'Far too important my love.' They laughed. He seemed so terribly far away. She had forgotten his smell and the cut of his hair; she missed his warm flesh in her bed and his strong arm around her shoulder. She couldn't ask him about when he might come back as it was not discussed over the phone; anyone could be listening. Neither of them could open up; he couldn't tell her how he really believed he was doing or how he felt about his losses and, similarly, she couldn't tell him of her loneliness and her terror, of her tiredness and how she wept alone. Both tried to make the other feel loved without telling the truth as the truth hurt too much and so they talked of the weather and how dinner had been and how Will still got a stocking from Santa and had sat on their bed to open it. She had bought him joke books, chewing gum, sweets, chocolate, quizzes, a mug, a hot water bottle, mosquito spray, medical kit, a cooking stove, three cookbooks entitled, '*Surviving on a jungle diet*', '*Delicious meals with just three ingredients*' and '*Foraging for dinner*'.

Jem's card ran out but he smiled. The voice of his wife and one of his children had made him happy. Now he had to get back to work.

Mark was nervous. He had no idea what reception he might get from Maggie and he was tempted to pretend that he hadn't been able to get through although that wasn't fair on Bethany and Alex and he wanted to hear the voices of his children and tell them he'd see them soon. Maggie had jumped when the phone had rang. They had been dancing round the kitchen with dry gins in hand winding up their mother about her stuffing balls. It was a family tradition on Christmas Eve that, dancing to Christmas music, the kids would make the prized stuffing balls. They would mix prime sausage meat with chestnuts and Paxo and place them lovingly in a tray to go in the oven the next day. Mum, however, had forgotten to get chestnuts; she'd had them in her hand and then she'd seen something else and put them back and completely forgotten but this was a likely story and her children loved the opportunity to get her going. Maggie's sister was older and had three children; her brother was younger and had none. Benjamin was gay but couldn't bring himself to tell mum and dad. Maggie was astounded that they hadn't guessed but it wasn't something that her parents' generation discussed along with other taboos such as orgasms, cancer and breasts. The older children looked after Alex and Bethany who thoroughly enjoyed being fussed over. Maggie's sister, Lizzie, had two girls and a boy, just like her own mother. They were ten, eight and six and the eldest loved being the first, and therefore the most grown up, of all the grandchildren. Maggie was glad she'd come home; at first she'd thought she couldn't face it especially seeing Lizzie and Graham together but she was glad she'd changed her mind. Bethany was better behaved and given constant attention, they were all fed to bursting as mum lived in the kitchen and she felt more rested than in a long time. Her and Benj danced to Kylie Minogue and Maggie felt a little tipsy. She had completely forgotten about Mark.

'Hello.' She sounded breathless.

'Merry Christmas.'

'Mark! Merry Christmas! Bethany! Alex! It's daddy!' The two children shouted with joy and ran to the phone. Mark started to say to Maggie that he wanted to speak to her first in case his card ran out but he didn't get chance.

'Daddy! I love you Daddy! Merry Christmas.'

'Merry Christmas darling, did Santa come?'

'Yes! She squeaked. He gave me dollies, high heels, hand bag, scooter…'

'Goodness me! How did he carry all that?' Silence.

'Bethany, can you hear me?' The line crackled and Mark's heart sank; he'd been in the queue for twenty five minutes.

'Bethany?'

'Daddy?' The line came back and Mark rubbed his eyes.'

'Can I speak to mummy?'

'Daddy!' Alex's voice came on and he began to cry.

'Home, daddy.'

'Soon, big man, you wait!' Alex smiled and nodded and dropped the phone on the floor.

'Alex?'

'Alex?'

'Sorry, he dropped it.' Maggie was back on. Silence, the damn thing went off again. He heard a dead tone and tried again. She answered straight away.

'Fucking thing.'

'Well at least you got through.'

'Yeah, how are you?' What could she say?

'Ok.' She lied.

'Benj and Lizzie are here.'

'Oh, say hi from me. Wish your mum and dad merry Christmas.'

'Of course I will.'

'How are you?'

'Ok.' He lied.

'Good.'

'What time did the kids wake up?'

'They were good; they didn't come into me until gone eight.'

'Wow! That's officially a lie in!'

'I know. And it's a good job because I stayed up late drinking port with Benj.'

'I'm jealous. I sneaked a bit of that miniature you got through, it tasted great.'

'Have you been out today?'

'Yes.'

'Right.'

'Maggie, I've got one minute left.'

'Ok, stay safe.' She meant it.

'I love you.' Maggie closed her eyes.

'Love you too.'

'Maggie I'm sorry it wasn't great on R&R, I'll make it up to you, I promise.'

The line went dead.

Jane's mother's house was chaotic and noisy. Jane had two sisters and both had four children; they seemed to like big families. With partners and in-laws too, that made a total of twenty three for lunch. James would have made twenty four but that would have to wait until next year. Jane's mother was born to hostess and she was good at it. She had been making sauces and gravies for the freezer for weeks and had iced the cake last night as the children watched in awe as she created a winter scene out of swirls of icing, adding characters made days ago from modelling paste. The grandchildren ranged from eighteen (Ella's eldest) to three (Maud's youngest - a recent 'surprise'). Granddad John sat fixed in his arm chair and was used to the noise, he read his paper and now and again asked for a cup of tea or, towards the afternoon, a sherry. The sisters huddled in the kitchen drinking wine and the men watched TV with children or played *Nintendo*, Wii or Xbox, all of which had been brought in the backs of cars. There was a slight issue with game choice as the eighteen year old wanted to play *Call of Duty* and of course the younger ones didn't yet understand the difference between reality and fantasy and preferred Pepa Pig. Christian and Tom played well together being only one year apart and they happily broomed cars about and helped one another do puzzles. Harry wanted to keep up with his older cousins and tried to convince his mum to let him play cert 15 games. Jane gave in, he was a good boy and what harm could it do? Ella had fifteen year old twins who played cert 18 games, how could you stop them these days when all their mates did it? Surely they wouldn't all become serial killers because of *Grand Theft Auto*? Luckily, mum and dad's house was big enough to accommodate the different age groups in different rooms but when all doors were flung open it sounded like an amusement park; excited shouts and hoots, Milla and nine year old Lilly chasing one another dressed as princesses, Dad getting slowly hammered in his chair, Dean Martin belting it out in the background, giggling from the kitchen where the sisters were getting slowly pickled and aromas floating through the air like delicious magic all combined in a chaotic fuzz that beat with the passing minutes. No-one heard the phone. James tried again. He smiled to himself; he knew what they'd be doing, he could picture the scene; John in his arm chair, probably asleep by now; the girls in the kitchen and the kids zooming about all over the place. God, he wished he was there. The phone was answered on his second attempt. It was Ella's husband Brian.

'Brian, it's James. Merry Christmas mate.'

'James!' He held his hand to the mouth piece and shouted.

'Jane! Someone get Jane! Sorry, James, someone's gone to find her, you know what it's like here. Kids are all good;

Milla's a little beauty isn't she? How are you keeping? Keeping your head down we hope.'

'Yes, not bad Brian. Not bad at all. Nearly there now. Jealous of you lot, I can taste Ida's potatoes.' James's mouth watered. He waited. He had saved up his minutes for two weeks knowing that Ida and John's house would be chaos on Christmas day, he longed to be there. Jane sometimes clashed with her mother but god she knew how to look after them all. James loved it there and Ida spoilt him. She came to the phone now.

'James! Merry Christmas, darling! Jane is coming now, I'll get the children.'

'Thanks Ida, merry Christmas! Save me some!' Ida loved feeding James; she didn't know where he put it but it was a pleasure to keep filling his plate up and see him devour it, they all missed him this year, he always joked about and threw the children up and down or played football in the snow with the boys. She hoped he was staying safe and those awful Taliban or whatever they were called came to their senses and let their soldiers go home instead of running round stoning women and planting bombs. She had read of a stoning only last week and it had made her feel ill; it was well thought through, the woman's arms were buried along with half of her body so she couldn't defend herself when the missiles came. At the end, the bloody mess was scraped up and put in a bag. It could take the woman twenty minutes to die. Who would do that? She didn't understand and she never asked James why he was there. Why couldn't girls go to school out there? What kind of people were they to come up with more and more complicated and barbaric ways to kill soldiers? Every time a vehicle was upgraded with new armour then new ways of getting though it emerged; soldiers were being sent home missing arms and legs and it broke her heart to think of the mothers of the boys who never made it home apart from under a union flag.

'James.' Ida closed all the doors to the halls and smiled at her daughter. She was doing so well; James should be proud of her.

'Jane.'

'It's mad here.'

'Of course it is. I wish I was there with you.'

'I know. I love you. Merry Christmas.' Ida had gathered the children and let them into the hall.

'Ok, who do you want first?' They all crowded round the phone except for Harry who held a back a little.

'Harry?' He accepted the phone.

'Merry Christmas, Dad.' James smiled and felt his heart beat faster.

'Merry Christmas, buddy.' He passed the phone to Lucas.

'Happy Christmas, Dad! I beat Harry on Star Wars!' Harry rolled his eyes. James bet that he had let him win because his son was like that. Lucas passed the phone to Milla.

'Happy Christmas, Daddy! Santa brought me a *One Direction* movie!' Even Lucas still believed in Santa Claus and Harry was sworn to secrecy; he looked at Jane who smiled. Then the phone was passed to Christian.

'Merry Christmas, my big man, are you looking after mummy for me?'

'Yes, Daddy. Tom has a DS!' James made a note for next year. Wasn't three a bit young for a DS? They got younger and younger; well, next year Christian would be five. The children scattered and went back to their games. Ida closed the door again.

'I miss you.'

'I love you. Can't wait to get my hands on you, not long now, babe. This week has been a killer; I keep waking up thinking I'm still with you.'

'I know. I haven't changed the bed yet.' James thought of their bed and what they'd done in it and he felt himself go hard. He faced away from the others in the queue and tried to think about cold showers or something.

'Have you had a Christmas dinner?'

'Yeah, plastic turkey, nothing like Ida's but it was ok smothered in gravy and cranberry sauce. It would have been better with a bottle of claret but you'll have to get John to save that for next year.'

'I think he's already asleep. Everyone sends their love.'

'Thanks, give them all mine, too. I wish I was there with you, I bet you'll have the best day.'

'Without you, no, but I know what you mean.'

'Did the kids get up early?'

'Christian did but he came in with me. The twins were up eating chocolate at six apparently and they've thrown up.' James laughed.

'How's Harry?'

'Oh he's alright, being spoilt of course.'

'Good. You are amazing, Jane.'

'I love you.'

'Love you too.'

'I will try and ring again tomorrow.'

'Ok.' They hung up and Jane stood in the hall for a few seconds looking at the phone. This time next year, she thought, she would have him here and it would be the best Christmas ever.

Chapter 28

*Breakfast at BGHQ (Battle Group Head Quarters) to a
bystander would have seemed a civilised affair but to those in
the know, 9 Platoon had patrolled late last night and were
scheduled to patrol again at 1800 and so the Platoon
Commander was enjoying a late bite to eat. Another young
officer- Carter- sat opposite him and joked about the fake
bacon and eggs which was in fact a kind of ham that came in a
tin and powdered scrambled eggs reconstituted with oil and
butter. They discussed their patrols and damned the lack of
supplies and men due to R&R. Now the CO was away, too, and
although the 2i/c was a formidable character he wasn't
Colonel Jem. Attitudes around BGHQ had slipped and morale
was low. The young Commander - Copper to his mates on
account of his ginger hair - was scheduled to clear several
routes for a convoy bringing food, ammo, batteries and water
tomorrow. They were also tasked to make secure a route to
allow the engineers access to the area to bring in wood,
sandbags, cement mix and barbed wire for a new PB - the
CO's wet dream. Copper was seriously undermanned. He was
down to two sections (he usually had three); the Platoon Sgt
was to lead one and Copper the other. As Copper ate his
breakfast he noticed leftover talc on his uniform (used to
denote cleared routes on the ground) and felt a tinge of
annoyance; he hadn't noticed it before, he should set a better
example. The young officer was eager to know more details
and an idea formed in Copper's head.*

'Carter, what are you doing tonight?'

'You asking me on a date?'

*'Kind of. Look I know you're not BARMA status but you
did OVERWATCH right?'* OVERWATCH *was a one day*

course in IED search that they all did when they arrived in theatre.

'Yes.' A knot formed in the young officer's stomach. Would he get to go out? He was bored sat behind a desk in HQ and wanted a piece of the action. He couldn't lead a whole section but he could easily stand in as a number two behind the VALLONMAN if Copper could find two more soldiers confident and experienced enough to lead the clearance. Carter didn't take much convincing and Copper needed bodies on the ground. The 2i/c was out on the ground visiting a FOB and so Copper took the decision that he could be informed later. It was only a clearance patrol; the area had been patrolled umpteen times in the last month; it was the safest deemed route for the engineers to bring in their kit with only one choke point, a junction with deep drainage gulleys.

1740 HRS (1340 GMT)
Carter's heart raced at around 130 bpm as he dressed quickly in the disappearing light. God it was cold. He felt like a naughty schoolboy but he wouldn't be first line; that was the BARMAMAN's job. All he had to do was walk behind and keep his ass alert. They could see their breath as they formed up to leave. The soldiers felt buoyed at the presence of another officer and were relieved they weren't short. It was a nervous time for the Commander; he was unsure about focus and morale and needed to get the lads back into shape after R&R; he also had to take their minds off the long countdown to the spring. Carter felt like a virgin; his uniform was clean and he was freshly shaven, he felt like a rooky among vets; this was a chance to prove himself.

The three sections worked their way down a narrow alley that had been cleared by 7 Platoon yesterday. They had no visual due to the pre-dawn haze but the audio came back as zero threat. It had been raining and it had turned to miserable sludge and it was mind numbingly cold; the men wriggled their fingers inside their gloves to maintain circulation. The alley seemed sinister to Carter but he hadn't had the benefit of patrolling here on a daily basis; two metres wide by four *metres high wasn't bad odds considering there were compounds all around and Copper had attended Shuras in these very compounds. Farm land (the green zone) surrounded them and a river ran the length of the road on the right hand side after an intersection emerged beyond the alley. Carter felt in good hands.*

1845 HRS (1445 GMT)

An explosion took the BARMAMAN by surprise. Firstly, it was behind him, how could that be? He had walked over that spot seconds ago; secondly it threw him into a wall. He heard Copper on the radio and shouts but he couldn't see anything, the light was shit and the rain dulled what little they could see; why had they come out tonight? Copper was calmly giving a RV point in coordinates and demanding a QRF (Quick Reaction Force) to meet him at the grid reference. Radio noise burst into a series of orders and crackles; names could wait, form had to be followed. An Incident Control Point (ICP) was set up inside a friendly compound and the Platoon Sgt shoved his men into doorways and on roofs; who was it? They didn't know but they thought it was the young officer who had joined them last minute. Knots twisted in Copper's stomach; he would be pasted by the CO for this. Copper's OC, James Blandford, was also out on the ground and not far away; he had probably heard the explosion as it sounded like a crack of thunder and was stored deep in the memory of every serving infantryman. James had heard the grid reference and knew full well that radio silence would shortly follow. A helicopter could be heard in the distance, god that was quick. The victim might have a chance. James wanted to get to the incident yesterday and charged a likely CSgt to get him over there like 'shit off a shovel' on the back of his quad bike retracing his own steps cleared in the last half hour. He had given the go ahead for Copper to use a young rookie; had he made a mistake?

Carter lay on the ground. He couldn't feel his legs but there again he couldn't feel anything. A medic was injecting him and Copper was holding his hand. What the fuck was going on? As the sun finally left the earth, he saw Afghans on the tops of buildings muttering to themselves and pointing. Were they outside? Surely they should get inside and safe? It was cold and still raining. Copper was shouting and it was hurting his head; where was he? Suddenly, he felt sick. All had fallen quiet; just the patter of rain and distant voices until nothing remained. He was aware of being lifted and a female said, 'over 50% of body's blood supply.' Then, various figures and bleeps and finally, take off.

1600HRS GMT

When Jem finally came home, he looked tired and generally pissed off. In fact Chrissy was a little tired of his grumpiness and, since his return two weeks ago, had got used to taking herself out for a coffee or just to the Barracks to see Dave and discuss various issues. So far, his leave had consisted of three visits to *Amber Lynn*, two funerals, the opening of a local Community Centre and three readings at Church, lunch with The Mayor and his wife and hours on the phone to relatives of those whose lives had been destroyed over the last six months. She didn't resent this aspect of his personality; no, it showed his commitment and that was to be commended, but he remained grumpy and distracted even when he was with her at home supposed to be enjoying a meal. He would constantly eye his phone and she remembered what Maggie had said about the point to R&R. She had considered the possibility of a short holiday but she had stopped asking. Even when Jake had visited, Jem had given his apologies for being called into the office. This was a total lie and in reality he simply couldn't stay away. He had spent hours talking to his 2i/c and she wondered dryly if he'd rather be sleeping with him than her tonight. She had been wandering over to Jane's more and more making Jane hope more than ever that James would never make CO despite it being the pinnacle of his career so far.'

Chrissy sighed; she should have expected it; even before he'd got home he'd called from Dubai and told her he'd arranged for three generals and their wives to come for supper from Brigade. She had served homemade squash soup to start, followed by lamb shanks in minted jus with courgettes, peas and roasted beetroot. For dessert she had kept it light and served dates soaked in brandy topped with crème fresh, pistachios and honey.

Jem's first instinct was to give his wife a greeting kiss; Chrissy offered her cheek but he didn't even notice and got papers out of his bag and started to read and tut. She might as well not be there. She jumped at his phone. She couldn't wait to have her real husband back for post Tour leave; this imposter would be banished, along with his phone.

'Col. Yes. Yes. Fuck! Thanks. Family informed? Right. I'll be five minutes.' Oh god. Jem rubbed his eyes and Chrissy stopped fiddling with supper and went to him. She didn't know what else to do apart from place her hands on his shoulders.

'Young officer, first time out on the ground; filling in. James's Company. Shit!'

He kicked a stool and it toppled over. This was their last night together; tomorrow, early, he would be picked up by a private car and driven to Brize Norton for his long journey back to hell and there was nothing she could do that would make him feel any better about it. He threw his coat back on and kissed her briefly and looked into her eyes.

'I might be late.'

'I know.'

'I'm leaving early.'

'I know.'

'Sorry.'

'I know.'

He left.

Chrissy wondered if Jane had cooked tonight and if not would she want some of her fillet steak that would otherwise be thrown in the bin. It was only 4.30 and Jane would probably be out at the children's various clubs. She had only just started the marinade for the steak and so she supposed it could go in the freezer. She texted Jane.

'You in?' A replay came back a few minutes later as Chrissy was staring at the fat scallops she had bought for their starter. A final romantic meal she had thought.

'Back at 5, watching tennis, yawn.'

'Can I call?'

'Please do, take me away from all this x' Chrissy called.

'Hi Jane, texts haven't gone out yet but there was a fatality this afternoon, it was James's Company. I was wondering if you wanted dinner, it's all ready; it was supposed to be for Jem but he has gone into camp and I doubt he'll be back early.'

Jane felt numb. Was James ok? How close had he been? How many more before they came back? She didn't want to think about food but something in Chrissy's tone told her that she needed some company.

'Can you bring it here so we can get the kids into their beds?'

'Of course!' Chrissy sounded pleased.

'About 6.30 and we'll have a glass of wine to start?'

'Perfect, see you then.'

By the time Lucas had finished his tennis lesson, his mother had become very quiet. Jane could only guess what her husband might be doing now and the guilt and loss he would be feeling. Jane thought of the soldier's mother not for the first time and her eyes burned. Harry was at a friend's and this was a godsend because he could read his mother's eyes only too well. Milla had been watching her brother and playing with Christian nicely for a change.

'Good match, Luke. Well done.' Jane ruffled his hair. He smiled at her but she looked away and became silent again. Maybe he hadn't been that good after all. Adults were so serious and very puzzling.

'Mum! Wait!' Milla had had her brother's shoes off and Jane hadn't noticed. She wanted to get home, she wondered if James had tried to call. If he had he would have been bitterly disappointed. She looked distant and irritated and Lucas dropped into a sulk. She needed a glass of wine. The drive home was quiet as Jane daren't turn the radio on in case the news was quicker to spread than normal. The media weren't

253

allowed to report a fatality until NOK had been informed; sometimes this was slow and sometimes it was quick, what if she turned on the radio and the news was already out? She thought about the young man's family again and wondered who it had been. Chrissy hadn't expanded on the phone. When they pulled up outside the house it was dark already and Jane yearned for spring, indeed for any sign of new life and hope. Her children bundled into the back door and as usual, dropped various soggy bundles of layers and woollens on the floor for her to pick up. They were usually shouted back and under duress would eventually claim said articles and hang them up, but Jane couldn't be bothered tonight. She went to the fridge and poured a glass of wine; it warmed her and made some of the tension ease away. She checked the phone and there was a missed call at ten to five but the number was unknown; he wouldn't call now, comms would be down for hours until the area was secured and all those involved informed. She sighed and started tea. The children could have something orange that went into the oven tonight. She was amazed at how the bad news sapped her strength and wondered how it must affect the men on the ground. How did they pick themselves up and carry on? How did they patrol the same areas where a beloved comrade had died? How did they not run away? She wondered if desertion still carried the death penalty; how bad must it get to drive them over the edge?

She kept the kitchen noiseless; she didn't want to be a part of any news or connection with the outside world. She let the darkness enter and left the lights off; only the light over the cooker burned. She sipped her second glass of wine and allowed herself to become morbid. Finally, she decided to serve tea and lifted chips and crumbed orange things off the oven tray. She let them cool for five minutes and then called the children. By the time they sat up at the table, the lights were on and Jane's demeanour had improved. Jane had made a paper clock to help Milla tell the time and she brought it to the table. Lucas kept wanting to butt in and Milla grew frustrated.

'Let her do it, Luke, you already know, now stop it please.' Her eyes pleaded with him and he looked down. Christian wanted to help and kept getting ketchup on Milla's side of the table.

'Yuk! That's disgusting!' Milla overreacted and Jane sighed. Why couldn't mothers sign off for a night when they weren't in the mood? Couldn't children come with an 'off' switch? But then she thought shamefully that some of her children would be turned off more than others and she might just forget to turn them back on again!

'What's so funny, mum?'

'Oh, I was just fantasising about you lot having 'on' and 'off' switches and how peaceful the house would be.'

'Mum!' Lucas feigned disgust but felt grown up because mum had used adult language.

'What's fastisyse?'

'Fantasising is wishing for something.' Lucas pretended he had known this already.

'Right, bath time. I want you in bed on time tonight, Chrissy is coming over to cook mummy dinner and I do not want to be disturbed.'

'Can we stay up?'

'No.' Jane winked at her daughter. They bounded upstairs - did they ever run out of energy? Jane ran a bath. Harry had showers usually but he wasn't here tonight so the younger ones could enjoy their bath for a little bit longer. Christian was yawning already and Jane heard the door go downstairs wondering if it was Harry or Chrissy. It was Harry.

'Do I have to have a shower tonight, mum?'

'Come here, let me smell you.' Harry recoiled.

'No, you'll last another day.' He went to his room happily.

'Did you eat?' She called after him.

'Yes.' That could mean anything.

'What?' She shouted.

'Chicken and chips and peas.' That'll do. He shut his door.

She had begun to let Milla bathe on her own as she became older and wanted to spread out and sing; unlike the boys who wanted to fight with sea creatures and pretend to die grisly deaths in the open water. She put Christian to bed with a cup of warm milk and he stared at his Teddys. Lucas wanted to read on his own and so Jane could concentrate on Milla. When she checked on Christian the next time, he was fast asleep and she breathed a sigh of relief. One down. The door went again and this time it was Chrissy who set about opening cupboards and finding dishes.

Milla didn't want to get out of the bath but Jane was in no mood to fight. She counted to five and then grabbed her daughter by the shoulders and lifted her out, she weighed a ton and she realised she wouldn't be able to lift her for much longer. Milla sulked.

'I'm hungry.'

'Would you like a bowl of grapes?' Jane was close to bursting, she just wanted to get downstairs and be fed and fall into bed. Milla always just wanted one more thing.

'And a glass of milk?' Milla nodded again. Jane tucked her in and received a pinkie promise that she wouldn't get out of bed. When Jane went downstairs, Chrissy was busy preparing plates and frying onions.

'Mmmm. I'm looking forward to this!' She was secretly happy that Jem had been called away. She went back upstairs with Milla's milk and grapes and checked Harry and Lucas. Harry was reading and Lucas was flat out; it had been a long day. Sports days always were.

In the kitchen, she sat down heavily. Chrissy had already topped her glass up and got herself one.

'Who was it?'

'Phil Carter, young 2nd Lt.' Jane held her head in her hands, she knew Carter (he was never called Phil). He had been round to their house for BBQs and Company drinks and he was a cheeky young charmer. She thought of James.

'I remember his girlfriend at last year's summer ball; she fell over and hit her head on the vodka luge; mind you I think she was only a date for the evening.' She smiled; he had been so handsome and young and full of life. James had said that he showed the most promise but he'd been shifted to HQ last minute to James's disgust but he could do nothing. Jane and Chrissy fell silent.

A plate of scallops, bacon and black pudding with some kind of jus over the top was plopped in front of Jane and her eyes widened.

'I hope you're not expecting a leg over.' Chrissy laughed. They cleared their plates in silence. Jane was feeling warm and merry as Chrissy busied herself. She couldn't even bring herself to tidy up; she could do it tomorrow. Next, a fat, juicy steak was placed in front of her and she blobbed mustard and blue cheese dressing next to it. Maybe she should go to the gym tomorrow? She had been meaning to get back into her fitness for months now but it just hadn't happened. Maybe she should just stop making excuses and go. It was about time her and Maggie had a coffee anyway.

'That was divine, Chrissy. Jem is a fool. What can he achieve tonight anyway?'

'Well, he just wants to be in control. Dessert?'

'I'm stuffed, what is it?'

'Mint chocolate mousse.'

'Oh well maybe I can squeeze it in.' And she did. The house was quiet. They hadn't bothered turning any music on.

'Thanks Jane. I needed that. Jem goes back tomorrow.'

'I haven't done anything Chrissy, I have just sat here and been waited on.'

'Just the company.'

'I know. I'm sorry Jem leaves tomorrow, it hasn't seemed like two minutes.'

'I know. Can I tidy up?'

'Let's do it together.' By the time they had finished, they were both yawning with emotional exhaustion and Chrissy got her coat.

'I'll collect my dishes in the morning.' She left and Jane sat in the dark and had one more glass of wine.

Chapter 29

Jane slept deeply but Milla woke her with a start at 8am. Oh god, she would be late and she had forgotten to text Maggie to wait for her. Did she really want to go? She looked in the mirror and decided to throw make up at the problem. Harry had got the children their breakfast.

'Oh, Harry, you're a star.'

'No problem, mum.' Her mouth felt sticky and her eyes felt droopy. Maybe it wasn't such a good idea to go to the gym; after all she might drop dead. Come on, Jane, she said to herself; excuses excuses.

'Can we do school dinners today?' Jane pleaded. They all agreed. Good. She combed hair, brushed teeth, checked uniform, found homework, turned off the TV, found car keys, thanked the lord they had cleared up last night and found odd shoes. They fought for space around the door but they made it in time. As Jane walked away from school she breathed easily and smiled. The sky was blue and it was a stunning day. She had purged herself of something last night and she felt a little at peace. She would go home and change and catch Maggie at the gym.

At the gym, Jane noticed Maggie's car in the car park when she went back to her own to collect her forgotten water bottle; it was going to be one of those days. The changing rooms were packed and hot as they always were in winter, she wondered which lunatic was in charge of the heating and why they thought that ladies who had got their heart rates up to 180bpm would need extra heat. She slung her bag to the back of a locker and grabbed a towel. Maggie would be way ahead by now. Jane felt a little nervous; it had been a while. She looked around quickly for her friend but couldn't see her; oh well, she was probably in a squash court or she might even have taken a class; she would see her after. Jane concentrated hard and an hour passed easily. She was pleased with herself not only that she had remembered the exercises but also that it hadn't hurt that much. She felt good and went to take a shower. Maggie wasn't in there. Never mind. She decided to wash her hair which was always a treat at the gym because her army shower dribbled water so she was freezing by the time she'd washed her body never mind her hair too. The showers at the gym were huge and water sprayed hot and steamy and she luxuriated in it. One day they would own their own house and she would spend as much as they could afford on the shower. Wrapped in fluffy towels she padded back to the changing room and bumped into Maggie.

'Ha! I knew you'd be here! Caught you!' Maggie looked terrified and her chest started to go red and blotchy.

'Are you ok?'

'Did you see me?'

'What? No I couldn't find you, did you do a class?' Maggie shook her head and stuttered...

'No, I... erm.' She looked away. Realisation hit Jane. The two women stood in silence and faced one another.

'Coffee?'

'Yes.' Maggie's locker was round the other side and she disappeared. Did she still have time to make something up or had she blown it?

Jane dressed mechanically. Ok, so she wasn't at the gym; that much was clear. Maybe she was wrong but the look of guilt and being found out might as well have been an advert in a Sunday glossy and why did she need a shower? Oh Maggie, why? That was a stupid question, she knew why but she was playing with fire and it wouldn't solve anything; mind you, if it was Peter then it could have its benefits. She pushed the thought away and thought of what it would do to James. Did Mark know? Of course not. She did her make-up quickly and joined Maggie. Maggie smiled weakly.

'I'll get you a coffee.' Jane left and went to the café. She wondered if Alex was in the crèche, my my, a lot of thought had gone into this. Peter strolled in and looked very pleased with himself; it was obvious that he had just come into work;

there was a spring in his step and Jane knew for sure that it was him.

'Hello, Jane, where have you been?'

'Oh, life got in the way.' Scumbag, I bet you know she's married.

'Back to it now then?' He suddenly looked ugly and over tanned.

'Well, we'll see. Don't want to overdo it and my family comes first.' A flicker crossed his face and he laughed nervously.

'Of course. Well, see you then.' Maggie came in as he was leaving and they looked away from one another. It was definitely him. No doubt.

'Jane you surprised me, I didn't expect to see you.'

'I intend to become a goddess once more so I thought I'd catch you here.'

'I was…'

'Busy? Look, Maggie, I think I've worked it out. I'm not your mum; I'm not going to give you a lecture.' Maggie looked down.

'Shit.'

'I won't tell a sole, Maggie. I presume no-one else knows? It's your business but what I will say as your friend is that you need to be careful; what is this going to achieve?'

'It was just a bit of fun, he makes me feel…alive.'

'I bet he does.'

'You're jealous.'

'Of course I am! Who wouldn't be? But it doesn't mean I'd do it. I couldn't hurt James like that.'

'It's different for you, besides Mark will never find out.'

'I wouldn't be so sure, these things have a way of …emerging.' Maggie chewed her lip.

'So?'

'So, what?'

'What's he like?' Maggie hid her excitement at finally being able to share it with someone.

'Incredible.'

'Get away! Never, he's a pup.'

'Well, he knows what to do and it's addictive.'

'How many times have you seen him?'

'About six.'

'About six?'

'Ten.' Maggie looked ashamed.

'When did it start?'

'After Mark went back.'

'That's why I never saw you.'

'I'm sorry; I was so angry and needed to escape The Patch for a bit.'

'So what happens now?'

'Nothing. We get posted again and it's all over.'

'What about your marriage?'

'What about it?'

'You don't think this will change it? Infidelity is all about what's wrong, not what's right so do you want to fix it?'

'It's impossible; Mark is so fixated he's become a stranger.'

'How do you know? You've hardly been together for the last two years.'

'Precisely.'

'So, leave him then.'

'I've thought about that but I can't.'

'Why?'

'Money.'

'But isn't happiness more important and besides you'll do it again, there'll be a Peter wherever you go.' Maggie hadn't thought of this.

'You're hurting my head.'

'I'm sure that's not all that hurts.' Maggie opened her mouth but it just reminded her of the last thing that was in it.

'Oh, Maggie, Maggie, Maggie. I just don't get you. I'm not married to him; I don't know what it is you hate so much but I just see two people struggling at the stage in life where kids are a nightmare and two people who fell in love for a reason. Have your fun but be prepared for the pain.'

'That's a bit deep.' Jane raised her eye brows.

'Ok, I'll shut up now.'

'Did you get the text?'

'No, Chrissy came round last night, he was a young officer; Phil Carter, you know, the one that played rugby, tall, big smile, always joking around.' Maggie couldn't place him and then remembered being introduced to someone called Carter because she had wondered what his first name was. It was last summer at the COs BBQ and Carter had been drinking beer with a group of young officers; they had been loud and it had made Maggie yearn to be single again. Carter had been very attractive and she felt shame that she thought this when now he was dead and being flown home to his mother in a box. It was sobering and she forgot about Peter.

'Is Jem still here?'

'He left this morning.'

'I never saw him.'

'I don't think Chrissy did either.'

'Why does she put up with it?'

Jane wanted to scream, *because she fucking loves him; it's called commitment!*

'I don't think he does it on purpose,' her voice was ironic, 'it's his job, he'd be the same in any other job - just as driven and committed.'

'But not dead.'

'No but that's the risk they take,' she was talking about James now, 'they can die crossing a road or falling off a cliff, or swimming in strong currents, Jane was becoming heated. 'They don't *want* to die.'

'Sorry. I'm not cut out for this whole *supporting-your-man* thing.'

'None of us are, Maggie, there's no magic solution. You'll get through it, you just need some time.' Maggie doubted it, but her friend seemed so sure, what did she know?

'Did you expect marriage to be easy?'

'No, but it would be nice to have a husband now and again.'

'You have.'

'Where?'

'In here.' Jane placed her hand on her heart and Maggie wished that she had ten per cent of her belief in love.

The sun shone through the gym café window. It was glorious. Maggie looked at her watch.

'I need to get Alex.'

'I can't wait till spring; this winter has gone on forever. I'll walk to the crèche with you.'

Once home, Jane had mixed feelings; she had felt buoyant and proud after her workout but her conversation with Maggie had left her low again. She looked at her calendar; 10 weeks to go. This side of Christmas was worse than the other side; it crawled along painfully and each day seemed longer. Jane seemed to sit for hours at her kitchen window watching for any hint of spring; her mornings were quiet unless she went to the gym and she would hug her coffee mug and watch for signs of life. She was not interested if Maggie continued her affair and didn't ask. When they shared coffee the subject never came up. As the weeks passed, each woman dug into her reserves and held on tight.

One day, Jane was sat at her window with the heating on and a squirrel shot across the grass followed by another; they tussled together and as soon as she moved they fled into a bush and up a tree. Jane spotted a lonely snow drop under the same tree; she had to squint but it was there and she swore the day was brighter. February had been the worst; the cold had been unbearable and her energy ebbed and flowed; they merely existed. Less and less attended coffee mornings or anything social at all; she went to the gym and lived in an automatic fugg; the children were tired and drained as well and they argued over tiny things like who had the most sausages at dinner or who had hidden their shoes. Jane continued to give in and let her standards slip. Chrissy came and went in this coat or that and snow continued to fall until almost March. Their skin was pale and almost light blue as they yearned for light and sun and their shoulders seemed lower in their jackets. The total stood at 31 dead, 84 injured and they all prayed that it would not change until the men were safely out of theatre. Finally, she dared to believe that spring was on its way.

The day she saw the squirrel, Jane received a letter from James and it warmed her as the squirrel had. She willed the day to move faster but the clock tick-tocked stubbornly and slowly. She toyed with the idea of going to the Families Office but changed her mind. Chrissy had gone out and she dreaded to think where Maggie was. She couldn't choose a book off the shelf and didn't want to bake or make chutney. Her mind drifted to the funerals she had attended and she wondered what morale was like out there now. James had said that the most dangerous parts of any tour are the first few weeks and the last few; the former due to lack of experience and the latter due to lack of focus. The wives had been informed of the return date of their men and there was the usual pang of jealousy over those who would get them home sooner rather than later. Of course, the return of a thousand men had to be staggered and the Battle Group taking over had to enjoy a proper hand over. It was kept fair, though; those who had left first would return first and vice versa, however it was slightly different for officers who generally did seven months rather than six either due to tying last minute issues up or giving their seat to other more needy soldiers, for example, one that might be attending a funeral. Whenever James finally returned home, she knew that his last day in theatre was definite and couldn't be changed; how long he hung around in Salatin after that was anyone's guess and then there were two days decompression in Cyprus where soldiers would get drunk and fight and purge themselves of the edgy aggression picked up on tour.

When she left the house to collect Christian, she noticed more colour that hadn't been there before and it lifted her spirit somehow. She looked at her calendar; two weeks. This would be the longest two weeks of their lives. Stay focused, she willed him. For the first time in what seemed like a life time, the school run was done in daylight and it was a beautiful thing. Was it her imagination or did people look happier? More alive and willing to pass the time of day and smile? Yes, she thought so. Jane had £6,000 in her savings account and felt proud of herself. She had been browsing through glossy holiday magazines and was shocked at the prices; it would take all the money she had saved to take a family of six away. Sod it, they deserved it. She could do with some sun on her body; they had earned it.

Chapter 30

Plans for the return parade were well under way. There was a lot to do and Chrissy had roped in various volunteers to help. With families and friends invited they expected hundreds to turn up. There would be a parade through the city – thousands were expected to turn out for that - and then a family day back at the Barracks before which, the men would be awarded their medals by various dignitaries and veterans. The date was set for the first week of April so the men had chance to finalise kit and decompress before leave; setting a thousand soldiers free amongst the general public straight after theatre would be a disaster and so for most of them they would be working a few weeks after their return. Of course, the news was met with grumbles as they would be itching to get away but the reason for it was generally understood and accepted.

All the OCs in theatre found ways of focusing their men before repatriation started. Of course, the Americans spent much longer in theatre but the debate was endless and would no doubt rage for years to come; what was the optimum time? Mistakes had already been made as men became either flippant or risk averse and uptight. Moustaches had appeared and personal hygiene slipped. VPs (vulnerable points) were maybe not checked as vigorously as men trawled through an area for the hundredth time that tour. There was a fine line between being boldly battle hardened and smugly self-assured and no-one wanted their men to cross it. Commanders tried to think of interesting and novel ways of keeping their men's attention. CSMs threw surprise checks and parades for kit and cleanliness and came down hard on those who had slackened sending a clear message to everyone; the tour was not over yet, so drop your cocks and fall in.

By now, every soldier knew his date for departure and they couldn't help but dwell on it and count down. For some, the adrenaline kicked in and they couldn't wait to get out and patrol feeling victorious and proud; for others, every patrol became harder knowing they had made it this far and might still not make it home. Mates joked and smoked and some started packing personal items ready to leave. Pin ups came down and porn was handed back and swapped; there would be no more of that at home. But then they wouldn't need it because they'd be shagging like rabbits every night. The men felt like their balls would explode at the thought of touching a woman; it could be their wife, girlfriend or one night stand, the soft flesh was all the same, it was just that some meat meant more than others.

Mark smoked one last fag before his patrol. He was stuck between winding down patrols to err on the side of caution and so not lose any more men, and the mission, which was to keep pushing until the very end. Today was a routine patrol and they had never been hit in that area before. There was one VP; a spot prone to regular flooding and out of sight of any sanger. If they had vehicles with them, they would stop two hundred yards short and man the ground for two reasons; one to display ownership and, two; if anything happened they could give chase. Today there were no vehicles. It was blisteringly hot even at six in the morning; summer was on its way and would be punishing for the next Battle Group. He didn't know which was worse; the heat or the cold. Neither, he thought; the downright winner in any climate and sworn enemy of the soldier was the rain, and, thankfully, there would be none today. Dust could be seen swirling in the early morning light and Mark thought how beautiful it was. He thought of Maggie and how he couldn't wait to get back; he had thought of jacking it all in to make her happy but what would he do? He would look around when he got back, he could talk to Uncle Jack who worked in the city.

Mark had seen James last night who had accompanied some soldiers to his FOB before he shipped out. Lucky bastard. He had been in excellent spirits but had just one more patrol to complete and like himself, was out on the ground now. They had spoken of their post op leave and what they were doing; Mark had felt a sting of jealousy as James had told him his wife's plans for a grand holiday; he would be lucky if Maggie wanted to stay married. She was so volatile; he couldn't even speak to her over the phone now without her losing it over the slightest thing. Yesterday it had been Bethany. Mark had given his opinion of an argument between mother and daughter and he had been accused of taking his daughter's side; he couldn't fucking win. She had hung up and he had pretended to chat for a while longer in front of the queue for the sat phone. What a pathetic OC he was; blown out by his own wife, he couldn't let the men see. Last night, he had found it hard to sleep and he wondered what was left for him if he couldn't keep his marriage going. Maggie had changed so much since having Bethany; one day she had been totally in control and a bundle of fun and life and now she was vicious, short tempered and depressed. He tried to push it out of his mind but at 3am had given up and got up for a fag; the CSM was up too and they went over the Ops for today. Mark's CSM was a rock of a man. Jack 'the stack' Clinton had been born in combat '95 and drank whiskey from his baby bottle so the saying went. The men had endless fun making up anecdotes about him and Mark knew he made the Company what it was; he was his right hand and his mucker. The orders came from Mark of course; he made the decisions, but Jack implemented them and kept a lid on discipline, they were a formidable unit and they had felt their losses keenly.

'Can't sleep, Sir?'

'Nah. You?'

'Nope.'

'Three days to go, Sir.' They looked into the cloudless sky; the stars in Afghanistan were stunning all year round. Soon, they would be out of here but the stars would never leave them.

Later, as they moved over the ground, each man was left alone with his own thoughts, fears and demons. The tour flashed through their memories like pages of a journal in full Technicolor; the ups and downs, the losses and tragedy, friends lost and friends made. The villages were always quiet at this time of the morning after the first call to prayer. Some lights shone and the odd dog strayed into their path but it was generally a safe area; they had had no trouble before although there had been some movement logged by one sanger two nights ago. The rifleman hadn't been able to make out a particular form and so it could have been an animal that he was seeing through his night vision and it was momentary but it had to be logged.

On the top of a hill, a man in winter robes looked through the sight of a Russian Dragonov sniper rifle. The dawn light worked in his favour and he watched the men snaking in a line close to one another. Some looked around but most concentrated on keeping to the footprint of the man in front. The Company reached the green zone and would soon cross the bridge. The man looked through his sight; two soldiers joked, they were going home soon; he knew their rotation, and another army of devils would replace them. For a while, they would be as naïve as girls and they would pick them apart; then would come the real war until this moment right now when they went soft again.

The Sgt leading the first Platoon raised his hand and the Company stopped. Had he seen something? A message made its way to Mark. The man in the robes looked through his sight again. This was a man of high importance and the British pandered to him; they nodded and followed him like women. He counted his breaths; he had been taught by his father as a little boy to fire on the fourth breath. He had killed Russians, British, Americans and now British again. His mother had been taken away by four Russian soldiers and his father had been tortured by the British. He had seen his nephew blown up by an American plane and his family had danced in the streets when the towers had fallen in the land of the free. He counted silently; his breath could not be seen as he had learnt to conceal it. His heart slowed as he breathed four breaths in through his nose and eight out of his mouth, silently. He placed his finger over the trigger; rags covered his wrists and his nails were black from months of hiding in his own country.

In a moment of pure madness, Jack the Stack lifted his helmet momentarily to wipe his brow. The shot sliced straight through his jugular vein at the moment that 95% of his blood was being transported through this flimsy piece of nature's least complicated or protected engineering miracle. Only a momentary hesitation had given the sharp shooter his window; his helmet had been raised only a fraction of an inch. He fell to the ground instantly. Jesus. Jack had been standing three feet away from Mark and he grabbed the signaller and barked, 'sniper! Take cover.'

'Sniper fire, one-nine-four-seven-seven-seven. Repeat, sniper fire, one-nine-four-seven-seven-seven. Man down. Wait out over.' The radio was silent as the chain flared into motion once again. The watchman informed the Adjutant who informed the CO and in England, the OC Rear was put on standby. Three comrades dragged Major Clinton's body to a nearby wall, their blood pumped fast and they went into survival mode. They knew a MERT team would be on its way but they also knew that Jack 'The Stack' was dead. The ground was red and the men bowed their heads. Mark shuffled on his elbows with the radio attached to the signaller. Two Platoons had given the same co-ordinates for the direction of the shot but the necky bastard had probably disappeared by now. Mark sent orders for scouts but the second shot blasted him onto his side. His last thought was where the fuck was he hit? He had body armour on and he was lying down. He felt no pain but he knew it was serious because he could feel nothing else either. He knew it was bad; his legs had stopped moving and he was vulnerable. He was dragged away and the radio burst into life once more;

'CONTACT: WAIT OUT... OC... fuck.' Mark passed out.

In BGHQ Col Jem stared at his Adjutant who thought he was about to be killed by a flying object or worse; the CO's pistol. Jem's face turned red and then purple and he threw a paper weight at the wall which knocked off a picture of his sons; it shattered to pieces and no-one moved. The Adj had seen some explosions of temper but nothing could have prepared him for this.

'Get the fuck out and find out exactly what happened, and shut the fucking door.' Jem was shaking. He had to stay focused and he had to make sure that it wasn't an incident that could have been prevented. He knew they'd take casualties before the tour gave up its last breath but this was a disaster for morale. He needed to get someone to C Coy and quick; the men would be in shock and half of them were still on the ground; the word would have spread by now and they would be a liability. That was some sniper, he thought. Probably been doing it all his life. He wished he could wring his neck. They had never had one single incident in that area, his stomach knotted; had he failed to push the enemy back? Were they becoming more confident? No, he mustn't think like that, they'd made progress, it would be a lone ranger; fucking unlucky. He needed to do something but couldn't be rash; he needed to boost morale but the chances of visiting all four main FOBs in quick succession was almost impossible. He would arrange radio calls instead. Now, where the fuck was his adjutant?

OC Rear Party called Dave Proctor. It was 3.30 in the morning and Dave knew that at that time there was only one reason for the phone to ring. They had three weeks to go for godssake until the last man returned. He blinked and reached for his phone; just as he thought, OC Rear, it read.

'Morning, Sir.'

'Dave. Two casualties, one incident. Both family cases.' Dave couldn't believe what he was hearing. Two immensely experienced officers, two good men. But death didn't favour the weak, it swathed erratically through the best meat anytime, anywhere. He would need Chrissy for this.

Chrissy was dreaming of bells and woke in a sweat realising that it was her phone. Jesus, what was the time? Her phone said 'Dave' and her stomach turned over. It wasn't Jem because no-one would be informed by phone but it must be someone important else Dave would wait till morning and deal with it himself; unless...unless it was someone close. It had to be an Officer. She heard Jack Clinton's name and she couldn't believe it; she couldn't take it in. Who would tell Marie? Oh god, she had seen her yesterday and they had chatted about post-op leave. Then Dave dropped the bomb shell and Chrissy began to shake. Oh god, Jem; what were they doing? How could this happen, now? He'd said they'd lose focus but she hadn't believed him. It would hit the news hard and Chrissy dreaded the fall out for the families. Who should she go to first? Maria or Maggie? Dave said Maria. Of course. Maria. She felt sick. She pulled on her clothes in the dark and felt desperately thirsty. She wanted to ring Jane but felt enormously selfish but then she thought what would Jane do? She knew that Jane would be mad with her should she keep it from her until she received the text and who knew when Dave would send it? Not in the middle of the night of course, but she might not reach Jane in time. She texted first. Maybe Jane kept her phone by her bed like they all did.

Jane was having trouble sleeping too and she wondered if she would sleep at all until James came home. The text made her jump and she cursed herself as Milla was in beside her. She reached over her and squinted.

'Can I come over?' Oh Christ, it was Chrissy. She told herself over and over again that it wasn't James; Chrissy wouldn't be allowed to inform, it would be three of them face to face including a Padre, but what if Chrissy had thought it would be better to wake her first and not have them banging the door down? What if they were all at Chrissy's waiting while her friend gently roused her? Her stomach heaved and she made it to the toilet just in time to release the bile and it tasted hideous, she rinsed her mouth and her hands shook. No, No, No; it just wouldn't happen like this. She padded downstairs and put a small light on in the kitchen, unlocked the door and waited. A tiny knock was taken away by the wind and Chrissy came in fully dressed. Jane put her hand to her mouth and shook her head.

'It's not James, Jane.' Oh thank God. But who was it? She looked into her eyes and Chrissy couldn't get out the words. Jane went to her and Chrissy let herself be held. She let out seven months of anger and loss. Seven months of looking women in the eyes and watching their faces crumple as their lives fell about around them. Seven months of dreams about funeral music and the union flag being folded and passed to women in black. Seven months of disconnection with her husband and avoiding the news. Seven months of standing on streets shaking a bucket. Seven months of watching children trash playgrounds and hound their mothers. Seven months of looking into the eyes of the injured and lying, saying everything was going to be ok. Nominally, the papers were full of how injured serviceman could go on serving but who had heard of an infantryman in a wheelchair? No infantryman would thrive as a store man or indeed behind a desk. Eventually they would have to face up to the truth and start discharging. The charities knew it and the MOD knew it. Her shoulders heaved and Jane joined her. They sat on the floor and Chrissy waited for Dave to call.

It was one of the worst days of Dave's career. He had been a Colour Sgt at Sandhurst when Jack Clinton had gone through. He remembered his swagger and prowess on the rugby pitch. Mark had been ahead by a few years and he'd known the young subbie in Northern Ireland. Maria and Maggie were both nice ladies and he had spent time with both of them in different circumstances. Dave's day was mapped out for him in the early hours and he wouldn't get to bed until much later. He hated involving Chrissy so intimately but it was necessary especially as Chrissy knew both wives so well. She had said she was going to Jane Blandford's and would wait for him there. A dim light shone in the kitchen and Dave knocked lightly not wanting to wake the children. The door was open and he went in. He found the two women sat at the table with coats on, whispering. They had a glass each and Dave suspected they hadn't been drinking water.

'Want one Dave?'

'No, it's a bit early for me.'

'It is for us too, but it'll be a long day.' Chrissy spoke for them both. Dave knew that this one had tipped them all over the edge and he dreaded to think whose ear had borne the brunt of it from Col Jem; probably the Adj as usual.

'I've seen Maria but not Maggie. Their families have been informed and cars have been sent as they both want their parents with them. There's not a lot more we can do now.' Dave's visit to Maria had been something he would prefer to forget. They had three children; the eldest was ten and the twins were nine; ages stuck between childhood and adolescence. At least Maggie's were only four and two; she wouldn't have to tell them for a while yet and they might not understand even then. He had left the CNO (casualty notifying officer) with Maria and the CVO (casualty visiting officer) was on his way. The Padre stayed also. Maggie had a relative ten minutes away and she had been located and was with her niece; the children were still asleep. Dave had marked in his diary the arrival of the first Company home; Mark's, and it was in exactly two days' time. Life sucks, he thought.

Jane was up for another whiskey but Chrissy covered her glass. 'You need sleep; you have kids to take to school in the morning.' Jane laughed. As if she would sleep now. She thought of Peter and wondered when the last time Maggie had shagged him might have been. She wondered if there was life after death and if sins could be seen by those who had passed. It was five o'clock and a hint of light could be witnessed shining through the kitchen window; a heavenly sight indeed, spring was on its way and hope eternal sprung from Mother Nature's loins. Not quite.

Jane hadn't smoked since Uni but joined Dave and Chrissy outside for one. It made her head spin and Chrissy put her to bed. The whiskey and nicotine did their job and Jane collapsed into a slumber; even Milla slept through the commotion and Chrissy and Dave snuck out into the dawn. Birds had started to sing and grey clouds hid behind the orange sky. Traffic could be heard in the distance and life had started once again. Chrissy was struck, not for the first time, by the freedom of her life, she walked down the street unmolested, she peered around unthreatened and wandered in the gloom unchallenged. She thought of what Jem was fighting for and imagined how it might feel to not be able to do those simple things; walk down the street, enjoy the night sky, stroll through the neighbourhood. She refused to believe that they had got it all wrong and that reports from Kabul indicated that it had all been for nothing; how could it be so? How could so many lives go unrecognised and be sacrificed for nothing? They had to believe; mothers had to believe, sisters, girlfriends, daughters all had to believe that death was not in vain. The war might not be won but the mission was not to conquer it was to improve life for those left behind and subjected to brutal rule for so long. Of course, cynics saw the war as a clearance of unnecessary obstacles to new oil pipe lines and Chrissy had no doubt there was truth in this, but she refused to let dishonour mar the sacrifice of Jem's men. Regardless of one's political leaning or historical appreciation, they had a duty to uphold and the Battalion could be proud of what they had achieved. There was talk of the US taking over most of the FOBs and Chrissy wondered how the OCs would view this; would they regret their losses or hand over gracefully to their allies? How would the locals react? Would it escalate violence or promote order? No-one knew. Jem would be home soon and would receive his next posting order shortly after that. Would she forget?

'Try and get some sleep, Chrissy.'

'Ok, call me if you need anything. I doubt I'll sleep. Please don't hold anything back.' Dave nodded.

Chrissy spent the next few hours dosing by her fire wrapped in a blanket. She had lied to Jane that she wanted no more whiskey and cradled a glass until the sun finally cracked through the mist. She had no children to take to school and she could sleep it off when her body finally told her to. She would allow herself this bit of indulgence. The fire and the whiskey finally took its toll and she drifted off around 6am just as Milla was waking Jane who felt like shit.

Jane brushed her teeth and made a strong cup of tea. She felt numb; familiar now. She moved around the kitchen automatically and Harry knew the signs and helped his mother.

'School dinners today, Mum?' Bless him. She held him tight and he manned up to the task. He had no idea why but his instincts told him when he needed to be strong for his mother. When dad came home, everything would be ok again and he could laugh like a child but not now.

Her head pounded through sheer exhaustion and she drove to school in a haze. She was relieved to drop Christian off and drove back home in a dream. Should she visit Maggie? Of course she should but what would she say? She was fucking someone else, how could she couple that with grief? Besides, she had Auntie Patricia with her. Jane decided to close her doors and windows and hibernate for the day. Giving had lost its allure. She sent a simple text to Maggie saying 'I am here xxx' She would let Maggie decide. She pulled James's pjs from a cupboard and threw them on. Once under the duvet, she calculated that she had two and a half hours before she collected Christian. Could it get any worse? She turned off her phone and fell into a deep sleep.

Chapter 31

April

As the men returned, women booked appointments with hairdressers, beauticians and nail technicians. They coiffed themselves to within an inch of their lives making sure that they were ready for their men. There was another reason also; the BBC was present at all of the scheduled Company returns. No drama was needed though as the image of a busload of battle weary men entering a gym hall of waiting wives and families carrying banners such as 'we love you daddy' or 'my daddy is a soldier' to the haunting sound of five bugles sold itself. Cameramen shot fabulously unrehearsed reunions beautifully and interviews were taken. It was prime time TV. Microphones were shoved into the faces of men meeting their babies for the first time or proposing to girlfriends or kissing wives long and needfully. Some wives across the country could not watch the footage as they would never hold their loved ones again and the sight of others doing just that was just too painful. James and Jem were on the same flight back and Chrissy and Jane waited nervously in the hall. Of course, the media knew that the CO was returning home and so it had attracted even more attention and the hall was full to bursting. It was late and some children had fallen asleep wrapped in banners on tables and chairs while the mums sipped coffee and checked their make-up. Harry was fidgety and wrapped his fingers on a table top; Milla was becoming bored and had lost her initial fervour, she sat on Jane's knee with Christian and swung her legs. Lucas was off playing with a friend on the gym mats. Dave Proctor suddenly looked excited and shouted, 'five minutes.' There was a buzz of excitement and some children cried with the pressure. Wives and girlfriends straightened skirts and jackets and sprayed perfume; Milla began to smile again, Christian was asleep along three chairs.

A line was being formed at the front and Jane was worried that the children would not see their father; the media was blocking the view of some of the families; Jane stood on tiptoes and tried to keep a weary Christian on her hip, he was becoming heavy like a dead weight; Milla bounced up and down and Harry took her and Lucas to the front.

The bugle call made her jump and the first of the men rushed into the hall frantically darting their eyes around and finally making contact and melting into the arms of those they had missed so desperately. Jane saw James and saw him bend down to his three eldest. Harry nuzzled into his neck and Milla almost knocked him over; cameras flashed and some people screamed, some sang. Jem was last in and snuck in almost imperceptibly as, by that time, the cameras were on kissing couples and men holding babies. He kissed his wife slowly and not too hard; it wouldn't do in front of the men; he was still on duty and they had interviews to give, indeed, at that moment, Dave steered a BBC journalist over to them and Chrissy held her husband's hand. She knew they would have to wait until everyone had gone; just another part of his job as Captain of the ship. After the interview, Chrissy helped Dave tidy cups and put chairs straight as families began to leave chatting animatedly and laughing, some saluted Jem as they left as a mark of respect. Chrissy looked for Jane but she had gone already; she smiled to herself and then remembered Maggie. She hadn't seen Maggie since that awful day when she had left for her mother's. She had looked gaunt and even thinner; the children were as delightful as ever and excited to be going on another holiday. Maggie hadn't told them; it could wait, they were too young. Her mother had not wanted her to drive but Maggie had insisted, saying that it focused her mind. She would not be telling her mother that she almost crashed twice; once because the low sun glare confused her vision and the other because she had almost nodded off and had to stop to rub her eyes. She ignored the children and they played and fought in the back but Maggie had let them; she was numb and wouldn't know what to do anyway; she couldn't shout, or even talk that well, she floated in her own universe and found herself parked outside her mother's house some three hours later. Ella and Benj had been there and she had fallen into their arms. Later that night she'd had to be put to bed utterly pissed and crying; Benj had stroked her face and lay with her for a long long time.

Maggie hadn't even spoken to Jane. Jane had rang the house and knocked but Dave had said that she was sedated most of the time and an Auntie was looking after the kids and had virtually moved in. Then she left. Without saying goodbye. Jane wondered if she would ever see her again and she became teary when she discussed it with James. James had held her and the tears came stronger and stronger as she let go the tension of the last seven months. She had seen Peter at the gym looking forlorn and knew instantly that he hadn't seen her either or spoken to her; good, thought Jane; her life would be complicated enough from now on without him.

The day of the parade started cloudy but by ten o'clock, the sun shone down through blue air and the trees swayed, proud of their new leaves. Women left jackets at home and children wore bright colours. James took her breath away when he dressed in his uniform with his medals on his chest and today he would get one more. Chrissy had said that Anita Dent would be there to collect Lee's medal but some other bereaved wives and families had wanted to stay away and have their son's or brother's or husband's medals sent on to them. Dave respected their wishes and made the appropriate arrangements. Jane wondered what Maggie would do. She had tried to call this week and left messages but none had been returned; maybe she wanted to forget that Mark had ever been in the army? Maybe she couldn't face it? Everyone was different. Every time she walked past her empty house she would peer in as if expecting Maggie to wave from behind the curtain and put the kettle on.

Harry looked so handsome; he had an ironed shirt on and had let Jane do his hair; he was getting so tall and would be going to big school next year and then her baby would be lost forever. James had to leave before his family as the men were being bussed into the city and they would be forming up in the grounds of the Mayor's house. Both Jane's and James's parents had come and the house was full to the brim; mothers fussed over James and hurried the children. They would all meet after the medals parade back in the barracks and then the party could really start. Dave and Chrissy had organised a band stand, bouncy castle, trampolines, candy floss stalls, hall of mirrors, burger stands, two bars and, later, three bands. The party would go well into the night and way beyond children's bedtimes. Several female band members might keep a few lucky soldiers company in the block or in a local hotel and tomorrow, post tour leave would officially start. Adrenaline pumped around The Patch and women were in love once again. Couples smiled deeply into one another's eyes remembering tender moments after they had returned and children hung on to daddies and looked up to their returning hero who, in turn, swung them around and tickled them. Older children had their hair ruffled and teenagers were taken to the club for a game of pool or to the cinema.

Jane looked at herself in the mirror; she wore a new beige suit with an orange scarf around her throat and orange accessories; James had called her beautiful. She wanted to make him proud and she wanted the importance of the day to be reflected in her outfit, she wore a hat as a lot of the wives would and as an officer's wife she would be sat at the front on a comfortable chair with a blanket for the medals ceremony. They drove into the city and were astounded by the crowds, people had begun to form up along the route that was protected with barricades; some places had crowds fifteen deep and Jane took her family to a spot that she knew would be quieter. The sun shone and it actually felt like April and Jane briefly thought back to January and February when she had believed cruelly that it would never end. They had made it.

They heard them before they saw them. Colonel Jem was at the front and then the Companys came behind led by their OCs. James looked formal and focused but as he marched past he winked cheekily at the children and they giggled. Crowds clapped and cheered and Jane watched as he finally disappeared. Mark's Company was led by his 2i/c and he marched tall and strong for his commander. Jane held her breath; she didn't want to cry in front of the children. They cheered until the very last troops had marched past and the crowd started to disperse. Both sets of parents chatted about how good the parade was and how James had looked the smartest but that they all did themselves justice and how awful for the ones who weren't there.

Contrastingly, the atmosphere back at the barracks was subdued as they all waited for the men to return formally and finally to familiar territory. The buses arrived and family and friends had squeezed into all corners of the parade square. The noise subsided and a cheer went up as the men climbed from their coaches and lined up in Company's and Platoons. There was a delay as they formed up properly; they would march onto the square and be presented with their medals and James had warned Jane that this might take some time; awarding medals to a thousand men was not going to be quick. Jane noticed that the injured had formed up as well and they stood with crutches or sat in chairs proud and dignified. A hush descended, but after half an hour children started to run around and play chased by embarrassed mothers. It didn't matter though, they were children after all. Seven guests gave out medals; generals, the mayor and The Duke of Sunderland had come along as guest of honour and would make a speech later. Jane had ribbed Chrissy about having royalty in her house and Chrissy had told her to sod off. Chrissy and Jem would be on duty until tomorrow when they could finally leave for a five week cruise. Until then, they couldn't hold each other and walk hand in hand; they had duty and honour to up keep and Jem set a shining example to his men by staying focused and committed to the last day. Chrissy herself had been asked to present medals and Jem kept his eyes front as she carried out her task. She had known that Maggie was coming all along but had wanted to keep it as a surprise for Jane; they would have a small gathering at her house afterwards with Mark's family. She looked radiant and stood erect and gratified. Jane spotted her and her heart jumped; she had come. She was bursting to wave but knew that it would have to wait; would she hang around afterwards? She craned her neck and saw Chrissy bend down and pin a medal onto Mark's chest. He shook her hand and they chatted for a while. Maggie laughed. She wore gloves and held on to Mark's wheelchair at the front of his Company flanked by his officers. Jane saw Maggie gently wipe her eye as Chrissy moved off and she placed both her hands on Mark's shoulders and he smiled.

THE END